Within
Every Flame

Publisher's Cataloging-in-Publication Data
Names: Peterson, Alanna, author.
Title: Within every flame. / Alanna Peterson.
Series: Call of the Crow Quartet
Description: Seattle, WA: Rootcity Press, 2021.
Identifiers: LCCN: 2021906311
ISBN: 978-1-952149-05-4 (pbk.) | 978-1-952149-06-1 (epub)
Subjects: LCSH Post-traumatic stress disorder—Fiction. | Family—Fiction.
| Friendship—Fiction. | Iranian Americans—Fiction. | Asian Americans—Fiction.
| Northwest, Pacific—Fiction. | Science fiction. | Adventure fiction. |
BISAC YOUNG ADULT FICTION / Thrillers & Suspense
| YOUNG ADULT FICTION / Diversity & Multicultural
| YOUNG ADULT FICTION / Social Themes / Mental Illness
Classification: PS3616.E84268 W58 2021 | DDC 813.6—dc23

Book design by Unflown | Jacob Covey

Printed and bound in the United States of America
First printing 2021

Published by Rootcity Press
Seattle, WA
rootcitypress.com

Within Every Flame

ALANNA PETERSON

CALL OF THE CROW QUARTET

BOOK THREE

ROOTCITY PRESS

SEATTLE

For Cora,
who has always known
the wisdom of the moon

December

Once the rumbling ceased, the cosmonauts relaxed.
The ship had held.
They had done it: they were finally free.

As they floated away from Earth, Mikhail turned to Natasha,
certain he would see his ecstatic grin reflected on her face.
<u>She was not smiling</u>.

"What's wrong?" he asked.

"It's only...."
She indicated the rapidly receding Earth with her gloved hand.
"I didn't expect it to look so small."

—Viktor Zolotov, *Keepers of the Moon*

Richard Caring, former CEO of Nutrexo, found guilty of criminal charges

SEATTLE, WA – In front of a packed courtroom in downtown Seattle, a federal judge declared Richard Caring guilty of criminal conspiracy. This was the latest in a string of guilty verdicts for key players in the Nutrexo scandal that shook the city last summer.

Caring headed the Nutrexo corporation, which manufactured iconic products such as Blazin Bitz and Coolixir, to much acclaim in prior decades. He was well-known not only as a successful businessman but as a pioneering philanthropist. The Women in Science program he started in the mid-90s was seen as a much-needed investment in female scientists, who formed a large percentage of Nutrexo's ranks.

However, one of these scientists, Dr. Tara Snyder, is the alleged perpetrator of last summer's shocking events. During court proceedings, Caring's legal team outlined the evidence indicating Snyder's responsibility for both the bombing at Nutrexo headquarters and the abduction of four Seattle youth, who were held against their will at a Nutrexo facility and forced to participate in Snyder's unethical experiments.

Caring denied any involvement in these events. He maintained they were driven entirely by Snyder, who will not stand trial until next spring. However, the prosecution laid out evidence, including testimony from two of the abducted youth, that showed Caring was indeed aware of the abduction and attempted to cover it up in order to protect his company. This allegation was corroborated by several people in Caring's inner circles. Ultimately, the judge declared the guilty verdict and sentenced Caring to eighteen months in a federal penitentiary.

The verdict strikes the final nail in the coffin for the Nutrexo corporation. After the events of the summer, it was forced to lay off thousands of employees, halt production on its food products, and spin off its subsidiary companies, including the pharmaceutical giant Genbiotix. Though recent acquisitions of Nutrexo's capital assets have cushioned the blow somewhat, the economic shock waves of its downfall continue to be felt around the region.

Andi

ANDI LIN STRETCHED HER FINGERS ABOVE THE PIANO KEYS. A new melody was floating around in her head, and she'd been itching to work on it all day. But now that she was finally ready to start, she could barely concentrate. Mental images from earlier kept intruding: the polished wood of the courtroom bench in front of her, Cyrus's hand in hers, the judge arriving to read Richard Caring's verdict....

Stop. Don't think about Richard. She managed to steer her brain back into composition mode, but just as she was finally beginning to immerse herself, someone stepped into her room. She stopped playing and looked up.

"No, no, keep going," her dad said. He parked himself in her desk chair and strummed an E-minor chord on his acoustic guitar. "That was sounding good."

Andi turned back to her electric keyboard, wishing she'd put on her headphones. She plucked out a few hesitant notes before falling back into a groove, though it felt different now. Something had tightened inside her. She hated it when people listened to one of her works in progress, especially when it was still in its messy beginning stages. Though she'd explained this to her dad several times, he never seemed to get it. He thought the early phase of songwriting was the best time for collaboration.

Sure enough, her father was soon humming along, murmuring lyrics. She could practically see him sketching out the song in his head, mapping out the chord progression, dividing sections into verse/chorus/ verse. Turning it into one of *his* songs, the way he always did.

She stopped again, leaving him strumming in silence. "Oh—sorry, Dad. Just noticed the time. I've got to get ready. Brooke's expecting me."

Her dad looked hurt. "But we were just getting started—let's run through it one more time. I'll record it so we can work on it later."

He fiddled with his phone. His sleeves were rolled up, so Andi could see the thick black tattoos against his white forearm, the Chinese characters that spelled her name: 林安地. They covered the track mark scars that dotted his left arm, souvenirs from his long-ago heroin addiction. He'd gotten the tattoos, he said, so that any time he was tempted to start using again, he'd have a permanent reminder of why he needed to stay clean.

The sight of them made Andi feel even worse. He was just trying to spend time with her. Why did she have to be such a jerk about it?

"Okay. One more time," she said. Her dad wanted to write a song for the new Mile Seven album together, and she'd resisted him for too long. Maybe if she gave him this one, he'd let her get back to her own compositions. Most of the songs she'd written so far were solo piano, though sometimes she dabbled in adding digital beats and synth loops, and she dreamed of writing multi-instrumental pieces someday.

She'd worked on probably a dozen different pieces in the past month. Even though she'd been neglecting her school work and just about everything else, those moments at the piano had kept her afloat. And, she kept telling herself, they were necessary: any day now, Vanesa Rosales would be sending the rough cut of her documentary about farmworkers, and Andi would be helping to select music for it. Vanesa had also been open to her writing a few original pieces to accompany the film.

Andi's dad had been thrilled by this news, and had put her in contact with a friend who had written musical scores for advertisements and TV series. She'd met with Glenn a few times, and he'd given her helpful critiques of the short pieces she'd been working on. With his encouragement—and letter of recommendation—she'd even applied for several undergraduate music composition programs.

Not that Andi's mother knew about that particular detail; Andi had let her remain under the impression that she was applying pre-med to all her chosen colleges. Andi had even kept it from her dad, who tended to look down on academia and the "pretentious" classical music scene. There was no way she'd get in anyway, when all the other applicants had undoubtedly spent half their lives writing songs.

Though, in a way, Andi had too. She'd always composed little melodies inside her head, but until recently, she hadn't dared to think she could write something that other people might actually listen to. Even now, she wasn't sure that was true.

But Vanesa seemed to have faith in her, as did her dad, of course, and his friend Glenn—and the person who had set this whole thing in motion. Naveed.

Andi couldn't hold back a heavy sigh. She planned to drive up north to visit him tomorrow, but wasn't exactly looking forward to it. He'd expect a play-by-play of the trial, and she'd be forced to think about Richard Caring again, forced to remember that moment right after the judge handed down the verdict—

Without meaning to, she banged out a dissonant chord, and her dad looked up from his guitar questioningly.

"I'm sorry," she said. "I can't do this right now."

Once her dad stopped recording, he asked, "Everything okay?"

"It's fine." The words sounded unconvincing, even to her.

"I know it's been a stressful week," her dad said. "But it's over now. The trial's done, and they found Richard guilty. That's worth celebrating, right?"

"Yeah. It is." It wasn't over, though, not really. Tara Snyder's trial, the one Andi dreaded even more, was still looming over them. But that was still months away. According to the lawyers, it probably wouldn't begin until late spring.

Andi's phone chimed and a text from Brooke appeared on the screen. "Let's finish this later," she told her dad. "Brooke's waiting for me to come pick her up."

He nodded. "Right. I'll keep working on it, and we can try again tomorrow? It would be perfect for the last track."

Andi agreed, and as she closed her door she heard him descending to his studio in the basement. She wondered if the song would retain any trace of her original melody by the time she heard it again.

Once he was gone, she changed into a plain black t-shirt, leggings, and a long army-green jacket. She laced up her heaviest boots and went extra thick with the eyeliner; tonight, she and Brooke were going to see an afro-punk band at a nearby club. A few weeks earlier, Brooke had presented Andi with a convincing fake ID, and she had made good use of it ever since. It was so liberating not to be limited to all-ages shows anymore.

Even though he'd probably used a fake ID all the time during his own teenage days, her dad had always firmly refused when Andi used to beg to attend 21-and-over shows, so she'd been careful to select venues that he would never set foot in. Which wasn't that hard; he pretty much only listened to music made by white hipsters, but there was a whole world of amazing musicians that Andi had discovered by avoiding them. Now, she craved soulful hip-hop and trancey EDM and even, in small doses, experimental jazz. After every show, she felt her mind opening to new ideas, new genres.

And loud punk music would be perfect for tonight. She had just texted Brooke that she was on her way and shoved her phone into her coat pocket when a knock on the door startled her. She opened it to see her mother standing there, with a pained look on her face that immediately set Andi on edge.

"Everything's going to be okay," her mom said distantly, as if trying to convince herself. "It's nothing to worry about."

Statements like these were probably the things that caused Andi to worry the most. "Mom? What's wrong?"

Her mother stepped into Andi's room and opened her arms, gathering Andi into a hug. "I just got off the phone with your ah-ma. She... told me... that she's... she's been diagnosed with colon cancer."

Andi was seized by an immediate rush of dizziness. "Cancer?" It came out in a wobbly whisper.

"Don't worry, it sounds like they caught it early. She'll be starting treatment right away, they want her to do a round of chemo first, but she may need surgery too. So—our trip might go a little differently than planned."

Andi hugged her mother back, still in shock. She had spent the first six years of her life in Berkeley, being raised by Ah-ma and Ah-gong while her mother finished college and her dad bounced back and forth between tours and rehab. Ah-ma was like a second mother to Andi. The thought of losing her was unbearable. "That's okay, it doesn't matter if we don't have time to visit colleges. I'm just glad... it's good that... that we can be with her."

"Thank you, bǎo bèi. It's going to be okay," her mother said again. Then she pulled away and looked quizzically at Andi, no doubt noticing her heavy eye makeup. "Going out tonight?"

"I, um, don't have to?" It felt wrong to leave, though screaming away her anxiety sounded even more appealing now.

"You should go. Be home by midnight, okay?"

"I will." Andi gave her mom another hug. "I'd better take off—Brooke's waiting for me to pick her up. Love you, Mom."

"Love you, too," her mother said. Andi closed the front door behind her and bolted outside for the freedom of her car. Technically, it was her mom's Sentra—but in the evenings, it was all hers.

Andi fought back tears all the way to Brooke's house, flooded by memories of Ah-ma, of the many BART rides they had taken to Oakland's Chinatown, where Ah-ma bought vegetables at the market and lit incense at the temple and drank tea with the old ladies, the musical tones of their Mandarin washing pleasantly over Andi. She remembered one trip where a vendor had caught her attention by holding up a black-haired cloth doll. "Ten dollars," he had said. "But you can have it for five." Andi took a long look at the doll and told him, "Eight dollars, and that's my final offer." Ah-ma's friends all laughed, thinking that the poor American child didn't understand how haggling worked, but Ah-ma got it. "She's beautiful, isn't she," Ah-ma had said to Andi. "It's insulting to the doll to suggest that she's only worth five dollars."

Andi pulled over in front of Brooke's house, hoping she might have a few moments to collect herself. But Brooke was waiting outside, taking one last drag from her joint before snuffing it out and sliding into the passenger seat. Andi didn't mind the skunky aroma of lingering cannabis tonight. In fact, she almost wished that Brooke would offer to share, but Andi had long ago made her straight-edge position very clear. Her whole early childhood was clouded not only by her father's absence as he struggled to get sober, but by all the secrecy and lies surrounding his addiction. She really wasn't interested in repeating history.

Brooke gave her a hug before cracking the window open. Only then did Andi notice how widely her friend was grinning. "So, I have some news!" Brooke said.

Even though the news was apparently good, Andi held back a sigh. Now how was she supposed to bring up Ah-ma's diagnosis, or her feelings about Richard Caring's verdict, without being a buzzkill?

"What is it?" Andi asked.

Brooke didn't seem to pick up on the wariness in her voice. Must be nice, being stoned. "My sister's moving out of the dorms into her own apartment in Boulder—and she said I can come live with her for a few months! I can finally get out of this place. I'm so excited!"

"But what about school?" There Andi went with the buzzkill, but she couldn't help it, because her brain was screaming, *No! Please don't leave me, please don't.*

"It's all online. I can do it anywhere. I'm almost done, anyway. Only a few more requirements to fill before I can graduate."

"So, Colorado, huh? Won't it be... snowy?"

"But I love the snow! Anything's better than all this gray." Finally, it seemed to dawn on Brooke that Andi was less than pleased about this. She wiped her phone's screen with her thumb. "Hey—it won't be forever. Just a few months. I'll be back before you know it."

Andi felt very numb all of a sudden. She turned up the radio, which was playing some old-school funk anthem she'd never heard before. "I love this song," she muttered by way of explanation.

After they listened in silence for a few minutes, Brooke started talking about the bands playing at tonight's show. Part of Andi wanted to yell, *don't you dare change the subject!* and ask Brooke why the hell she was so excited to get out of Seattle, then vent about Ah-ma and the trial and the song her dad was probably butchering right this very second, but she didn't want to ruin the evening. So she kept it inside and pretended everything was fine.

But this act didn't last for long. Because after they had found a parking spot and walked over to the back of the line, Andi saw something that made her grip Brooke's arm in shock.

One of the people in line was opening a blue cellophane bag of chips, with a redesigned brand logo that Andi had to read twice. Even then, it was hard to believe what she was seeing. These snacks hadn't been on the market since Nutrexo shut down, and they were part of the reason that Richard Caring had just been sentenced to eighteen months in federal prison. But the bright red mini-chips he held in his other hand left no doubt.

Blazin Bitz were back.

Naveed

SATURDAY, DECEMBER 12

NAVEED MIRZAPOUR WATCHED FROM THE DINING HALL WINDOWS as Andi's car approached. Lately, nothing in the world thrilled him more than watching that silver Nissan coast between the rows of trees lining the road to Englewood. The maples had been flaming red when he arrived in autumn, but now were skeletal versions of their former selves, their bare branches cutting dark patterns into the perennially gray skies.

Beside him, Koffka wagged his tail, also eagerly anticipating Andi's visit. Englewood had several service dogs, but Koffka, an enormous yet gentle German shepherd, seemed to have appointed himself as Naveed's personal guardian. Not that Naveed was complaining in the least.

He turned away from the window so that Andi wouldn't see Koffka and him staring out at her like two excited puppies—only to find that Max was taking a seat in the chair next to him.

"Hey, Max. What're you doing out here?" Naveed asked. Max usually didn't show up in the dining hall during visiting hours.

Max raised his head, and Naveed looked him in the eye. It had taken him a while to be able to do that. Max had come to Englewood after he'd put a gun in his mouth and attempted to blow his head off—but only succeeded in obliterating the right side of his face. When relating the story in group therapy, where everyone studiously avoided looking at his sunken forehead, the dent in his cheek, the skin-covered hollow where his right eye should have been, Max had shrugged and said, without emotion, "I've fucked up everything my whole life, makes sense I'd fuck that up too."

Naveed knew how that felt. He'd liked Max immediately.

"My step-mom's visiting today," Max said now. "You wanna hang out with us, play some Monopoly? She always lets me win, like I'm a four-year-old or something. It's insulting."

"Maybe. But not until after Andi leaves," Naveed said.

Another voice came from behind them. Naveed didn't have to turn around to know who it was; that mocking tone could only have come from Dennis. "Oh, so *that's* why you were drooling on the window. Your girlfriend's coming today?"

"She's not my girlfriend," Naveed said, then immediately wished he hadn't. It was better not to engage with Dennis. Every conversation they'd ever had was uncomfortable, maddening, or disturbing—or some combination of the three.

Apparently, this one would be no exception. "She's not? Great. 'Cause I've got yellow fever, and there's only one cure." He made a thrusting motion with his hips.

If the nurses hadn't been watching, Naveed would have shoved him right into the window, hard enough to shatter the glass. Instead, he had to settle for saying through clenched teeth, "If you touch her, if you even *talk* to her, I am going to cut that racist tongue right out of your mouth. And that's just the first appendage you'll be losing." He turned his *don't-fuck-with-me* glare up to full wattage.

Miraculously, it seemed to work. Dennis shrugged and drifted away from the windows, muttering something that Naveed didn't care to hear.

"She's coming." Max angled his head toward the windows. "See you later, yeah?"

"Yeah," Naveed said, still rattled. As he made his way through the dining hall, he felt someone staring at him, and turned around, expecting it to be a nurse silently evaluating his tight jaw and clenched fists. *Patient appears angry. Will remove him from common area so he doesn't pose a danger to visitors.*

But it wasn't a nurse. It was one of the other patients, a girl sitting by the windows overlooking the vegetable and herb gardens in the courtyard. She had just arrived at the beginning of the week. Englewood was a residential treatment center for mentally ill teenagers—though they'd recently started a transitional program for young adults over 18, like Naveed—but this girl seemed much younger. She sat in her wheelchair across the dining room, staring at him intensely while sucking on the end of one of her braids. He looked down at Koffka, not wanting to stare back, and gave the dog a rub behind the ears. Even though he couldn't feel Koffka's coarse black fur beneath his fingertips, his presence somehow brought Naveed's blood pressure down a few notches.

Moments later, Andi walked through the door. He smiled at her, but his grin faltered when he noticed the dark circles under her eyes, the strained expression on her face.

Maybe Richard Caring's trial hadn't gone well. He'd been waiting all week to get the report from her, since he didn't have access to the internet thanks to Englewood's strict media restriction policy. Most of the time he was glad to be in the dark about what was going on in the world—he had plenty to work through in therapy without knowing what people were saying about him out there. But sometimes it drove him crazy to be so cut off from everything.

Andi made her way across the room. Even though they didn't usually hug, she looked like she could use one today. But he could see Dennis out of the corner of his eye, once again making thrusting-hip motions, and decided against it.

Instead, he said, "Hey—I'm glad you're here. Want to walk around outside?" It was gray and drizzly, but she was still wearing her rain coat.

She nodded, but didn't say anything. He led her over to Fiona, one of the nurses, since he had to ask permission for everything around here.

Luckily, Fiona agreed to let them go. "Sure—you can go all the way to the barn if you want, since Becky's out with the horses. But don't forget your poncho. And don't stay out too long."

"Thanks. We won't," Naveed said. Fiona worked with the younger kids; she didn't know that he never went anywhere near that barn.

He put on one of the plastic ponchos hanging by the door into the courtyard, each of them a violent shade of orange exactly the same color as a prison jumpsuit. He probably looked ridiculous, but Andi still didn't say anything. Her silence bothered him. Was it because of the trial? Or something else?

As soon as they got out the door, Koffka keeping his faithful pace on Naveed's right side, she spoke. "Thanks. I needed some fresh air." The words were quiet, half-whispered. She cleared her throat. "Ugh—can barely talk today. Went to a show last night and lost my voice."

Naveed was relieved that this was the reason for her silence. "When we get back inside, I can make you some tea," he suggested. "We have a great blend for sore throats."

"Maybe. But I can't stay too long today," Andi said. "Got a ton of stuff to do before I leave next weekend."

Despair pierced through Naveed's heart. She'd be in Berkeley for the entire winter break, meaning that he wouldn't see her again until after he completed his twelve-week program and left Englewood in early January.

"Are you sure?" He hoped he didn't sound desperate, but didn't want her to leave too soon. Whenever she came, he felt like he was being recharged, filling up with enough power to endure the week ahead.

She didn't answer. Her expression was far away, as if she hadn't heard him.

"Is everything all right?" Naveed's anxiety was mounting fast. "Is it—is the trial over?"

She adjusted her hood. "Yes. They found him guilty of criminal conspiracy. Eighteen months in prison."

"Eighteen months? That's it?"

"I know. Pretty much a slap on the wrist. But at least it's something, right?"

Naveed kicked a rock, trying to release his anger in an "acceptable" way. "It's bullshit! He signed off on that Blazin Bitz project knowing it would harm millions of people."

"He's a rich white guy with a really good lawyer. It's lucky he got any jail time." Andi's eyes were on her feet. She opened her mouth, as if she was about to say something more, but quickly closed it again.

Naveed fumed beside her. He wanted to keep railing against the unfairness of the criminal justice system, but they passed a nurse walking with a younger patient and her parents, and he kept his mouth shut.

He and Andi stepped through the courtyard gate and meandered into the back trails, where it was muddier. The air was damp and the moss on the trees glowed bright green in the drizzle. Being out here made it easier to avoid getting lost in his anger about Richard Caring, since there were lots of pleasant details to focus on instead: the jingle of Koffka's collar, the wet slap of their footsteps in the mud, all around them the sound of water falling on evergreens. He wanted to distill this moment, to bottle it up into a vial and take sips of it whenever the crushing loneliness descended on him, as it usually did mid-week.

But then he came around the bend and stopped short. He hadn't intended to get so close to the barn, yet there it was, looming up in front of him.

Before he could turn around, the wind blew it right toward him. That unmistakable barnyard stench of ammonia, of manure—

Instantly, everything changed. His heart fluttered into overdrive as panic flooded his body. He tried to fight it with rationality, the way he'd been working on in therapy with Dr. Young: *you're safe, it's not going to hurt you, it's just a fucking barn, take a deep breath and calm down.* But he couldn't breathe, that was the problem; already he was spiraling back in time, he was losing control—

He tried to resist the nightmarish images that threatened to start playing inside his head. If he could focus on something real, he might be able to get back on top of this, but he was too embarrassed to turn toward Andi so he looked down, and there he saw Koffka pressing against his legs, staring up at him with furrowed brows. He bent down and gazed into the dog's dark eyes—and that simple action, somehow, brought him back. He could hear the raindrops on the hood of his poncho. All he could smell now was the green forest. The barnyard stench had gone away. Grateful, he took a deep stuttering breath.

Andi was kneeling beside him. "You okay?"

He nodded. "Fine. Just a little… out of breath."

Her eyes flicked toward the barn in the distance. She understood; she always did. "You know," she said, "Think I'm ready to go in. A cup of tea sounds perfect."

They made their way back inside. But instead of leading her to the dining hall, Naveed took her through the doors that led to the dispensary. He was still on the edge of veering back into panic, hyper-alert and aware of every detail. The sweat prickling his forehead. The crinkly sounds his poncho made when he hung it up. Their footsteps squeaky on the wood floor. Naveed prayed they wouldn't run into Dennis when he was this keyed up. Just seeing his round, sneering face would probably trigger him to lose whatever self-control he still had.

Both the medical and herbal dispensary windows were closed. Naveed had forgotten that they never dispensed meds or tinctures during visiting hours. He'd been trying not to rely on benzodiazepines the way he used to, and had found that the herbalist's tinctures and teas made a good substitute. Sometimes they weren't strong enough to stave off a panic attack, but right now he just needed something to take the edge off.

He knocked on the closed window, hoping someone would be inside and come to his rescue, but nothing happened. So he banged harder, louder; still nothing. Koffka gave a warning yip, *calm down,* but he couldn't stop, he needed it, he needed it so bad, he was *not* going to lose it in front of Andi—

"Hey." Her steady voice jolted him back. She was covering his curled-up fist with her hand. "Stop. No one's there."

He froze, staring at her lovely slender hand on top of his own ugly scarred one. Normally he disliked being touched, but for some reason this didn't bother him at all. Maybe because he couldn't feel it, thanks to the damaged nerves in his hands.

On an impulse, he took her hand in his and pressed it against his rapidly-beating heart. Now he felt her touch for real, and it was like each of her fingertips was sending a beam of calm straight into his chest. He closed his eyes, breathing in and out, feeling her palm against his sternum, slowing his heartbeat, returning him to his body.

"Ahhh." The sigh of contentment escaped his mouth before he could stop it, and he opened his eyes to see a curious half-smile on her face. To his surprise, he realized he was smiling, too.

"Is everything okay over here?" A nurse stepped out from the shadows. Distantly, Naveed wondered how long she had been watching, but couldn't bring himself to care.

"It's great," he said as Andi pulled her hand away. "We were just heading back to the dining hall."

Naveed felt like he was walking on air. Well, he always did, thanks to his nerve-damaged feet, but right now it was actually an enjoyable sensation. They found a quiet table in the corner, and he filled two mugs with hot water at the beverage station to brew each of them a cup of licorice root tea. Thankfully, Dennis was nowhere to be seen, though Naveed felt like nothing could ruin his good mood right now. He asked Andi about the shows she'd been to since her last visit and the songs she was writing, and even worked up the courage to ask her about the documentary. Andi told him that Vanesa hadn't sent it yet, which Naveed was glad to hear. He hadn't been in a very good place during the filming, and he had no idea how they were going to portray him—or how Andi would react to seeing him at his craziest.

Eventually, though, he noticed her discreetly checking the clock on the wall, and knew she was getting ready to leave. Three more weeks until he saw her again. He wasn't sure he could take it.

His family was planning to visit the next day, but it wasn't the same. He had really messed things up with them last fall, and every time they came, he always felt like he was performing. *Look how happy I am! See how well this is working?* It was very tiring. He dreaded having to be around them all the time once he got discharged, painstakingly rebuilding his parents' trust and working through his complicated relationship with his brother.

As he sat across the table from Andi, though, he found himself daydreaming about leaving with her right now, getting in her car and leaving this picturesque prison. Then he'd never again have to suffer through another of Dennis's snide remarks, or be in the dark about what was happening out in the world. He'd been doing well these past few weeks. He would be fine on the outside. Wouldn't he?

"I'd better head out before it starts getting dark." Andi stood up and pulled on her jacket.

Take me with you, he thought. "Okay," he said.

Andi fumbled with her zipper as he walked her to the door. She rang the bell and waited for a nurse to escort her through to the other side, the place where he wasn't allowed to go.

"See you in a few weeks," she said before turning away.

Don't go, he thought. "Okay," he said.

She stepped through the threshold and was gone. Naveed returned numbly to the dining hall, where Max waved from behind his Monopoly board. Naveed greeted Max's step-mom and pulled up a chair. Koffka, mercifully, sat down on the other side of Naveed. He rubbed the dog's ears as he watched the tail lights of Andi's car blazing their path between the trees, until she rounded the bend and disappeared from sight.

Roya

SUNDAY, DECEMBER 13

ROYA NEVER KNEW WHAT TO EXPECT DURING A VISIT TO ENGLEWOOD, but she couldn't have imagined what was waiting for her that rainy Sunday in December.

She and her parents had come prepared with board games and a deck of cards, knowing that they probably wouldn't get out for a walk today in the driving rain. Cyrus had stayed home since he had some big tests coming up and had already gone to see Naveed the previous week. It had been almost a month since Roya had gone. Even though it was nice to see her brother, there was something painful about that place, a sadness that seeped out of the walls.

Today Naveed seemed healthier than the last time, much less coughing, which was good. But something was distracting him. She kept having to remind him when it was his turn, and at one point he forgot which game they were playing. After they finished their round of Hearts, Maman suggested Rook, but he said he wasn't in the mood. Instead, they got out

Scrabble. Roya held back a groan—she hated that game. Naveed invited her to join his team, which just meant she got to pick the tiles out of the bag. She never thought of good words to play.

After she picked their tiles, she looked around the dining hall. Not too many visitors today, so the room was quiet. Roya was glad. Sometimes the other patients made her nervous. Especially—not that she'd ever say so out loud—Naveed's friend Max, with his scary, dented face.

There was a girl in a wheelchair sitting by the windows, staring out at the kitchen garden. Roya had never noticed anyone in a wheelchair here before. Maybe she was new? Roya couldn't see her face, but the thing that kept grabbing at her heart was that the girl wore her hair in two braids, just like her old friend Kasandra. She still thought about Kass every day, even though she hadn't heard from her in months.

"B-R-I-D-G-E," Baba spelled as he set his tiles on the board. "Triple letter score on the B."

"Good one." Naveed laid out the tiles for their word. Q-U-E-S-T. "Double word score. With a Q!" He held his hand up for Roya to high-five.

That used up most of their tiles, and as she reached into the bag, feeling those smooth cold pieces with her fingers, it dawned on her that Naveed had given her that job not because he knew she liked it, but because he couldn't do it. His hands didn't feel anything; how would he be able to tell how many tiles he had without looking? For some reason, the thought made her really sad. As soon as she'd arranged the tiles on their little wooden bench, she said, "I have to go to the bathroom. I'll be right back."

The bathrooms were within their sight, so they let her go without giving her a hard time about it. She went to the ladies' room and locked herself into a stall, a quiet small comforting place, and willed herself not to cry. It was stupid to get worked up over her brother's situation when he was doing fine now. And she knew from the way her parents acted that she was supposed to look as cheerful as possible whenever she was here, even if she didn't feel happy at all.

After washing her hands, she paused in the doorway and looked at the girl in the wheelchair again. Roya could see her much more clearly from this angle.

No. It couldn't be… could it? Roya stepped closer. The girl turned toward her, and Roya froze in amazement.

She knew that face. Those long braids, those tangled teeth.

It seemed impossible—but she was here! Kasandra was *here*!

Roya hadn't seen Kass since they'd met on Lopez Island the summer before. Not long afterward, things had fallen apart for Kasandra's family. Her grandparents, who had raised her, were now dead—actually, her grandfather Alastor had tried to kill both of Roya's brothers, but that was another story—and Orcinia, where Kass had lived her whole life, had been shut down because her grandparents were growing illegal drugs there. Kass had been sent to a facility on the mainland where she'd stayed until they found her a foster family. Back in late October, she'd written a letter saying she would send Roya her new address, but she never had.

Roya glanced at her family, but they were hunched over the board, talking intently about something. Good: they were distracted. She veered over to Kass, and couldn't restrain herself from giving her friend a big hug. No one noticed. "Kass!" she whispered. "I'm so glad to see you, I think about you all the time! What are you doing here?"

Kasandra hugged her back, but she didn't smile. "Things didn't work out with my foster family." She looked down at her wheelchair. "There was… an accident, and I hurt my feet. I can't stand on them for very long right now. But they'll get better. What are *you* doing here?"

Roya wanted to know more, because Kass's feet didn't look broken or anything, though she couldn't really tell because of the thick socks and large slippers Kass wore. What kind of accident had it been? And why was she at a mental health center instead of a regular hospital? Had someone hurt her? Just the thought of that was painful, but it was obvious Kass didn't want to talk about it, so Roya sat down in an armchair and answered her question. "I'm visiting my brother."

"Ah. I thought he looked like you. I was hoping it was him, so that he could lead you back to me. Although... I've been trying other methods. I really missed you."

"I missed you, too." Roya wondered what Kass had done. Had she gone so far as to try blood magic? She thought about the spell Kass had taught her many months ago, the one that had brought Naveed back after he ran away from home. She'd considered using it to find Kass, but she hadn't wanted her friend to return in the same terrifying way that Naveed had.

Roya leaned forward. "I've been wanting to tell you, Kass. The blood magic worked. I did it just like you said, and he came back."

"That's good." Kass glanced at Naveed. "He's a very messy person, though, isn't he?"

Roya followed Kass's gaze. Her brother's beard was a bit scruffy, but she'd definitely seen worse. "Messy? What do you mean?"

"His energy. It's all blocked up and tangled. Like a big ball of yarn with a bunch of knots that won't come out."

"Oh. Definitely." Roya couldn't see things quite like Kass could, but the description was accurate.

"If only I had my athame," Kass said. She must have noticed Roya's confused expression, because she clarified, "My ritual knife. I could've used it to get his energy flowing smoothly again. Although I don't know if I'd be able to do it right. Nan probably could, but...."

Kasandra's voice trembled, and Roya took her hand. She didn't want Kass to get too sad about her dead grandmother, so she tried to change the subject. "I kept waiting for a letter from you. Why didn't you write to me?"

Kass avoided her eyes. "My foster dad didn't like me taking anything of his. Once I took a stamp and he caught me and he asked what it was for but I didn't want him to find out about you, so I lied. He also didn't like people who lie."

Roya squeezed Kass's hand, but let it go when she heard her brother calling her name. "I need to go talk to my family for a second," she told Kass. "I'll be right back."

Naveed watched her as she walked back to the table. "Found a new friend?" he asked.

Roya was about to tell them, but something stopped her. Something in Naveed's face, in her parents' eyes. Kasandra's grandparents, especially Alastor, had caused Roya's family lots of trouble. And Kass was Roya's secret friend; she'd intercepted all of Kass's letters and never told anyone they'd kept in touch. If she told them now, how would they react? Would they not want her to talk to Kass? It seemed very likely, and Roya couldn't bear the thought. So she said, "She seemed lonely. And she's really nice. Is it okay if I go talk to her some more?"

The three of them exchanged glances. Maman said, "All right, Roya-jaan, but we won't be able to stay much longer."

Naveed's face darkened, and Roya felt bad about not spending more time with him, but even so she turned away. Kass was smiling at her, which was almost enough to make her forget everything else.

When Roya got back, she whispered, "Does anyone here know that you're Alastor's granddaughter?"

"Just the staff," said Kass. "They won't tell, though. Not unless I do first. Which I haven't."

"Have you talked to my brother?"

"No. I don't usually talk to people unless I have to."

Roya understood that. "You shouldn't tell him who you are. Or that we knew each other before. I'm worried they won't let me talk to you if they know."

"Why not?" Kass looked at her blankly.

Was it possible that no one had told Kass everything that had happened? Roya certainly wasn't going to be the one to explain it all. She barely understood it herself. "Because your grandfather hurt my brothers," Roya said slowly. "I'm not sure how Naveed would react if he knew who you are. He can be a little scary when he gets angry.

So please don't tell him, okay?"

"Okay." Kass chewed on the end of her braid. They sat in silence for a minute. Then Kass spoke again. "I was in the hospital for a long time before I came here. Staring at the ceiling. I would have conversations with you in my head. I wanted you to come visit me so badly. No one ever came to see me."

"I would have come. If I'd known where you were."

"I know. But—do you know what's the worst thing?"

"What?"

"When I left the island… when they came and took me away, I had to leave right then. I didn't get to say goodbye. And they took away everything I had, gave me new clothes, new shoes that were so uncomfortable. They didn't let me keep my old things, they just got rid of them because the new things were 'better.' They wanted me to forget everything I knew there. But I didn't forget. And I can't stop thinking about what I left behind." She paused. "So when I talked to you in my head, I always asked you to do one thing for me."

"What's that?"

"Go back to the island. Get our Book of Shadows. I don't think those men who raided the cabin would have found it. Nan always kept it hidden, because it's sacred and she wanted to keep it safe from the acolytes. So in my head I told you where to find it, and you brought it to me so that I'd have something to read, so that I could figure out the right spell and then it would be better and all the hurt would go away."

Roya wanted so badly to do this for Kass, but it didn't seem possible. How could she convince her family to go back to Lopez? "I'll find it," Roya finally said. "I don't know how. But I will. You need it, Kass. It belongs with you."

"It's okay," Kass said. "It's not important anymore, because you're here. We found each other again, and that's all I wanted." They scooted closer, holding hands tightly, and stayed that way until Naveed interrupted them, saying that he needed Roya's help with the Scrabble game.

She shot Kass an apologetic glance, and Kass nodded knowingly. So Roya went back to her family. But every time she looked over to the windows, Kass grinned at her, making happiness bloom again inside Roya's heart.

Cyrus

MONDAY, DECEMBER 14

"WELL, IT FINALLY HAPPENED." CYRUS SLID INTO THE CHAIR next to Dev, who barely looked up from his laptop. It was lunch break at the community college where they were enrolled in an accelerated high school program. As usual, they were spending it working on their website.

"What, the moon's open for space tourism? Never thought I'd see the day," Dev deadpanned, his eyes already back on his screen.

"I wish. No, but it's almost as good. One of our fans wants to eat lunch with us! Shea, you know, that girl in pre-calc—"

"Yeah, I know who Shea is. You only talk about her *all the time.*"

"I do not. Anyway, I guess she watches our show, and she wanted to ask us something. You know what this means? We did it. We're officially the kings of the internet!"

"The internet is not a monarchy," Dev pointed out. "It's a little more democratic than that, but we're certainly not presidents. At most, we're maybe… junior senators."

"Okay, fine. The junior senators of the internet! Akh, that doesn't sound nearly as good. Damn you and your semantics." Cyrus rifled through his backpack for his sandwich.

"Hey, I don't make the rules," Dev mumbled, but Cyrus knew that he, too, was secretly thrilled at the success of their web series. Earlier in the fall, they'd started uploading a weekly show where they fictionalized their triumphs and humiliations as high school/community college students. (So far, the series was heavy on humiliations.) Instead of filming it on their phones, though, they recorded their voices and Dev created charming cartoonish animations to serve as the visuals. Dev's on-screen persona was a friendly-looking devil creature; Cyrus's was a one-eyed cyborg.

Lately, their channel had been rapidly gaining subscribers and their content was averaging tens of thousands of hits every day. Dev had convinced Cyrus to start monetizing, and after allowing advertisements on their videos, they'd had some pretty impressive earnings. Way more than Cyrus had made when he'd worked in a fancy restaurant over the summer.

While Dev focused on the show, Cyrus had finally begun making progress on their next mobile app. Downloads of their original offering, *Pacific Northwest Quest*, had dropped off, and Cyrus had decided to take a different tack instead of making a straightforward sequel. He was over the whole princess rescue trope, and had started building the bones of something completely new.

His successful digital life made Cyrus feel like he was on top of the world. Well, as long as you didn't squint too hard and happen to see the older brother who had checked himself into a mental institution, or the little sister who barely spoke anymore, or the crabby overworked parents, or the girl who had dumped him and then started spending a ton of time with said institutionalized older brother. As long as he didn't dwell on any of those things, life was pretty grand.

"Hey." Shea plunked down beside them and took a granola bar out of her backpack. She tucked a strand of short auburn hair behind one ear and pushed up her round-ish clear-framed glasses. Cyrus never had the gall to look at her for too long, settling for short glimpses while the pre-calculus professor drew swooping curves and complicated functions on the whiteboard, but now that she was so close he noticed the pale freckles that dotted her cheeks. Beneath her cardigan, she was wearing a very tight t-shirt with a picture of an 8-bit unicorn stabbing its horn through the neck of a modern CG lion.

Yeah. He was totally in love.

"Hi, Shea. Um, thanks for eating with us." Cyrus prayed that this lunch would not end up as one of the humiliation scenarios on their show.

"I hope you're not going to talk about me on *Devil & Cyborg*," she said, as if reading his mind.

"Of course not," Cyrus said. "And I hope you're not here to ask me about my brother." It was a running gag on *D&C*, all the girls who talked to Cyrus but really just wanted to know what was going on with Naveed. Every episode, he came up with something more far-fetched. (Cyrus really, really itched to talk about Englewood on the show, because that place was bizarre, but he did have standards.)

"Why would I do that? I already know he's attempting a solo trans-atlantic flight on his hand-carved, pedal-powered biplane," Shea said.

Cyrus was speechless. She had been paying attention!

"I'm not here to talk about *D&C*, actually." Shea took a bite of her granola bar. "Well, not the show anyway. You mentioned that you're working on a new game, and I was wondering if you'd heard about GameCodeX."

Dev glanced at Cyrus. "Yeah, we've heard about it. But isn't the competition in February? There's no way it'd be ready in time."

"Maybe not, if it's just the two of you. But what if you had help?"

"Are you saying... you want to work with us?" Cyrus tried not to sound as eager as he felt.

"Maybe I am," Shea said. "My friend Todd and I entered last year, and it was amazing. You know about the prize, right? A marketing budget of $1 million a month for a year?"

"Weren't there a bunch of strings attached, though?" Dev asked.

"Well yeah, it's backed by investors, so you have to repay them. But you keep all the profits you make on top of that. The whole idea is that it's like a real-world training program for forming a startup. Anyway—we were planning to submit a new app this year, but none of our ideas panned out. We have tons of back-end experience, but we really suck at UX stuff."

"So Todd would want to be in on this too?" Cyrus wasn't sure how he felt about that, though it would be nice to delegate some of the more tedious tasks to a couple of underlings. "Is he a *D&C* fan?"

She shrugged. "Actually, he thinks the content is kind of childish, but he's impressed by your website. He's a great coder. And a hacker, too, which comes in handy sometimes."

Cyrus thought about it. A marketing budget that big would broaden their reach way beyond their current following. He and Dev had big dreams: they wanted to expand their digital media offerings to include a podcast, maybe a blog, definitely more games and apps. To crank out content at that level, though, they'd need to get more people involved, so they'd figured that was way in the future… but maybe it wasn't as far away as he'd thought. Plus, he'd get to know Shea better, even though this Todd guy was apparently part of the package.

He was about to respond when Dev said, "Sounds interesting, but I'm not sure we have time. We've got so much to do with the show, with school… we'll have to discuss it."

Cyrus found himself nodding. Dev was right—it was crazy to think that they'd be able to get something good together in two months. But maybe, with a little time pressure, he'd be able to stop procrastinating.

"You don't have to commit to anything. Just let me know if you want to set up a meeting with us. But the registration deadline is coming up next week, so we should get together soon." Shea wadded up her granola bar wrapper and zipped her backpack shut.

"Okay," Cyrus said. "Okay, yeah, we'll think about it."

"Who does that Todd guy think he is?" Dev said once she'd left.

"Calling *D&C* childish."

"Well, he obviously doesn't have good taste in content. But, I don't know, maybe we should do this? Even if we don't win, it would be good exposure. And you know that sometimes I need a fire under my ass to get anything done."

Dev sighed. "Sad but true. Still… we barely have any time to put this together. Plus, if we won, it might just make things more complicated. Why bother getting investors involved? We'd be fine just finishing the game and launching it ourselves."

"I guess. But it doesn't hurt to put ourselves out there, right? I bet we'd learn a ton. And who knows, we might be pitching a startup to those same investors someday. Besides, if Shea and Todd want to help us get ready for the contest by doing the back-end work, we should definitely take them up on that. It could save us a ton of headaches."

"I don't know…." Dev trailed off.

"We should at least meet with them, see if that Todd fellow seems legit. Shea's awesome, though, isn't she? I mean, did you see her shirt?"

Dev shrugged noncommittally. "She seems all right."

"Are you kidding? She's super hot."

"I guess, but… what really matters is how well she codes, right?"

Cyrus clenched his teeth as a burst of annoyance flared up. Dev had been so PC about certain things lately, even going so far as to scrap a few of the jokes Cyrus had made from *D&C* after deeming them sexist or racist or homophobic or whatever. Most of the time Cyrus thought Dev was being way too sensitive, but defending the jokes felt gross. After all, his family had been on the receiving end of Islamophobic vitriol far too often. He'd decided it was best to stick with non-offensive humor, and resisted getting in an argument with Dev over any of it.

"Besides," Dev continued, "Don't you think it's too soon? After Andi?"

"What does she have to do with anything? That was ages ago," Cyrus said, as if he hadn't been counting the days since they'd officially broken up. (It had been 87, to be exact.)

Dev shot him a skeptical look. "Come on, Cy. I know you still like her, and now that she's. You know." *Spending so much time with your brother* was the censored part of that sentence. "If we're going to be working with Shea, maybe you should try to… rein it in a little."

"Because you think I'll blow it with her, too?"

"No. It's just not a good idea to get romantically involved with your colleagues. Haven't you seen any sitcom ever made?"

"Okay, I know I've been hung up on Andi for a long time, but I'm totally over her now, and it doesn't bother me at all that she goes up to the cabin almost every weekend," Cyrus said. Truth be told, it *did* irritate him, just a tiny bit, that Andi spent so much time at "the cabin," which was how he and his family referred to Englewood in public.

He didn't want to discuss this further, so he took a bite of his turkey/mayo sandwich. It was the most boring lunch in the world, but he'd barely had time to slap it together in the morning. All quarter, he hadn't been able to bring himself to buy anything at the cafeteria, and wouldn't eat food prepared by someone he didn't know. Only food in sealed packages or stuff he made at home. Being poisoned by a crazy hippie and going into sudden cardiac arrest—yep, he was only sixteen but he'd already had a heart attack—then spending days in the hospital puking up what seemed like every meal he'd ever eaten was not an experience he cared to repeat. He tried not to let the resulting paranoia show too much, but it nibbled at him slowly. Silently.

He checked his phone to distract himself as a new text from Andi appeared on the screen. The sight of it made his heart flip in a weird but pleasant way. It was just that he missed her, he told the judgy-faced Dev who lived inside his head. As a friend. That was all.

She had texted him a picture of a bag of Blazin Bitz the other day. THEY'RE BACK I CAN'T BELIEVE THIS, she'd written. What should we do about it???

He had never responded, because honestly he didn't *want* to do anything about it, but admitting that made him feel lazy. So he braced himself, figuring her latest text would be something else Bitz-related.

But it wasn't. Have you seen the news about Viktor Zolotov? So crazy. You like sci-fi, right? Did you ever read any of his stuff?

Cyrus thought about writing a snarky reply that not every nerd on the planet was into sci-fi—he personally didn't care for it—but he was too curious what she meant. So he clicked the link she'd texted and started reading.

> Authorities have now identified the human remains exhumed last month in Orcinia, the Lopez Island "retreat center" run by Alastor and Zennia Yarrow. Three men, one woman and two infants were found buried on the property. One of the bodies has been confirmed as that of Viktor Zolotov, a Russian-born science-fiction novelist who disappeared in the 1990s. Cause of death could not be determined, but one curious finding offers a potential clue: the body had no right hand.

The turkey sandwich churned in Cyrus's stomach. No matter how much he tried to rid his mind of the things that haunted him, they just kept coming back.

Andi

FRIDAY, DECEMBER 18

ANDI SHOOK OFF HER WET JACKET AS SHE STEPPED INTO THE Coalition for Food Justice's office. She hung it on the coat hook, careful not to splatter raindrops onto the nearby box of rolled-up posters and protest banners.

Brooke looked up as she entered the cramped conference room. "Yay, you made it! Just in time, too. The intern was supposed to be here, but they're running late and I've been doing everything myself." She gestured at the white post office bin filled with hundreds of envelopes.

"Your mom hasn't been helping?" Andi asked.

"She and Mahnaz were in meetings all morning, plus they have a ton of reports and stuff to wrap up by the end of the year. These mailings should've gone out weeks ago, but... with the trial and everything...."

"Yeah. I know." Andi winced. She'd spent the past week desperately trying *not* to relive Richard Caring's trial. She'd also avoided mentioning Ah-ma's cancer to anyone. Saying it out loud would make it feel too real. "How can I help?"

Brooke showed her all the enclosures: the letter asking for tax-deductible year-end donations, written and signed by CFJ's co-directors, Naveed's mom Mahnaz and Brooke's mom Kelly; the self-addressed return envelope; the small flyer printed on bright yellow paper advertising a protest in January.

"What's this about?" Andi held up the flyer before stuffing it into an envelope. "A rally against Blanchet Capital? Who are they?"

"I don't know that much about it. Mahnaz printed a bunch and asked me to include them in the mailings. They're some sort of financial company, a private equity firm, I think. Not sure how that fits in with CFJ, but they're probably just trying to get the word out. I'll still be in Seattle that day—I'm not leaving for Boulder until the week after that. Wanna go?"

Andi had no desire to go to a protest ever again. "I don't know...."

Luckily, she didn't have to elaborate, because Mahnaz walked into the office then, taking off her own sopping coat and hanging it next to Andi's. Andi steeled herself: she had an idea she wanted to run by Mahnaz and Kelly, and Brooke had assured her that this would be the best way to catch them.

"Andi-jaan!" Mahnaz hugged Andi, kissing both of her cheeks before sinking into a chair and taking a stack of envelopes to seal with a wet sponge. It seemed like every time Andi saw her, more white strands were visible in her curly dark hair. "Thank you for helping out. How have you been?"

Mahnaz's affection always made Andi feel warm inside. "Pretty good," she lied.

"I've been meaning to thank you for your testimony at the trial. I think it really helped convince the jury—and now Richard Caring is behind bars. It was a huge victory, and it wouldn't have happened without you."

Andi wished she could feel as good about it as Mahnaz apparently did. She could still picture Richard Caring's face as the judge stated that he'd been found guilty for attempting to cover up Dr. Tara Snyder's many crimes. He had looked stony and unrepentant. Andi got the impression that he didn't care at all about what he'd done: he was just furious that he'd gotten caught.

She'd been unsure whether the jury would agree that the once-beloved CEO of Nutrexo was guilty. Richard Caring's lawyer was ruthless, systematically tearing down Mahnaz's reputation, repeatedly referencing her Iranian-Lebanese heritage and her involvement in "organizations attacking American values." He had succeeded in getting Cyrus's testimony thrown out because he was in an "unfit mental and physical state" when he'd heard Richard confess to the cover-up.

But he hadn't been able to strike down Andi's testimony of what she'd overheard Richard Caring say to his Senior VP, Mark Williams, at a party the previous summer—especially since Mark later took the stand and corroborated what she said. He told the jury that both he and Richard had known about the harmful research Dr. Snyder had been carrying out at SILO, her research facility. He said that they hadn't known all the details, but had approved the project hoping that it would benefit both Nutrexo and Genbiotix, their subsidiary pharmaceutical company. Mark had already pled guilty to his conspiracy charges, but had only been sentenced to six months in prison since he had been unaware that Dr. Snyder had abducted four research subjects: Andi, Naveed, Cyrus and Roya.

As Richard Caring's verdict was being read, Andi had squeezed Cyrus's hand so hard that he whispered in her ear, "Could you ease up there, A? I can barely feel my fingers." Then she heard the judge say that he'd been found guilty, and relief swooped through her. But the judge had gone on: *eighteen months in a federal penitentiary.*

That was disappointing, but he deserved every minute that he'd spend in prison, every instant of disgrace. Just as Andi was about to turn to Cyrus, whom she could feel beaming beside her, Richard Caring caught her eye instead. He stared at her with so much hatred that it felt tangible, like he'd launched a heavy stone her way. That stare communicated something very clearly: *I'm going to make sure you pay for this.*

The moment didn't last long, because Cyrus pulled her into a hug and spoke into her ear, "We did it! No, *you* did it. You did it, A!" Andi tried to soak up his happiness. But when she glanced back at Richard, he had turned his seething, furious gaze to Mahnaz, who didn't notice because her head was buried in her husband Sam's chest. Though it had all been over within a few seconds, it still haunted Andi, over a week later. The violence of that stare....

Eighteen months, she kept telling herself. *Eighteen months is a long time.*

But it wasn't, not really. Andi certainly didn't want to bring any of that up with Mahnaz now, anyway, so she kept her eyes on the letter she was stuffing into an envelope. "I'm just glad it worked out. He needs to be punished for what he did. Hopefully Dr. Snyder's trial will go the same way."

"I hope so." Mahnaz gathered a stack of sealed envelopes and began straightening them into a neat pile as she asked, "Are you planning to go to the cabin this weekend?"

Andi felt heat rising to her cheeks and angled her head downward, hoping to hide in the shadows of her long black hair. It was stupid, she knew, but all week long she'd been revisiting that moment when Naveed had pressed her hand to his chest, the electric jolt that his touch had sent radiating through her arm, her entire body. The sound of his contented exhale; the sight of his brilliant smile; the conversation they'd had afterward, focused on all the things that mattered to her.

Andi's attraction to him, which she'd been successful at denying ever since he'd made it clear that he loved her as a sister, swelled up to the surface. Again and again, she tried to push it down, but it was like a round ball in water, and kept bobbing back up. It was something about the way he had looked in that moment. The glow that came from him. The way he seemed... more like his old self.

She felt bad for thinking that, for feeling more attracted to him when he seemed healthy and sane. And she did love him, no matter what mood he was in, but some visits she'd been counting down the minutes until she could leave, because he was so distant or distraught that she didn't know how to help him. The visit last weekend, though... that time, she *had* been able to help, and she just wanted to stay close, to feel that spark glowing inside.

"I can't," Andi said now, directing her words to the envelopes, trying to erase Naveed's smiling face from her mind. "I'm flying to Berkeley in the morning. But—I've been wanting to ask you something."

"Sure," Mahnaz said.

Andi forced herself to look up, hoping the blush had faded. "It's about Blazin Bitz," she said. "Have you seen that they're back on the shelves? I did some research—apparently a bunch of people kept lobbying to get them back, so some other food company bought the brand."

Mahnaz frowned. "I did see that. I've been meaning to look into it, but... well, you know. These past few weeks have been too busy."

"So is CFJ going to do anything about it?" Brooke interjected. "Someone needs to push back."

"I've already talked about it with Kelly. It's not something she wants to take on right now, but I've been thinking about some options. We could start circulating a petition, but there's no way I could get to that until January. It might even be later than that—there's a chance I'll be taking some time off early next year."

"Really?" asked Brooke. "Why's that?"

"Nothing's for sure yet. But if it works out, I might be going to Iran for a few weeks. Farhad, you know, Khaleh Yasmin's son, he's getting married in February, and she offered to fly me out with her."

"Wow! Good for Farhad. That's exciting," said Brooke.

"I can't believe he's getting married," Mahnaz said. "I still remember when he was a little boy, before he grew up and moved back. Naveed thought he was the greatest person on the planet. He followed him around everywhere. Farhad was like his big brother. I'm just—I'm so happy for him." She dabbed her eyes with the corner of her sleeve.

For some reason this conversation was making Andi uncomfortable, and she wanted to steer it back on track. "It's okay if you're too busy to work on the petition," she said. "What if I wrote it? A draft, anyway, and you could edit and post it? That way we don't have to wait to get the word out."

"That would be wonderful, Andi-jaan," Mahnaz said. "If you have the time."

Andi had a feeling that she'd have plenty of time over the next few weeks while sitting with Ah-ma during her chemotherapy infusions. She also needed to make some progress on the documentary score—Vanesa had finally sent her the rough cut, which she hadn't watched yet—but she would need to work on that at night when she could focus. The petition would be the perfect daytime distraction.

The door opened and Kelly peeked her head into the conference room. "How's it coming?" she asked.

"Still got a long way to go." Brooke indicated the large stack of unstuffed envelopes. "But Andi and I have to head out in about an hour. We're going to a show tonight."

"That's fine. Thanks for helping out," Kelly said.

Mahnaz got up and headed for her desk, saying that she needed to send out a few emails. Kelly, though, picked up one of the flyers about the Blanchet Capital protest and frowned. Then she, too, left the conference room.

"Did you get a chance to listen to Invisible Noise yet?" Brooke asked Andi.

"No. Not yet."

"They're amazing. You're going to love the show. Here, I'll put them on." Brooke closed the door, then began playing Invisible Noise's debut album through her phone's speakers. Andi was just starting to get into the music when she heard Kelly's voice through the thin walls.

"Mahnaz, what's this flyer about?"

"Oh, right," Mahnaz said after a moment. "Akilah asked if we could help spread the word, and I figured our mailings would be perfect."

"I thought we agreed that we needed to be more strategic about which protests to promote. Especially after what they said about you in the trial. We need—*you* need—to be careful. Besides, the rally is about Blanchet Capital's role in the for-profit prison industry. It doesn't have anything to do with food, it's not in our scope—"

"It is, though," Mahnaz said. "Blanchet *does* have connections to the food industry—their PR branch creates advertisements for lots of different food companies. Not to mention their land grabs in Africa that are destroying peoples' farms and livelihoods. It's all connected. And we need to fight back." She paused. "Besides, what happened at the trial shows that we're making progress. We need to keep pushing while we still have momentum."

Kelly's voice was almost a whisper. "Don't tell me that you're actually planning to go to the protest."

"Of course I am. I'm not going to let them intimidate me out of taking action against the next greedy corporation to move into that building. They're not Nutrexo, but they may as well be. It's like a shape-shifter—its face may have changed, but it's still the same demon underneath."

Kelly's chair squeaked. "We need to stay focused on the CFJ's core mission, promoting food justice. We just don't have the capacity to take everything on."

"But maybe it's time to broaden our scope. After all, capitalism is the root of all the inequality, the oppression, the racism—"

"Mahnaz. I get what you're saying, but... after everything that's happened...."

"Will you pass me another stack of those flyers, Andi? Right behind you," Brooke was saying.

Andi returned her attention to the conference room, to the growing stacks of stuffed envelopes. She handed the flyers to Brooke, still thinking about what she'd overheard. She and the Mirzapours had been successful in shutting Nutrexo down, in bringing its CEO to justice—but now, just months after the scandal, another corporation had moved into their building, and Blazin Bitz were back by popular demand. Genbiotix was still around, and they were actually profiting from the superbug Dr. Snyder had unwittingly created, since they made the only antibiotic that could treat MRK. It was just like Mahnaz had said. Different face, same demon.

The phrase echoed in Andi's head even after she and Brooke left an hour later for the all-ages Invisible Noise show. They stood in the front, waiting for the lights to go down, defending their turf with sharp elbows. Andi was mentally working on her anti-Blazin Bitz petition when Brooke nudged her shoulder. "Hey. See that guy over there? To your left, by the speakers. He's totally checking you out."

Andi glanced that way to see a college-aged white guy smiling at her. He was broad-shouldered, muscular, with an unruly mop of brown hair—and dimples. Really cute dimples.

She looked away quickly. Lucky for her, the house lights dimmed just then, and the opening act came out on stage. All through their lackluster set, she could feel his gaze straying her way. But Brooke was probably wrong, Andi thought. He wasn't checking her out, he probably recognized her from the news or something—her photograph had been all over the place during Richard Caring's trial—and was trying to figure out where he knew her from.

But when Invisible Noise came onstage, Andi was instantly swept away. It was the best kind of show, the kind that sent electric energy coursing throughout the entire room, so that even the most self-conscious of hipsters started jumping up and down and screaming out lyrics.

Most people had their eyes on the lead singer, a Kenyan-Scottish man whose magnetism was undeniable, but Andi kept watching the one woman in the band—who happened to be Asian—drifting between playing backup guitar, keyboard and violin. On one of the songs, she shredded an incredible violin solo. It was the best thing Andi had heard in ages.

After the show was over, Andi didn't file out with the others right away. She wanted to stay there, where the magic afterglow of an amazing show still hung in the air, instead of driving home to pack for her depressing "vacation."

Besides, the music had inspired her. A new melody was floating around in her head, one that she thought might work perfectly for the documentary. It was a melancholy song, for those poignant moments in the film, and really would be better with violins....

Andi was about to record a voice memo on her phone, wanting to capture the melody before it floated away, when she heard a deep voice behind her.

"Have we met before? You look so familiar."

Andi turned. The guy from earlier smiled broadly, his dimples on full display. He was pretty much the same height as Andi, but now that he was close, she was acutely aware of the bulk and chisel of his muscular arms and shoulders.

"Um, no, I don't think so," Andi said.

He held out his hand. "Well, then, nice to meet you. I'm Jed. Amazing show, right?"

She shook, noting his firm, strong grip. "Yeah."

"What's your name?" he asked.

Andi pulled her hand back. "Sasha," she said, giving the name printed on her fake ID. "And this is my friend—"

"Elise," said Brooke, following suit.

Jed nodded at Brooke before returning his gaze to Andi. There was something fiery about the way he looked at her, something that unleashed a sudden heat throughout her whole body. She was usually wary of white boys like him, after a brief freshman-year fling with a guy who'd expected her to be a stereotypical obedient Asian girl and tried to get into her pants on the first date. But Jed was brimming with a friendly, laid-back charm that was hard to resist.

"You go to shows often?" Jed asked. "I'm new to Seattle, and could use some help finding the good ones. Maybe you could text me some suggestions?"

"Um…." Andi was very selective about who she shared her phone number with, but he had a hopeful look in his eyes that she didn't want to destroy. Besides, she wouldn't exactly mind seeing him again.

"Here, give me your number," Brooke said.

He recited it for her, and Brooke entered it into her phone. "Well, see you around, I hope," he said, giving Andi one last smile before turning to leave.

Brooke was still thumbing at her phone. "What was his name again?"

"Jed, I think."

"I'll never remember who that is—I'll put him in here as 'Dimples.'"

They stepped outside. The drizzle had stopped, but the wet, salty air hung thickly around them. "He's super into you," Brooke said. "If you want me to send you his number, just say the word."

"Okay. I'm not sure yet."

Brooke stopped. "Hold on—over there. Isn't that the violinist?"

It was. She leaned against the wall of the club, her face illuminated by her phone.

"We should go over there. Tell her how much we liked the show," Brooke said.

"I don't know. She looks busy," Andi said.

"Come on. Don't be shy."

Reluctantly, Andi followed her over. The woman was even more glamorous, and more intimidating, up close. "Hey, great show," Brooke said.

The violin player looked up from her phone. "Oh, thanks."

Brooke poked Andi, who, in her nervousness, started babbling. "Yeah, you were amazing. That violin solo… it was so kickass… I've never seen anything like it…."

"Yep. Punk rock violin always surprises people." She slid her phone into the pocket of her leather jacket. "Do you play?"

"Me? Oh, no, I'm not… not a musician."

"Don't be ridiculous, Andi, you totally are," Brooke said. To the woman, she added, "She's an incredible piano player. Even composes her own pieces."

"Oh?" the woman tilted her head.

"Not really," Andi said. "I've just been dabbling in songwriting—"

"By which she means that she's been working on music for a documentary film," Brooke added.

While Andi appreciated Brooke's faith in her, she didn't want this woman to get the wrong idea about her being some sort of musical savant. "That's true, but I've actually, I mean, this is all new to me." She stopped short of saying, *I'm making it all up as I go. I honestly have no idea what I'm doing.* "Anyway, tonight, seeing you play... I was thinking that it would be great to have some violin in the mix."

"What's the documentary about?" the woman asked.

"Migrant farmworkers." Andi really needed to watch the film so that she could provide a better description.

"Sounds bleak. You'll definitely need violins," the woman said. "You know what? I do session work sometimes. Look me up if you need someone to play for you. Patricia Duong. I've got to go, but it was nice meeting you. Good luck, yeah?"

She turned to go back inside. Brooke flashed Andi a cheesy grin, and she found herself filled with a soaring lightness. It was a good thing gravity was holding her down, because otherwise she would probably float all the way up to the moon.

Naveed

NAVEED PADDED INTO THE DINING HALL ON SATURDAY MORNING, only half-awake. Around dinnertime the night before, his nerve pain had flared back to life for the first time in weeks. It felt like he was stepping across an endless bed of needles as he walked back to his room. Once there, he stripped off his slippers and socks and lay down, frustrated. It had taken so long to find an SSRI antidepressant that kept his mood balanced without unbearable side effects, and also kept the neuralgia manageable—but apparently it wasn't as effective as he'd thought.

He listened to a guided meditation while telling himself that that this was temporary and would soon pass. But the pain kept him awake most of the night and caused him to miss morning yoga, a ritual he'd initially scoffed at but had grown to enjoy.

By mid-morning, though, it had receded, so he got dressed and headed to the dining hall. No point in cleaning himself up too much, since no one was coming to visit him today. He didn't want to think about the fact that he wouldn't see Andi again for weeks.

He brewed himself a cup of green tea. Max was nowhere to be seen, and Koffka was sitting near the girl who wore her hair in braids. Naveed slumped into a chair at an empty table. Yep. There it was again, that crushing loneliness he knew so well.

Not that he could complain. He was incredibly lucky to be here at Englewood, he knew that. Even so, the last few months hadn't exactly been easy.

His stay hadn't gotten off to a great start. Not long after he'd arrived in October, Dr. Young decided he should try equine therapy with the horses. When he'd stepped inside the barn for the first time, the smell of manure hit him like a brick to the jaw. The horses in the stalls. Their black, long-lashed eyes. Instantly, he was back in that other barn at SILO, reliving everything again. In his mind, he was running from them all: from Dr. Snyder and Alastor and the police and everyone who'd ever tried to hurt him. In reality, he bolted for the forest but tripped on something and fell into the mud where he couldn't breathe, couldn't find the air, was certain all those phantoms were descending upon him and he was going to die.

After that, Dr. Young had tried exposure therapy to get him to face his fears. During their sessions, they walked a little closer to the barn every day. It took weeks before he could stop himself from turning around the second it appeared on the horizon. One day, though, he managed to step right up to the door. But the second she opened it and the manure smell hit him, he was off in panic-land again.

The fever came that night. It lasted for a week and was accompanied by a chest-rattling cough that made him unable to sleep. The whole time, his thoughts had wheeled in anxious overdrive. He'd long suspected that the antibiotics they'd pummeled him with the previous summer had failed to contain the multidrug-resistant *Klebsiella pneumoniae* that had nearly killed him; he imagined pockets of it still surviving in his body, waiting to re-emerge. But according to Englewood's staff physician, it wasn't MRK, just a bad case of bronchitis, a virus that would go away on its own.

The physical recovery was one thing, of course, the mental recovery yet another. During his illness, Nate had come back, whispering in his ear, reminding him of what a burden he was, what a waste of space.

Their therapy sessions shifted to focus on this instead. The way Dr. Young saw it, Nate was the personification of his depression, and Naveed needed to learn how to live with that self-destructive voice whenever it came back. She also helped him work through the "internalized ableism," as she called it, that made Naveed see his physical and mental limitations as character flaws. According to her, every time he didn't give in to Nate, every time he endured being struck down with nerve pain or bronchitis or a panic attack, he showed how strong he truly was—even if it didn't look like what society had conditioned him to see as strength.

It sounded nice in theory, but he still thought the whole thing was unbelievably stupid. He didn't want to fight battles inside his head while looking, on the outside, like a helpless bedridden lump. He wanted to do important things out in the world, but right now he couldn't even think past the confines of his own self. His was a hidden war that he feared would never be over.

"Good morning, Naveed!" The cheery voice interrupted his thoughts. Becky, one of the administrative staff, set a box down in front of him. "Delivery for you!"

"Thanks," he said. The box had already been opened, as usual, and searched for contraband. Still, his excitement grew when he saw that it was from Khaleh Yasmin. She always sent good stuff: homemade rosewater-scented rice-flour cookies; tins of imported pistachios; rich, soft dates. This time, he opened it to see six fresh pomegranates. Nestled among them was an envelope.

There was a card inside wishing him a happy Shab-e Yalda. A pang of loneliness hit him hard. The holiday was one of Naveed's absolute favorites, and he'd be missing it this year. He'd always loved staying up late at Khaleh Yasmin's house, gorging on pomegranates and watermelon as they celebrated winter solstice with poetry games and dancing, surrounded by a wild, raucous energy that always made Naveed feel so at home.

A piece of folded paper was also enclosed. Naveed opened it to see a printed-out email written in Persian. It was from Yasmin's son Farhad, who lived in Tehran. He read it twice, then crumpled it up and threw it in the nearest garbage can.

"What's this?"

Dennis had come out of nowhere. He fished the wadded paper out of the trash can and sat down next to Naveed.

Naveed grabbed for it, but Dennis jerked away, spinning in his chair so that the letter was out of Naveed's reach. He let out a low whistle, then bent his head toward Naveed conspiratorially. "So, what are you planning?"

"Give that back," Naveed said.

"Tell me: where's the attack going to be? I'm sure the FBI will want to know the details."

Naveed allowed himself to briefly imagine strangling Dennis. Then he focused on his breath, on the sounds in the room around him, trying to will his anger to subside. But he felt like he would be running from racist stereotypes his whole life, and this ignited something deep inside him, a rage that couldn't be easily controlled. But he had to stay on top of this, had to take the high road, or else Dennis would win.

Naveed hid his clenched fists under the table. "Why, Dennis?" he asked, his voice quiet and controlled. "Why do you keep fucking with me?"

Dennis leaned forward. "Because I know what you people are capable of," he said. "And I know you were really the one who killed the CEO of Bountiful Earth. It's complete bullshit that you're not in prison right now."

That was it. Naveed's vision clouded: he needed to get out of here, now. He grabbed his box of pomegranates and burst through the doors to the courtyard. He wished Koffka was there beside him, but it was probably better to do this alone.

Naveed left the courtyard, veering off the trail into the forest. He stopped when he saw the perfect tree, a gleaming white birch, and cradled a pomegranate in his hand. He couldn't feel its leathery skin, but could sense the weight of it in his palm, this fruit full of arils packed with sweet juice.

He stepped back. He took aim and flung it at the tree. It exploded with a satisfying *crack*, spraying its purple-red juice all over the pristine birch bark. The fruit fell, cracked and bleeding, onto the forest floor. He was going to throw another, but changed his mind: he wanted to destroy that first one fully, so he seized a fallen branch and started attacking it, the juice spattering everywhere, and oh that release felt good, it felt *good, good, good*.

But he couldn't enjoy it for long, because soon he felt eyes on him. Someone was watching.

He turned around slowly.

Fiona, the nurse, was directly behind him. Flanking her on both sides were two other nurses, forming a semi-circle around him. For a second he almost lost himself, flashing back to that night on the pier when the police had surrounded him, the electric jolt of their tasers, the explosion of pain as they slammed his head into the wet wood. He tightened his grip on the branch and turned again quickly, just in case someone was advancing on him from the other side. No one was there.

"Why don't you put that stick down," said Fiona calmly.

He took three deep breaths, anchoring himself back in this moment. Then he did as she said. The branch dropped to the ground with a quiet *thunk*. "I want to see Dr. Young," he said, also very calmly, hoping to set them at ease.

"I think that's an excellent idea. Come with me," Fiona said. One of the other nurses picked up the box of remaining pomegranates, folding the flaps down so he couldn't see them. As if the fruits themselves had provoked his rage. Before she closed it, he noticed the splatters of juice bleeding into the sky-blue tissue paper, and looked down at his hands.

They, too, were pricked with sticky droplets.

After they had installed him in Dr. Young's office and gone to find her, Fiona handed him a warm wet towel and sat with him while he scrubbed off his hands and face. He didn't say anything, and neither did she. When Dr. Young came in, she took the reddened cloth and left.

"Do you want to tell me about what happened?" Dr. Young asked as she sat down behind her desk. She tucked her long silver hair behind her ears, regarding him with her incongruously youthful face, open and nonjudgmental as ever.

"I know how it probably looked, but I didn't lose control. I knew what I was doing. I was angry and needed to get it out, but I didn't want to hurt anyone." This wasn't exactly true. Naveed would gladly have done the same thing to Dennis's face.

But he knew it was the right thing to say, because her chin dipped almost imperceptibly down, then back up, a tiny involuntary gesture that he'd come to read as a nod. "What made you angry?"

He wasn't about to tell her what had happened with Dennis. She seemed to think that, just because the two of them shared a PTSD diagnosis, it should be easy for them to find "compassion" for each other. It had also been Naveed's experience that white people—even those who considered themselves progressive, like her—were very good at forgiving, ignoring, or explaining away the racially-charged comments of other white people, and he really didn't want to hear her siding with him right now.

It must have taken him too long to respond, because she prompted, "I heard you received a package. What did the letter say?"

He looked up, relieved to have something else to talk about. Besides, he *was* upset about that. "It was from my friend Farhad. He's getting married in Iran this February. He invited me to the wedding."

"And that's what made you angry?" She didn't sound confused, just curious.

"Well, yeah. Obviously I can't go—I'm on probation until October. I can't leave the state, let alone the country."

"And he knows this?"

Naveed started to answer that he did, but the more he thought about it, the less sure he was. He'd barely talked to Farhad in months. Khaleh Yasmin knew that Naveed had been convicted of misdemeanor theft for taking off in Brennan Walsh's rental car after the CEO was killed, but maybe she was fuzzy on the details of Naveed's probation. "I'm not sure," he finally said.

"How would you have felt if he *didn't* invite you?" she asked.

It was so annoying when she was right. Naveed opened his mouth to protest, but what came out was, "I hate having to miss out on things like that. And it isn't just the wedding, they also sent me a card for this holiday we celebrate on winter solstice. I'm missing that too, since I'm here, and it's, like, my favorite."

He hated himself for sounding like a sulky little kid, but all Dr. Young said was, "Tell me more about that."

So he did, realizing as he talked that he was glad to be missing the celebration this year. Everyone would be so happy for Khaleh Yasmin; maybe they'd even beam in Farhad and Zahra via video chat. Naveed's parents would get in on the fun, telling the story of how the two of them had met at a Yalda party years before, when his dad was a civil engineering freshman at the UW and his mother had just started her PhD in molecular biology, and their hands had touched as they'd both reached for the last wedge of pomegranate.

If Naveed were there, he'd be the cautionary tale, the flip side of hope and love, his despair and resentment leaking unpleasantly into their celebration of returning light. He'd be the black hole that people avoided for fear of it swallowing them whole.

Naveed kept talking to Dr. Young, not saying any of this, telling her, instead, about another Yalda party, one that he remembered particularly clearly, even though he was only nine at the time. That was the party when Maman had gone into preterm labor, and Baba had whisked her away, and Naveed and Cyrus stayed with Khaleh Yasmin, sleeping on a hard futon in the basement while the rest of the adults carried on upstairs. Roya had been born four days later, on Christmas morning.

It killed Naveed that he wouldn't be there to celebrate Roya's own ninth birthday with her, since she probably wouldn't want to spend half the day sitting in the car for the four-hour round trip to Englewood and back. "I want to go home," he said suddenly.

Dr. Young raised her eyebrows in that slight, almost-imperceptible way. "You only have a few weeks left in the program," she said. "I'd strongly advise against leaving early. The transition can be difficult; that's why we set the process up the way we do. We should do one more family therapy session, get you set up with an outpatient therapist and psychiatrist and support group, spend some time setting goals...."

She droned on, but Naveed stopped listening. Despite all her protests, she couldn't stop him—he was a legal adult who was here voluntarily. He could sign his own discharge papers. All that was required for his probation was to continue mental health counseling, but he didn't have to be an inpatient. He vaguely remembered signing a financial agreement that stated he'd be billed for the full twelve weeks even if he left early, but that wasn't an issue; Maman had assured him that his stay would be covered by their health insurance.

A knock on the door interrupted Dr. Young's seemingly-endless list. Fiona stuck her head inside the office. "I'm so sorry to interrupt, but this man says you had an appointment?" The door opened further to reveal a white middle-aged man Naveed had never seen before. He was dressed much more formally than the standard Englewood visitor, with precisely styled sandy-blond hair, a dark blue suit jacket, and sleek, well-polished Italian loafers.

Dr. Young glanced at the clock. "Oh! I'm sorry—"

Naveed stood up. "I'll go. We can talk later."

But the man was already stepping into the office. "Actually, I'd like to speak with him too, if I may."

Naveed's heart hammered, his guard instantly up. Before Dr. Young could say anything, the man said in a rush, "I'm Tim Schmidt, from the CDC. I work with the National Center for Emerging and Zoonotic Infectious Diseases, and we've been following the global spread of MRK—it was recently classified as an official epidemic in Mexico. We've been receiving reports of lingering health problems among survivors of the disease, and want to study the long-term effects of severe MRK infections. We would just need you to provide a few blood and tissue samples, sign a medical record release, that sort of thing—nothing too invasive, and the information would go a long way in helping others with this disease."

It took a minute for Naveed to digest this. It wasn't at all what he expected. But before he could say a word, Dr. Young was stepping between them. "Mr. Schmidt—"

"Dr. Schmidt," he corrected.

"Dr. Schmidt, I did not give you permission to speak with him about this." Her firm tone barely disguised her anger. "Please step outside, and we can meet when I'm finished with my session."

Tim Schmidt seemed nonplussed. "Of course. My apologies."

Dr. Young ushered him out the door. When she sat down again, she exhaled audibly. "I am so sorry. Are you all right?"

She made it sound like he'd been beaten up or something. "I'm fine."

"I wasn't aware he was going to ask you that, and I would never have allowed him to talk to you if I'd known. What he said—that must have been very triggering."

Dr. Young must really be flustered if she was suggesting how he felt, rather than asking him. But she was right; it *had* triggered something in him, just not in the way she thought. He was overcome by a sense of curiosity, and a strange vindication: perhaps his suspicions had been correct. Maybe he was right; maybe some form of MRK lived on inside him, and in other survivors too.

"The epidemic—what's happening in Mexico right now—you know that it's not your fault," Dr. Young went on.

"I know." They had been over this frequently, though this was the first time she'd ever called it an epidemic. Which itself was more vindication: despite her assurances that cases of MRK would eventually peter out, he'd known that this would happen. He knew, too, that it *was* his fault. He was Patient Zero. He'd started this all.

But maybe, now, he could do something to help.

Dr. Young was staring at her computer. "Really, I'm fine," Naveed repeated. "Can I go now?"

"All right," she said. "But if you need me… my door's open."

Naveed stood up and left her office. Tim Schmidt was sitting in one of the chairs across the hallway, a briefcase at his feet. When he saw Naveed, he stood up.

"I'm sorry about that. Didn't mean to interrupt," he said. "But if you ever want to hear more about the project, here's my card."

Naveed glanced inside Dr. Young's office, knowing that she wouldn't approve, but her eyes were still fixed on her computer. Without saying a word, he took the business card and slipped it into his pocket. As he walked down the hall toward his room, he couldn't resist looking back one last time, but Tim Schmidt had already disappeared.

Cyrus

SUNDAY, DECEMBER 20

ON SUNDAY MORNING, CYRUS FINISHED THE LAST BITE OF HIS scrambled eggs and brought his plate to the sink. Maman was scrubbing something invisible on the counter.

"I'm heading out," he told her. "Be back in the afternoon."

She looked up, but didn't answer right away; it seemed to take her a minute to process what he'd said. "Aren't you coming with us to Englewood?"

"Sh—oot, I forgot you were going today. It's just, we have this important meeting scheduled. Dev needs to be there, and this is our last chance before he heads out to Kolkata for two weeks. Can we go tomorrow instead?"

"No, tomorrow won't work. We'll be getting ready for the Yalda party at Khaleh Yasmin's."

Oh yeah. That. Now Cyrus felt worse, because her exasperated tone transmitted her unspoken words very clearly: *your brother really wants to see you. We're all making the effort, why can't you?*

This was much harder for Cyrus than it was for the rest of them, though. His relationship with Naveed had been strained since the previous summer, when Cyrus had blown up at his brother at the worst possible time, and Naveed had responded by overdosing on painkillers and later running away from home. Even though they'd gone through several painful therapy sessions together, he knew Naveed hadn't fully forgiven him, and visiting him dredged all that baggage up again so Cyrus tended to avoid it, which he knew wasn't helping, but it was just so *hard* and he was so busy and visiting Englewood took up an entire day and there were so many other things he'd rather be doing and and and....

Maman was watching him with furrowed eyebrows, like she was reading his mind. "Okay, how about this: I'll go see him tomorrow on my own," Cyrus said. "I can take Roya if she wants to come. That way it'll be easier for you and Baba to help Khaleh Yasmin get ready."

She nodded slowly. "All right. We'll need your help with the food, though, so don't be back too late."

"I won't. We'll be back way before the party starts." Cyrus wasn't exactly looking forward to sitting around while a bunch of Iranians had poetry throw-downs in a language he could barely understand, but at least the food would be good.

His phone buzzed. "Oh—Dev's already on the train. I'm running late. See you later." He bolted out to his car before she could respond. Once in the driver's seat, he inhaled deeply as he turned the key in the ignition. Ah, that smell: the warm and musty smell of his car. His parents had surprised him with it for his sixteenth birthday in September. He was still amazed they'd remembered his birthday at all, considering all the other shit that had been going on at the time. It wasn't exactly the car he would have chosen if he'd picked it out himself, but he'd instantly fallen in love with the black late-model Honda Civic hatchback. Now, it was his inner sanctum. It might be littered with to-be-recycled empty soda cans and tons of papers from school, but it was *his*.

He wished he and Dev could carpool, but thanks to Washington state law, Cyrus wasn't allowed to have non-family passengers until he'd had his driver's license for six months. Dev didn't turn sixteen until April, so he had to catch the train up to the U-District, where Todd lived.

By the time Cyrus found parking and texted that he was outside, he was only seven minutes late. Much to his delight, Shea opened the front door. "Hey," she said. "Dev just got here—we're setting up in the basement."

She led Cyrus to a narrow stairwell off the kitchen, and he followed her down to the basement, a wide room with low ceilings. Todd and Dev were both sitting at a dining table that looked like it had never once been used for its intended purpose. It was buried under piles of laptops and cables. In an open closet in the back of the room, under the glow of multicolored LED lights, Cyrus noticed a crazy-amazing PC battlestation setup: two wide-screen monitors, a cushioned gaming chair, wall-mounted speakers. It was all he could do not to drool.

"You must be Cyrus. Come on in, pull up a chair." Todd was tall and lanky, not the usual burly programmer build, though he avoided eye contact and had pale, sun-starved skin and terrible posture, so those things checked out.

Cyrus sat down and unzipped his backpack. They made small talk for a minute while he and Dev set up their laptops.

"Okay, so what's the game about?" Shea asked once they'd gotten settled.

"We'll show you what we've got so far," Dev said. "It's hard to explain without looking at it."

Cyrus was glad that Shea had chosen to sit on his side of the table; Dev and Todd sat opposite them. So far, there had been no signs that Shea and Todd were an item—no loving glances, no lingering touches or cutesy nicknames—which made him happier than he cared to admit.

He opened the app on his phone, and Shea leaned in closer. Her hair smelled like lemon zest. He forced himself to concentrate. "So the game is pretty simple," he said. "It's called *Bugpocalypse 3K*. The first level starts in a grassy field that's been invaded with a nuclear swarm of insects.

The catch is, some of the bugs are good, and if you smoosh those you'll actually lose points. Like, here, these shiny green ones. And these little black ones. But the big red bugs—they're bad news, so smash away."

Shea smooshed a red bug and it disappeared with a pop, a sound effect Dev found that had been labeled "bubble wrap." They had paired this with a tiny vibration, which, in Cyrus's opinion, made it extra satisfying.

"Yes. Killed it dead!" Shea exclaimed.

"The purpose is to smash as many of the bad bugs as you can while leaving the good bugs. The level ends when you kill off all the bad ones. The more good bugs left in the end, the higher your score. The first level starts off with a high ratio of bad bugs to good ones, like 80/20, but the ratios change as the levels go on. Eventually the ratio is completely opposite, and there are way more good bugs than bad."

"Can I try?" Shea asked, and he handed over his phone. Todd was already smashing away across the table, a steady *pop - pop - pop* emitting from Dev's phone. Both of them, Cyrus noticed, exclaimed in triumph whenever they had a good run, and cried out when they accidentally smashed a good bug. Cyrus and Dev met each other's eyes across the table and smiled. It was the first time they'd shared the game with anyone, and both Shea and Todd seemed to be genuinely enjoying it.

When they finished the level, Cyrus took his phone back. "What do you think?" he asked.

"It's pretty great," said Shea. "But how many levels are there? They're over pretty fast. You don't want people to run through the whole game in ten minutes."

It was a valid point. "To be honest, I haven't gotten that far yet," Cyrus said. "We've only completed five levels so far."

"And they're all with the same bugs? Just different ratios?" Todd asked.

"Yeah, same bugs," Dev said.

"Maybe you could design different skins for every level, or every five levels or something," said Shea. "Like, I don't know, an underwater one with good fish and bad fish. No—that's stupid, but you know what I mean."

Dev was nodding his head. "Yeah. Yeah, I like that."

"Is there a social component to it at all?" Todd asked.

"Not really. There's a global high score that users try to beat, but that's all we've got so far."

"Hmm. It would be way more fun as a social game," Todd said. "Like, you could challenge a friend or a random person. They'd share the same view as you, so it would be a race to find all the bad bugs before the other one does."

"Or you could have two modes, a competitive and a cooperative option," said Shea. "Like, pitting yourself against other people, or choosing to team up with someone else to fight the evil bugs before you run out of time."

Cyrus looked at Dev. "I don't know. It's a good idea but it sounds really complicated to pull off. I'm not sure we have time—"

"It's not *that* complicated," said Todd. "I've done stuff like this before. I could work on a beta version if you want."

Dev shrugged. "Worth a try, don't you think?"

"All right," Cyrus agreed.

"Oh, and a design note," Todd said. "Can you make it more obvious which are the good bugs and which are bad without relying so much on color? I'm actually colorblind, so it's hard to tell red from green."

"Whoa, sorry, dude," Dev said. "Good point. We can totally fix that."

"Can I see your code?" Shea asked.

Cyrus pulled it up on his laptop, but she only looked at it for a minute before shaking her head. "The problem is, there's not enough variance between the levels. So it'll get boring really quick."

"Cy and I were thinking about changing the layout of the levels," Dev said. "Like having an image gradually appear in the background as you kill the bugs. Maybe even designing it so the good bugs spell out a hidden message when you finish the level, to make it more satisfying."

"Ooh, I like that," Shea said, rubbing her hands together.

They spent the next hour brainstorming. Cyrus sent Todd and Shea the code, and they all pored over it on their individual laptops as they made plans for dividing up tasks. Shea offered to take care of registering them for the contest, and they all agreed to reconvene after Dev returned from his trip.

Before he and Dev left, Cyrus excused himself to the bathroom on the other side of the gamer closet, trying not to be jealous of the fact that Todd had his own awesome coder-cave in his parents' basement. Cyrus wished he had this much room to spread out in. It had been nice not having to share a room with Naveed being gone, but even so his family was always clomping up the stairs and yelling at each other across the house, constantly interrupting his train of thought and making it hard to concentrate on anything. If he had a place like this, though....

But he soon stopped thinking about that, because he noticed something atop a stack of magazines by the toilet. It was a book—and not just any book. On the cover, two figures in space suits stood before a white expanse dotted with craters, gazing at the faraway Earth in the sky. The title was printed in tall yellow letters below. *Keepers of the Moon*, by Viktor Zolotov.

Cyrus shivered involuntarily. He washed up and took the paperback with him when he returned to the main room. "So you're reading this, huh?" he asked Todd. "How is it?"

"I got that copy years ago," Todd said. "Just finished reading it for the eleventh time."

Okay, so obviously Todd knew about it before it was cool. "What's it about?" Cyrus asked.

Todd launched into the summary with great enthusiasm, as if he'd been waiting his whole life for someone to ask. "Well, the story starts in this alternate-history Soviet Russia—"

Dev interrupted. "Hey, no spoilers. I'm only a hundred pages in."

"Your first time? Oh, you are in for a treat." Todd looked excited.

Cyrus, on the other hand, was not. "You're reading it too, Dev?" He couldn't quite say why this felt like a betrayal, but it did.

"Yeah. It's really good so far."

Cyrus kept his mouth shut as Todd continued, "So. Alt-history Soviet Russia. A group of rebel scientists and thinkers—comrades of people killed in this bloodbath similar to the Great Purge—start drawing up plans to build a new society on the moon."

"They wanted to escape," Dev chimed in. "To create an independent, self-sustaining colony."

Cyrus glanced at Shea, wanting to share an eye-roll with her at the expense of these two fan-boys, but she was frowning at her laptop screen. She looked cute when she did that.

Todd was talking now. "It takes years, but they build a rocket out of scavenged metal and the chemist—he's the main character, Mikhail—builds an apparatus to harvest and concentrate oxygen from the atmosphere. The botanist, Natasha, brings a whole bunch of plants and seeds and soil.

"So they get to the moon, and they have to be in their suits all the time to protect against the crazy-high solar radiation, and they build all these connected structures and greenhouses. But one day, Natasha tears her suit and ends up getting infected with what turn out to be these alien life-forms that live on the moon, tiny bacteria-like things. But they're not harmful, at least not at first. They're, like, symbiotic. They help her figure out how to work with the materials on the moon, how to get the plants to grow."

"Whoa, whoa, stop right there," Dev said. "I just got to the part when Mikhail finds out about the Little Strangers."

Todd made a motion like he was zipping his lips. "I'll say no more. But once you finish, there's some awesome fanfic you should check out. Especially if you ship Milinsky. I can send you the link… I mean, if you're interested."

"Hell yeah," said Dev. "Mikhail and Belinsky are the perfect couple."

Cyrus wasn't exactly sold on the book, but he also didn't want to be left out. So he asked Todd, "Would you mind if I borrowed your copy?"

"If you're careful with it," Todd said nervously, as if worried Cyrus was going to light it on fire or something.

After he and Dev said their goodbyes, Shea stopped Cyrus as he was about to head up the stairs. "Thanks for giving us a chance," she said, extending her hand. "Looking forward to working with you."

They shook hands. She held on for a few seconds longer than was strictly necessary, and he could still feel the ghost of her touch even after he'd closed the door and stepped outside into the grey December afternoon.

Roya

ROYA WOKE UP ON HER BIRTHDAY TO A CAT SNIFFING HER FACE. Pashmak was curled up on the pillow, her little nose inches from Roya's own.

"Do I smell good, Pashi?" Roya stroked the cat's head, and Pashmak purred in response. Roya took that as a yes.

She checked the clock, but it wasn't even six yet—too early to get up. There was no way she'd be able to get back to sleep, though, not with this antsy sense of anticipation flooding her whole body. This year, more than any other, she was hoping she'd get the gift she wanted most of all.

She'd been begging her parents for it ever since her first conversation with Kasandra. "All I want," she'd told them, "is to go on vacation to Lopez Island. Even if it's just for a few days. Remember, Maman, how nice it was there? I want to go back."

"I'm not sure, Roya-jaan," Maman had said. "Baba and I aren't able to take much time off of work."

"We could just go for a weekend. It would be the perfect time! We don't have any plans, other than visiting Naveed, and Kourosh doesn't have school."

Baba shook his head. "I don't think we can find a good place on such short notice. I'm sorry, azizam. What else might you like?"

So it hadn't seemed very likely, but then again, today was also Christmas. Even though her family didn't celebrate the holiday, this made her birthday feel extra special somehow. It was the kind of day when miracles could happen.

Plus, she was excited because she'd get to see Kass today when they went to visit Naveed. She fantasized about telling Kass that her wish had come true, that she'd be going to Lopez and would do everything she could to get Orcinia's Book of Shadows back to its rightful owner.

It was cold in the house but cozy in her bed, so for a while she stayed under the quilt cuddled up next to the purring Pashmak. Around six, though, she was ready to get up, so she put on a sweatshirt and went downstairs to survey her pile of presents. Maman had set up the birthday table, as she did every year, decorating it with pine boughs and pretty candles and a bowl of fresh fruit and nuts still in the shell. Roya counted eight gifts, mostly from her parents and Cyrus but also something that looked like a book from Auntie Leila and several small presents from Khaleh Yasmin. There was nothing from Naveed, of course.

His absence tugged at her, like it did from time to time. It seemed like this would be the new way of things: he would leave for a while, he'd come back, and then he'd leave again. One day he'd move out for good. She didn't want to think about that.

There was a faint noise coming from the front of the house. Like a tree tapping its branch on a window. Roya decided to ignore it. But a moment later, she heard it again. This time she noticed the pattern. Tap, tap, tap-tap-tap, tap, tap. Naveed's knock.

Could it be? She pushed aside the curtain on the front window and saw her brother under the porch light in his coat and hat, his breath puffing out into the cold air, holding a pink bakery box. He smiled when he saw her.

Roya stared at him. It didn't make any sense. What was he doing here?

His smile faded, and she let the curtain fall back. She opened the door—but then the alarm, which she had forgotten about, began to beep warningly, so she had to close the door in Naveed's face and run to punch in the code before it went off and woke everyone up. That done, she returned to the door and opened it again, a million thoughts running through her head. *If he's here, then we won't be visiting him today, but I told Kass I would come see her on Christmas....*

Naveed looked deflated by now, so she apologized. "I forgot about the alarm. What are you doing here? We were supposed to visit you today."

This wasn't going well. Her voice sounded mad. He was still standing outside, holding that box, rocking from foot to foot. "Nope, now you don't need to! I'm home. For good. Can I come in? It's cold out here."

"Oh. Sorry." She held the door open.

He stepped inside and set the box on the coffee table. Then he sat down on the couch to take off his shoes. "Anyone else up yet?" he asked. "I know I'm early, but I figured you'd be awake and I was just... excited. To surprise you for your birthday." He sounded so sad that she forgot about her own sorrows for a second and leaped onto the couch next to him.

"I *am* surprised." Roya hugged him. "I thought you weren't real. That I was dreaming. But you're here! You're here." She snuggled into him. He smelled like the outside.

"I brought you something," he said after a minute, handing her a wrapped gift from his coat pocket. "It's not much, but I hope you like it."

"Thanks." Roya added it to the birthday table, knowing her parents would want to watch her open it.

"Oh, and doughnuts!" Naveed added. "Want first pick?"

He opened the pink box, and Roya chose one with chocolate frosting and coconut sprinkles. Her favorite—he'd remembered. She felt bad for not jumping up and down with happiness when he arrived, which was obviously the reaction he'd been expecting.

As Roya took a bite and her mouth filled with sweetness, Maman appeared at the top of the stairs. Naveed stood up, and Maman brought her hand to her mouth, tears in her eyes. Then she flew down the stairs, and they were hugging, and she was kissing his cheeks, saying, "You're home. You're home. I can't believe it!" Then, calling up the stairs, "Saman! Kourosh! Come see who's here!"

They came down, and Roya was glad for the flurry of excitement, because it gave her a minute to collect herself. She pushed Kass out of her mind. Maybe she could still figure out a way to get to Englewood today. Somehow….

"Are you just here for the day? How did you get here so early? Did someone drive you?" Maman was asking.

"No, I checked out yesterday," said Naveed. "I only had about a week left in the program, so it wasn't a big deal to leave early. Dr. Young was headed to Seattle anyway, so she gave me a ride back, and I crashed with Andi's dad last night so I could surprise you when you woke up. I missed you and… and I wanted you to know how much I appreciate all that you've done for me. I know it's been hard and I've caused you a lot of problems, but it's going to be different now. You don't have to worry about me anymore."

Maman and Baba were both openly crying by now. Cyrus was looking down at his phone, like always, but Roya could tell he was a little misty-eyed. Now would have been an appropriate time for her to get her own tears out, but nothing came. Her family was together again. Why couldn't she be happy about it?

They sat around for a while, eating doughnuts and cracking walnuts and drinking tea. Soon Baba went to the kitchen to make French toast, Roya's favorite breakfast, and Roya jumped at the chance to go outside and collect fresh eggs from the chicken coop. As she set them gently into the wire basket, she whispered to the chickens, so low that only they could hear, "What's wrong with me?"

The chickens clucked quietly. Inside her mind, Roya went back to her last birthday, when Naveed had given her the wooden flute that now sat untouched on her highest bookshelf. So much had changed since then. She shivered and the eggs knocked together, but didn't break. Roya sat for another minute in the quiet dark with the chickens, then turned and left the coop.

After breakfast, Roya opened her presents. Her parents had gotten her new clothes—how boring. Cyrus gave her a card with a sketch of the three-layered raspberry-chocolate birthday cake he'd be baking for her, which she couldn't wait to eat later. The present from Naveed turned out to be a framed picture that he'd drawn, which had her name written in Nastaliq calligraphy, surrounded by pretty geometric designs. Baba exclaimed over it, wondering if he'd made it at Englewood, but Roya only half-listened as Naveed went into detail about the different art supplies he'd used. She knew she was supposed to like it, but it really wasn't that exciting. It definitely wasn't as good as a handmade flute. Still, she didn't want to seem ungrateful, so she gave her brother a big hug and told him that she loved it.

She was about to bring her presents up to her room when Baba stopped her. "Wait, there's one more thing." He pulled one final gift from behind the fruit bowl.

Heart thumping, Roya opened the wrapping paper. Inside was a small wooden box. A crescent moon was carved into the top. "It's beautiful," she said. "It's perfect. Baba—did you make this? For me?"

"Just for you, Roya-jaan," Baba said.

Roya opened the lid. The inside smelled like cedar, and it was just large enough to fit a few treasures: a smooth rose quartz and a pearly white shell. But Roya's eye was drawn to a folded sheet of paper underneath them.

She removed the paper and unfolded it. At the top was a picture of the house on Lopez that Auntie Leila had rented last summer. Underneath that were the words, *Your reservation is confirmed. You're going to Lopez Island!*

Roya lowered the paper in disbelief. "Really? It's really true?"

"It's really true," said Maman.

"What does it say?" Naveed asked.

"We're going to Lopez!" Roya read the rest of the confirmation. "In just a few days! We're really going! Oh, thank you, thank you!"

"Lopez Island? Awesome. I can come too?" Naveed looked bewildered.

"Of course!" Maman said. "We won't be able to stay for long, I'm sorry about that, Roya. But we were able to rent the same place—it happened to be available for a few nights before the new year."

"It's perfect," Roya said. "It's perfect, Maman. I can't wait."

As soon as she could get away, she retreated to her room. She lay on her bed, thinking about what she'd pack for their trip to Lopez, but soon enough her thoughts drifted to Kass, who was probably sitting at Englewood all alone right now, staring out those big windows waiting excitedly for Roya, who would never come.

Without warning, the tears erupted. She buried her head in her pillow and let them flow.

Some time later, when her sobs finally petered out, Naveed knocked on her door. "Hey, Roya. Can I come in?"

"What is it?" she asked thickly.

"I just wanted to tell you something," he said.

"Fine." She turned her face so that her hair hid her eyes.

He ducked his head to avoid the sloping ceiling and sat on the edge of her bed, like he'd done thousands of times to tell her bedtime stories. For some reason, this made her even sadder. She swallowed back another sob.

He stared at the floor, drumming his fingertips on his knees. "Do you remember that dog at Englewood who would sit with us sometimes?"

"Of course."

"That was Koffka. All the dogs were great, but Koffka... it felt like he understood me."

Roya wasn't sure where this was going. "Wait... are you saying... you're going to get a dog like that?"

"I don't know. Maybe someday. Actually, Becky—one of the admin staff—helped me apply for a service dog before I left. So we'll see. But there's a long waiting list. It sometimes takes years to get one."

"Oh." Roya wiped her still-running nose on her shirt, glad he wasn't looking at her.

"Anyway," Naveed continued, "Yesterday, Koffka was right by my side all day. Like he knew I wouldn't be there much longer. When it was time to go, I took him to the girl in the wheelchair. Your friend. I told her I was leaving, and I... I told her how he likes to be scratched under the ears, how he loves raw broccoli. Asked her to keep an eye on him for me, and she said she would." He stopped drumming his fingers. "So don't worry, she and Koffka won't be lonely. They have each other now. But before I left, she did say, 'Tell your sister to write to me.' If you wanted to write her a letter sometime, I'm sure she'd appreciate it."

"Okay." Relief rushed through Roya. If Naveed had told Kass he was leaving, then Kass would know why Roya didn't show up for their promised Christmas visit. She'd know that Roya hadn't abandoned her.

Naveed got up to leave, but she stopped him. "Wait. Naveed, I'm sorry if it didn't seem like it earlier but... I'm so glad you're home."

"It's okay," he said. "It's good to be back."

As soon as he closed the door, Roya wiped her eyes, feeling much better. Everything was going to work out. Even if she couldn't visit today, Roya could still write letters to Kass, and after she got the Book of Shadows back from Lopez she'd find a way to get it to Englewood. She sprang up to search for a piece of paper, not wanting to waste another second before telling Kass the good news.

Andi

FRIDAY, DECEMBER 25

THE FIRST WEEK OF ANDI'S VACATION PASSED IN A WHIRLWIND, much of it spent in sterile clinic rooms where Ah-ma had her chemotherapy infusions. Andi and her mother sat with her at each session, listening to audiobooks or watching Chinese soap operas, trying to distract themselves from the constant reminders of illness and mortality.

During the long hours at the clinic, Andi spent lots of time working on her petition, which was much more difficult than she thought it would be. No one seemed to care about Blazin Bitz's return, with the exception of the brand's many supporters. And since only the original flavor was being sold, not the kind that included the super-addictive component Tara Snyder had created, there was no outcry about potential health risks—even though, as Andi found during the course of her research, there was plenty of evidence to link consumption of junk food to various metabolic diseases.

She decided to play up this angle, but for a while wasn't sure who the petition would be addressed to. It wouldn't do any good to ask Hannigan Foods, the company that had acquired the brand, to stop selling them. Instead, Andi chose to target the grocery store chains, asking them not to stock Blazin Bitz on their shelves. But the more she worked on it, the more Andi doubted any of this would make a difference. Even if she collected thousands of signatures, why would the stores care? They were probably making tons of money now that people finally had their Bitz back.

It wasn't until the night of Christmas Eve that she made an interesting discovery. She'd been about to send a draft of the petition to Mahnaz when she found an article outlining the corporate restructuring that had happened during Nutrexo's downfall. The whole thing was incredibly confusing, and Andi was thankful the author had included a helpful infographic. As she pieced it all together, though, she only became more disturbed.

Nutrexo hadn't really gone away. All of its major brands had been sold to other companies. Most of the food products went to Hannigan Foods, their longstanding rival. But their agrichemical holdings, the seed and fertilizer and weedkiller brands, had all become part of Genbiotix, which had spun off as a separate company.

Strangely enough, Andi discovered as she dug deeper, Hannigan itself was a recent acquisition of an even larger company. Andi almost laughed out loud when she read the name: Blanchet Capital. The same financial firm that was moving into the old Nutrexo tower.

So, basically, Blanchet owned Blazin Bitz now. It was exactly like Mahnaz had said: *Different face, same demon.*

Andi sent a link to the article, as well as the petition she'd drafted, to Mahnaz. Then she texted Brooke, who was equally aghast after Andi filled her in. Brooke promised she'd go to the protest against Blanchet, which would be happening a few weeks after Andi returned to Seattle. You want to come? Brooke asked. We could invite Dimples ;)

At the mention of Jed, Andi's heart lurched unexpectedly. She did kind of want to see him again, and felt like she should show up for the rally, but she wasn't as fearless as Brooke or Mahnaz. Instead, she wrote a noncommittal, Not sure. Maybe.

She couldn't find sleep that night. After tossing and turning for a while, she got up and cleared space on the small desk that still had several trinkets on display from her preschool era, including a lump of dried clay that was supposed to look like a dog and a framed drawing of her mother and grandparents standing under a rainbow.

Before she'd left for Berkeley, Andi's father had presented her with a Christmas gift: a portable 25-key MIDI keyboard that she could plug into her laptop. She'd been itching to play around with it, but had dropped into bed exhausted every night and hadn't had a chance yet. She hadn't even watched the documentary, although she knew Vanesa was waiting on her. Tomorrow, she thought. She could watch it tomorrow. Tonight, she needed to lose herself in music.

For the next few hours, she did. It was amazing how much better she felt when she was composing, in her own world where she had control over everything. No one was looking over her shoulder, no one was second-guessing her decisions or co-opting her vision with their own. This was freedom. Escape. When she finally crawled back into bed close to two in the morning, she fell asleep quickly.

After her late night, Andi didn't wake up until almost noon on Christmas. Groggy, she checked her phone to find a bunch of texts wishing her a happy holiday, many of them from her dad. She wrote him a short response. Just woke up. Merry Xmas! Miss you.

Minutes later, he replied, Me too Peanut. I think you'll be getting a happy surprise today tho!

For some reason, this message unleashed a swell of anxiety. Andi told herself she was being stupid—it was a perfectly normal thing for him to say, especially on Christmas morning. But at the same time, she wished he'd just tell her what it was. She was not exactly a fan of surprises, even if they were supposedly good.

She combed through her other texts, trying to let that go. Cyrus had sent a message asking, u up yet? Got time for a video chat?

She replied, Slept in late, just got up! Maybe this afternoon.

Andi pulled on her clothes and made her way downstairs. Her bedroom was on the top floor of her grandparents' narrow three-story duplex, next to the room that used to hold the Buddhist shrine where they prayed twice a day. They had recently moved it to the first floor to spare Ah-ma the long climb, but the scent of incense had seeped into the walls. To Andi, it smelled like home.

She stopped by the shrine before heading into the kitchen and lit three sticks of incense, offering up prayers to her ancestors. *Please, protect Ah-ma. Help her get better. Please.* Though she'd felt funny about it at first, burning incense or joss money and leaving offerings of fresh fruit or green tea had become part of her daily routine, too. She didn't know whether any of it would actually help Ah-ma, but she figured it couldn't hurt.

When she finally made it to the kitchen, Andi's mother and Ah-ma were sitting across the table from Ah-gong, who was pouring tea from an Yixing clay pot into a glass decanter. Ah-ma smiled at Andi; she looked pale and old and her hair was thinning rapidly from the chemo, but it was good to see her out of bed.

"Merry Christmas, bǎo bèi!" Andi's mother said. "Just in time for gōng fu chá."

Ah-gong pinched a tall aroma teacup with bamboo tweezers and rinsed it with a splash of hot water from the kettle. Then he poured tea from the decanter into four of the aroma cups. Andi took hers and waited for Ah-gong to rinse another teacup for her, this one normally-shaped. Once he had, she placed it upside-down on top of the aroma cup and flipped them both over, letting the spring-green liquid flow into the teacup. She held the now-empty aroma cup up to her nose, inhaling the scent. The tea was sweetly perfumed, bright and floral.

Andi's mother flipped Ah-ma's cup for her, then Ah-ma lifted it to her lips and tapped two knuckles on the wooden table—a symbol for "thank you." She sipped her tea loudly, aerating it as it entered her mouth.

"Can you tell what it is, Andi?" Ah-gong asked. It was a game they'd been playing ever since Ah-gong started his tea importing company, Lu Yu, when she was a toddler.

Andi sipped from her teacup. "Baozhong?" she guessed, though she wasn't sure. It had that floral scent, so it could be Lishan. No, Lishan had a sharper note at the end, a different aftertaste.

"Ah, still got it!" he said with delight. "Winter harvest."

"Hěn hǎo hē," Andi said, because the tea was very good.

Ah-gong finished his tea and poured fresh hot water over the leaves in the pot to make another infusion. Then he stood up to retrieve something from the kitchen counter. "We were going to wait for xīn nián," he said, referring to Chinese New Year. He handed her a white envelope with both hands. "But since you won't be here then, we wanted to give this to you in person."

Andi slid the back flap open with her thumb. She opened the card and found an inscription inside. *Dear Andi, we know you are on to great things. That's why we are happy to provide you with whatever you need (tuition, room and board) for your college education at any California university. Love, Ah-ma and Ah-gong.*

Wait... what? They were paying for college? For *everything*? She wouldn't have to worry about taking out loans or scrounging up financial aid or working a part-time job? It was incredibly generous, and Andi knew she should feel relieved and grateful, but something was off. It was like sitting down at the piano and starting to play a song, and having a jangly mess come out instead of the beautiful melody you'd expected because you'd positioned your fingers on the wrong keys.

She read the inscription again, and this time pinpointed what was bothering her: the stipulation that it had to be at a university in California. She'd humored her mother by applying to Stanford, UC Davis, and UC Berkeley, but in her heart she had known that she'd end up at the UW. Seattle was where her family was—her parents, of course, but also her other family, the Mirzapours. After everything she'd been through in the last year, she wasn't sure she was ready to strike out on her own yet.

Unless, that is, she got into USC. She'd applied to the school because its music composition program was one of the best in the country, and its proximity to LA meant that she'd have the opportunity to make connections with people in the film industry. Vanesa had actually gone there, and she'd spoken highly of it.

Andi wondered if Ah-ma and Ah-gong would still honor their offer if she went to USC to study music. Not like she'd get in anyway—she shouldn't even dream about that.

But why had they specified California schools? Did they think UW was inferior? Or was there something else going on?

She was still having this internal monologue when she looked up and realized that everyone was staring at her. "Wow," she said, breaking the silence. "This is... amazing, I just... I can't believe it! Thank you so much!" She sprang up and hugged everyone.

After eating a late brunch, Andi climbed back upstairs to her room, ready to take Cyrus up on his video chat. Maybe he would parse out this new development with her. He might be at Englewood with Naveed by now, but maybe he hadn't left yet.

So she tried calling him, and he picked up right away. She could tell from the bunk beds in the background that he was in his bedroom. "Andi! How's your Xmas going?" He actually pronounced it that way, *X-mas*.

"It's fine. Weird, but good? I don't know. Is now an okay time to talk? I thought you were going to Englewood today."

"Well. About that." Cyrus grew straight-faced, and Andi's heart sank. Had something happened? Oh God, she didn't think she'd be able to take that. No, wait, he'd answered smiling... ugh. She had no idea how to read these cues.

"What's going on? Is everything okay?" she asked.

"Hold on a sec," Cyrus said maddeningly, then his screen went dark. When it came back on again, she saw two faces: Cyrus and... Naveed?!

Andi may have shrieked a little. "What? Why? You..." she sputtered. "You're home?"

Naveed was beaming. "Surprise! Checked out yesterday."

Andi could barely register what was going on. Out of the blue, she thought about Jed with his irresistibly cute dimples. But Naveed's smile was somehow a million times more beautiful, maybe because it was so rare. "I can't... wow! That's amazing! You must all be so happy."

A strange sadness descended on her. She wished intensely to be there, with all of them, having a big celebratory meal together.

"I stayed with your dad last night and surprised everyone this morning," Naveed said. "I swore him to secrecy—he didn't tell you, did he?"

"No." Andi thought about the text he'd sent, relieved that this must have been the "happy surprise" he was referring to. "Hey, speaking of Dad... are you guys having a big dinner? Maybe you could invite him over?"

"Already did," Naveed said. "But I guess he has plans with one of his bandmates."

"Which one?" Andi liked some of his bandmates a lot more than others. Charlie was a total stoner, and she always worried about him having a bad influence on her dad.

Naveed wrinkled his nose while he thought. It was adorable. "Kyle? I want to say Kyle."

"Oh, Kyle. That's good."

"Okay, Andi, one more surprise." Cyrus was practically bouncing up and down. "I sent you an email—a present from us."

"Wait, but you said you didn't do Christmas! I didn't get you anything, you shouldn't—"

Cyrus cut her off. "Hogwash. Open it up! Open it up!"

Andi was still stunned to have Naveed's face smiling on her screen. She could hardly tear her eyes away, but once she finally did, she was even more surprised. She had to read the email twice before it finally sank in.

"You got me Digital Performer?" she asked. She'd been coveting the music composition software for ages, but it was so expensive that she hadn't been able to justify buying it. "How did you know?"

"You mentioned it once when we were talking," Naveed said. "Kourosh and I—well, all of us really—wanted to do something special for you. I mean, where would we be without you, Andi?"

"You guys." Andi didn't know what to say. "It's so generous. I can't... it's just... thank you."

"Our pleasure. Let me know if you have any problems downloading it or anything," said Cyrus.

They talked a little longer. Cyrus told her about their upcoming trip to Lopez Island; Naveed and Andi made plans to go for a run around Seward Park when she got back home. Not once did Andi mention the gift her grandparents had presented her. She had no idea how Naveed would react to that.

After she ended the call, Andi started downloading the software to her laptop and flopped down on her bed, completely drained.

Naveed was back home. That was good, of course it was good, but... it had been hard enough to keep him out of her mind while he was at Englewood. What was it going to be like, not having that distance? If he was around all the time, texting her, running around the park with her, wanting to meet up after school—how would she control herself?

Andi smoothed the blanket beneath her. *Be like Ah-ma*, she thought. *Don't worry about what the future will bring. Focus on right now.*

A few minutes later, her computer dinged: her new software had finished downloading. She sat up. Whatever happened—or didn't happen—with Naveed, she knew exactly what she needed to be doing right now. She clicked through old emails until she found the link to the rough cut of the documentary.

It was time to get to work.

Cyrus

CYRUS COULD HARDLY BELIEVE IT: HIS WHOLE FAMILY WAS ON vacation together. Even more unbelievably, there hadn't been a single catastrophe—and everyone was actually enjoying themselves.

He was sitting on the sofa in their Lopez Island rental with his laptop, temporarily alone. His parents had taken a walk to the beach, and Naveed and Roya had gone on a bike ride. Everyone had been surprised when Naveed decided to bring his bike along, but Roya had eagerly said she would bring hers too. The first time the two of them had gone out together, Cyrus and his parents had been nervous wrecks, waiting for their phones to ring with news of the latest disaster. But they both returned laughing and breathless, and when Naveed was in a genuinely good mood, he was like a hot-air balloon that lifted the rest of them up.

Of course, he wasn't always so cheery. Cyrus had felt bad on Roya's birthday when Naveed walked into their bedroom and saw the extent to which Cyrus had taken over. He'd moved into the long-coveted full-sized bottom bunk, and had been using the top as storage for dirty clothes and textbooks. Had he known his brother was coming home, he would have cleaned up a little. But as it was, Cyrus worried it looked like he'd moved on. Like Naveed had been forgotten.

Naveed hadn't said anything, just stood there with his jaw clenched tight, the thin scar on his cheek glowing pinker than usual. Cyrus knew there were all kinds of storm clouds brewing inside his mind, but he didn't want to cause an explosion, so he'd quickly started gathering his stuff and joking about his slovenly ways. That had seemed to diffuse the tension.

He had not looked forward to that first night, either, remembering the months of waking up to hear Naveed coughing or screaming or freaking out. But they'd both slept fine, and even though Cyrus kept waiting for his brother to break down, he seemed wonderfully, refreshingly... normal. Sure, he was spaced out sometimes, and he took forever to do simple things like getting ready in the morning, but it was much better than it used to be. To Cyrus's relief, Naveed didn't seem to be mad at him anymore, and the two of them had been getting along surprisingly well.

Now, Cyrus heard tires on gravel outside, and looked out the window to see his brother and sister arriving on their bikes. They didn't seem unhappy, exactly, but they definitely weren't in the same ecstatic mood as the last time.

Cyrus saved his *Bugpocalypse 3K* code as they walked through the door, disappointed to see them back so soon. He'd barely gotten any work done, and it was much harder to concentrate with them around. "How was the ride?" he asked.

Roya shrugged, unclipping her helmet. "It was fine."

"Yep. Fine." Naveed rifled through the kitchen cupboards, pulling out a glass and filling it with water.

"You guys hungry?" Cyrus asked. "I was trying to figure out what to make for dinner."

"Whatever's fine. We just had some trail mix, so we're good for now." Naveed sank onto the couch after draining his glass and picked up *Keepers of the Moon,* which Cyrus had thoughtlessly thrown onto his desk back at home after borrowing it from Todd. Though Naveed usually liked more highbrow literary stuff, he seemed to be enjoying it, and Cyrus had found himself unable to mention the bizarre connection between Zolotov and Orcinia. He didn't think there was much danger of Naveed finding out, though, since he tended to stay away from reading the news.

Roya climbed up the ladder to the loft bedroom. "Yeah, whatever you make will be good," she said.

Cyrus was slightly annoyed at the lack of guidance. He closed his laptop and started some rice, thinking he might make a simple khoresht with potatoes and lentils. That didn't have anything on Naveed's hit list in it. He still refused to eat meat and dairy, and couldn't stand the smell of bread. Which pretty much ruled out 90% of normal food.

After a while, Naveed put down his book and joined him in the kitchen. "Need any help?"

Cyrus didn't want Naveed wielding knives, so he said, "You can peel the potatoes. I already washed them. You don't have to take all the skin off, though. Leave a little."

"Sure thing, boss." Naveed started washing his hands in the kitchen sink. Cyrus turned away, because there was something really intense about the way he did it, scrubbing every inch of them with soap and then taking ages to wash them off.

After what seemed like several minutes, the water was still running, and Cyrus glanced over to see Naveed's hands wringing under its stream. "Okay, okay, that's good enough. You're wasting water," he said, but Naveed didn't respond. Cyrus marched over and turned the water off. For a second, Naveed stood there, hands still scrubbing each other. They were red, and Cyrus mentally kicked himself for not checking that the water temperature wasn't too hot. He handed his brother a dish towel.

Naveed blinked, then took the towel and dried them off. He picked up the vegetable peeler and started scraping, as if none of that had happened. With a mischievous grin, he asked, "So, do you and Shea have any plans for New Year's Eve?"

Cyrus couldn't hold back a smile. He and Shea had met up a few times to work on the app, and so far things were going marvelously. "Akh. I never would've told you about her if I knew you were going to give me this much grief."

"What? I'm only making conversation." Naveed batted his eyelashes in mock innocence.

"Oh, no, you're not." Cyrus stopped short of saying anything more, because it was still something of a sore spot for him. They'd never talked about it, of course, but every time Cyrus mentioned Shea he could practically hear his brother's thoughts. *Oh good, he's over Andi. Now she can be mine.* Cyrus didn't know why that always sounded so cackly in his head, like it should end with villainous laughter. Well, okay, he *did* know: he was still uncomfortable at the thought of Naveed and Andi ending up together, but it seemed inevitable now. Instead of bringing any of this up, though, he said, "As a matter of fact, we do have plans. We're going to spend a totally romantic evening together debugging the app. It'll be awesome."

"Nice," Naveed said. He set the potato he was peeling down on the counter to inspect something on his hand, then returned to the sink to wash it off. "Hey, so I was wondering... when are you and Dev going to make the next episode of *D&C*?"

The question surprised Cyrus. "Well, we were going to work on one while he's in India so that we could do an episode about his adventures there. But his internet's spotty, so it'll have to wait. Why do you ask?"

Naveed turned to face him. "Kourosh, you don't have to do this if you don't want, I know it might not fit into your vision and everything but... I was wondering if maybe sometime I could be on the show? As, like, a guest star?"

Cyrus could hardly believe it. This was something he'd dreamed about, since it was guaranteed to rake in the views. Naveed had never done a single interview or made any public statements since the original Nutrexo ordeal over the summer. If he were to appear on *D&C*... well, it would probably break the internet. But Cyrus hadn't wanted to ask, knowing that Naveed probably wasn't interested.

"I'd have to talk to Dev, but I'm sure that could be arranged," Cyrus said carefully. "What did you have in mind?"

"I don't know. I'm tired of hiding. Before someone else beats me to it, I need to come out."

Cyrus must have looked startled, because Naveed continued, "As mentally ill. I want to be honest about where I've been these past few months. I mean, I don't exactly *want* to put myself out there as a poster child for PTSD, but I feel like I have a responsibility. After meeting all those people at Englewood. Knowing how much people suffer because of the stigma around mental illness."

"Wow, I think that's great, but… I mean, we never talk about serious stuff like that. People come for the humor."

"I know. I won't go too dark, I promise."

Cyrus hesitated, trying to come up with a good way to phrase the next question. "You don't think it would… you know, fan the flames for those nutjobs who think you're a…." He trailed off, aware of Roya's presence in the loft above them, not wanting her to hear him finish the sentence. *A terrorist.* Cyrus had no idea if Naveed was aware of the many ridiculous conspiracy theories swirling around online—people saying he'd really killed Brennan Walsh and had taken out Alastor and Zennia too, despite the fact that there was actual video evidence of the latter showdown that clearly proved his innocence. Cyrus was glad that, for the most part, the trolls had stopped spouting these theories on *D&C* video comment strings, so that he didn't have to deal with them directly anymore—but he knew they were still out there, building their own communities of anger and hate. He tried really hard not to think about that too much.

Naveed scooped his cast-off potato peels into a neat pile. Despite his efforts at hiding it, Cyrus heard the bitterness in his voice. "They'll jump on anything I do. But this is important. Like I said, I don't want to hide anymore, and this is part of who I am, so I want to get it out there."

"Well," Cyrus said, "I guess we could go ahead and record something, then Dev and I can talk about whether to post it after he listens. But you'll need to choose a stage name and give him some artistic direction on how you want him to draw you."

"Deal. You're a cyborg, right? So I should be something similar. Maybe a robot—but one that's a weird half-animal hybrid. Like a wolf or something, maybe."

"Okay," Cyrus said slowly. "Yeah. That sounds good. We could call you... Navotron."

"Perfect! Let's do it." Naveed looked at Cyrus expectantly.

"Now?"

"Sure. I already know what I want to say. Might as well get it over with."

Cyrus didn't want to wait, knowing that his brother could easily sink into a crappy mood and change his mind. He chopped the potatoes as fast as he could, and as soon as dinner was simmering on the stove, he made Roya promise not to bug them, set up his laptop and mic in the downstairs bedroom, and closed the door.

Once he'd made sure Naveed was ready, Cyrus started recording. "Greetings, humanoids," he began, as always. "Cyborg speaking. Devil's off on a grand adventure this week, but I've got a special guest today. My brother."

"Greetings." Naveed leaned closer to the mic. "It is I, Navotron."

Something about the lighthearted, playful way he said it made Cyrus remember things about his brother that had been buried over the last half-year. How charming he could be. How much he'd loved acting—and how good he was at it.

Cyrus cleared his throat. "So. You're just back from... where, exactly? I can't keep track anymore."

"Well," Naveed said, "I, too, have been on a grand adventure."

"Oh? Do tell."

Naveed's tone grew slightly more serious as he said, "I think most of you know how the story starts, so I won't bore you with that. Let's just say that we—Cyborg here, and Devil too, and a few others—all fought in a great war against the forces of evil. Yeah, that's right, Devil's on the good side. Minds blown yet?"

He paused, and Cyrus nodded encouragingly, not feeling the need to interject anything. Naveed continued, "So. During the fight on the battlefield, I was hit. The wound was bad, but it wasn't lethal. One day, just as I was finally starting to recover, the ground opened up at my feet, and something grabbed onto my ankle and pulled me down.

"I fell into a very dark place. It was like a cave, a subterranean realm with endless passages. I wandered and wandered, but couldn't find my way out. Every so often, without any warning, the demon who had dragged me down would appear, and he'd pass his shadowy hand over my eyes and I would be flooded with memories of horrible things I'd seen in battle. I couldn't escape. I'd be forced to sit there and watch while they repeated on a loop, over and over.

"After a while, I only wanted it to end, and I tried to make it stop. I took drastic measures. My system was rebooted. And by some stroke of incredible luck, I woke up back on the surface. But it wasn't long before the shadow demon dragged me down into the cave again.

"After wandering for many weeks, I found a cavern with a spring that flowed along the rocks, and all these plants that grew in the slivers of daylight shining from a small hole far above. There were other people there. People who had been through the caves, people who were also stalked by the demon. People who proved that I wasn't alone.

"But the most amazing thing about the cavern was the long rope ladder that went all the way up to the hole at the top. There were people up there, too. They called down to us. 'Climb up,' they said.

"To people who've never been in the cave, it sounds so easy, right? Just climb the ladder. But they have no idea how treacherous that ladder is, how frayed and unstable. The thing is, to them it looks sturdy, and they don't understand why it's so hard for us. We tell them about the shadow demon, about what he'll do if he finds us trying to escape, how he'll drag us back down, maybe even so deep that we'll never find our way out again. But this frustrates the people on the surface, because it doesn't make sense to them. They've never seen the demon, so they don't believe it exists. Some of them yell at us as we try to climb out, saying that it's our fault for falling into the cave in the first place, that we brought it on ourselves. That only makes it harder to keep going.

"With lots of help, I finally made it up that ladder. I'm back on the surface, for now. But I've been through this long enough to know it won't last forever. The shadow demon, he knows me. He wants me to come back. I might get dragged down again. But it won't be as hard next time. Because I know how to find the ladder. And the climb isn't as bad when you have other people helping you.

"So if any listeners out there are in the cave right now, just remember: this isn't your fault. You're stronger than you think. You can make it back to the surface. And no matter how deserted it might seem down there, you aren't alone."

Cyrus was too choked up to say anything. Luckily, Naveed wrapped it up on his own. "Well, I've got to zoom. See you again soon, eh, brother? Thanks for having me on the show."

"Anytime." Cyrus cut the audio and started backing up the file right away.

Naveed looked over at Cyrus. "Was that okay?"

It was definitely a departure from their usual programming, but Cyrus knew Dev would love it. "Better than okay. It was perfect."

"I'll send you some links to put in the description. Resources and stuff," Naveed said. "Anything else you need?"

"No. I think we're good," Cyrus said. He opened his email and had already begun composing a message to Dev before Naveed had even left the room.

Roya

WEDNESDAY, DECEMBER 30

ROYA HELD HER BREATH AS SHE CLOSED THE FRONT DOOR OF the cabin on Lopez. Darkness engulfed her, but she didn't dare switch on her flashlight yet. Right now, the moon would have to do.

If she'd had her way, she wouldn't have to visit Orcinia in the middle of the night. But she hadn't managed to convince her family to let her go "exploring" on her own, and her second-choice plan, to go with Naveed while they were riding bikes, had failed miserably.

It probably hadn't been a good idea to go there with him. But she'd found herself unable to resist veering off the main road when she saw the tall front gate. Naveed was still behind her, and she tried to make it look like she was taking a random detour, but when she came up next to the metal gate she slowed enough to see if she could pull it open. She couldn't, of course: it was locked. She touched the symbol engraved around the lock, one she recognized from the book Kass had showed her long ago. Two orca whales swimming in a circle. If only she had the key....

Naveed came up beside her then. "What are you doing?"

She drew her hand away from the gate. "I... I don't know. It's pretty here, don't you think?"

He didn't answer. He was staring at something behind her, and she turned to see what it was. A scrap of yellow police tape, caught in a tree branch, was fluttering in the wind, its big black letters yelling, "POLICE LINE—DO NOT CROSS."

Naveed shivered. "Let's go, Roya."

"But...." She trailed off, unable to think of any reason to stay here longer, let alone go inside. The book was so close, and she knew exactly where to look for it. But he would never let her go in.

"Come on. We're leaving," he said firmly, and had seemed distant for the rest of their ride. Roya wondered if he knew something was up.

So she had to wait until her whole family was asleep. Which took *forever*. Naveed tossed and turned for hours after they'd gone to bed, and she drifted off at some point. When she woke, she could hear him dead asleep beside her, the quiet whine of his breath. Cyrus, naturally, had been sleeping the entire time. Her parents were in the bedroom on the main floor, which was the other obstacle. But Roya could tell by listening to the sounds of their breathing that they, too, were completely out. So she grabbed the backpack she'd prepared and snuck out the front door.

She put on her jacket as she walked. It was very foggy outside. The beam of her flashlight reflected back at her, seeming to illuminate the entire island.

Roya knew exactly where to go, though, and she'd come prepared. Before they'd left home, she had snuck into Baba's workshop and found a pair of heavy-duty wire cutters that she'd slipped into her bag. Kass had warned her it might be hard to get in. The fence wasn't very strong in places, so climbing over it wasn't safe.

She followed the road to the main gate, then walked along the perimeter fence into the woods. Once she came to a spot that was clear of brambles, she pulled out her wire clippers and cut a straight path through the joints in the fence, like Kass had done once. Then she slipped inside.

Orcinia was just as she remembered, only sadder. Before, everything had been well-tended and cared for, but now it had fallen into neglect—kind of like her own family's garden. She peeked into one of the acolytes' canvas tents, because she was curious what was in there, and found a row of cots underneath a mess of garbage: dressers opened with all the contents gone, bedclothes tangled up on the ground, beetles scuttling away from the flashlight's beam.

Roya stepped backwards, letting the tent flap fall. The air here felt like a pillow against her nose. The fog seemed thicker, too. She could barely see the wooden cabin where Kass had lived.

She wanted to turn around and leave. It felt like something was waiting for her here. In this fog, in this abandoned place, ghosts felt like a definite possibility. What if Kass's grandfather, Alastor, had found a way to leave a piece of himself behind? He might have come back to this place to protect it. To make sure it was not disturbed.

But then Roya thought about Kasandra at Englewood. About Kass sitting in her wheelchair, speaking with quiet urgency as she told Roya what she must do.

No, she couldn't chicken out when she was this close. She had to do this. For Kass. She was almost there. The house was empty, Kass had been certain of that, and there was no such thing as ghosts, and Roya would go in and get the book and be back in bed before anyone had a clue she was even gone.

She plodded up the steps of the cabin. Her feet felt heavy. Her footsteps seemed so loud, even though the fog tried to dampen the sound.

Roya turned the door handle. It was not locked. The hinges squeaked when she opened it.

The smell hit her first. Dank and musty, yet sharp. Exactly like her basement smelled when Pashmak accidentally got locked inside and peed on the rug to express her anger at being trapped.

Roya scrunched her nose up. She decided to leave the door open.

The house was a mess. The police must have searched it and not cleaned up after themselves, which seemed pretty rude. Either that or robbers had come through afterward. In fact... what if there were robbers here right now? Once the possibility occurred to her, she found it hard to shake. Between thoughts of ghosts and police and robbers and trapped cats, Roya was finding it harder and harder to keep calm.

Find the book and get out, she told herself. She listened to Kass's voice inside her head. *The Book of Shadows is hidden inside a false wall in the kitchen cupboard. Look for the bottom shelf, the one with the bowls on it. At the very back, the wall slides up—just press against it while you're pushing up and it should slide open.*

But when she arrived in the kitchen, Roya saw that it, too, was in disarray. Dishes were all over the countertop, some of them broken. She moved the debris aside and set her flashlight down while she climbed onto the counter.

Roya balanced on her knees and angled her flashlight so it lit up the back wall. She followed Kass's instructions, but they didn't work.

Maybe it wasn't this section? She moved her hand along the wall and tried again in another place. Still nothing. But the third time, she found it: the wall slid up nice and smooth. And behind it, facing forward, was the leather-bound Book of Shadows. She loaded it into her pack—then noticed another one behind it. This book was smaller, and bound not in leather, but in loosely-woven fabric.

Roya took that book, too. Then she moved the false wall back down— *she* was going to respect the house, even if the police hadn't—and eased herself back onto the kitchen floor.

Now she could go. But there was one more thing Roya wanted to do before she left Orcinia. She wanted to find Kass's special knife, her athame. And she knew exactly where to look.

She returned through the front door, leaving it open to air out the house in case she needed to inspect it more later. Roya descended the porch stairs, then found the little door that led into the root cellar. She pushed it open and crawled through.

It was much as she'd seen it that morning with Kass so long ago. Unlike the rest of the house, it was undisturbed. Rows of red and golden-skinned apples still lined the shelves. It made Roya sad to think that no one would ever eat them, so she stuffed a few into her backpack.

She searched and searched, gently, replacing everything in its original position when she was done, but there were no magical objects anywhere. She was debating whether to go back into the main house when she heard footsteps clomping up the stairs above her.

Roya froze. This was a mistake, such a mistake, she never should have come, and now someone else was here, a robber or the police or maybe even Alastor's ghost. All of those options seemed equally likely, and equally terrifying.

But then she heard a voice. "Roya? Are you in there?"

Naveed? What was *he* doing here?

She probably should have called out to him, but she didn't. He'd been fast asleep when she'd left. How could he possibly have known where she'd gone?

Now that she knew it was just her brother, she wasn't scared anymore. If anything, she was annoyed that he'd interrupted her search. But this was actually very bad, she realized—because if he found her, he'd tell their parents and she'd get in huge trouble and they'd search her backpack and find the Book of Shadows and take it away and Kass would never get to see it again and she would be so mad about Roya's failure that she wouldn't want to be friends anymore.

But if he was in the house now, Roya could probably sneak away and be back "asleep" in her bed before he returned. It was her only option, really, if she wanted to keep the books safe.

She was crawling out of the root cellar, about to sprint back to the hole in the fence, when she heard something heavy falling, followed by her brother's frantic yell.

Roya shouldered her backpack. For the briefest of moments, she thought about leaving anyway. But... she couldn't abandon him.

She sighed and climbed back up the stairs into the dark cabin. Naveed wasn't yelling anymore, so she paused, listening for his voice.

When she swept the beam of her flashlight through the house, something winked back at her from the end of the hall: a reflection of her flashlight in a mirror, which was mounted on a narrow table. Upon it was a collection of magical objects. There were candles and crystals and incense—and a chalice Roya recognized, the one with the engraving of Hekate looking forward, backward, and straight ahead.

Roya's heart leapt. Maybe she had another chance of finding Kass's athame after all.

But first she needed to find her brother. Cautiously, she crept through the hall. Probably the two of them were alone in this house, but she couldn't be sure. Her skin was prickling, as if it detected another presence nearby. But she couldn't give in to fear. Had to keep putting one foot in front of the other.

She found Naveed in a room off the main hallway. There was an open trap door on the ground. His voice floated up from it. For a second Roya was confused: he was in the cellar, where she just was? Impossible. She would have seen him fall in.

Then, as a tickly chill rolled down her neck, she remembered one of Kass's letters from long ago, when she'd talked about her punishment after she'd been caught talking to Roya. *Grandfather gave me twelve hours in the Box.*

Roya aimed her flashlight into the hole. Sure enough, Naveed was inside. He was standing up, which was good; that meant he hadn't hurt himself when he fell in. But the Box was very deep, and he was clawing at the smooth dark walls, roaring nonsensically. When she shined the light at him his eyes were full of terror and rage.

A thought fluttered across her mind, one she was ashamed of, but still felt disturbingly true. *Don't let him out. If you do, he's going to kill you.*

Because the person in the Box didn't seem like Naveed at all. It was like… like he'd been possessed or something. Like some angry spirit had flown into him from beyond the grave.

Alastor, Roya thought, and shivered.

"Hey," he yelled. "Hey! Get me out of here!"

What was she supposed to do? She wanted to help, but not if it meant he was going to hurt her. He was hollering now, a stream of escalating curses, which only made her more afraid.

An image of the magical altar sprang to her mind. If only she could find Kass's athame....

Roya tried to ignore Naveed's screams as she left—*No wait, wait, don't go, get me out I SAID GET ME THE FUCK OUT OF HERE*—and returned to the hall to inspect the altar. She straightened up the cloth beneath the objects, then the objects themselves. To her disappointment, there was no athame scattered among the crystals and candles.

Roya picked up the chalice and stared at the image of Hekate. "Where can I find Kass's athame?" she whispered to the goddess, imagining her question swirling through the air, mingling with the fog, drifting into the cup of the chalice.

No answer came to her, but she didn't want to leave this precious object forgotten inside an abandoned house. Roya stepped into another room to look for something to wrap the chalice in so that it wouldn't break inside her backpack.

Like all the rooms, it was a mess, with drawers turned out and clothes all over the place. She held up a heap of fabric, then realized she recognized it: a small linen shift, like the ones Kass used to wear.

This must have been her room! With renewed energy, Roya scoured the piles until—like magic, like actual magic!—she found it: the leather sheath that Kass had so often worn knotted around her waist, the dark handle of her athame sticking out.

Roya tied it hastily around her own waist, then wrapped the chalice in the linen shift and zipped it into her bag. She had, miraculously, found the athame. Now all that remained was to use it.

When she returned to the Box, she searched the room until she found a rope ladder rolled up in the corner. Only then did she approach the trapdoor.

Naveed was still carrying on inside. He still sounded very angry.

Without hesitation, Roya drew the athame. It was substantial. Heavy. It seemed to have its own vibration. A tiny hum. She walked around the Box, tracing a circle in the air. She didn't really know what she was doing, didn't know the proper incantation for this sort of thing, but it felt right in a way that she didn't need to question.

She thought about Alastor's ghost, but the idea wasn't as scary now that she was holding the athame. She looked down at the Naveed-that-wasn't-Naveed. Then she slashed across the top of the Box and whispered, "Leave him now."

Naveed fell to his knees. Roya watched in amazement, because as she'd drawn the knife across the Box, she had felt the tiniest bit of resistance, a subtle catch in the air. As if she'd just cut invisible strings.

He was sobbing now. "Please," he said quietly. "Please."

The change was so sudden. The athame's vibration traveled up Roya's fingers, giving her a deep thrill that felt incredibly, wonderfully powerful. Naveed had probably come here convinced that she was lost or in trouble and needed to be saved. But instead here she was, saving him.

"It's all right," she said comfortingly, hooking the rope ladder into place and unfurling it into the Box. "I'm here. Just climb out, and we'll get you home. Everything's going to be okay now."

As she replaced the magical knife in its sheath, its protective energy continued to pulse all around her. She was no longer worried about Naveed discovering the books. She had the knife now. The knife, two books, and the chalice, all of which were filled with magic. With these in her grasp, the possibilities were as numerous as the stars beyond the fog.

Naveed

WEDNESDAY, DECEMBER 30

NAVEED WOKE UP IN A FOREST.

So. That was interesting.

He was walking. Following someone holding a flashlight, the beam bouncing ahead of them. Couldn't see much. A thick fog surrounded them, wisping around the trees. He tripped, and the person turned around to pull him back up.

"Come on. We have to keep going." It was Roya. She didn't sound afraid, exactly, but there was a harsh note to her whispered words.

What was going on? It felt like he had just awakened from a nightmare, one he couldn't quite remember. Whatever it was, it had left him with a vague yet unshakeable terror that clawed at him still. He was so drained. Exhausted. Didn't want to keep walking. His knees hurt. His feet, too. Nerve pain waking up again. Invisible needles stabbing in with every footfall. Along with that, the certainty that he wasn't supposed to be here. Wherever *here* was.

He stumbled again. This time Roya didn't catch him and he fell, landing on his hands and sending a fresh jolt up his arms. Lying there in the midnight forest, his scattered brain began trying to piece things back together.

Oddly enough, the first thing he thought about was *Keepers of the Moon*. He'd finished reading it that evening, and was still unsettled by the ending. The book had started out as a straightforward human-vs-alien story, but it played out in unexpected ways, with the microscopic, bacteria-like aliens—the Little Strangers—both helping and hindering the humans, so that it wasn't at all obvious how it would unfold. When Natasha died after giving birth to a little girl with suspiciously shimmering skin, Naveed felt as bereft as Mikhail. The novel ended on an enigmatic line: *Mikhail reached for his wailing daughter, whose hands glowed with points of light, as if she held every star in the cosmos on her tiny fingertips.*

Given the context of the rest of the novel, it wasn't clear why Mikhail was reaching for his daughter. To pick her up, to comfort her? Or to kill her, to protect the colony from the aliens he believed had invaded her body?

It all felt real to him in a way that no fictional story had in a long time. *It's because I'm on the moon,* he thought drowsily. *I'm there right now, and the Little Strangers infected me too.* Because that was how it felt, like each phantom pinprick in his hands and feet was a point of light, a miniature star, a burning ember.

But he wasn't on the moon. He was at Englewood? In the forest after a freak-out in the barn? Smashing pomegranates into the dirt, going to see Dr. Young, being interrupted by that CDC researcher, Tim Schmidt... no, that wasn't right, all of that had happened a few weeks ago, he'd left Englewood but Tim Schmidt's card was still in his wallet. Because maybe that could help him find out if the Little Strangers—no, the MRK bacteria—were still there inside him, biding their time, waiting....

But Roya was here too. Wasn't she? "Roya?" he whispered into the dark.

"Get up." She touched his hand and he cried out, but she didn't let go. "Be quiet. We need to leave."

"Where...?" The searing sensation of her touch made it impossible to say anything more.

"Come on." She tugged on his arm. There was a soft urgency in her voice that he latched onto. He let her pull him up out of the dirt.

Walking was hard. He was clumsy at the best of times thanks to his unfeeling feet, but now he not only had to focus on staying upright, but also on forcing himself to keep going after every agonizing step. He wouldn't let himself cry out again, kept his lips shut tight, but tears were streaming out of his eyes and his whole body was shaking. The walk back to the cabin was going to be very, very long.

Ah, that was it! But no sooner had he remembered this—they were on Lopez Island! Staying at a rental house!—than he got a mental picture of a different cabin, an open doorway, a dark hole—

Sweat beaded his forehead, his upper lip. Nausea burned in his throat. Better stop that train of thought and swivel over to safer memories. Like sitting around the table after dinner earlier that evening, playing Rook with his family. Yes, that was good. Or it had been, until Maman had mentioned that she'd made arrangements to go to Tehran for Farhad's wedding in February. Naveed had excused himself shortly afterward and went up to the loft to finish reading *Keepers of the Moon*.

There had been other good moments in the day, though. Recording the episode of *D&C* with Cyrus, finally getting that confession off his chest and out into the open. Riding bikes with Roya. That had been pleasant... until....

Naveed wanted to steer away again, but this time he couldn't. Because he remembered. Their bike ride. Roya turning off the road, pulling up to that iron gate. The emblem engraved around the lock: two orcas swimming in a circle. He'd seen that symbol before, carved into the bone-handled knife with which Alastor had killed Brennan Walsh.

Roya had led Naveed straight to Orcinia.

And with that memory, it all came together. How he had startled awake in the night to a mental image of Roya standing in front of that gate.

Why had she seemed so drawn to it? How had she even known it was there? Did she have any clue that Alastor, who had tried to kill both Naveed and Cyrus, had come from that place?

He had waited for his heart to slow down, listening for the rhythmic breaths of his brother and sister to anchor him. But he could only hear Cyrus's quiet snore. He sat up, careful not to knock his head into the slanted loft ceiling, and crawled over to Roya's spot.

She was not there.

So that was it, that's why he had struck out in the middle of the night, despite knowing it was a terrible idea. He was still on probation; if he got caught for even a minor offense like trespassing, he could go to prison. But he'd felt an indescribable pull toward Orcinia, he had just *known* somehow that she was there, and couldn't stop worrying that she was in danger.

He shuddered as other images arose in his mind. Canvas tents in the fog, a still pond in the distance, gutted greenhouses. Mountains of dirt surrounded by fluttering police tape. And, farther away, a wooden cabin. With its front door wide open.

Deep breaths, he told himself, not permitting himself to go back there, imagining he was back at Englewood and this was some sort of elaborate exposure therapy designed by Dr. Young. He pretended that Koffka was right there, the way he had been all those times when Dr. Young had forced Naveed to look at photo after photo of paper cuts and bloody noses and skinned knees to deal with his fear of blood. It had worked then, sort of; he'd been able to stay conscious most of the time, though Naveed knew that Koffka, who had a way of gently distracting him, was the biggest reason for his progress.

This is not real, he told himself. *It's just another one of her tests, and if I pass, they'll let Koffka stay with me.* This charade gave him the strength to keep walking, even though he wanted nothing more than to curl into a ball on the ground.

But soon enough, another obstacle stretched before them, glinting in the beam of Roya's flashlight.

"The fence," he said, staring up at it. "How...?"

"I made a hole somewhere," she said, and Naveed remembered something else—scrambling alongside a tall chain-link fence like this one long ago at SILO—the memory was so foggy—

"You dug a hole under the fence," he murmured.

"No. I cut a hole *in* the fence," she corrected. "And I think it's close. By those tents—yeah, right there, see where it bends in?"

Naveed followed Roya to the opening. She tried to crawl through, but only got halfway before stopping with a soft *oof*. Her backpack was stuck—it was too full to fit through the hole.

"Your pack," Naveed said. "You need to—"

"No! I've got it. It's fine." Roya lowered down to shimmy through the hole on her belly. She glared at him from the other side as she stood up and dusted her hands off. Everything about her stance said, *I don't need your help.*

She seemed angry. He still wasn't entirely sure what had happened back there in that abandoned cabin, but he had obviously messed things up somehow.

Naveed pulled himself through the hole. Stumbled behind her through the woods. Once they finally made it out to the road, he sank to the ground, too tired to go any further.

"Come on." Roya nudged him. "Don't quit now. We're almost home."

Naveed turned away from her. Everything was catching up with him now. Heart thudding too fast. Nausea still burning his throat. He swallowed it back. "Why, Roya? Why did you go there?"

Roya looped her thumbs into her backpack straps. "I just wanted to explore. Don't worry, I won't tell anyone you were there. I know you're afraid of getting in trouble."

Naveed shook his head. It didn't make any sense. Exploring that place now, in the dark of night. "No," was all he could say before another surge of nausea forced him to close his mouth.

"All that matters is that everything worked out. You're fine. We'll go home, you'll get some more sleep, and everything will be okay."

Naveed gathered his strength and stood again, holding back another cry as he put weight on his feet. He'd have to grill her later, at a safer time in a safer place, when he felt better and his head wasn't so muddled.

They rounded the bend by the house and started coming down the driveway. The fog wasn't as thick here, and Roya had turned off the flashlight. A group of crows lined the ridge of the roof. They cackled and cawed as Roya approached.

Naveed froze. His heart drummed inside its bony chest-cage, *thudthudthudthud*, so fast that there was barely a space between beats, he wasn't quite sure how to breathe anymore, and then he caught a movement in the kitchen window. Everything seemed blurry, mystical, like the mist rolling coolly against his cheek, the fog wisping against that window. A faceless, shadowy form moved inside it.

It's not over, said a familiar voice inside his head. *It's never over.*

Oh. Hi Nate, Naveed thought wearily. *You're wrong. It's over. We're back at the cabin. We're safe here.*

You're never safe, Nate said. *And you do realize why Roya's mad at you, right? You ruined her vacation. Like you ruin everything.*

Not true, Naveed countered. Nate kept chattering, but Naveed tried not to listen. Instead, he turned his attention to Roya, who stood with her back to him, facing the house.

She raised her arms. "Okay, crows, you need to leave us now. We have to be very quiet. Don't want to wake anyone up."

As if understanding, they took flight, fluttering away from the roof, quickly swallowed up by the moonlit clouds.

Roya turned around, and for a second she looked much older than nine. It was almost like he was seeing a future version of her, one that was tall and confident and powerful.

But when she spoke, her voice sounded the same as always. "Let's go inside," she said, and Naveed followed her wordlessly through the door.

Andi

THURSDAY, DECEMBER 31

ANDI SAT IN THE SUNSHINE ON HER GRANDPARENTS' BACK PORCH, hunched over her laptop and keyboard. She had watched Vanesa's documentary, *Blood Apples,* dozens of times since Christmas, but felt like she could still watch it dozens more without tiring of it. Every time, her awe of the film grew deeper.

Vanesa had crafted it perfectly. Naveed's story was woven throughout, but only as a subplot. The overarching narrative was focused on the farmworkers, especially Ramón and Marisol, as well as their daughter Gabriela and the baby that almost didn't survive after Marisol came down with MRK while pregnant.

That footage was especially heartbreaking. Ramón slumped in the waiting room, hands covering his face; the clock on the wall ticking and ticking; little Gabriela swinging her feet and working on a coloring book, looking dazed, like she didn't know what was going on. The doctor speaking quietly in untranslated Spanish. Ramón's crumbling face.

The screen fading to black. The words, *There is a shortage of the antibiotics she needs. None are currently available. Without them, she is not likely to survive.*

The sun set. It rose again. Then the screen displayed snippets from an email string: Naveed alerting Genbiotix about a spike of MRK cases in the Yakima Valley and begging them to send rindamycin to the hospital in Sunnyside. Genbiotix's response that they wanted to help and would send a shipment right away.

There were shots of nurses in infection control gowns hanging IV bags of the antibiotics, as seen through the narrow windows of closed hospital doors. And finally, several days later, the doctor telling an exhausted Ramón that Marisol's condition had dramatically improved, though their son was later delivered by emergency C-section.

Towards the end, Naveed appeared in a short interview. He was in the woods somewhere, and the shot was stark, just his face against the leaves. It must have been taken at Englewood, Andi guessed. "The people who pick our food work so hard," he said. "And yet, we give them nothing. They deserve the same basic labor protections as every other worker in this country. They deserve the right to stay home when they're sick. To care for their families, for their children. They came here for something better, and we've failed them."

The documentary ended on a shot of Ramón's family several months later. Back on the road again, that tiny baby bundled into its massive car seat, heading down to California for the winter. Ready to keep on picking.

The beauty and poignancy of the movie had moved Andi in a way that few others ever had. This was no ordinary documentary, she realized. This was going to be *huge.*

As long as she could get the music right.

The more Andi worked on it, though, the more confident she felt. Her new equipment must have given her superpowers or something, because suddenly everything was *working.* The scraps of songs floating around in her head were finally fitting together just right, and after getting some direction from Vanesa over the course of the week, she knew which moments needed accompaniment, and which to leave silent.

She'd been sitting outside on New Year's Eve, headphones on, toggling between the film and Digital Performer, for hours probably. Working on the film was much more pleasant than obsessively checking the number of signatures on her Blazin Bitz petition, which was pitifully low. Mahnaz had reassured her that they'd try another push after the holidays, but Andi was still disappointed with the lackluster response.

There was a Meyer lemon tree against the back fence that kept blasting its citrusy perfume right into her nose. The light falling on her skin felt so good. A strange thought rushed through her: *I could get used to this.* She hadn't realized how much the relentless Seattle gray was dragging her down.

But even thinking that felt treasonous. She didn't want to leave Seattle behind. Because what would Naveed do without her? How would he react if she left?

She hadn't mentioned any of this to him yet. He had seemed really depressed when she'd talked to him the day before, since his neuralgia had apparently flared up again, and she didn't want to pile on. She wanted to be there for him. But... she wanted to be *here*, too. Free from distraction, able to escape into the one part of her life where she felt truly at peace.

But as she worked, she noticed that Naveed was an invisible companion, silently influencing every musical phrase, every rest, every chord. He was woven into her music the way he was into the film: seamlessly, subtly. She wondered if he would hear that when she finally played it for him someday. The thought both thrilled and terrified her.

Now, she toggled back to the film, trying to decide whether to add music to one particularly heart-wrenching moment. The camera had been focused on Naveed, who was picking apples at the top of a tall ladder. His pace was much slower than the other workers, who filled their bags quickly with apparent ease. He started descending the ladder, but his foot slipped and he fell sideways, arcing limply through the air, landing hard on his shoulder. The supervisor didn't even seem to care. He just tossed Naveed a bottle of water and told him to get back to work.

The scene felt so stark without music, but Andi worried that adding any would make it too melodramatic. It was a tough call. She watched it several more times before deciding to go by Vanesa's aphorism: *When in doubt, let the moment speak for itself.* She left it as it was, even though the sound of his body hitting the ground made her stomach drop every time.

Then Andi heard her name. She minimized the browser window, but it didn't matter: her mother had been standing behind her. Watching her watching him. For some reason, this made Andi incredibly embarrassed, maybe even more so than if she'd been caught kissing him. She took off her headphones, trying to act nonchalant, but she could feel her cheeks burning.

"We just got back. I figured you might be hungry, so I brought you some jiǎo zi," her mother said, placing a plate of potstickers on the table.

"Oh. Thanks."

"Making progress?"

"Yeah. It's coming along." Andi wished she could skip the small talk and get back to work. But her mother sat down, so Andi took the hint and closed her laptop. She picked up a dumpling with chopsticks and nibbled it tentatively.

"That's good." Her mother tilted her face toward the sun. "Nice day, isn't it? Maybe we could head into the city for the afternoon. We haven't spent much time over there this trip."

Andi had no desire to brave bridge traffic or stuffed commuter trains to play tourist in San Francisco, so she said, "That's okay, I'm happy just being here. How'd Ah-ma's clinic visit go today?"

Her mother frowned. "It's really hitting her hard this week. Getting worse before it gets better. But it *will* get better. It will."

How do you know? Andi wanted to ask. She looked away to hide the tears springing to her eyes, desperate to talk about something else. "Mom…

are you sure they're going to be able to afford my college tuition, on top of everything else? With all the health care costs? I heard Ah-gong talking about Lu Yu the other day, it sounds like business hasn't been going so well—"

"Andi." Her mother said it sternly. "Don't worry about any of that. They've been saving and investing for a long time so they could do this for you. They want you to have the advantages that come with getting a good degree."

Andi knew what her mother was really saying: "good degree" was code for a practical, high-status field, like medicine or business or engineering or law. Not music. Definitely not music.

She had originally hoped to please everyone by double-majoring, going pre-med with the intent to eventually become a psychiatrist, and minoring in music to satisfy her itch to compose. But she wasn't so sure anymore that she'd be able to handle a college course load that intense. The past semester had been difficult; she had barely managed B-minuses in most of her classes.

Maybe that was what this was about. Her grades had been posted a few days ago, and she knew her mother was disappointed. So she tried to steer the conversation elsewhere. "But they want me to go to a school in California, and... I don't know. It's hard to think about leaving Seattle."

Her mother arched her eyebrows. "But you applied to lots of schools here. I thought Berkeley was one of your top choices."

"It is, but... I don't know, Mom."

"They think it would do you good to live in a new place for a while," her mother said. "After everything that happened to you in Seattle. And California's your home, too. You were born here, grew up here."

"It's just... I'd really miss everybody."

"Is this about Naveed?" her mother asked.

The question caused heat to flare in her cheeks again. "No. Well, maybe a little. Mostly about you and Dad."

"Andi, listen to me," her mother said. "Your father and I don't want to hold you back. And if Naveed really cares about you, he won't hold you back either."

Andi was stunned. As if there was any doubt that Naveed cared about her! And he would never, ever want to hold her back. The dumpling she'd eaten sat heavily in her stomach. This was so uncomfortable. She wanted to yell, *Abort! Abort!* and stop the conversation right this minute.

But her mother continued, "Besides, you shouldn't base your plans around your father and me. He'll be going on tour in the summer, and who knows where we'll end up." She drummed the patio chair with her fingertips. "Actually, there's something I wanted to talk to you about. I'll be staying in Berkeley longer than planned."

Andi sat up straighter. "You're not flying back with me?"

"It's going to be a long road for Ah-ma," her mother said. "And Ah-gong is so busy with Lu Yu. I need to be here. I need to help take care of her."

"But what about work?"

"I'm taking leave for six weeks. Then we'll re-evaluate."

"You'll be gone for six weeks?" Andi wasn't sure why this was hitting her so hard, since she'd spent most of the conversation wishing her mother would go away.

"It'll go by fast," her mother said.

"You're probably right." Andi stood up, her chair's legs scraping the patio. "You know, I need a break. Think I'll go on a quick walk."

She didn't turn back to see her mother's expression, just walked right out the gate. Then she ran. She ran down the sunny streets, even though she was only wearing flip-flops on this warm winter day. She ran all the way to campus, only slowing once her ankles threatened to give out.

Andi couldn't stop thinking about her mother's announcement and everything it meant. She and her dad would be alone. There were some definite pluses: he'd probably let her do whatever she wanted; he wouldn't nag her about school or care if she spent a lot of time with Naveed. But she'd undoubtedly get stuck doing all the chores he never seemed to get around to, like running the dishwasher and folding the laundry and making dinner. All definite minuses. It stressed her out just thinking about adding more to her already full plate.

She sat down on a bench beneath a grove of eucalyptus trees, remembering how she and Ah-ma used to come here back in the pre-Seattle years while her mother was studying. Back then, the Campanile tower had seemed so tall, like a rocket ship about to launch into the sky. She thought about Ah-ma then, how she'd sat on this very bench years ago, calling out items for Andi to find in a nature scavenger hunt: ten eucalyptus leaves, a stone that wasn't gray, a feather, a pinecone. She thought about Ah-ma now, crippled by nausea and fatigue, her penciled-in eyebrows, her disappearing hair.

Abruptly, Andi stood up and jogged back off campus, wandering until she found a hair salon with a sandwich board positioned outside proclaiming *walk-ins welcome* and a sticker on the window noting that she could pay by phone.

She opened the door, combing her fingers through her long hair until one of the stylists stopped flipping through a magazine and turned toward her. "What can I do for you?" they asked.

"I'd like a haircut," Andi said. "I want it really short. But I want to keep this." She indicated the hair she had gathered in one hand. "I'll be donating it."

The stylist led her over to a chair. Before she had a chance to change her mind, she sat resolutely down, closing her eyes as they draped a cloth over her shoulders and began to cut.

January

They stared at the rip in the fabric.
It was tiny, only centimeters long,
yet large enough to change everything.

Mikhail flew into a panic:
the Little Strangers were all around them,
their suits the only protection against invasion.
Natasha covered the tear with one hand,
took Mikhail's with the other.

"It'll be all right," she said,
and though he normally could not hear her
through the muffle of his helmet,
her voice came to him loud.

Natasha. He could not lose Natasha.
He would do anything to keep her.

—Viktor Zolotov, *Keepers of the Moon*

Andi

SUNDAY, JANUARY 3

ANDI STOOD ON THE CURB AT THE AIRPORT LOOKING FOR HER father's car. She was back in Seattle after her first-ever solo airplane flight, and the city was just as gray and dreary as she'd left it. The mist seemed to settle underneath her skin.

She couldn't help feeling abandoned by her mother, despite the assurances that she'd return soon. In the morning after breakfast, she had followed Andi to the back porch to help her pick ripe lemons.

"I'll miss you, bǎo bèi," she said. "Just call me if your dad isn't pulling his weight, and I'll talk to him."

"Yeah, okay," Andi said.

"I want you to focus on your school work," her mother said. "I know you've been working hard on your little music project, but now that's school's starting up again, that's where your priorities need to be. Your grades this last term still matter."

The scent of the lemons suddenly felt cloying. Andi's project was not *little*. There was nothing small about that film, or her contribution to it.

"And I'm sure it will be nice to have Naveed back in town," her mother added. As if he'd been on vacation or something. "But don't let him distract you too much."

"*Mom.* I get it, okay?"

"Look, I know what it's like to love someone with their own demons," her mother went on. "But I've also learned that it's unrealistic to think you can change someone. You're not here to save anyone else, or to fix them. That's something they have to do on their own. And Naveed has lots of other people helping him—it shouldn't have to fall to you. You have a bright future, Andi. None of us want to see you throw your life away."

Andi pulled a lemon so hard that a large piece of stem broke off too. She tossed it into the bag with the rest and tied the handles into a knot to indicate that this picking session—and this conversation—was over. "You know, I'm going to miss you, Mom. But I'm glad you'll be taking care of Ah-ma. When someone you love needs help, it's important to be there for them."

She left her mother standing on the patio, a lemon still in her hand. When they parted at the Oakland Airport a few hours later, both of them pretended the conversation hadn't happened and hugged each other goodbye.

Now, Andi scanned the circling cars, feeling odd. When her father's Highlander slowed next to her, she had a strange moment where she didn't even recognize it. Like she'd been gone for years, or had returned a completely different person with a different set of memories.

Her dad sprang out of the car and gave her a massive hug before observing her at arm's length and exclaiming about how different she looked with short hair. Andi forced a smile, knowing that she'd be hearing that a lot today. As he tossed her bags in the trunk, Andi slid into the passenger seat, still unable to shake her sense of disquiet.

He glanced over his shoulder as he pulled away from the curb. "Just you and me for a while, huh?"

"Yeah, I guess." She really didn't feel like talking about it. Her father seemed lost in his own thoughts, tapping his fingers on the steering wheel, and Andi grew aware of what was playing on the speakers: Stars' "On Peak Hill," a totally depressing breakup song. Was the whole world trying to keep her and Naveed apart? There wasn't anything *to* break up, anyway. They weren't even technically together.

She turned the volume down, and her dad opened his mouth as if to say something, but she didn't want a lecture from him about keeping her priorities straight. Instead, she said, "Hey Dad, I think I finally have something listenable for this documentary score—but it still needs more layers, maybe some percussion? And there's this violin player I might ask to collaborate... but first I'd like to hear what you think."

That seemed to snap him out of his reverie. "I'd love to help! I've been working on some new songs lately, too. Including the one we started before you left. Do you want to help me write the lyrics for it?"

Andi cringed inside. In her opinion, it didn't need lyrics; the melody told a story on its own. But she didn't want to argue with him about it, so she said, "I don't know if I'll have time for that. But I can't wait to hear how it turns out. Oh, and I'll have to show you that software Cy and Naveed got me. It's amazing." She paused, trying to sound extra casual about the next part. "By the way, when we get home I need to head over to their house. We stopped by Berkeley Bowl on the way to the airport and got them a few things. Oh, and don't worry, I brought you those cheesy breadsticks you like."

"This day just keeps getting better," her father said.

They rounded the corner of I-5 that gave them their first glimpse of the city. Andi thought the sight of the tallest tower in the downtown skyline might make her even jumpier. In addition to unpleasant Nutrexo memories, it brought to mind the upcoming protest against Blanchet Capital, as well as her Blazin Bitz petition that no one seemed to care about. But instead, she just felt a swell of relief at being home.

After dumping her luggage at the house, digging through the linen closet and packing up a few tote bags, she texted Cyrus on the way out her back gate. You at home? I'm walking thru the alley now.

He was standing inside the kitchen door, eyes on his phone, when she tapped on the window. "Hey, A!" he said as he opened it. That was what he called her now; he said he liked the way it made him feel vaguely Canadian. She waited. Just like she'd thought he would, he did a double take. "Whoa. Your hair! It's so… short!"

She ran her fingers through it, wondering if he was going to add anything like, *Looks great!* Or, *I love it!* But he didn't. Instead, he looked back at his phone screen. "Come in, come in."

He led her into the dining room, which was messier than usual. His laptop was open on the table. A stack of school textbooks and his backpack were piled next to it.

She handed him one of the bags. "I brought you something from Berkeley."

"Aw, you didn't have to—" He stopped when he opened the bag. "Meyer lemons! Hell yeah! Look how many—there must be, like, two dozen in here!"

Andi couldn't stop a grin from spreading across her face. Cyrus was probably the only teenager on earth who would be thrilled to receive a bag full of lemons. "Picked them from my grandparents' tree this morning."

"Wow. I'm so excited. What should I do with all of these? Maybe I'll make some lemon curd? Or—preserved lemons! Definitely. Lemon meringue pie? Hmm."

When he set the bag on the table, Andi noticed the novel on top of his stack of textbooks. She picked it up. "*Keepers of the Moon,* huh? You reading it?"

Cyrus made a noise somewhere between a snort of betrayal and sniff of exasperation. "No. Naveed's obsessed with it, though. The whole thing creeps me out, so I told him I had to give it back to Todd. I never should have let him read it—now he'll probably go poking around online and find out about Zolotov's body being found in Orcinia. Honestly, I don't even want it in the house anymore." He took it from her and stuffed it into his backpack.

Andi stepped into the living room and plopped onto the couch, tucking her feet underneath her. It was so cold here—she'd have to get used to this climate again. "How's he doing today?"

Cyrus sat down at the opposite end. "Not so great. His hands and feet hurt so much that he literally cannot get out of bed. Just has to lie there completely still. Which of course makes him super depressed. Been some real fun times around here."

Andi cringed. "If it's that bad… are your parents going to take him to the doctor?"

"Maman got him an appointment at the neurology clinic in a couple days. I think he has therapy with his new shrink too. Anyway, you can guess how thrilled he is about all that. But… it'll get better. It always does. And I know he'll be glad to see you."

Andi looked at the steep staircase leading upstairs, thinking of how endless it seemed to her, even with her normally functioning feet. "Is Roya up there, too?" she asked.

"I think so. Probably in her bedroom."

So Andi headed upstairs with her remaining bag of gifts and knocked on Roya's door. She peeked her head in to see Roya hurriedly hiding something—it looked like a small book—under her pillow.

"Oh—hi Andi. I didn't know you were coming over. Do you need something?" Roya asked.

"Um, no. Actually, I brought you a little birthday gift," Andi said as she rifled around in her bag. Of course she couldn't find Roya's present right away, which only prolonged the awkward moment. Roya was obviously in the middle of something and hadn't appreciated the interruption.

"Ah, here it is." Andi held out a narrow box. Inside was a row of four chocolates, each shaped like a different bird.

Roya examined them. "They're pretty. Thanks, Andi. That was nice of you."

"Sure. Enjoy." Andi backed slowly to the doorway, flustered. "See you later?"

"Mmm hmm. Please close the door," Roya said. She reached back toward her pillow as Andi closed it.

Hopefully the visit with Naveed would go a little smoother. His doorway across the hall was open, and she could see him sprawled out on his bottom bunk, eyes closed, palms upturned. A low, soothing voice was playing from his phone's speakers—maybe he was listening to a podcast, or a guided meditation or something. She wondered if he was cold; he just had on a t-shirt and pajama pants rolled up above his knees. No socks. No blankets. And it was drafty up here.

But when she entered the room, she felt the warm blast of a space heater, and saw his sweatshirt and wool socks heaped on the floor. She remembered him telling her, once, about how the nerve pain made the tiniest things, like fabric against his skin, feel excruciating.

She tried not to stare at the scarred hands that he usually hid under long sleeves, tried not to remember peeling the rope away from his wrists in Dr. Snyder's lab all those months ago. But the image came anyway, the sight of his raw, ruined skin—

She lurched toward the corner of the bed, seized by a rush of light-headedness, and sat down just in time.

"Hey. You're home," said a sleepy voice behind her. She turned to see Naveed looking at her with a brightness in his eyes that she decided to count as an almost-smile. He told his phone to pause, plunging the room abruptly into silence. "And you cut your hair!" he added. "It looks... it's beautiful."

Andi ran her hand through it again—she'd never realized how much of a nervous habit touching her hair was until it was all gone. She closed her eyes, because she could barely stand the sweet, earnest way he was looking at her.

"Are you okay?" he asked.

"Yeah. I'm just... tired," she said. But she was fine, of course; her problems always felt small compared to his. "I'm sorry. That you feel so crappy."

"I think it's getting better? Maybe." He moved his head slightly, though his limbs stayed sprawled like a starfish. She was sitting next to his left foot, and had a bizarre, sudden impulse to tickle his toes, even though she knew it would send a lightning bolt of pain straight through him.

She looked at his thin face, his shadowed eyes, his stubbly chin and greasy hair. She wondered when he'd last showered. There was a dankness in this room, but it was hard to say whether it was coming from him or the space heater. "I wish I could give you a hug," she said.

"Let's try," he answered.

That surprised her. "Um, okay. I don't want to hurt you, though."

"Impossible," he said, and there it was, that little upward twitch of his lips. She didn't care anymore about what her mother had said about priorities, throwing her life away, etc. She would have suffered through a million of those painful conversations just to see that tiny smile.

She settled herself in the space between his elbow and knee, then leaned forward into him, wrapping her arms behind his back and elevatoring him up. It would have been a lot easier if she'd straddled him, but even just thinking that sent a quick, dizzy rush spiraling into her brain. Once he was upright, she hugged him, hard, and burrowed her face into the curve of his neck.

"Aahh!" He sounded startled, and she pulled her head up. Oops. Maybe he'd brushed his hand against something, or she'd gotten too close that time. She was never quite sure how much touch was okay with him.

"Sorry," she apologized.

"No, it's fine," he said. "It just tickled. Please don't stop."

She wouldn't dream of it. His neck was really sweaty, but for some reason it smelled insanely good, and she wanted badly to kiss it—to lick it. To taste him. To wrap her fingers in his hair, to slide one leg across his lap....

Abruptly, she pulled back, and started arranging the pillows behind him with one hand, then easing him down into a sitting position. "Stay right there. I brought you something," she said.

She got up, still feeling a bit wobbly, and retrieved her Berkeley Bowl bag. Without saying a word, she took out a red-checkered tablecloth and spread it next to him on the bed—he moved his legs closer together to make more room, clearly intrigued—then she turned her back while she arranged some food on a platter on the desk.

"What are you doing?" he asked.

She carried the platter over to the bed. It was piled high with bunches of tiny champagne grapes, rosemary flatbread crackers, and a vegan cheese-style product made from cultured nuts.

"We're having a picnic," she said, sitting cross-legged next to him.

"Wow, thanks, but... I'm not really hungry," he said.

"Of course you are. Look, I went through all the trouble of carrying this with me on the plane and making sure the cheese stayed cold—plus I haven't eaten since breakfast and I'm not going to sit here devouring all the food I picked out for you while you watch, so you have to eat some." She hadn't meant to say all of that out loud, but his rejection was frustrating.

"Okay," he said, as if gearing himself up to do something incredibly difficult. He reached for a cluster of grapes, but as soon as his fingers touched them he inhaled sharply and drew his hand back. "I'm sorry," he whispered. "I can't right now. This fucking neuralgia."

Andi felt like an idiot: she should have known. Shouldn't have gone off on him like that. But she knew how to fix this. Without saying a word, she plucked a few grapes and held them to his mouth, imagining him taking them from her with his teeth, his tongue... then kissing the sweet juice on her fingers....

But he didn't open his lips. Instead, he jerked his head away. He had the strangest look in his eyes, like someone had drawn a shade over windows. Like somehow, this gesture that she'd intended to be sweet—maybe even a little romantic—had been the exact wrong thing to do.

Of course it was. He was not attracted to her in the way that she was to him; he'd made that abundantly clear in the past, and now it was written all over his face.

She dropped the grapes back on the platter and stood up, knowing that staying any longer would only make things worse. An ocean rushed inside her head as she mumbled something about how she was feeling kind of weird and needed to go.

If he answered she didn't hear, because the most important thing was finding her way out of that room. But she wasn't quite ready to face Cyrus again, so she sat at the top of the stairs to collect herself, forehead on knees, inhaling the scent of grapes still clinging to her fingertips.

Roya

TUESDAY, JANUARY 5

ROYA WAS IN A BIND. SHE NEEDED TO DELIVER THE BOOKS TO Kass, but wasn't sure how she could possibly get back to Englewood.

Her parents were too busy to take her. Naveed still wasn't feeling well and wasn't allowed to drive anyway. Cyrus was out of the question—it had been hard enough to convince him to visit Englewood while Naveed was a patient there. And she was pretty sure she needed to have an adult with her, too. They had rules about things like that.

At least the magical objects would be safe in the meantime. She'd wrapped the Book of Shadows, the chalice, and the athame in Kass's linen shift, then bundled them all inside an old towel and hid them deep under her bed. The apples were down there too, lined up against the wall. They seemed too special to eat somehow, and since it was dark and cool there, just like in the root cellar, she figured they would keep. Roya was the only one who could fit underneath her bed, so there was no way anyone else in her family would snoop around and find her Orcinian treasures.

But the little book was small enough to carry with her, so she kept it zipped inside the secret pocket of her coat. This one was not at all like the Book of Shadows: it was written in different handwriting, and from the few pages she had read, it looked to be a made-up story. She hadn't gotten very far, though, because every time she started reading someone barged in on her, and she couldn't risk getting found out.

After school on the first Tuesday after break, Khaleh Yasmin came to pick her up. When Roya saw her waiting with the other grown-ups outside the school gates, adjusting her blue head scarf against the winter wind, she couldn't help feeling disappointed. She loved Khaleh Yasmin, but Roya wouldn't be able to disappear into the little book under her watch.

"Your maman's still at the neurology clinic with your brother," Khaleh Yasmin explained in Persian as they walked home. "I thought we could go get some ice cream. Or a cupcake?"

Everyone was always trying to bribe Roya into happiness with sweet things. Not that she minded. "A cupcake sounds good," she said.

At the bakery, Roya picked one out for herself and one for Naveed. She'd been avoiding him as much as she could, but to her relief he hadn't brought up anything about Orcinia. Still, she felt horrible about the whole thing. Everyone seemed puzzled by his sudden decline after he was doing so well, but she knew: this was all her fault.

When they got home, Maman still wasn't there, so Khaleh Yasmin set up some watercolors and Roya painted until she heard the front door open.

Maman set down her purse and took off her shoes and coat by the door, while Naveed kicked off his slides and started making his slow ascent up the staircase.

Roya rushed to the bottom of the stairs. "I got you a cupcake," she told him.

He didn't turn around. "No thanks."

"Okay, maybe later, then," she said. He only grunted in reply.

Maman kissed Roya on top of her head and gave her a side-hug. "Merci, azizam. That was thoughtful of you." She looked so tired. Roya wished she'd brought Maman a cupcake, too. "Here, let's make him some chai nabaat. How was school?"

Roya went into great detail about how her class had been so rowdy in the hallway after lunch that they weren't allowed to go to art, which wasn't fair because Roya was being quiet but she still got punished anyway, and Maman said, "that's too bad," from time to time while Khaleh Yasmin cleaned up the watercolors.

The kettle started singing its boiling song. Roya perked up as Maman poured the hot water onto Naveed's special sleepy tea, the one he'd brought home with him from Englewood....

She picked up the box. "Maman, do you think we could go back to Englewood sometime? Like maybe this weekend? My friend there misses me, and I want to visit her again."

Maman looked surprised. "Oh, Roya-jaan—no. We don't have time to make the trip back up there—we've got a lot of things to catch up on this weekend."

"Or next weekend? It doesn't have to be this one."

"No. I'm sorry. It's just too far away. You can be pen pals, though. It's always nice to have someone to write to, isn't it?"

Roya wasn't terribly surprised by this answer, but it was still disappointing. "I guess so."

Maman took the box of tea from her and put it up on a high shelf. "Why don't you go see if you can find any flowers outside? We can put them in a vase on his tray."

Roya doubted she'd find any flowers in early January, but she knew what Maman was trying to do. Get Roya out of the way so she could talk to Khaleh Yasmin.

She put on her shoes and coat at the front door, then stepped outside. No flowers anywhere. She could cut some bare branches, she supposed, but wouldn't he just find those depressing?

Roya took a short detour into the chicken coop, but even the hens couldn't cheer her up right now. Maybe the little book would be a good distraction. She removed it from her coat, but couldn't concentrate on the words, and her fingers were freezing. So she moved it to the pocket of her sweater and came back inside a few minutes later.

"I didn't find any flowers, but can I take his tea to him?" Roya asked once she'd returned to the kitchen, where Maman and Khaleh Yasmin were talking in hushed voices.

"Of course." Maman added rock sugar and a few ice cubes to the tea, then put a straw on the tray too, in case his hands hurt too much to hold the mug.

Roya carried the tray upstairs, careful not to slosh. When she entered his room, he was in his bed facing the wall, possibly trying to sleep. She nudged his shoulder anyway. "Brought you some chai nabaat."

He didn't answer. She had no idea how to fix this, but she had to try. She set the tray on the desk and snuggled in behind him.

"You planned it," he said suddenly. His cold words felt like ice cubes against her skin.

"Planned—planned what?" she stammered.

"You must have brought something with you. To cut the fence. You weren't just exploring—you went in there for a reason. Why were you there that night? What were you looking for?"

Roya was glad she didn't have to look at his eyes. Instead she stared at his back. His wingbones jutted toward her accusingly. The little book inside her sweater pocket seemed to grow heavier, as if he'd turned it to stone. She wanted to tell him, but she also knew it was very important not to give up Kass's secret. And if he knew the truth, it might even make him worse. Even though it hurt, she said, "I don't know what you're talking about. What night do you mean? What fence?"

"You know," he whispered. "You know exactly what I'm asking. So tell me. *What were you looking for?*"

"You're not making sense," Roya maintained, even though she felt all twisted up inside. "Did they give you some medicine at the clinic? I think it's confusing you."

"Stop it. Stop lying to me." He turned around so fast that it startled her, and she tried to scoot away but fell out of the bed, coming down hard on her right hand.

He was staring down at her. When the sharp ache in her wrist receded, she met his gaze.

Never before, never ever in her life had he looked at her like that. So angry—no. Not just angry. *Furious.* Like he wanted to hurt her.

It was different from when he'd been trapped in the Box. Then, he hadn't been himself. His fury had come from somewhere else, or maybe it had been Alastor's. But this rage, this hatred, was coming from him, her brother, the Naveed she'd known all her life. And Roya was responsible for all of this; she had lied, had betrayed him deeply. She scrambled to her feet and got out of his room fast.

Khaleh Yasmin's voice floated up from downstairs. She and Maman were having a conversation in Persian about things they probably didn't want Roya to hear.

Roya hurried into her bedroom and shut the door, then sat against it in case Naveed tried to get in. Which of course he didn't. She hugged her knees to her chest, squeezing them as tightly as she could.

She would have to find a way to get him to trust her again. And she didn't know how to do that without telling him the truth. But she also couldn't risk him getting mad about the magical objects and taking them away.

Maybe... maybe she could tell him *after* she returned them to Kass. Yes, that would work. There wouldn't be any need to keep the secret once they had been given back to their rightful owner.

The thought cheered Roya. She pulled the small book from her pocket and held it in her hands for a minute. Something about it felt so comforting. The cloth cover, maybe, which was slightly padded, and soft to the touch. It would be hard to give it up, but it didn't belong to her. Still, right now she was in desperate need of an escape. She opened it to the first page and began to read the handwritten words inside.

Katerina and the Little Strangers

On the night we are to leave the moon forever, the cabbages began to sing.

The song started while I watered the plants in the greenhouse; it was faint at first, but now I can no longer ignore the sound. It's not singing, exactly, not like the nursery songs Dr. Belinsky used to sing to me. This is more of a hum, a deep vibration. It builds into a crescendo so loud that I drop my watering can, spilling the precious water all over the floor.

That brings me to my senses, and I begin scooping the puddles up with my hands, redistributing them to the plants closest to me. All the while, the humming continues.

I position my head close to the nearest cabbage, so that my ear is right next to the leaves. The hum grows louder, thicker, more word-like. It almost feels like the plant is trying to talk to me.

Which is impossible. Right? I close my eyes so that I can listen harder. With great effort, the cabbage finally forms two words: COME OUTSIDE.

My head snaps up with the shock of the suggestion. Outside? I cannot go outside. I don't have the proper suit for that; my mask will not allow me to breathe out there. Dr. Belinsky has told me many times: if I ever leave the dome, I will die.

Certainly, I have dreamed of escape. I am only allowed to be in the greenhouses during the long dark night when the grow lights are off. This makes it easy to see the landscape stretching before me, the ridges and craters, the sky freckled with millions of stars, the blue planet that Dr. Belinsky once fixed his telescope on so that I could see the place they left behind. I nodded my head when he told me it was blue because most of it was covered with water, even though I knew that could not be true. Who would leave a place where water was so plentiful?

Most of the time, though, I stay inside my living quarters, a room and a bathroom off of Dr. Belinsky's suite. He talks, sometimes, of the other cosmonauts, but whenever someone rings him, I am to disappear. I only ever met one of the others, and that wouldn't have happened if not for the incident with Sergey.

Sergey. Thinking of him sends a wave of fear rippling through me. Sergey had heard voices too. And it had not ended well for him.

I decide to ignore what I'm hearing, even though it is now being repeated by what seems like every cabbage in the greenhouse. Another word has been added now: my name. COME OUTSIDE, KATERINA. COME OUTSIDE.

"No," I whisper aloud, then open my eyes, deciding I should return to my room, perhaps lie down for a rest. But I am immediately dazzled. I think for a moment the grow lights have turned back on, and my fear turns into panic: I should not be here. I cannot let myself be seen.

As I stumble out of the room in my still-too-big isolation suit, I realize something odd about that light. It's not coming from the grow lamps at all. It's coming from the cabbages. They're shimmering, each leaf dotted with tiny star-like points of luminescence, and their song grows louder and louder and louder still. KATERINA, COME OUTSIDE! COME OUTSIDE!

I run through the secret corridor to my room. Once safely inside, I take off my isolation suit, happy to be rid of the bulky fabric that makes my skin leak sweat.

I stop when I pull my fingers out of my gloves. My hands are glowing. Just like the cabbage leaves.

I don't know what to do. I let my suit fall in a heap on the floor and inspect myself. My hands, my arms, my entire body glimmers with constellations.

Into the bathroom for a timed one-minute shower, scrubbing at my skin to make the light go away. It does not. It's as though it is part of my skin. Through the splashing water I can still hear the hum.

COME OUTSIDE, COME OUTSIDE.

I try taking a short nap next, but nothing changes. The relentless chorus is starting to drive me mad.

I need to tell Dr. Belinsky, I know that. I also know how he will look at me, with his kind but scrutinizing eyes; how he will listen to my heart with his stethoscope and feel my lymph nodes with his gloved hands and record these new symptoms in the notebook he keeps about me and my disease.

This isn't related to my disease, is it? I hope with all my might that this is just a passing sickness.

I don't want to end up like Sergey.

The thought is enough to make me hesitate to ask Dr. Belinsky for help. But he is all I have. The only other person in the colony I've ever met is Dmitri, but I don't know where his living quarters are, and I can't wander the halls looking like this. I can't wander the halls at all. Leaving my quarters is too risky, according to Dr. Belinsky. For me, and for everyone else.

Most of all, I know, he does not want Mikhail to find out about me.

And I don't want that, either.

I towel my hair dry and pull my isolation suit over my linen work clothes, then travel the back corridor that connects Dr. Belinsky's quarters to mine. As I walk, I can't stop seeing Sergey, chained to the pipe in that locked room. The wildness of his eyes. The way he screamed and screamed—INVADERS! OUTSIDERS! YOU NEVER SHOULD HAVE COME!—before ripping that pipe from the wall and trying to smash his way out. Mikhail gave orders to cut off the oxygen supply to his room. They let him suffocate in there. They were that afraid of him.

That won't happen to me... right? Dr. Belinsky would never treat me that way.

But Mikhail might. I've only seen him once, on Sergey's last night; I was in Dr. Belinsky's exam room when he barged in and Dr. Belinsky ushered me into a closet just in time. So I only caught glimpses of him, his steely eyes and tight fists. I could hear those things in his voice, too. "A man of conviction," Dr. Belinsky always says. Mikhail does not hesitate to do whatever needs to be done.

Whatever happens, I'm certain Dr. Belinsky will protect me. And if anyone knows how to help, it is he. Perhaps he even has a pill I can take to fix this.

My anxiety grows as I step closer to his office door. The spaceship is to depart in secret later this night, though Dr. Belinsky told me earlier that there has been a delay. It will probably be another forty hours or so, he'd said.

Will that give me time enough to recover? What if this is still happening when they're ready for launch?

If it is… will they leave without me?

I don't want to even consider this possibility. The only person they're planning to leave behind is Mikhail.

I'm about to open the door when I see, through the small window, that Dr. Belinsky is talking to Dmitri inside. Thinking it best not to interrupt, not to show my face to Dmitri while it's still glowing, I turn to go. But then—

"What did you tell Katerina?" Dmitri's voice is loud. Even though he is beyond the thick door, it's as if he were standing in the corridor right next to me. I don't have time to figure out why I can hear them so clearly, because Dr. Belinsky is talking now, and I need to know his answer.

"I told her that we are leaving in forty hours."

"So… she thinks she's coming along?"

"That's what she's been led to believe, yes."

I'm so stunned I cannot move. What does Dr. Belinsky mean by that—has he been lying to me?

"But perhaps she could come?" Dr. Belinsky adds. Now he sounds like he's pleading with Dmitri. Even though his words are somewhat comforting, I don't like the weakness in his voice. He is usually so authoritative. "She could stay in her isolation suit, and she could live with my sister Ilyana Petrokova, near the Volga River in Syzran, ulitsa Pushkina 84... Katerina would be safe there."

"No. We can't bring her to earth with us. The risk of contamination is too high—"

"My studies lead me to believe that the creatures aren't air-borne. They spread by physical contact. And I don't think they're necessarily dangerous. She's always exhibited normal human behavior."

Dmitri keeps talking as if he hadn't heard. "Assuming the ship even makes it through re-entry, we probably won't land anywhere near Russia. And none of us have any plans to return to the land where we are fugitives."

"It's been twelve years. There may have been a revolution in the meantime. They may welcome us back with open arms."

"Unlikely. Besides, if anyone finds out about Katerina's... condition... which they most certainly will... she will be quarantined. Tested. Viewed as a curiosity, a specimen. Is that what you want?"

Dr. Belinsky exhales. "No. But I still think—"

"There is no other way. She must stay here."

"With Mikhail? The same person who abandoned her outside the dome as an infant—who left her out there to die? It's a miracle she was still breathing when I got to her. Next time, she may not be so lucky."

Instead of answering, Dmitri says, "I will not allow her on the ship, and that is final. But you, Fyodor—we need you. So be ready. My estimate is twenty hours. We need to launch before Mikhail finds out. I'm worried he suspects something."

"Ironic, isn't it." Dr. Belinsky sounds resigned. Like he's done fighting. "We started out trying to build utopia, and ended up creating a totalitarian system just like the one we left."

The men are still talking, I see when I peek through the window one more time, but I cannot hear them any longer. Instead, the hum returns.

I try to fend it off. I need to process what I've heard. But I can barely think.

COME OUTSIDE, KATERINA, COME OUTSIDE. The walls are saying it now. The whole dome, vibrating with these instructions.

Something comes together inside my head. Dmitri said that Mikhail had taken me outside the dome after I was born. I should have died instantly—but I was still breathing when Dr. Belinsky saved me.

Maybe he's been wrong all this time. Maybe I don't need a spacesuit after all.

I head straight for the airlock before I can lose my nerve. This might kill me.

But it might not.

I punch the button, and the door slides open.

Cyrus

FRIDAY, JANUARY 15

"WELL, WHAT DO YOU THINK?" CYRUS ASKED AS HE SET HIS backpack on Todd's floor after school on Friday. "Ready to publish the beta version and get our first round of testers?"

Dev and Todd were working side by side, heads bent together in front of Todd's screen. Shea was camped out in her usual armchair. Her freckles glowed in the light of her laptop. "I don't think it's ready," she said. "Just tried it on my phone—it's pretty buggy. Keeps freezing up."

"It's a game about killing insects. It's supposed to be buggy," Cyrus joked, trying not to let his frustration show. He'd barely slept the past few nights putting the finishing touches on the app, and he and Dev had both tested it without running into any problems.

"Har, har," said Shea. "You know what I mean."

"Works on mine." Todd's eyes didn't lift from his computer. "But we're not ready anyway. Dev and I just got this idea—don't look yet," he said, as Cyrus craned his neck to see the screen. "Want to finish it first."

Todd was supposed to be figuring out how to incorporate ads into the free version of the app. He and Dev seemed a little too captivated to be working on that particular task, but Cyrus bit his tongue.

"I have something to propose, too," Shea said. "After we get the bugs worked out."

Cyrus couldn't hold back a sigh this time. He was itching to move on to the next phase of development, but it looked like it might be another late-night coding session. Maybe he could stay over at Dev's tonight. He had been spending a lot more time there lately, since his own bedroom had become a place to avoid. His brother's unrelenting misery was getting harder and harder to take.

Cyrus had tried everything he could think of to help Naveed feel better. The *D&C* episode they'd recorded on Lopez had been immensely successful—views were approaching the as-yet unprecedented ten million milestone. Cyrus had read him every single one of the nice comments that continued to roll in, people from all over the world thanking Naveed for talking about what it was like living with mental illness.

Of course, Cyrus had skipped over all the trollish ones. He kept trying to moderate them out, but they continued popping back up like evil dandelions. There had been one particularly unsettling string of comments from a user called fleshpuppet69, starting with a disturbing tirade.

> Don't fall for this BS. He's trying to sound all noble and shit but I know him personally and he's very hostile, constantly threatening me with violence & dismemberment. He has serious anger issues and one day he's going to explode and then you will all be sorry he wasn't locked up like he should be.

Cyrus had immediately deleted it, which had caused fleshpuppet69 and a bunch of his troll-friends to flood the comments with complaints about how he was restricting free speech and dire warnings about the coming attacks that Naveed was plotting.

After blocking and reporting the users, things had died down, but Cyrus was still perplexed at the intense level of contempt this video had inspired. Sure, people talked shit about *D&C* sometimes, but they didn't generally stoop to this level. It was like everyone was willing to give Cyrus the benefit of the doubt, whereas with Naveed they always assumed the worst. Why was that? They were brothers, had been through similar experiences....

There were a few things, of course, that Cyrus didn't want to believe would make a difference, even though he knew deep down that they did. Cyrus was light-skinned, easily passing for white. He never called much attention to his Iranian heritage. Naveed, on the other hand, had darker skin, Middle Eastern roots that he proudly flaunted, and PTSD on top of that.

So it bothered Cyrus, to say the least, that he was reaching new heights of cultural acceptance and internet fame while his brother struggled with the most basic of tasks... all the while facing not only his own demons, but the trolls who graphically wished him dead.

Nevertheless, the past few weeks hadn't been easy for Cyrus either, which was probably why he felt so defeated by this small setback. Well, whatever; time to dive back in to the task at hand. Coding was a nice escape. A place where things made sense, where logic always prevailed. Cyrus needed that more than ever lately.

"Okay, so what's the problem?" he asked Shea once he'd settled onto the couch and pulled up the code. "What were you doing before it crashed?"

They worked on troubleshooting for a while. Since Cyrus never had issues on his phone, Shea let him fiddle with hers. The action felt weirdly intimate; her phone was an extension of her, and it was like he was peering inside her brain. Not that he was poking around or anything, but he was stroking the screen that she had touched, and there was something about the action that felt mildly thrilling.

Eventually, he figured out the problem, which had to do with an incompatibility in her phone's OS. After he made the fix and sent her the new version, he held his breath while she tried again.

"So far, so good," Shea said. "Let me play a few levels just to be sure."

He exhaled. If only all of his problems were so easy to solve.

To distract himself while she played, Cyrus got up and wandered over to Dev and Todd. "What're you guys working on?"

Dev toggled back to the code, but before he did, Cyrus saw an image on the screen that was unmistakably Dev's work: a moon surface dotted with glass domes.

"Just brainstorming." Dev stared at the screen, but he and Todd were still smiling. What, they had inside jokes now?

Then it hit Cyrus: it must be from that book they were both obsessed with. *Keepers of the Moon.*

He suddenly felt very sour, but tried not to show it. Instead, he slumped onto the couch.

Shea must have sensed his dejection. "You look tired," she said. "Rough week?"

"Yeah, you could say that."

"You should probably lay off the mango juice."

In spite of himself, Cyrus grinned at her *D&C* reference. He and Dev had recorded their last episode shortly after Dev had gotten back from Kolkata. Cyrus at that point had barely slept in days, and Dev was loopy with jet lag. It had been their most bizarre show ever, including a fantastical tale that Dev invented on the spot involving a flying cow, a chai wallah, and a tree full of magical mangoes. After they'd posted it, Cyrus felt a little embarrassed about how inebriated they sounded. In retrospect, he wasn't sure if that was the best way to welcome their thousands of new subscribers, but it had been performing respectably.

"Appreciate the advice." Cyrus sprawled out on the couch. If only he hadn't downed two cups of coffee on his way to Todd's, maybe he'd be able to take a short nap. But he felt wired and jangly, pumped up on too much caffeine.

To his surprise, Shea closed her laptop and tucked her knees up into her chair. "So. I watched that *D&C* video. The one with your brother."

Great. She'd probably fallen in love with Naveed and was going to ask how he was doing, and Cyrus would have to lie because he still felt the need to hide the extent of his brother's struggles.

But she continued, "My little brother has Down's. I love him to death, but sometimes it can be kind of rough, you know. To watch the world tear him apart, and not be able to help him every time. And... to be so invisible next to him."

Cyrus closed his eyes. His heart thumped uncomfortably.

"It fucking sucks to have no control over shit like that," Shea went on. "But we don't, so we just have to get on with it. At least we can control the machines." She gestured at her computer. "I like being able to tell something what to do, and having it literally follow my every command."

"Me, too," said Cyrus. "At least, until our algorithms get so advanced that the machines learn to think for themselves."

Shea looked like she was about to respond, but Todd interrupted. "Okay, we're ready. Sorry about that. Just coming up with ideas for another skin—this one's totally cosmic." He and Dev exchanged a smile. "What did you want to talk about, Shea?"

"Oh. So, you know how we've been trying to figure out how to make our presentation stand out more? I have an idea. Shouldn't be too hard to implement either. I think we should add a short mood survey each time the user plays, both before and after the game."

"What does mood have to do with anything?" Dev asked.

"It could give us some really interesting data," Shea said. "Like, you could see whether mood changes after playing, or compare whether playing in competitive mode impacts mood differently from cooperative mode. All sorts of things."

"Yeah, but who's going to analyze it?" Todd asked.

"Me, of course," said Shea. "Good training for my future career as a data scientist."

"We have less than a month to get the app tested and put a presentation together. You really think you'll have time for that?"

"I'll make time," Shea said stubbornly. "Trust me, we'll stand out if we have a meatier presentation instead of just doing a demo of the app."

Dev looked at Cyrus. "What do you think? Is it doable to incorporate that?"

Cyrus was already plotting out how he could add it. "I don't think it would be too difficult. And it seems like a good idea to me. Probably will only take me a couple of hours. Especially if you help out, Dev, by getting that new skin in there."

"I can do that," Dev said.

"Great," Shea said. "I've already mocked up a database." She sat down on the couch next to Cyrus, so close that he could once again smell her lemon-zesty hair.

They hadn't worked on it for long before Dev got up and said that he had to get going. As he slid his laptop into his backpack, Cyrus asked, "Hey Dev, would you mind if I spent the night tonight? We could bang out some of this code. Maybe even record the next *D&C*, get ahead for next week."

An odd look flashed across Dev's face, but it quickly relaxed into his usual neutral expression. "No, sorry, not tonight. Actually, Cy, I've been thinking—we might need to put *D&C* on hiatus for a few weeks. I haven't had any time to animate the last episode yet, and I think we need to prioritize the app for now."

"Oh." Cyrus tried to hide his disappointment. Working on *D&C* with Dev was always the highlight of his week. Even so, he had to admit that taking a break from the show made sense. He wasn't all that good at functioning on only a few hours of sleep, and probably wouldn't be able to keep up his current pace for long. "Okay. I guess that's a good idea."

"Great. I'll make the announcement," Dev said. "We'll get back on it after the contest. Anyway—better run. See you all later." Dev swung his backpack onto his shoulders and headed up the stairs without even a backward glance in Cyrus's direction.

Andi

FRIDAY, JANUARY 15

ANDI GLANCED AROUND THE BUSTLING RESTAURANT WHERE Brooke had told her to meet. She felt uneasy about joining this group of people who had just gone to the Blanchet Capital protest, since she'd skipped out on it herself. Brooke had texted her updates throughout, though, and the worst thing that had happened was that turnout wasn't as good as they'd hoped. There had been no disasters, to Andi's great relief.

Brooke had insisted that Andi join her at the post-protest happy hour gathering, because there were some people she wanted Andi to meet. Since she and Brooke had plans afterward anyway—it was Brooke's last weekend in town before moving to Boulder, and they had mapped out two epic nights of show-hopping—Andi didn't want to turn her down. She suspected that Brooke was trying to help by introducing her to potential new friends, but this was unnecessary. Andi didn't have any time to spare for new friendships.

She didn't have much time for anything, actually. Despite what she told her mother during their daily text conversations, Andi had barely been keeping up at school. She had been almost entirely focused on her music. Earlier in the week, she'd sent her documentary compositions to her dad's friend Glenn, who had ripped them to shreds. Well, that was how it felt; he'd said a few nice things, but still the underlying message was, *This isn't good enough.*

After a few days where she'd seriously considered scrapping her original pieces and just choosing royalty-free tracks instead, she had woken up in the middle of the night understanding what he'd really been saying: *This is pretty good, but I know you can do better.* It was true; upon listening to them again, she could hear the places where they veered toward the generic and overwrought.

She'd approached the songs with renewed purpose, and had been trying to follow Glenn's advice. *Don't go with the first thing that comes to your mind. Dig deeper. Find something unexpected—that's where the magic is.* But that wasn't easy, and even as she sat through each school day trying to concentrate on vector equations and the symbolic meaning of the green light in *The Great Gatsby,* it consumed the corners of her mind.

After school, she often stopped by the Mirzapours' house to hang out with Naveed, who had been in a dismal mood for weeks but always seemed to brighten slightly at her presence. She'd been careful not to get too close physically, sitting on the opposite end of the couch or at the foot of his bed. He didn't talk much and seemed disinterested in watching shows or movies together, so she brought over her homework, thinking out loud as she worked on her assignments.

Every night after she made herself dinner—boxes of cereal and cans of soup were her friends these days, since her dad was constantly holed up in the basement working on new songs—she would sit at her keyboard and try to dig deeper. But she wasn't coming up with much, and that was frustrating.

She hoped that a fresh infusion of live music tonight would leave her inspired. First, though, she had to get through dinner. She'd been standing at the entrance to the restaurant searching for Brooke's head of shocking-purple hair for what felt like forever when she saw Mahnaz waving at her.

Andi headed over to her table, where about a dozen other people were sitting. Most of them looked to be in their twenties, but there was one gray-haired older white couple, as well as a middle-aged Black woman. Mahnaz stood and hugged Andi, planting kisses on either cheek before offering her a chair and introducing her to everyone.

"You're the one who wrote the Blazin Bitz petition, right?" asked the middle-aged woman. Mahnaz had introduced her as Akilah, an organizer for Black Lives Matter.

"Yeah." Andi tried not to let her disappointment at its pitiful performance show in her voice.

Akilah broke into a smile. "Thought so. I signed it. How's it going? You delivered it yet?"

"No," Andi said. "Still trying to collect more signatures. But I'm not sure... I don't know that the grocery stores will even listen."

"Maybe not. But you'll never know unless you try," Akilah said. "Hey, have you thought about a boycott?"

Andi had already resigned herself to the fact that most people simply didn't care about Blazin Bitz. "I don't know. Do you think there would be enough support to make a difference?"

"There might be." Mahnaz turned to Akilah. "Maybe we could join efforts? The Blazin Bitz brand is technically owned by Blanchet Capital now, after all. Might be a good way to tie into your campaign against them."

Akilah was nodding. "Yes! I was going to tell you, Mahnaz—I recently read that Richard Caring used to be on Blanchet's board of directors. Probably why they picked up so many of Nutrexo's brands."

At the mention of Richard Caring's name, the room faded away. Andi was instantly transported back to the trial. The sentencing. The violent way Richard had looked at both her and Mahnaz.

It took a lot of effort for Andi to wrestle that image out of her mind's eye. But Akilah's voice brought her back to the conversation at hand, and she was able to shove the memory back into the depths where it belonged.

"You know who you should talk to, Andi?" Akilah nudged the young woman beside her, who had a nose ring and wore her long dark hair up in a topknot. "Laurel, we're thinking a Blazin Bitz boycott could be a nice concrete action for us to take, so we can keep up the pressure and show Blanchet that we're paying attention to them. Maybe you and Andi could figure out how to promote it?"

Laurel turned to Andi. "Sure. What did you have in mind?"

"I... I don't know. I haven't really thought about it and... I'm new to all this," Andi stammered.

"No worries!" Laurel said. "Sounds like a good project for this artivist collective that I'm part of."

Artivist? Andi had never heard the term before, but a warm glow spread through her as she pieced it together. A fusion of art and activism. She had been thinking of her musician self as distinct from the part of her that wanted to fight for justice—but maybe the two parts didn't have to be separate after all.

"We could draw up some sketches," Laurel was saying. "Make a video, maybe. Like a satirical Bitz ad."

"Yeah," Andi said. "That would be perfect!"

"I bet my friend Tadao would have some ideas—he studied marketing in college. He could make it look really legit."

"Let's do it," said Andi. "I can help with the music, maybe write a jingle or something. But I'm working on this other project right now, so I don't have much time for the next few weeks."

"That's okay." Laurel took out her phone. "Our next meeting isn't until the end of January anyway. You should come."

"Sounds great," Andi said truthfully. Laurel texted the details, and Andi was adding her to her contacts when Akilah slid her chair away from the table.

"I've got to head out," she said to the group. "Great to see you all, but it's time to get back to work."

"Don't go yet," Mahnaz said. "This *is* the work." She gestured at everyone sitting around the table, and Andi felt another rush of warmth as the meaning of these words sunk in. Maybe activism wasn't just about waving protest signs and creating petitions. Maybe it was about moments like this, too. Meeting other people who cared. Making connections.

Akilah laughed. "Truth, Mahnaz. But I can't stay." Mahnaz stood up to hug Akilah just as Brooke walked toward their table.

"So sorry I'm late!" Brooke said as she sat down in Akilah's empty seat. "What did I miss?"

Andi and Laurel filled her in on their idea for the anti-Bitz campaign, and the three of them brainstormed for a while. Brooke wanted to help out, even though she'd be in Boulder before their next meeting. Andi didn't want to think about that... but, she had to admit, it felt good to know that she'd have plenty to distract her from Brooke's absence.

Brooke and Andi ordered a hummus plate to share, but bit by bit, the others departed. Laurel promised to keep Andi in the loop about the next meeting. Mahnaz left soon after, hugging both Brooke and Andi before she made her way to the door.

After she'd gone, Brooke leaned back in her chair. "I hope my mom's able to keep up with all the CFJ stuff while Mahnaz is gone. I feel bad that we're both leaving her. Think you might be able to help out with a few things?"

Andi definitely didn't have room on her plate for yet another commitment, so she avoided answering. "Wait. Where's Mahnaz going?"

"She's leaving for Iran at the end of the month. For Farhad's wedding, remember? She'll be gone most of February."

Andi had completely forgotten about Mahnaz's mention of this back in December when they were working on mailings. Instantly, Andi thought about Naveed. She knew how much he'd always wanted to go to Iran, and it must be painful that his mom was able to see his "big brother" get married while he wasn't even allowed to leave the state. Was this part of the reason he'd been in such a bad mood lately? If so, why didn't he just tell her? She would understand.

Though maybe she wasn't one to talk; she'd barely told him anything about what was going on in her life, never even mentioning Ah-ma's cancer or her own mom's absence.

Brooke's voice startled her back to reality. "You look a little stressed. If you're too busy, don't worry about it. She'll survive."

Andi rubbed her forehead. She missed having long hair to twirl between her fingers. "I don't know. Can we talk about something else? Which show should we hit first?"

Brooke sipped her pomegranate mocktail. "How about the one at Neumo's? They're having a DJ showcase—we can check it out, head somewhere else if it's lame, or just dance all night and forget about everything."

"Sounds perfect," Andi said. Her midnight curfew was a thing of the past now that her mom wasn't there to enforce it. She'd texted her dad that she was spending the night at Brooke's, but even if she hadn't done that, he probably wouldn't notice if she didn't come home until two in the morning.

"Ooh, and I have a surprise for you!" Brooke added. "I texted Dimples! He's going to meet us there."

Andi wasn't sure how she felt about that. She kind of wanted it to just be her and Brooke tonight.

Brooke must have sensed her hesitation. "Come on, it'll be fun! If you're not into it, we can ditch him and go to the show at the Crocodile instead. I just thought it might be a good way to blow off a little steam."

Andi didn't talk much about Naveed to Brooke, since she was his ex and all, but she wondered sometimes how much Brooke had gathered about her true feelings for him. Maybe Brooke was right, though. Maybe hanging out with Jed tonight *was* what she needed, a pleasant distraction in the form of a cute guy with dimples.

Before heading to Neumo's, Andi steered Brooke into a nearby drug store, where she bought two Red Bulls and drained them both on the way to the venue. Brooke usually used her fake ID to its fullest extent, helping herself to a drink or two from the bar, but Andi had no desire to tempt fate, and settled for the legal mind-altering effects of lots of caffeine and sugar.

By the time they got inside, Andi was already feeling wired, and when she saw Jed standing alone in the crowd, she pushed her way towards him.

He saw her approach, but there was no recognition in his eyes. When Brooke materialized at her side, though, a smile spread slowly across his face. "Whoa, Sasha, I didn't recognize you," he shouted at Andi over the din of the crowd.

She'd forgotten that she'd told him her fake name. Good thing she hadn't blown her cover right off the bat. "Oh yeah. Cut off all my hair."

"Nice." He brushed her bangs to one side, and she felt a brief burst of pleasure at his touch, but ruffled them back into place as soon as he took his hand away. She didn't want him asking about the scar on her forehead.

The atmosphere was definitely not conducive to talking—the first DJ had already started, and the music was extremely loud—but that was fine by Andi. Emboldened by the energy drinks, she took his hand in one of hers and Brooke's in the other, and led them to the dance floor.

For a while, they stayed close together, but Andi soon lost her eye on Brooke, because she was paying so much attention to Jed. He danced right beside her, and she found herself closing the distance between them so that she could feel his body against hers, his taut biceps, his sweaty skin....

She couldn't help imagining that he was Naveed, though it was impossible in so many ways. Even if they were together, he would never come to a show with her, not with all these people bumping up against each other, all this jostling and dancing and joyous exaltation, in this place that was like her cathedral.

And maybe it was the potent mix of sugar and caffeine and music and exhaustion and long-repressed tension, but Andi found her hands wandering Jed's chest, and his hands did the same, and when he pressed his lips to hers she didn't hesitate, not for a second, she tasted his warm mouth and felt his smooth teeth with her tongue. She held his face in her hands and he didn't make her stop. She touched his dimples with her thumbs and he didn't pull away. He swept her sweaty bangs aside and kissed her scar and she didn't care. She just wanted more of this, and more, and more, and more.

His hands had gotten below her shirt and were edging along her waistband, and she was thinking *yes,* when she heard a yelp and felt cold liquid trickling down her back. She turned to see Brooke standing behind her.

"Oops, so sorry, I spilled my drink!" Brooke laughed, but there was a strange look in her eyes and suddenly it all changed; the music seemed too loud, and everything was throbbing, Andi's heart beating so fast, she could hear it pounding in her ears, all that caffeine, too much, and Jed was looking at her hungry and she thought *oh my God what am I doing this is so so wrong.*

"I... I've got... to go...." she said to Jed, stepping backward towards Brooke.

"Don't," he said. "We were just getting started."

"No, I... no," said Andi. Brooke was pulling her back now, but Jed grabbed hold of her other arm.

"At least give me your number," Jed pleaded. "I want to see you again."

She made a bizarre sound, a mix between a snort of disbelief and a nervous laugh. The whole thing felt so ludicrous, and the sound she'd made seemed hilarious for some reason, and once she started laughing, she couldn't stop, it was tripping out of her mouth like an extension of her pounding heart. She laughed and shook her head, *nope,* realizing what a mistake all of this had been.

"Andi, come on, let's go!" Brooke yelled at her, pulling hard, and Jed's grip broke but Andi couldn't bring herself to turn around. She was aware that everyone was staring at them. Still, she kept laughing, but it wasn't really laughter anymore, it was dangerously close to weeping.

Brooke led her outside. "Are you okay? He looked like he was going to rip your clothes off right there on the dance floor." She paused. "If you were having a good time, I'm sorry, it just seemed like… I couldn't tell…."

The air was so cool on Andi's hot skin. Every piece of her felt so alive, so fiery. They walked away to a quiet residential street, where Andi sat down on the curb, and Brooke let Andi bury her head in her shoulder as the laughter inevitably turned into tears, and even though she couldn't stop blubbering enough to say anything out loud, all Andi could think was, *Oh, Brooke, I am going to miss you so much.*

Naveed

THURSDAY, JANUARY 21

AFTER TWO HOURS UNPACKING CRATES OF PEANUT BUTTER AND canned soup at the food bank, Naveed was completely out of energy. So, even though he still had almost an hour before he was due to pick up Roya from school, he ducked his head into the back office.

"I've got to head out," he said to the director, whom he sort-of knew from various CFJ fundraising events. "See you tomorrow."

She glanced up from her computer screen. "Great, thanks for your help today."

Naveed signed himself out. Two hours down. Only ninety-eight left to go.

Earlier in the week, he'd gone to the courthouse for a mandated visit with his probation officer. As always, it was an unpleasant experience. His PO had told him in no uncertain terms that he needed to start making progress on his community service hours. Naveed explained about his neuralgia, that it was difficult to walk and use his hands when it flared up, though in truth the pain had been much more tolerable since the doctors upped the dose of his SSRI. His struggles with Nate were what had taken so much out of him these past weeks, had made it impossible to focus on anything or carry on a conversation or even get out of bed most days. But he knew that wouldn't sound like a plausible excuse to his PO, who regarded him with the disinterested expression of a man who heard sob stories all day long.

Thankfully, though, Nate had finally backed off. Naveed was relieved to be thinking more clearly, even though the meds made him feel light-headed and emotionally numb. Supposedly these side effects would subside as he adjusted to the higher dose, but he wasn't sure that would actually happen. Still, in his world, this was considered an improvement, so he'd take it.

Andi's visits had kept him going throughout the past few weeks. She came to see him almost every day after school, and would sit in his room doing homework, mumbling to herself as she typed on her laptop. He watched the dim winter light fall on her adorably short hair; he loved how well he could see the shape of her face now, her delicate ears, that cleft in her chin. Once upon a time, he probably would have found her irresistibly attractive, but the meds extinguished those emotions too. Besides, he didn't want to get romantically involved with anyone ever again, not after what he'd done to Brooke, all the ways he'd hurt her. It was a good thing, he reminded himself constantly, that he'd drawn boundaries around his and Andi's relationship from the start.

Far less pleasant were the appointments to which Maman or Khaleh Yasmin shuttled him, mostly follow-ups with neurology and his medical team, who insisted on doing a bunch of painful tests that all came back inconclusive. Then there was the psychiatrist who managed his meds, as well as the new therapist he'd only seen once. Because of some insurance issue, he wouldn't meet with her again for six more weeks. It was incredibly daunting to start all over with someone new, and Naveed hadn't been able to open up to her in his first session, especially with Nate there whispering that she couldn't be trusted.

He definitely couldn't tell her about what had happened that night on Lopez Island, especially when he wasn't sure himself. Had any of that even been real? Roya hadn't known what he was talking about when he'd confronted her. Was it only a vivid dream… or had it been some sort of psychotic episode? If so, did that mean that the hallucinations he'd experienced in the fall weren't just a side effect of the tricyclic antidepressants he was taking at the time? Was there something deeper wrong with him?

He wished he could pop into Dr. Young's office and talk it all over with her. He really missed the constant mental health support he'd been given at Englewood. True, he'd learned lots of coping skills while there, but plunging back into the real world felt like being forced to fend for himself on the streets after leaving a loving family. And Koffka… it was unbelievable how much he missed Koffka.

He tried to shift his focus back to the present as he stepped into the gray afternoon. The air was misty, so he pulled up his hood and shoved his hands into his coat pockets. He fumbled around with his unfeeling fingers until he sensed the small weight of the pocketknife in his palm. He'd found it tucked away in the kitchen junk drawer, and had sharpened the blade. When he'd tested it on the leathery skin of a pomegranate, he was pleased at how easily it sliced through.

One of these days, he would need to buy a proper knife, a switchblade he could open with ease. Though he knew better than to read the comment string on the D&C video featuring "Navotron," he was well aware that it had summoned the trolls. He knew, too, that most of what they said was just talk, but he needed to be able to defend himself if they ever came after him in the real world.

Naveed headed toward the shopping district further down the road, thinking he'd sit for a minute on one of the benches dotting a nearby green space. He kept to the far right of the sidewalk, since everyone else had a faster pace than him. He hated how slow he was now.

As he neared the park, he looked up and saw someone he recognized approaching from the other direction, her vibrant purple hair shining as brightly as the smile on her face.

"Hey, Naveed!" Brooke had a heavy canvas bag slung around one shoulder. She stepped off the sidewalk into the grass and dropped it to the ground beside her feet. "It's good to see you."

Naveed raised his left hand in an awkward wave, since he was still clutching the knife inside his right pocket. "Hey, Brooke. Good to see you, too."

"I was just stocking up at the co-op. Got a long drive ahead of me tomorrow. Did Andi tell you I'm moving to Boulder for a few months?"

Naveed wasn't sure whether she had or not. His mind had been such a jumble lately that he'd had a hard time holding onto details. "Yeah, that's great! Finally getting out of Seattle, huh?"

She smiled again, though there was a hint of sadness in her eyes. "Oh hey, I'm glad I ran into you. I've been meaning to text you about this, but it keeps slipping my mind—my mom has this friend who gets really bad nerve pain because of their diabetes, and they grow their own cannabis, it's good organic high-CBD stuff, and they make these capsules that have been super effective in helping manage their pain, so I just thought, I mean, if you're interested, I could put you in contact with them so you could try it out?"

"I can't," Naveed said. "I'm still on probation. I've got to do random drug tests and stuff, and if there was any detectable THC...."

"But it wouldn't be illegal if you're using it medically, right? Can't your doctor get you a prescription?"

"Doubt it. My neurologist says there's not enough evidence—"

"That's because they can't research it! Just because cannabis is a Schedule 1 substance thanks to arcane, racist drug laws!" Brooke exclaimed. "Maybe you should ask your other doctors, or go see a naturopath or something. I really think it could help. And it's way better than relying on the pharmaceutical industry. I was just reading this disturbing article the other day about Genbiotix... did you know that they test their drugs on *dogs*? It's disgusting. And yet everything they're doing is technically legal."

Naveed's unease grew. Dogs? He thought about Koffka, locked up, trapped in a lab being pumped full of drugs—

Stop. He couldn't get worked up about this now. He wished that he could stop using Genbiotix's meds, could boycott and fight against them in the way they deserved, but... their drugs were the reason he was alive, the reason he was here talking to Brooke right now instead of at home bedridden with debilitating pain and tormented by Nate's incessant urgings toward self-harm.

It is what it is, he told himself. *Can't fight Genbiotix if you're dead.* "I'll think about it."

That seemed to placate Brooke. She picked up her bag. "Just let me know if you change your mind. Well—I'm glad we ran into each other. Take care."

"You, too," he said, and she hurried down the street, back along the path to her house that the two of them had traveled together so many times before.

Naveed trudged on. He sat on a bench for a few minutes, too weary to even take out his phone, but then he noticed that passers-by kept hurrying past him and pointedly not making eye contact. Maybe they thought he was homeless. He hadn't bothered to trim his beard or tame his curly hair, and maybe it was unusual to sit in the winter drizzle on a wet bench staring into space. But he was tired. Crashing. Frustrated that only two hours of being back in society could do this to him. And he still had time to kill before picking up Roya.

He was about to pull out his phone, thinking he might text Andi to see how her day was going, but froze when he saw two police officers approaching him.

He withdrew both hands from his pockets, dropping the knife inside, and rested his palms on his knees. *No sudden movements,* he told himself. *Keep calm and they'll walk right by.* But he wasn't calm, not at all; he was sweating now, his heart racing, as the vise grip of panic squeezed his chest.

Even though he tried not to let them in, the memories flooded back: the night of his arrest on the pier, when the officer had slammed his head into the ground, the jolt from the taser paralyzing him, his arms twisted and cuffed, the knee in the small of his back, how they had held him down for what felt like ages as icy wind pierced through his soaking wet clothes, but lucky for him he passed out at some point and couldn't be revived by the medics, so he woke up in the hospital instead of the police station. Even though he was later cleared of all murder charges, the cops had insisted that their use of force was justified. There would never be an apology. He was expected to be satisfied with his shitty consolation prize: they hadn't killed him. They had let him live.

The injustice of all this—not only his own situation, but that of the countless Black and brown people who hadn't been so lucky—grated against that pocket of rage deep inside him, the rage that he worked on a daily basis to keep quarantined. Even the emotion-numbing meds couldn't fully take it away. It stalked him at every turn, especially out here, away from the safety of his home. Dennis's voice echoed in his mind: the things he'd said about Andi back at Englewood... the attacks he'd accused Naveed of plotting....

The worst thing was that Naveed had to shut up and take their abuse. Because if he lost control, if someone pushed him hard enough to unleash this fury, he wouldn't be able to hold back. And then he'd become the killer everyone expected him to be.

As the cops came closer, he pasted his most charming smile on his face. *Kill them with kindness,* he thought. That had always been Maman's approach. "Afternoon, officers," he said as they walked by. One of them nodded, but the other gave him a long, piercing stare that made him sweat even harder. To his relief, though, they didn't stop. Only once they were a safe distance away did he lean back into the bench and return his hands to his pockets, heart still hammering.

He opened a meditation app on his phone and went through a few breathing exercises. Which actually did help. But by now he was getting cold, so he got up and continued along his way, moving slower now. He couldn't wait to pick up Roya and go home.

On his way past the bookstore where he used to work, he stopped short when he noticed the window display. It was devoted entirely to *Keepers of the Moon*, with a lunar landscape made from painted cardboard forming the backdrop.

Seeing the cover again sent goosebumps rising on his arms. *Her hands glowed with points of light, as if she held every star in the cosmos on her tiny fingertips.* He'd spent many sleepless nights listening to the audiobook, which was narrated by a man with a soothing voice and a slight Russian accent. It had been hard to focus with Nate competing for attention, though, and he often wished he had a paper copy.

On a whim, he opened the door. It was warm inside, but the shop only felt vaguely familiar, as if he were returning to some faraway city he'd visited once as a child. He hadn't gone in since the work shift in early June that had turned out to be his last.

He didn't see anyone he recognized as he made his way to the sci-fi section. Annoyingly, a preppy-looking white employee abandoned the box of books he was restocking and followed Naveed, making a big show of straightening up nearby shelves that were already perfectly tidy. Was the whole world going to treat him like a criminal forever?

With all the dignity he could muster, he picked up a copy of *Keepers of the Moon* and made his way straight to the checkout counter. Naveed rang the bell for service, half-hoping that the preppy guy would be forced to help him, but he'd gone back to restocking.

While he had his back turned, a familiar voice said, "Hi, can I help you?"

He turned around, surprised that his old friend Ethan was standing behind the register. The last time they'd texted had been in August, when they'd made a lunch date that Naveed had never intended to keep; he'd used it as cover for his plan to run away from home. At the time, he'd been certain he'd never see Ethan again.

"OMG, Naveed!" Ethan exclaimed. "I almost didn't recognize you!"

Naveed set the book down. "Hey, Ethan. I didn't know you worked here."

"Yeah, just started over winter break," Ethan said. "I was working at Bountiful Earth before that, but they got bought out recently and things were going downhill, so I bailed."

Naveed tried to suppress a wince at the mention of the natural grocery stores that had once been owned by Brennan Walsh. Ethan, too, looked slightly uncomfortable, as if he'd just remembered the connection, and quickly said, "Well, anyway, I'm glad you stopped by! Want me to see if I can take my break now? We could grab a bite somewhere and catch up?"

Why did Ethan seem so happy to see him? Naveed had been the worst friend imaginable. "I can't right now, have to go pick up my sister in a few." He paused. "Look, Ethan, I'm really sorry... about this summer and... not staying in touch...."

Ethan shrugged. "S'okay. Don't worry about it. I've been ridiculously busy since school started. Fall quarter was *insane.* But I've got this drama prof who's incredible—I know you'll love him too. Did you start up this quarter?"

Naveed blinked. College felt like such a distant possibility now; he honestly wasn't sure he'd ever get there. "Um, no, I couldn't defer my admission. I'll have to reapply."

Ethan's sunny expression faltered. "Really? That doesn't seem fair."

Naveed had nothing to say to that. Was *anything* that had happened to him in the past six months fair? He pushed the book over to Ethan. "I've got to go—will you ring me up? Oh, and I was wondering, do you have any other books by Zolotov? Did he ever write a sequel?"

Ethan looked down at the book, then back up at Naveed. "No, this was the only book Zolotov ever published. He disappeared right after that and... well, you know... don't you?"

"Oh, yeah, of course, I just wondered." Naveed could tell he was missing something that was apparently common knowledge, and tried to brush it off. Ethan rang up the book, and seemed to want to say something more, but Naveed reiterated that he was in a rush and said he'd see Ethan around.

As soon as he got a safe distance from the bookstore, he pulled out his phone and googled Zolotov's name. What he found nearly made him drop his phone.

> Human remains discovered at Lopez Island "retreat center" identified as belonging to author Viktor Zolotov.

Other words from snippets of news reports caught his eye: *Skeleton exhumed. Right hand missing. Unknown cause of death.*

Naveed tried not to see what his brain wanted to show him. That night on Lopez. The tall piles of dirt. The police tape. The moon shining bright above. The smell of that cabin. A deep hole from which there was no escape.

Next thing he knew he was running. He could barely breathe but still he kept going. If he ran fast enough, maybe he could stay here instead of getting lost in his head.

But then everything caught up with him: The police officer slamming his face to the ground – falling into a deep dark pit – Dennis's sneering face – Genbiotix's drugs saving lives – destroying them – someone coming at Koffka with a needle as he whimpered, shut in a cage – no – *at least you can take comfort knowing that you'll be making a contribution to the greater good* – NO – Brooke leaving – and Ethan – the past always catching up, always following – *it's not over, it's never over* – no escape, none, never ever never ever—

"Hello?"

Naveed spun around. "Andi?" he said, confused. That was her voice, but she wasn't here; the sidewalks were deserted, but this street was unfamiliar and he was sweat-drenched and out of breath. There was a sour taste in his mouth.

"What's wrong?" she asked.

Only then did he realize her voice was coming from his phone, which was pressed to his ear. She must have called him. Or had he called her?

"Naveed." She said his name quietly. "What's going on?"

His heavy breath fuzzed back at him through the phone. "I... I think... I think I'm lost."

"You're lost?"

He forced a laugh. It felt good to hear her voice, so rational and rooted in reality. Like he just had a small problem, one she could easily help with. "Yep. Can't figure out where I am."

"But you have your phone?"

"Oh! My phone!" Now his laugh was genuine. "The map. Right. Why didn't I think of that."

"Are you okay? I'm between classes right now, but I could come get you?"

"No, no, it's fine, I'll figure it out."

She was quiet for a second; he could hear the din of high school hallways, hundreds of buzzing voices. Then, "I mean it. I can leave if you need me to."

"No," he said firmly. "I didn't mean to... just got... confused for a minute there, I'm okay, really."

Another pause. The halls seemed quieter now. "You're sure you can find your way?"

He wasn't. But he was glad to have something else to preoccupy his brain. Now he'd have to figure out where he was and navigate home. Or, wait, to Roya's school. He pulled the phone away from his ear and checked the clock. Shit. It was nearly dismissal time. "Yep. I just needed to hear your voice, that's all. See you later?"

"Yeah. I have to go—but please text me when you get home."

"I will." Once he thanked her and hung up, he pulled up the map of his current location, replaying the whole embarrassing conversation in his head. He really should do something special for Andi, he thought as he started making his way towards Roya's school. She deserved a fucking medal for putting up with him, and for everything she did to keep bringing him back to himself, over and over again.

Roya

KATERINA AND THE LITTLE STRANGERS

I run into the night before trying to draw my first breath. I want to get as far away from the dome as I can. Far away from Dr. Belinsky. He plans to leave with the rest of them, and I will be all alone here with Mikhail.

It doesn't take long before I grow breathless. My heart flutters with panic as I inhale: it feels all wrong, like my lungs are being squeezed tight instead of inflating the way they should.

I stop, doubled over, trying again. Gasping, searching desperately for oxygen.

And then something happens. It's like flipping a switch, turning a spigot. My lungs fill, somehow, with an atmosphere they were not built to handle. It's impossible, but it's happening, and I don't even care why, because it feels so glorious to do this simple thing. To breathe.

My isolation suit billows in the low gravity as I bound farther away, and I shed it on the moon's craggy surface. When I do,

I notice that my skin is no longer glowing. I have gone dark: if anyone is watching from inside the windows of the dome, they will not see me.

There is a strange feeling in my chest now, like it's swelling, but it doesn't hurt; it feels good. All my organs feel like they have grown and are going to leap out of me, which I know doesn't sound like it would be a good thing, but...

It makes me think of something Dr. Belinsky told me. About the day they left their homeland, when the rocket miraculously pierced the Earth's atmosphere. How he felt a thousand emotions all at the same time: sorrow for leaving his sister behind, relief that their ship hadn't burned up, excitement for the new society they would create. But most of all: freedom. Like all paths were wide open.

That's it. I feel free, because I am free, for the first time in my life. Why didn't I come outside sooner? I shouldn't have believed Dr. Belinsky. What does he know, really? He's limited by his earth way of thinking, but I am a moon child. If I'd only known, I could have come out here all the time! Bounding across craters, filling my lungs with this strange air that only I can breathe.

The exhilaration of it is almost too much to bear. It's only after I've leaped far away from the dome that I realize the voices have gone silent. There is no more humming. It's wonderfully quiet out here, in this long dark night that lasts two Earth weeks. Dr. Belinsky often complains about the length of the night, but I've always thought it beautiful.

When I become tired, I slow to a stop. I think it might feel nice to dig my fingers into the dust, so I do. It glitters with luminescence, the way my skin did in the greenhouse.

"Hello, Katerina," says the dust. It seemed like it took the cabbages lots of effort to form human words, but the dust sounds quite nonchalant. "Thank you for coming outside. It is much easier for us to talk out here."

I lift a handful. "Who are you?" I ask the moon dust. It's sharp, clinging to my skin like glassy burrs.

"You probably know us by the name they have given us. The 'Little Strangers.'"

My breath catches in my throat. According to Dr. Belinsky, the Little Strangers are responsible for my disease. They're the reason I need to stay in isolation. The reason that anyone who walks on the moon's surface, or digs in the mines—the way Sergey did—must undergo an hours-long decontamination procedure afterward.

As if reading my thoughts, the sand says, "We find it offensive that they call us a disease. It is part of their flawed way of thinking, the assumption that things they do not understand are always sinister. We are not infectious agents. We are the Matryoshka, the mothers of all: trillions of tiny units that connect to form a singular consciousness. We have blanketed the moon since the beginning of time, but your people have killed many of us with their carelessness. And now the future of the moon is in jeopardy: their mining and digging have destabilized its structure. It may not remain intact much longer."

"I'm... I'm sorry," I stutter, because I'm not sure how to react. This goes against everything I have been taught, and yet... and yet, what they are saying feels true. What gives Dr. Belinsky and the cosmonauts the right to barge into this beautiful place, to cause so much destruction—to extract so much in order to force their earthly bodies to live, without caring about the consequences?

For some reason, I think of Sergey's words. INVADERS! OUTSIDERS! YOU NEVER SHOULD HAVE COME.

"Did you infect Sergey?" I ask. "Is that why he...?"

"Again, we are not infectious." The sand sounds indignant now. "They flatter themselves to think that they've kept a sterile colony. Their decontamination procedures are completely useless; we infiltrated the dome long ago. We blanket their skin, their walls. Sergey was... nothing but an experiment. He was highly susceptible to our suggestions. And he singlehandedly killed billions of us through his actions in the mine."

I'm quiet for a moment. "Why are you telling me this?"

"Because you are different. You are not like the rest of them. We can only live on their surfaces. But you—because we had already colonized your mother when she became pregnant, we are part of every single cell in your body. Just as we can allow you to do things most humans cannot—like breathing this air—you can allow us to live in places we've never gone. That's why we need you to be our savior, Katerina. We need you to bring us back with you when you go to Earth."

I think about this. "But if you're already covering everything, if you're all over them, too, and the spaceship—why do you need me?"

"The moon provides us with certain things we need to survive. Without them, we may not live through the journey. But you are a proper host. With you, we can thrive, and learn how to adapt to life on other planets."

"Sorry, I can't help." I sniff. "I'm not going. They won't take me on the ship."

"You'll find a way," they say.

To tell the truth, I'm not sure I want to leave now. There's so much I haven't explored yet, so many wonders to discover beyond the dome! But even as I think it, a small voice inside me says, Aren't you curious, though? Don't you want to see the blue planet up close? Swim underwater?

Having enough water in one place that a person could actually swim in it—this possibility has never occurred to me. It feels like an odd thing to think.

"So you've colonized them all," I say, trying to piece this together. "But are you able to... change them? Can you control what they think?"

"We can nudge. It takes great effort. And not everyone is susceptible."

"But since you're a part of me, you can 'nudge' me easily, can't you? You can make me do what you want me to do, even if I don't want to do it."

"No, your decisions are still yours. But this is crucial, Katerina. We only want you to understand how important it is that we leave on that spaceship."

"Then I want you to do something for me first," I say.

"What do you need?" the sand says, or my hand says, or the entire moon says.

"I need to know. I need to know everything you know about our colony."

"Very well, then. Close your eyes."

And I do. Despite the darkness, I see a bright light. It's warm, pleasant. And suddenly it's pierced by an insight so sharp it almost hurts. It feels limitless, bottomless, the source of all that is and all that ever will be. I see everything: the moment that Dr. Belinsky described, the cosmonauts gleefully leaving Earth. Embarking on the difficult work of building the colony. The whole group of scientists, all of them looking much younger, resting inside the dome for the first time without their helmets, once the oxygen circulation system is installed. One woman among them, a woman whom I've never seen, but have heard plenty about. Natasha, my mother.

She tosses her hair over her shoulder. A smiling Mikhail has his arm around her. Dr. Belinsky watches from the periphery, wincing as if in pain.

Then things speed up. Natasha and Mikhail smash their faces together and seem to be enjoying it. Then they are outside in their space suits, bounding across craters—until she falls, skidding across the surface. She and Mikhail stare at the ripped fabric in horror. Next she's alone, in the room I recognize as my own, looking very different, her belly like a round ball, and Mikhail talks to her through the intercom, telling her that she cannot see her plants anymore. And in another flash she is on her back, sweating and moaning, and Dr. Belinsky pulls a baby out of her, pulls me out of her, red with her blood and glowing brightly with the light of the Matryoshka. Behind me, she dims. Her eyes close. Dr. Belinsky tries to help, but nothing can be done. Mikhail watches through the glass with a look of disgust on his face. He steals in after she goes still, with his full spacesuit on, to take me. To bring me outside, where he carelessly sets me in the sand and turns his back.

It's all I can do to keep my eyes closed, because I feel his disgust also. I know why the Matryoshka are showing me this. They want me to know everything that Dr. Belinsky has kept from me all this time.

The visions keep going, showing Sergey's death and the subsequent building of the spaceship, but I can barely pay attention anymore. I watch all the way to the end, though. I watch Dr. Belinsky boarding a spaceship without me.

I tear my hands free from the sand, and the vision ceases.

I stand up and run, though of course there's nowhere to go. This new knowledge sickens me.

Mikhail, the tyrant leader, is my father.

And he tried to kill me. His own daughter. Yet Dr. Belinsky intends to leave me here with him, where he'll doubtlessly try to destroy me again.

But he can't destroy me if I destroy him first.

Andi

THURSDAY, JANUARY 28

EVEN THOUGH ANDI WAS RUNNING LATE, SHE PAUSED BEFORE opening the door to the recording studio. She could hardly believe she had made it to this point. Her dad had pulled some strings to arrange the session and book a sound engineer—but what felt the most miraculous to Andi was that her songs were actually done.

It was like something had been unleashed in her after that night at Neumo's with Jed. Finally, Glenn's advice to dig deeper had clicked. All this time, she'd been skating along the surface, where things were safe, but to make her songs great she needed to plunge down into the icy water below. Her first reaction was to turn away, afraid of what she might find in those depths, but she stayed to explore them instead. And then she poured everything she found into her music. Not just the fear, but every emotion, all of it, even the contradictions. The joy in the darkness; the darkness in the joy. When she'd sent it back to Glenn, he'd responded with only one word. *YES!*

After that vote of confidence, Andi had met up with the violinist from Invisible Noise several times. Patricia had contributed some beautiful arrangements, and Andi couldn't wait to hear it come together in an official recording. She had almost been moved to tears when she printed the finalized sheet music. That made it look so official, so... *real*. And it felt better than anything she'd accomplished so far in her life: she had written songs for an actual film.

Sure, she'd barely slept for days, and she was missing afternoon classes for this. Her mother would never have let that fly, but she was so focused right now on getting Ah-ma through chemo that Andi decided she didn't need to know. All of that left her mind, though, when she saw the room she'd be playing in. The soundproofed walls, the gorgeous polished-rosewood Steinway grand piano, the empty stands waiting for her stacks of sheet music.

"What do you think?" her father asked.

"Dad, it's incredible. A grand piano and everything."

"A serious piano for a serious musician," he said, just as Patricia walked into the room.

"Wow, this is a swanky spot." She adjusted her music stand and opened her violin case. "Nicely done, Jake."

"Being an aging rock star does have its perks," he said. "Let's get started, shall we?"

Before doing anything else, Andi snapped a picture of the piano and sent it to Brooke, who responded with a flurry of heart-eyed emojis. She'd only been gone in Boulder for a week, and her absence didn't quite feel real yet, especially since they constantly texted each other. It had helped, of course, that Andi had been completely distracted with her music.

As Patricia warmed up, Andi indulged in a few quick rounds of *Bugpocalypse 3K*. Cyrus had asked if she wanted to help test the app, and she'd found it to be a surprisingly good stress reliever. Exactly what she needed to quiet her nerves right now.

After a few minutes, her dad said it was time to start, so she silenced her phone and put it away. They ran through the main theme together, then it was Andi's turn to lay down the piano track. The others left to stand behind the glass with Brian, the sound engineer, who gave her the thumbs up when he was ready.

Andi's nervousness flared again. This reminded her of long-ago piano recitals, when she never failed to choke horribly the second the spotlight was on her. Those old fears returned, the worry that she wouldn't be good enough, that her fingers would trip as they always did and she'd clunk out all the wrong notes.

But then she looked at the sheet music. *Her* sheet music, the songs that she'd written, that she loved more than almost anything. She played the first notes, and they sounded so good in that room, in the reverent silence surrounding her, that she thought: *this is what I want to do forever.*

Everything else slipped away. She thought about the documentary as she played, about the images that would go along with her melodies, about Gabriela swinging her feet in the hospital waiting room, about Ramón and Marisol driving down the coast with their children in the back seat, about Naveed in the forest at Englewood saying, *we've failed them.* Naveed, Naveed, Naveed. Always there, in every note.

She didn't look up until the final chord had faded away, but when she did, she was surprised to see only two faces behind the glass; her father was no longer there.

Patricia opened the door after receiving an approving nod from the engineer. "Andi, that was amazing. Jake had to step out for a minute. He was a blubbering mess," she added in a faux whisper.

"You're up," the engineer told Patricia.

"Tough act to follow," she said as they passed each other in the doorway, and a giddy grin spread across Andi's face. She was still totally... well, *high* seemed the only word to describe it.

Andi's father returned shortly, his eyes still red. "Goddammit, I told myself I wouldn't cry," he said. "But I couldn't help it. You were such a pro in there. I'm just... I'm so proud of you."

At least one of her parents was supportive of her music career, Andi thought as she hugged him. They settled in to watch Patricia, who was shredding away on her violin. It was mesmerizing to watch, and when Andi snuck a peek at her father, he looked just as awestruck as she was.

"I told you she was good," Andi said to him.

"What was that?" He seemed unable to tear his eyes away.

"My point exactly," Andi said.

When Patricia finished playing, they took a brief break before Andi's father recorded some guitar and percussion for a few tracks. Andi thanked Patricia and told her she could leave if she wanted.

"That's okay. Think I'll stick around if you don't mind. See how it all comes together." Patricia took a sip of her diet soda.

"Sure. I'd love for you to stay," her dad said.

Andi grabbed a bottle of water and stepped outside, where the sun had finally broken through the ever-present cloud cover. She opened the texts that had streamed in from Naveed while she'd been recording.

She tensed up before reading them, unsure what to expect. Things had been a little rocky ever since that distressing phone call when he'd gotten "lost" last week. Thankfully, today's texts were benign.

Finished up at food bank!

Walking home now

It's taking forever, I'm slower than a sloth swimming in a vat of molasses

It's good tho, sweet and treacly

How's the recording going?

I can't wait to hear your music btw

Really I can't hold on much longer so when can I hear it?!!

Hey want to finally go for that Seward Park run later?

But hope you don't mind if we go slow (see aforementioned sloth)

Or it doesn't have to be that we can do whatever

Feeling great, just want to spend this beautiful day with you

Andi found herself smiling. A run around Seward sounded perfect.

She was about to text him back when something caught her eye in the parking lot.

The ground was sparkling. She blinked, confused. Then she realized why: the sun was shining on a carpet of broken glass.

Andi stepped closer. She'd left school at lunch and had driven her mom's car to the studio; one of the perks of having an absentee parent was that she had adopted the Sentra as her own. But now, her breath left her as she saw that both of its front windows had been smashed.

She bent to look inside the car, realizing that she'd stupidly left her backpack in the passenger seat. To her surprise, it was still there.

Andi returned to the studio, where she found her dad and Patricia standing by the espresso maker. Her father must have just said something funny, because Patricia was laughing so hard her eyes were tearing up.

"Dad?" Andi asked in a shaky voice. It felt oddly good to destroy the cheery mood.

"Everything okay, Peanut?" he asked.

"Um, I was just out in the parking lot. Someone broke into Mom's car. They smashed the windows."

"Did they take anything?" her dad asked.

"I don't think so. The weird thing is, I left my backpack inside— I know, I know," she said, as he opened his mouth to lecture her about her carelessness. "But it's still there."

"Did you check it? To make sure no valuables were missing?" he asked.

"Not yet." Andi grew even more breathless as she felt her pockets: she'd left her wallet in her backpack. She'd been in such a rush to start recording that she hadn't remembered to take it with her.

Her dad and Patricia followed her outside. Andi wanted to check her backpack right away, but had to wait while her dad took a few photos. As soon as he was done, she opened the car door and unzipped her bag. Her wallet was sitting on top of her school textbooks, not in the interior pocket where she always kept it. But her cash was still inside, her debit card, her driver's license, even her fake ID.

"It's all still here," she said in disbelief. It didn't make any sense—if they'd gone through her bag and found the wallet, why hadn't they taken it?

"Well, that was lucky," her dad said. "You should never leave your backpack out in plain sight like that—especially if your wallet's inside!"

"I know," Andi said, annoyed that he insisted on lecturing her. "I was in a hurry. I forgot."

Patricia went back inside to see if Brian had a broom to sweep up the glass. Only after she'd left did Andi notice something winking at her from the passenger footwell.

It was an empty bag of Blazin Bitz. Its foil lining glinted in the light. Scattered around it were crushed mini-chips dusted with red powder.

"Dad. Look." Andi pointed helplessly at the mess, unable to say anything more.

Her dad frowned. "Hmm. That's odd."

"But... why would someone leave *those*... of all things...."

"I'm sure it doesn't mean anything, Peanut," he said. "Something must've scared them off, I guess, and they panicked and dropped the bag. I'll go ahead and file a police report, but it was probably just some punk kid."

Patricia reappeared, followed by an apologetic-looking Brian, who was holding a broom. "So sorry this happened," he said as he began sweeping the pebbles of glittering glass.

"My fault. Shouldn't have left my bag in the car," Andi muttered. She couldn't shake the feeling that this was personal, and sank onto the curb, lowering her head onto her knees.

A moment later, her dad sat down beside her. "You all right?" he asked.

"Yeah," she lied.

"It's not a big deal," he said. "This kind of thing happens all the time."

"I know." Maybe he was right, and the bag of Blazin Bitz was just a coincidence. But she couldn't stop thinking about Richard Caring. It didn't seem likely that he was behind this; it would be an absurd way for such a powerful man to retaliate.

But maybe this was only a warning. Maybe it was a sign of more to come.

"I'll take care of it," her dad said. "I'll file the report, the insurance claim, drop off the car at the shop. Don't worry. We'll get it sorted out."

Though she was glad to hear it, a burst of resentment prevented her from thanking him. He'd barely been around lately, and suddenly he was acting like a devoted dad? He probably just wanted to look good in front of Patricia, she thought cynically.

"You want a ride home?" he asked at the same time that her phone buzzed. She glanced at it and saw another text from Naveed. What do you think? Seward? Somewhere else?

Andi no longer felt like running. She was completely exhausted. Coffee, that's what she needed.

"No, thanks," she said to her dad. "You should finish up here. But if it's okay, I think I might take off, hang out at a coffee shop for a while to get some homework done. I can take the train home later."

"Fine by me. Oh, and you don't need to wait up tonight. I'm going to go see Kyle's band at the Sunset up in Ballard."

That was more like the dad she knew. She wanted to say, *Can't you see that I'm a little freaked out right now? Please don't make me go home to an empty house.* Instead, she muttered, "Okay. Have fun."

He opened his wallet and handed her two $20 bills. "For coffee. And dinner. Sorry I haven't been around much—we should work on our song some more over the weekend."

"Maybe. If I have time." She took the money, then stood up and shouldered her backpack. "See you later," she said to the others, who had finished cleaning up and were heading back into the studio.

"Great job today!" Patricia said. "Can't wait to hear how it turns out."

"I'll send you the rough mix when it's ready," Brian promised.

Andi thanked them and turned away. As she walked, she texted Naveed back. Done in studio. Want to have coffee? She sent the address of a nearby café. It would probably take him a while to get there by train, but that would give her time to collect herself and start chipping away at her massive pile of homework.

He replied that he'd see her there, but her hopes of getting work done were soon dashed. She settled in at a cozy table near a sunny window with a double-shot latte, opened her physics textbook, and immediately felt a headache crashing down.

She closed her eyes, once more seeing the glass glittering on the asphalt. Seeing Richard Caring's glare. He hadn't done this, she knew, not personally anyway. But she had no doubt that he could still make things happen, even from behind bars. Still—why was someone after her? Why now? Her petition had gone nowhere. She had met recently with the artivists, and they'd begun working on a satirical ad to promote the Blazin Bitz boycott campaign that would officially start in a few months. Nothing had been announced yet, but even if it had, what did it matter to Richard? It wasn't like he was gaining anything from Bitz anymore.

Or was he? Andi remembered what Akilah had said, about how Richard Caring was on the board of the company that had bought the Blazin Bitz brand. But he would have lost that position since he'd gone to prison... right?

Her head pounded harder. She rubbed the scar on her forehead. She took another sip of coffee, then let her head rest on her folded elbows. Just for a minute. Just until the pain subsided.

Some time later, the dissonant screech of chair legs against the floor startled her awake. Naveed was sitting down across from her.

"Hey. That physics book must be a real page-turner," he said.

Andi hoped very hard that she hadn't been drooling. She tried to surreptitiously wipe her mouth without him noticing. "Oh... I was just... trying to study. Obviously it wasn't going so well."

He pulled his chair in closer to the table, and his foot accidentally brushed against hers. Feeling quite awake all of a sudden, she took a sip of her coffee, which had cooled considerably. At least her headache had retreated. For now, anyway.

"I'm glad you suggested this," Naveed said. "A run would have been too much after my exhausting two-hour volunteer shift." He slumped in his chair dramatically, smiling to show it was a joke, even though she suspected it wasn't really. "So how was your day? I want to hear all about the studio."

Andi closed her book and glanced at him, but quickly returned her gaze to her hands. She couldn't look at the curls falling over his forehead, at his eyes, his mouth… it was all so irresistible, but resist she must.

She didn't want to ruin his good mood by telling him about her mom's car. Something about this bothered her—it didn't feel right that she was always there for him, yet she couldn't tell him what was really going on in her life without worrying that it would send him over the edge.

But she didn't want to think about the break-in anyway, so she skipped over it completely. Instead, she showed him the pictures she'd taken in the studio and told him how amazing it had felt to play that perfectly-tuned, top-of-the-line grand piano. As she talked, her excitement returned. She couldn't wait to hear the finished product, professionally mastered and ready to add to the film.

Across the table, Naveed listened to every word, seeming to absorb her happiness. And in that instant she realized the exact future she wanted: she would get into USC and study music composition, and Naveed would move to LA too, and he could get acting jobs, and maybe they could collaborate on films together, and it would be sunny all the time and everything would be perfect.

It was an impossible dream, she knew. But it was beautiful one nevertheless.

Cyrus

THERE WERE ONLY TWO WEEKS LEFT UNTIL GAMECODEX, AND Cyrus was starting to think they might actually have a chance of winning.

He was glad, in a way, that Dev had suggested putting *D&C* on hiatus. Cyrus had enough to keep up with, especially now that school work was ramping up—how the hell was it time for midterms already?—but the downside was that it had been a long time since he and Dev had hung out alone together. Now, it was all *Bugpocalypse*, all the time. The four of them often spent long evenings in Todd's coder-cave, tweaking the app based on user feedback and getting ready to release the second beta version.

On Thursday afternoon after class, Cyrus saw that Shea had sent a message to the team. Can't meet tonight, but I put together some stats—interesting stuff! Look them over and maybe we can talk tomorrow.

Todd had messaged that it would be good to take a night off since he had other plans, and Dev had said, Studying now but will look at it ASAP.

Instead of going home to his distracting family, Cyrus headed to the library and texted Dev. Just got to library, where u at? Wanna study together?

The answer came quickly. Sorry can't

Cyrus pushed down a swell of annoyance as he settled in at a table. He missed hanging out with Dev, even if they were just studying side by side, so the terse response stung.

But maybe Dev was in the thick of something and didn't want to be distracted. Cyrus decided to turn his attention to the data.

He opened the file Shea had sent. She had compiled a lot of useful information, including results from the mood survey. She'd also reported on other metrics such as the number of times users opened the app and the duration of play—

Wait. Was that right? Cyrus looked at the numbers more closely. Shea's graph showed that the majority of users spent between 0 and 60 minutes per week playing the game—but about a quarter of users played it for 750 minutes or more. Cyrus did some calculations: that was almost two hours a day. He couldn't even imagine playing it for that long.

Shea had gone on to analyze these "heavy users" in more detail, noting that they often played for long spurts every few hours. Most of them only played the competition mode, and selected starting moods like "bored," "lonely," or, somewhat perplexingly, "snacky." Their ending moods weren't much better: "bug-eyed," "tired," and, again, "lonely." But still, they came back day after day.

This unsettled Cyrus, but he couldn't pinpoint exactly what bothered him. Just looked at the data, he wrote to Shea. Wondering about the heavy users. Can we talk?

Not now, she wrote back. In the middle of something. But it's exciting stuff right? We did it! Made an app that's totally addictive!

Cyrus literally dropped his phone. It fell to the table with a thud that seemed very loud in the hushed library. Several people sitting nearby looked up in surprise. "Sorry," he whispered, and they went back to their work. But Cyrus couldn't bring himself to pick up his phone again.

Making an addictive game hadn't been his goal at all. He'd wanted to make an app that lifted people's spirits a little, that was a healthy vent for frustration and a distraction from life's unpleasantness. Something that his brother could play in clinic waiting rooms, for example, to take his mind off of whatever tests or procedures or therapy awaited him.

Instead, he'd created a game that stole time from people without leaving them any better off than they were before.

That wasn't exactly true, though; Cyrus had skimmed over a chart showing that some users, especially the ones playing in cooperative mode, actually did report better moods after playing. That was good, he supposed, but he couldn't get the heavy users out of his mind.

And the word Shea had used. *Addictive.* It made him think of Blazin Bitz, which in turn reminded him of the video game he'd played while imprisoned in Tara Snyder's research facility. That was exactly what Nutrexo had been trying to do, wasn't it? Hook people on their "adver-game," immerse them in a world where Bitz grew on trees, so that it would burrow into their subconscious and the next time they were in the chip aisle they would mindlessly grab a bag or two....

Not that *Bugpocalypse 3K* had set out to do anything close to that, but all the same, he wondered: should an addictive game *really* be the end goal?

Maybe Dev could help him think through this. Hey have u looked at Shea's data yet? he texted.

No response. He fired off one more message. Well text me when u do there's something I want to talk to u about

Cyrus tried to get some work done, but couldn't concentrate, so he packed up and headed home. He texted Dev again and kept checking his phone, but Dev was disconcertingly silent. It really wasn't like him to ignore texts like this.

After a late dinner with Baba and Roya—Maman was at an evening meeting and Naveed was out with Andi, apparently—Cyrus could no longer ignore his growing worry. So he deployed the nuclear option and called Dev's phone. It rang and rang. No answer.

He waited a few minutes for a text back, but none came.

So he got in the car and drove to Dev's house. He needed to know that Dev was all right, that was all, he told himself as he walked through the dark side yard to Dev's window. The light was on. Cyrus peeked through the narrow gap in the curtains and froze.

Dev was in there, all right. Shirtless. Cyrus could only see the back of his friend's head, but his arms were plainly wrapped around someone, and from the way the two of them were moving, things were obviously getting hot and heavy.

Cyrus's gut curdled. He couldn't see who the other person was, but he knew.

Shea. Dev had stolen Shea from him. This must be why they were both too busy to talk this afternoon, why Dev had been so distant, why he'd put *D&C* on hiatus and avoided hanging out with Cyrus.

Cyrus was about to leave, knowing he shouldn't be witnessing this in the first place—but then Dev moved his head so that Cyrus caught his first clear glimpse of the other person in the room with him.

It wasn't Shea. No.

It was Todd.

Cyrus retreated to his car and backed out of the driveway as quickly as possible. He could barely believe what he'd seen.

Dev. And Todd. Together.

He took the long way home, then holed up in the downstairs office and tried to cleanse his eyeballs by watching random video game livestreams and viral clips of skateboard fails.

By the time he finally climbed into bed it was very late. Naveed was already in his bottom bunk, and the lights were off, but Cyrus wasn't sure his brother was actually sleeping.

"Hey, Naveed. You awake?" he asked.

"Yeah. Just got home—Andi wanted me to hang out at her place until her dad came back. What's up?"

Cyrus was still so upset about Dev that he couldn't bring himself to care that Naveed had been "hanging out" at Andi's until after midnight.

"Can I, um… can I tell you something? But you have to promise not to tell anyone. Not even Andi."

That seemed to intrigue Naveed. "Of course."

"Okay. So, long story short, I saw Dev." Cyrus couldn't get it out. He swallowed. "I saw Dev… I saw him hooking up with this guy on our app development team. Todd."

Naveed shifted in his bed. "Huh."

"I know, right? Not that I have anything against that, or whatever, I mean it's fine if he's gay, it's just that… I had no idea. None. I mean, how could I not have known? Did he feel like he couldn't tell me? And why *Todd*, of all people? Plus, Dev was the one who was like, 'you can't date Shea because she's a colleague. Haven't you ever seen a sitcom?'" Cyrus closed his eyes. "Akh. I have a gay best friend now. That feels so weird."

"Don't think about it like that. He's still *Dev*. Being gay is part of him, but it isn't all of him."

"I know that. In theory. It's just hard to wrap my brain around it. I guess I'm not as enlightened as you."

"You just need some time to adjust," Naveed said. "But you'll get there."

Cyrus couldn't hold back a tiny smile. "You sound like such a therapist."

"Not surprising. I've spent so much time with them, they might as well give me an honorary degree," Naveed deadpanned.

"Well, Dr. Mirzapour, while I'm on your proverbial couch… what do I do now? They didn't see me, so Dev doesn't know I know, but now that I do, I can't just pretend that I don't. And it's not like we sit around talking about shit like this. It's going to be so awkward."

"You need to tell him," Naveed said slowly. "But it's tough. It's like with Ethan. I mean, when we met, he was already out as bi. But he told me once how hard it could be, especially at first, to find an opening to talk about it with his straight friends. Maybe you need to make it easier for him to start the conversation, without putting him on the defensive by confronting him about what you saw."

Cyrus thought about that. There had been lots of times when he'd closed himself off to meaningful conversations. And—oh God—there were also those gay jokes he'd made on *D&C* that Dev had scrapped in the final cut. Not to mention Dev's continual lack of interest in talking about Andi, and girls in general. He'd probably been waiting for ages for Cyrus to take the hint. "That's a good idea. Thanks," he said, even though he still wasn't exactly sure how he was going to give Dev an opening.

"Oh, that reminds me of something—your app," Naveed said. "So, Andi loves the game and keeps asking me to play it, but when my neuralgia flares up… it's just not… a pleasant experience. And I know this probably isn't doable, but is there a way to enable voice controls or something? For people who have trouble with mobility or whatever."

"Hmm." Cyrus hadn't even considered this, but now that Naveed pointed it out, it seemed like a glaringly obvious issue. "I don't know if that would work with this game, but it's a good thought. I'll definitely look into it. Maybe tomorrow. Or Saturday."

"Maman's leaving for Iran on Saturday," Naveed said in a quiet voice. "I can't believe she's actually going."

It took Cyrus a second to catch up with his brother's train of thought; he was still thinking about *Bugpocalypse*. "Oh, yeah. That's coming right up."

"Did she… when she found out about the wedding, did she ask you and Roya if you wanted to go too?"

"Yeah. But I didn't really want to," Cyrus said uncomfortably. That made it sound like he didn't care about his heritage, which he did; it was just that he didn't feel as strong a connection to the country where his parents were born as Naveed did. "I would've had to miss too much school. And it's not like I know Farhad super well, he was always better friends with you, wasn't he? Baba couldn't take the time off work, so he said he'd stay behind with us. I'm not even sure if they asked Roya. Probably was too expensive to get her over there too."

"I wish I could've gone," Naveed said.

"You will. Someday."

Silence for a minute. Then Naveed yawned. "Well—I should try to get some sleep. Didn't get much last night."

"That's too bad. Nerve pain again?"

"Yeah. Sometimes I wonder if the meds are really helping. Or if it just flares up randomly, so it isn't necessarily the meds that make it go away, but they get all the credit even when it wasn't there in the first place. Does that make sense?"

"Kind of," Cyrus said carefully. "But that doesn't mean you can stop taking them."

"I know." Naveed's voice was flat.

"And I know you hate it, but they're necessary evils." Cyrus didn't have anything else to offer. None of that *it'll get better someday* crap, because Naveed would probably be dealing with this for the rest of his life. Which was way too depressing to think about. "Well, anyway. Thanks for listening to my TV-worthy drama," Cyrus added.

"Yeah. Good luck. Tell me how it goes." The mattress creaked as Naveed turned over. "Night."

Cyrus stared at the ceiling for a long time before eventually falling into a dreamless sleep.

The next day, he drifted through school zombie-like, despite the three cups of coffee he drained throughout the morning. At lunch, he and Dev sat together at a quiet table in the corner of the cafeteria. Cyrus tried to put on a *you can talk to me about anything* face, but Dev had opened up Shea's stats and was paging through them.

"Sorry I never got back to you yesterday," Dev said. "What did you want to ask me about?"

At the moment, Cyrus barely even cared about the app. Despite his attempt to sound neutral, his voice still came out grumpy. "Never mind. It was nothing."

Dev scrolled to another page. "Wow, those heavy users are something else, right? I had no idea anyone would ever play that long. Good thing Todd put in that social stuff—it's so much better that way. It's like a real game now."

"It was a real game before," Cyrus grumbled.

Dev glanced up from his laptop. "What's gotten into you?"

"I could ask you the same thing," Cyrus said before he could stop himself.

Dev tilted his head. "What's that supposed to mean?"

Cyrus swallowed hard. "Nothing. Never mind. Forget it. I have to go." He started packing up his things, but Dev stopped him.

"What. Are. You. Talking. About."

Might as well just come out and say it. Cyrus dropped his voice to a whisper. "Fine. I, um. I saw you with Todd last night."

Dev looked shocked for a second, but it soon gave way to anger. "You saw us? Where?"

"At your house. You weren't answering my texts, and I—"

"You were watching me? *Through my bedroom window?*"

"No, I wasn't *watching,* I just happened to see you... together... and then I left."

Dev's face hardened. "I knew you'd freak out about this. That you wouldn't understand."

"What the fuck, Dev. I don't care about *that,* I just can't believe you didn't tell me."

"Why *would* I tell you? After all your gay jokes? After all the ways I tried to show you, and you insisted on staying completely clueless?"

Cyrus felt like he'd been punched. "You know what? I'm just—I'm done. With you, with the app, with all of it. I don't like where *Bugpocalypse* is going, and I don't want to be a part of it anymore so take it and go have fun with Todd and I hope you win the contest and have a happy fucking life together."

Cyrus stood up so fast that his chair tipped over and clattered loudly on the floor. He could feel people staring, but he didn't care. He just needed to get away from here. He needed to get away from everything.

Roya

KATERINA AND THE LITTLE STRANGERS

It doesn't take me long to find Mikhail. His living quarters are away from everyone else's, in a building connected by a glass tube to the main dome. I watch him through the window, hating everything about him. His long gray beard. The way it grazes the table when he sits down. The way crumbs of the bread—made from the wheat I grew—get stuck in those coarse hairs. I watch him eat. I think about the Matryoshka infesting that bread, infesting all of him, without him even knowing.

I am cloaked in darkness outside the window; the Matryoshka on my skin have mirrored their surroundings. I wonder if I can control his mind. I want him to see me.

I want him to know that when he tried to kill me all those years ago, he did not succeed.

Mikhail turns to me, startled. Like he's seeing a ghost. Is that all I am to you? I think. Then let me show you how wrong you are.

I smash a window with a nearby rock. It breaks through so easily, and I find myself wondering how long it took them to make all this glass. Must have taken ages. And here I am, shattering it in an instant.

He screams. I step through the hole, enjoying the sight of him gasping for his precious oxygen, the oxygen that has already left, that will not save him.

Alarms sound in the distance. He manages to get the door open and retreats into the corridor, but I follow him through.

"Natasha?" he mutters. Even here in the oxygenated corridor, his face is so pale. If he got rid of that beard, I think, he wouldn't look so threatening. Not that I'm afraid: I'm drinking up his fear. It feels wonderful.

"Guess again," I say.

He swings his fist at me, which I'm not expecting. I duck to avoid it, but it catches me off guard, and I drop the rock I'm holding. I watch him run down the corridor to the main dome. Back towards the greenhouse.

I retrieve the rock and follow him at a leisurely pace. Though he's out of my sight, I know I'll be able to find him anywhere. He cannot hide from me.

But I'm not expecting what I see when I arrive at the greenhouse.

I hear the sounds first. A shout from Dr. Belinsky, followed by the ugly smack of fist against flesh, and another, and another. Then, Mikhail's voice. "She's alive? She's ALIVE?"

Dr. Belinsky says nothing, but I can hear his cries. The two men are distracted, and Mikhail's back is to me, which makes it too easy. I slam the rock into the base of his skull.

He falls to the ground in a satisfying heap, and I kneel beside Dr. Belinsky, who is half-sitting near a row of cabbage. It's not glowing anymore, I notice.

I reach towards him, ready to wipe away the blood that's

streaming from his nose. But he recoils. "Your suit," he says. "Where is your suit? You can't be in here if you aren't wearing it...."

"It doesn't matter," I tell him. "The Matryoshka—the Little Strangers—they're already here. They're everywhere. On you, on him, on these cabbages. They've always been."

It feels good to deflate him, to make him realize that I know things he does not. But it doesn't last, because I can't help feeling a bit sorry for him. There's something off about his eyes. I wonder if Mikhail knocked something loose inside his head.

I find myself saying, "You were going to leave me."

He stares, straight-faced. "No," he says. "No. I decided to stay. I'd never leave you here alone. Never."

The way he says it, I know he's telling the truth. The Matryoshka—they're the ones who lied. Or maybe they told me what I needed to hear, so that I would do what they wanted me to do.

But doesn't it matter what I want?

What do I want?

Who am I, anyway? What am I? Part them, part my mother, part... him.

I don't know whether I want to stay here, or whether I want to get on that ship with the rest of them and leave. The only thing I do know is this: Mikhail, my father, does not deserve a future. Here or anywhere.

"Katerina, please believe me," Dr. Belinsky says. His face is so bloody; he still won't let me touch him. "I'm so sorry I didn't tell you these things, but... I... you have to know that Mikhail... he's not who he says he is."

"I know. I know exactly who he is. He's my father."

"No, that's not... he's... he's someone else, on the outside... where they know him by a different name..."

It's an odd thing to say, but I'm no longer listening. I glance behind me to where Mikhail was just sprawled on the floor, only—

Only, he's gone.

"The ship," Dr. Belinsky whispers. Idiots—we were talking about it right in front of him. And now he knows.

We run. I follow Dr. Belinsky, since he knows the way and I do not. When we arrive, Mikhail is the only one standing at the base of the rocket, which sits underneath a small dome. The other cosmonauts are probably busy packing, busy preparing fuel and finding provisions. Hatred pours out of Mikhail's eyes.

"You were going to leave," he says coldly. "And when were you going to tell me?"

"We weren't." I expect Dr. Belinsky to get another pummeling for that, but Mikhail doesn't move. He actually looks rather amused.

"Doesn't matter. It's suicide—it'll never hold up." He reaches into his pocket and withdraws something. I can't see what it is until he flicks it on. The lighter's tiny flame burns bright in the darkness.

"Don't." Dr. Belinsky sounds frightened. "There's propellant all over this room. And the tank is already half full—you'll kill us all."

Now. It has to be now. Mikhail is inches away from the gas tank. One flick of the wrist and he can end it all.

What should I do? I ask the Matryoshka. But they are silent. They aren't going to help me. No one can help me. Only I can decide how this is all going to end.

As soon as Roya finished reading those words, she paged forward, frantic. Where was the end? What was going to happen to Katerina?

She found no answers. It was all blank, until—

At the very end of the small book was a messy note. It was scribbled so illegibly that Roya couldn't understand it at all. There were a few words she thought she could read. *Forgive. Finish.* But the longer she stared at it, the more incomprehensible the letters got.

All Roya could think was that she had to show this to Kass as soon as possible. She was the only person who would understand. The only one who would know what all of this meant.

Naveed

SATURDAY, JANUARY 30

THE MORNING HIS MOTHER WAS TO LEAVE FOR IRAN, NAVEED awoke feeling strange. He swallowed hard, trying to shake his sense of unease, but it only grew when he realized how scratchy his throat felt.

All week at the food bank, people had been coughing and sneezing and talking about the nasty flu going around this winter. Naveed had been feeling much better lately, and he really wanted to keep it that way, so he'd been careful to keep his distance and was constantly washing his hands. *You're fine*, he told himself. *Got the flu shot months ago. There's nothing to worry about.*

But such reassurances felt thin this early in the morning. He didn't want to lie around dwelling on his discomfort, though, so he got out of bed. He'd been trying to conserve the teas he'd brought back from Englewood, but maybe a good dose of immune-boosting herbs would stave off anything that was trying to take root. He pulled on a sweater and grabbed his phone, then headed downstairs.

It was barely five a.m., so Naveed was surprised to hear typing noises coming from the office as he stepped downstairs. The door was ajar. He peeked inside to see his mother at her laptop. "Morning, Maman."

She jumped. "Oh! You're up early."

Actually, he was almost always awake at this time, though he usually stayed in bed until the others started stirring. "Couldn't sleep. Thought I'd make tea. Want some?"

"Sounds lovely," she said. "I'll join you in a minute."

He started the electric kettle in the dark kitchen, rummaging through the cupboards as quietly as possible, and began brewing a pot of her usual cardamom black tea while preparing an extra-strong mug of his herbal blend. While he waited for them to steep, he searched the fridge for any forgotten jars of elderberry syrup, but there were none to be found. Which wasn't surprising; he'd gone through a ton of it the previous summer and Maman had been too busy to make more. The elderberry bush by the back gate was still dotted with shriveled, rotten berries.

There were several pomegranates in the fruit bowl, though, so he cut one into wedges. *More effective at fighting colds than a thousand oranges,* Maman liked to say. But as he sliced into it, as he watched the juice flow out onto the cutting board, he remembered being back at Englewood watching purple-red stains dripping down white birch bark.

And that, in turn, reminded him about Tim Schmidt, the CDC researcher who had showed up at Dr. Young's office. Naveed had thought about him often over the past week, since his mind went straight to MRK every time someone coughed. In his attempts to check whether there was a resurgence of the disease in Seattle, he'd spent way too many hours combing news about the epidemic. What he saw was undeniably bleak. Death tolls climbing, both in the U.S. and Latin America. Rindamycin had become so expensive, due to limited supply, that a full course of treatment now cost tens of thousands of dollars. Genbiotix's stock prices were soaring.

At one point, he'd texted Vanesa to ask if she was still in contact with Ramón and Marisol, and had learned that Marisol still struggled with constant fatigue and difficulty breathing. It probably doesn't help that she has a new baby, Vanesa had written. Plus, the air quality's terrible where they're living right now.

All of this had weighed on Naveed, but he hadn't been able to push through the paralyzing guilt to do something about it yet. Maybe it wasn't too late, though. He wasn't entirely sure whether the CDC's research project would be the best way for him to help, but at least he could find out more, learn what was really going on from people who knew things that the news outlets didn't.

He didn't want to contact Tim Schmidt directly, though. He needed some assurance that this research project was legit. So he put the pomegranate wedges in a bowl and brought the tea and fruit to the table. After he sat down, he searched the CDC's website on his phone. He didn't see anything about MRK listed in their current projects, and was trying to find contact information for the National Center for Emerging Zoonotic Infectious Diseases when Maman stepped out of the office. She smoothed her blue silk robe as she sat across from him.

He'd have to finish his research later. He clicked his phone off and took a pomegranate wedge from the bowl, peeling the thin white membrane away to reveal the swollen red seeds.

"So," he said to her. "You're leaving today."

"Yes." She paused. "Naveed-jaan, I… I want you to know that this is hard for me."

"We'll be fine." He plucked seeds from the rind one by one, wiggling them loose like teeth. "I've got a billion reminders set on my phone. I'm not going to forget to pick up Roya from school, don't worry. And I know when my appointments are, I won't miss any of them—Baba's fine with me taking the car, by the way, did he tell you?"

"He said your trial run went well. I'm okay with you driving short distances. But you need to obey all the traffic laws—don't give the police any reason to pull you over. And stick to surface streets. No freeways," she said. "What about your meds?"

"Got reminders for those too," he said. "I won't forget."

"You need to take them as scheduled. Every day."

"Every day. I know," he repeated, hating this conversation more every minute.

She dropped a sugar cube into her teacup, stirred it. "That's not what I meant, though, about leaving. This is hard... it's hard because... it's the first time I've been back since I was seven years old. It was a very different country before the revolution. The places I remember, the people I remember... none of them exist anymore."

Naveed stared at his cup. He'd been so focused on Farhad's wedding, on the unfairness of not being able to go, that he hadn't really thought about how it might feel for her to return to the country she and her own mother had once fled. How she'd be faced with constant reminders of loss: the prison where her father, an outspoken Marxist/Leninist, had spent his final days before being executed; the ghost of the apartment building where her entire family had lived before it was leveled by an Iraqi bomb, leaving no survivors. "I'm sorry, Maman," he said softly.

She took a pomegranate wedge and began picking at it. "Naveed-jaan, I grew up feeling like something was wrong with me. I struggled so much with my depression, but I couldn't talk to anyone about it. I don't want it to be that way for you. I want you to know that you don't have to hide your true feelings in this house. You can be disappointed to miss the wedding. You can be angry at me for leaving. I just wanted you to know that I'm conflicted about it, too."

"I'm not angry at you," Naveed said. He tended to think of her depression as something in the past, even though he knew that wasn't how it worked; it was always there, lurking on the horizon. And even though it was something they both had to deal with, even though he felt that she understood him in a way no one else could, they never really talked about it together. Here she was, opening the door to a conversation, yet he had no idea what to say.

The stairs behind him creaked, and he turned around to see Roya.

"Maman! Are you crying?" she asked.

Naveed looked up. It was true: her eyes were watery, her nose very red.

She was quiet for a minute, as if debating how to answer. "Yes," she said finally. "I am. It's just... I'm going to miss you all so much."

Roya snuggled into her lap. Naveed walked into the kitchen, not sure whether he was relieved or disappointed at the interruption. He felt off-kilter again, goosebumpy and constricted, like the walls were growing close. The house felt that way sometimes: like a prison cell, a thing he was trapped inside.

He stood in front of the sink, tracing invisible boxes inside his mind while focusing on his breath—*inhale for a count of four, hold, exhale for four, hold*—stacking up those nice orderly square breaths until he felt better. Then he washed his hands, found a saucepan, and started a batch of oatmeal. He wanted to look like he was doing something normal, even though all he could think about was how much he wanted to escape.

Cyrus wandered into the kitchen a few minutes later, at the precise instant that Naveed registered a toasty smell in the air.

"Shit." Naveed opened the smoking saucepan of burned oats.

Cyrus smirked. "Well done. No pun intended."

Naveed poked at the oats with his spatula. "I think just the bottom got burned. Maybe it'll still be edible."

"Smoked oats. Why not. Sending Maman off with quite the breakfast feast, huh? Should've waited for me to get up."

"What are you doing up this early, anyway?"

"Rough night," Cyrus mumbled.

Naveed couldn't hold back his curiosity. "Did you talk to Dev?"

"Yes. It did not go well and I don't want to talk about it, so let's just leave it at that, all right?"

"Okay. I'm really sorry."

"Same," said Cyrus. "I feel so gross about the whole thing."

"Hey, I was thinking..." Naveed said. "Do you want to, like, go some-where today after Maman leaves? Get away from everything for a while?"

Cyrus took down some bowls from the cupboard. "Actually... yeah. I like that idea."

"Ooh, I want to come!" Roya had just wandered into the kitchen. "Where are you going?"

"I don't know," Cyrus said. "You don't have anything going on today, Naveed?"

Naveed usually avoided working Saturdays at the food bank, when they distributed food to hundreds of people. The crowds were overwhelming. "Nope. I don't care where we go. Just want to get out of the city."

"Well, that narrows it down," Cyrus said. "So, what, a hike or something? Crappy weather for that."

"Do you remember last winter, when we went sledding?" Roya said. "Maybe we could do that?"

"It would be nice to see some snow," Naveed mused.

"I don't know how my car would do in the mountains, though," Cyrus said.

"Oh—can I ask Andi? Maybe she could drive us."

"Yeah! See if she can come," Roya said.

Naveed texted Andi, who said she was happy to take them, though she'd have to borrow her dad's car because hers was in the shop. This was news to Naveed, but he was just glad that she'd be able to join them. She even knew the perfect spot. It's off the beaten path, nice and quiet, she texted. Pretty far up north, past Englewood on Hwy 20, but I don't mind driving.

The next hour was a flurry of activity as they dug out snow clothes, searched for the wooden sled Baba had made years ago, packed lunches and thermoses of hot chocolate, and hunted down waterproof boots. Naveed was glad for the distraction; it made his goodbye with Maman much easier. She hugged him hard and he bent down a little so she could kiss the top of his head, and he told her truthfully that he was glad she'd be able to represent their family at the wedding. As Baba drove away to drop her off at the airport, she waved at them all, blowing kisses out the passenger side window.

Andi picked them up shortly afterward. Even if he didn't get to go to Iran, Naveed thought, at least he got to go *somewhere* today.

They headed north on the freeway. "Your dad has a pretty nice ride," said Cyrus from the back seat, head bent over his phone.

"Yeah. He was kind of weird about me borrowing it, but I doubt he's going anywhere today. He was sick last night—a stomach bug or something. Anyway, he's probably just nervous about me driving in the snow, but I checked the roads and they don't look too bad. This thing has four-wheel drive anyway."

"Naveed said we were going somewhere up north. Is it close to Englewood?" Roya asked.

"Actually, yeah. That's sort of on the way. We'll be going further east though," said Andi.

Roya leaned forward in her seat. "If we're going that way... do you think we could stop by real quick? My friend really, really misses me. And there are visiting hours today."

Cyrus looked up from his phone in the back. "I don't think so. No offense, but I can't imagine a more depressing side trip."

"You don't have to go in," Roya said. "I won't be long. And it would make my friend so happy."

"You can't go by yourself."

"I know. Naveed would come with me. Right, Naveed?"

Naveed thought about Roya's friend, the girl in braids who was always alone. He still remembered the tedium and loneliness of being an inpatient, and how even short visits from Andi made everything seem more bearable. He didn't especially want to go back, but at least he wouldn't have to worry about running into Dennis, who would have finished his twelve-week program by now. It would probably be good to check in with Max, who was a long-term patient and would definitely welcome a visitor. And, of course, there was Koffka. Thinking of the dog almost made Naveed not want to go at all; it had been hard enough to leave him the first time. But... it would be nice to see him again....

"Um." Naveed looked at Andi, but she had her eyes on the road. "What do you think?" he asked her.

She shrugged. "I'll take you if you want. But you shouldn't stay too long. Don't want to lose all our daylight."

"Fine, Roya. Let's go. But just for half an hour."

Roya bounced in the backseat, and lunged unexpectedly forward to hug Naveed from behind. "Thank you! She's going to be so happy."

Naveed settled into the passenger seat, watching the city roll by outside the window. Andi's phone was hooked up to the stereo, playing classical music at a low volume. He was too warm, already bundled in his knit hat and thick coat and waterproof pants and the heavy work boots that had taken forever to put on. He had his gloves on too, and was tempted to take them off, but he didn't want to touch anything if Jake had spread stomach bug germs all over the car. His throat was still scratchy, and he wished he'd brought some tea, and he was tired after getting up so early. And so warm. Too warm. But the music was so relaxing. He let his eyes close.

He must have dozed off, because the next thing he knew they were pulling up in the parking lot at Englewood. He lifted his heavy head. It felt like someone had been whacking his muscles with a meat tenderizer while he slept. His throat burned with that familiar swallowing-shards-of-glass sensation.

Naveed didn't want to get up, but he was here now, and Roya was waiting for him on the curb, so he staggered out of the car and through the sliding doors. In a daze, he told Iris, the receptionist at the front desk, that he and Roya had stopped by for visiting hours, and went through the whole security routine before stepping through the door to the dining hall.

He was getting his bearings, studying all the new faces and keeping his eyes out for Max, when he saw Koffka on the floor next to the windows. As soon as the dog caught his eye, he sprang up and trotted over.

Naveed wrapped his arms around Koffka's soft body, his tension dropping away as he fell into the dog's comforting presence. Koffka knew better than to lick him in the face, but he nosed at Naveed's hands until he took his gloves off, then lapped at them in appreciation. Naveed rubbed the dog's ears and Koffka smiled and Naveed could hear himself laughing and suddenly he never wanted to leave. The wholesome calm he felt around Koffka—he'd take that over benzos and mood stabilizers any day.

When he finally looked up, he saw that Roya had found her friend; the two of them were talking animatedly in the armchairs by the windows.

Max was nowhere to be seen, though. Naveed was feeling uncomfortably warm again, so he decided to check outside, and trooped out to the courtyard after checking in briefly with Roya. Koffka kept pace next to him. But the cold air didn't do anything to invigorate Naveed or wake him up. It just made his chest hurt. He slumped onto a bench to catch his breath. Koffka rested his head on Naveed's knee, gazing up at him with eyes that said, *Don't worry. Everything's going to be okay now. We're together again, that's all that matters.*

Naveed wanted to break into an unoccupied bedroom and curl up under a stack of heavy quilts with Koffka at his feet. But he'd have to settle for going back inside. Maybe one of the nurses could find Max for him. He was trying to find the energy to get up when he saw Dr. Young approaching.

"Naveed!" she said. "What brings you here?"

"Oh… my sister and I just stopped by to visit. I was looking for Max."

"Ah. Well, glad to see you've found Koffka." She patted the dog's back. "So, how have you been?"

"Um, I guess I…." He searched for a word that sounded positive yet realistic. "I've been adjusting," he finished.

"Good, good." She opened her mouth as if to say something else, then closed it again.

He wished he could confess everything to her, admit how hard it had been going back home, but he wasn't sure it was appropriate now that he was no longer her patient. Besides, he didn't feel much like talking at the moment. "Nice to see you," he said. "But I was just about to head back inside." He heaved himself to his feet and gestured for Koffka to turn towards the dining hall door.

"Wait. Before you go, I wanted to ask you something," Dr. Young said. "Tim Schmidt—you remember, from the CDC—he hasn't contacted you again, has he?"

"No. Why?"

"Oh. That's good. If he hasn't tried by now... it's probably fine...."

"Why do you ask? What's going on?" A chill rolled through him. He shoved his hands into his pockets, trying to stop himself from shivering visibly. Good thing Koffka was right there, or else he'd be properly freaking out right now.

"I'm sure it's nothing," she said. "But I followed up with the CDC afterward to file a complaint about his unprofessional behavior, and...."

She now sounded overly casual, like she regretted telling him and was trying to gloss over it. "They're not doing any research on long-term effects of MRK infections. And they've never heard of Tim Schmidt. Whoever he is, he doesn't work for the CDC."

Roya

SATURDAY, JANUARY 30

AS SOON AS THE CAR PULLED UP IN FRONT OF ENGLEWOOD, ROYA leaped out before anyone could change their mind. She could hardly believe her good luck at being here.

When Naveed had said those magic words—*Andi knows a place, but it's pretty far up north, past Englewood*—she'd dared to hope, and had slipped *Katerina and the Little Strangers* into the pocket of her winter coat. The Book of Shadows was too big, and she wasn't sure the nurses would let Kass have it anyway. The chalice and the athame were, of course, out of the question. Those would have to remain safely hidden in her room for now.

Roya had written a letter to Kass about her successful Lopez Island quest. Kass, too, had been very interested in the little cloth book, so as Roya read it, she wrote up summaries and sent them to her friend. But the story had ended so strangely, and there was that odd note a few pages later. *There's a note at the end but I can't read it,* Roya had written. *Will have to show you someday.*

And someday was finally here.

As Naveed shuffled inside the building, Roya remembered something: they were going to make her take everything out of her pockets. She could tell the truth that the book was a gift for Kass, but then they would go through it, and she'd have to explain what it was, and she was not about to do that right in front of Naveed. So as soon as the car disappeared from sight, she removed it from her pocket and slid it underneath the front waistband of her leggings.

Then she stepped inside the sliding doors, careful to walk like a person who didn't have a small book stuffed down her pants. Naveed was talking to the lady behind the desk in a flat monotone. He did not sound like he wanted to be here. Uneasiness tickled Roya's stomach. She wasn't sure if this visit was going to be good for him, and felt guilty for bossing him into it.

"My sister's here too," Naveed was saying to the front desk lady. "We're on our way to go sledding and thought we'd stop by to see—to see Max and—"

Roya could tell he was having trouble remembering Kasandra's name. "And Kass," she prompted.

"I'm sure they'll love to see you," the front desk lady said. "I'll need you both to sign in and empty your pockets. Including your phone, of course. You know the drill." She handed them each a plastic baggie. Roya noticed that Naveed had a pocket knife among his belongings, which he tried to hide inside a wad of tissues. He wasn't supposed to have knives, she knew, but maybe his parents trusted him to be careful by now.

Or maybe she wasn't the only one keeping secrets.

Once they'd returned their belongings, they had to stand in snow angel pose as the front desk lady scanned them with a metal detector wand. Roya prayed there was no hidden metal in the little cloth book.

To her relief, the metal detector remained silent. The front desk lady presented them both with visitor badges and buzzed them through the inner doors.

Roya held on to Naveed's hand as they walked down the short hall to the dining area. He was tense, she could tell, and that made her feel worse. So she squeezed his hand, but he didn't react, of course.

As soon as they entered the room, Roya looked around for Kass. She usually sat by the windows during visiting hours, even though no one ever came for her, because she liked to listen to everyone else's conversations.

Naveed left Roya's side before she spotted her friend. Koffka was trotting toward him with a big dog-smile on his face. Roya watched their happy, slobbery reunion, and her worry left. Her brother was okay. This had been the right thing to do.

Someone was tapping on her shoulder. She spun around to see it was Kass, who squeezed in a quick hug before the supervising nurses noticed.

"You're here!" Kass said. "You're really here! Right? I'm not imagining you?"

"No!" Roya laughed. "It's me. I'm here, but I don't have long—hey, you're out of the chair! Are your feet better?"

"Getting there," she said. "Let's go sit down, though. You have to tell me everything."

Roya glanced over at Naveed, who was rubbing Koffka's belly, oblivious to her. "Yeah. How about the chairs by the window?"

They settled in, and when Roya was sure no nurses were looking, she removed the book, which made sitting down a lot more comfortable. "This is the only one I was able to bring with me. You can keep it, but I didn't tell the front desk lady about it because I was afraid she'd take it. So it's not in the gift log."

Kass waved that away. "Don't worry, I'll figure out somewhere to hide it. Thank you. I still can't believe you were able to get the Book of Shadows. And my athame. The chalice."

"Me neither. I left them at home. I figured they wouldn't let you have them."

"Good thinking. I'm glad they're safe with you. But this is the one I wanted to see, anyway."

She opened it up and grew quiet. Naveed chose that time to tell Roya that he'd be back in a minute and she should stay right there. Kass said hello, and he greeted her back, but didn't seem to notice the little book. She watched him walk into the courtyard, Koffka trailing behind him.

Perfect. Now that he wasn't breathing over her shoulder, Roya could speak freely. She scooted closer to Kass. That's when she noticed her friend was crying.

"What's wrong?" she asked.

Kass wiped the tears away. "It's his handwriting. I thought it might be, but I wasn't sure."

"Whose?" Roya asked. "Alastor's?"

"No. Not his. My father's."

"Oh," Roya said. "Your dad wrote that? Why didn't he finish the story?"

"He must have written it right before he died," she said quietly.

Roya scoured her memory, trying to recall what Kass had said about her father's death. She remembered how it happened, because it had reminded her of her brother; he'd gotten a blood infection after some accident. When he was chopping firewood, that's what it was. Or that was the official story, anyway. *He shouldn't have made Grandfather angry.* "So you were... how old were you then?"

"I was five."

"Do you remember him?"

"Little things. I remember his voice, how he spoke differently from everyone else. Grandfather didn't want me to learn how to read, but Father taught me anyway. He used to play word games with me."

"Was he from Russia? Like the people in the moon colony?"

"Yes. He was a writer. But somehow he ended up in Orcinia and fell in love with my mother, and after I was born he said he never wanted to leave."

It made Roya sad to think about this, and she could tell it was upsetting Kass too. "Can you read what it says at the end?"

Kass flipped forward in the book. "Please..." She frowned. "Please... forgive me...."

"I think this word is 'finish.' Here," Roya said, but Kass pulled the book away to look at it closer.

After a minute, she lowered it. "I don't understand."

"But what does it say? Is it the end of the story? What did Katerina decide to do?"

"No, it says, or at least I *think* it says…" She took a deep breath before continuing. "'Forgive me, I cannot finish. Remember what I told you on the bluffs? It's all in here for you, someday when you too are ready to leave. I love you, K.'"

"'K'? Like Katerina?"

"Like Kasandra," she said quietly. "It's for me. But what does he mean? 'Remember what I told you on the bluffs?' I don't remember. I don't remember."

She gripped the book to her chest and hugged her knees in close. Roya looked around helplessly. What if the nurses kicked her out for upsetting a patient?

Luckily, Kass was a quiet sobber, and Roya was able to side-hug her for a minute without anyone seeing. She couldn't help crying a little bit too, thinking of how awful it would be to lose Baba. Or Maman.

"I'm sorry," she whispered when Kass came up for air. "I wish he wasn't gone, and we could just ask him what he meant."

Kass looked up. Her mouth formed a slow grin. "Yes," she said. "Yes! You have the book!"

"What do you mean?"

"The Book of Shadows." She wiped the tears off her cheeks with the back of her hand. "Here's what you need to do. Somewhere inside the book, there are instructions for another ritual we could use to summon the dead. I think there's a potion involved that's similar to the ceremonial tea we used to drink on new moon nights."

"But what if I can't find everything I need?" Roya asked. "And I don't know when I'll be able to come back. It was hard enough to get here today."

"We'll figure it out." Kass looked so hopeful that Roya couldn't bear to turn her down.

"Okay," she said. "Okay. Yes. We'll figure it out. Somehow."

"And—this is really important—I need you to bring something else, too."

"Sure. What else do we need?"

"Fire." Kass leaned forward, speaking so softly Roya could barely hear. "Fire is a gateway. 'Entire worlds exist within every flame'—that's what we used to say back at home. So bring candles. Matches. Whatever you can find. We won't be able to talk to him unless we have fire."

Andi

SATURDAY, JANUARY 30

ANDI WATCHED THE SLIDING DOORS CLOSE BEHIND NAVEED AND
Roya as they disappeared inside Englewood. Cyrus, meanwhile, had settled
into the passenger seat. "I need coffee, stat," he said as he pulled on his
seat belt.

"Any suggestions?" Andi asked.

Cyrus consulted his phone. "There's a spot nearby. Just a diner, but
I don't even care about the quality of the coffee. All I need is a caffeine
delivery system."

"How far is it? We don't have much time."

"It's about ten minutes away. But don't worry about it. If Naveed says
half an hour, it'll be at least forty-five minutes."

Once they had navigated to the diner and sat down at a quiet booth
by the window, they ordered two cups of coffee. "So you need caffeine,
huh? Long night?" Andi asked.

Cyrus rifled through the sugar packets on the table. "Yeah. Plus I
made the mistake of only having tea this morning. That stuff doesn't

have nearly the same punch, so now I have a splitting headache. Damn addictive substances."

"Were you up late working on the game?"

"No," Cyrus said with such forceful weight that she knew something was wrong.

"Everything okay?" Andi actually liked listening to Cyrus talk about his problems, since he usually spun them as humorous *D&C*-style rants.

"Not really. It's really not."

The server stopped by with the coffee pot and filled their mugs. Andi was hungry, so she ordered a slice of cherry pie. She asked if Cyrus wanted anything, but he shook his head. She asked for two forks anyway.

"You want to talk about it?" she asked after the server had left.

"Not now, not here," he said. "But thanks for asking."

"Well, I've been meaning to tell you how much I love *Bugpocalypse 3K*," Andi said. "I have some feedback—"

He held up a hand, signaling her to stop. "Thanks, but that's on the list of things I don't want to talk about right now."

"Oh. Okay, then."

His phone buzzed, and he checked the screen as Andi stirred some sugar and cream into her coffee and took a sip. Still too strong. She added one more packet of each.

Cyrus's face lit up. "I can't believe it!" He thrust his phone at her. "Look at this text from Shea."

Andi read it. Missed you last night. Want to grab dinner this weekend?

"What do you think?" he said. "She missed me! Does it sound like she's asking me out?"

"It sounds like she wants to eat dinner with you. I don't know whether it has romantic connotations or not. I'm probably not the person to ask."

Cyrus tilted his head. "Because you're my ex?"

"Sure, let's go with that," Andi said.

Cyrus sipped his black coffee. "Hmm. Not bad." He gulped more down before continuing, "Okay, what's up? Is there trouble in paradise with you and Naveed?"

Andi actually laughed. "When has our relationship ever been paradise?"

"True, true. But it's obvious that he loves you. Like, so much it's ridiculous."

"Oh, I know. He loves me like a sister. He's been very clear about that."

"Aha." Cyrus nodded knowingly. "So you've been family-zoned. And that's not where you want to be."

Andi raised her mug and took a long sip of creamy coffee. "That pretty much sums it up."

"Well, that sucks. Want me to talk to him?"

"No. Definitely not. I need to tell him myself."

"All right, I'll stay out of it. Ah, sweet, sweet caffeine," he said into his cup. "So, back to Shea. Should I tell her I can do dinner tonight? Or will that seem too eager?"

"Don't overthink it. If you want to go tonight, then go."

"Oh. Wait." Cyrus set his phone on the table. "I know what this is about. She probably just wants to convince me to come back."

"What do you mean, 'come back?'"

"To the development team. I kind of... quit."

"You *what*? Why would you quit? Isn't it your game?"

"Well, yeah. It's a long story," Cyrus mumbled.

"You can't give it up! There's something special about that game. I always play it right before I'm about to do something stressful, because somehow it gets my head into a better place. And oh my God, when I got to the convenience store level I almost died laughing." The level featured a snack shelf swarming with bad bugs—which were marked with dollar signs—and as you killed more and more of them, a bag labeled "Fiery Bitez" appeared. Pure genius.

This seemed to perk Cyrus up. "Really? That's exactly what I was going for. Not that stress relief is the main purpose, but I just wanted it to be a fun escape, you know?"

"Well, that's how it feels to me. There's something so satisfying about it."

Cyrus smiled a goofy smile, one that could have been a full-on grin had he not held back. But it faded quickly. "I think we might have done too good of a job, though. Shea put together some data on heavy users that was really disturbing. Some people play for, like, hours every single day. I guess that's technically a good thing, but... I don't know. It reminds me of NutrexoWorld."

"It's nothing like that game," Andi said.

"I know, it's just... everyone else is really happy about the heavy users, but I don't feel right about it. I don't want to be responsible for ruining someone's life because they get addicted to my game. Well, maybe that's overly dramatic. Not ruining their life, just... being a total time suck that keeps them from doing important shit."

"But aren't there things you can do design-wise to make games less addictive?" Andi asked. "I feel like I've read about that somewhere."

Cyrus nodded. "Yeah. I've seen that too. Not sure whether everyone would be on board with it, though, and besides...." He trailed off. "That's not the reason I quit. It had to do with something else."

"Okay. So you're just going to sit back and watch as the game gets so huge that in a few years, nobody will ever look up from their phones because they're too busy playing *Bugpocalypse 3K*?"

Cyrus's mouth twitched. "I don't think it'll ever be *that* big."

"Who knows, though? It might. And if you want to shape it into a game you're proud of, one that maybe even makes people's lives better, then you should get back on the development team. Don't give up on this, Cy."

The server arrived with Andi's slice of cherry pie. She handed a fork to Cyrus. "Want some?"

"Nah." He patted his belly. "On a diet."

Andi found that hard to believe, but she didn't push back. "More for me, then."

So she ate her pie and he drank his coffee and disappeared into his phone, but she pulled him back out of the vortex by telling him the feedback she had about *Bugpocalypse 3K,* which, in spite of his earlier protests, he seemed quite curious about.

It didn't feel like much time had passed, so Andi was surprised when she glanced at her phone. "Oops. It's already been half an hour. We'd better get back."

So Cyrus paid their bill and they drove back to Englewood. Andi expected Naveed and Roya to be waiting outside, but when she pulled up at the front curb, they were nowhere to be seen.

"Where are they?" she asked.

The worry must have seeped into her voice, because Cyrus said, "He's fine. If they don't come out in fifteen minutes, we'll go ask the receptionist to get them."

As they waited, Andi's phone chimed. It was a text from Brooke. OMG I'm at Bountiful Earth and you will NOT BELIEVE what I found on the shelves, she had written below a photograph of a bag of—wait, was that right?—organic Blazin Bitz.

Andi snorted in disbelief. She showed it to Cyrus. "Seriously? This is madness."

"Wow." He shook his head. "That's just—wow."

Andi texted it to Laurel. For our anti-Bitz ad? she wrote. You can't make this stuff up.

Laurel wrote back a minute later. this is perfect. you coming to the meeting on tuesday?

Andi replied that she would be there. As she lowered her phone, Roya skipped up to the car, grinning widely. Naveed followed, looking like her polar opposite. His hood was pulled up over his knit hat; his shoulders were slumped, hands shoved in his pockets.

"How'd it go?" Cyrus asked when Roya opened the back door.

"Great! My friend was *so* happy. I'm glad we came." She scooted over to let Naveed in, since Cyrus had made no move to give up the passenger seat. Andi glanced at Naveed in the rearview mirror. He was scrunched into the back, and she could only see the hooded top of his head. Everything about his body language said, *don't talk to me.* So even though she wanted to ask him what was wrong, she pulled away from Englewood and started heading down the tree-lined drive without saying a word.

She kept peeking back at him, but still couldn't see his face; maybe he'd fallen asleep again. Eyes on the road, she reminded herself, as she pointed her dad's Highlander—finally—toward the mountains. Snow started appearing on the pine trees as they gained elevation, but the roads were mostly clear. A little slushy, but at least they were free of ice.

The drive was longer than she remembered. She had gone to this sledding hill many times with her old best friend Marina, back when her family would invite Andi to their second home up in Marblemount and they'd spend a week during winter break skiing and sledding and snowshoeing. What had become of that place, Andi wondered, now that Mark Williams was serving his prison sentence?

At last, Andi spotted the landmark she'd been looking for: the rustic A-frame cabin that was around the bend from the sledding hill. She pulled carefully into the slush on the side of the road, where a few other cars were parked next to a tall snow bank.

"Are we here?" Roya asked.

"Yep. It's just a short hike in."

Roya squealed in delight. After they'd unpacked all their gear and pulled on their snow pants, they trudged through the deep snow into the woods, heading towards the quieter hills farther from the road. Naveed kept sinking down deep and falling over as he tried to struggle his way out, so Roya and Cyrus were laughing and pulling him back up, and to Andi's surprise Naveed started laughing too.

Cyrus and Roya moved on ahead, trailing their old wooden sled behind them. After a few minutes, Andi noticed that Naveed was lagging behind, and turned around to check on him.

"You all right?" she asked him.

He was just standing there, dazed. "I'm coming. Sorry, I'm slow. You can go on ahead."

"I don't mind," Andi said, stepping closer.

"I'm just…" He looked like he was conflicted about something; she figured it probably had to do with his visit to Englewood, so she waited patiently, trying to communicate with her eyes that he could tell her anything. But all he said was, "I'm really cold."

Andi trudged through the snow until she was standing in front of him. Cyrus and Roya were so far ahead that she couldn't see them anymore. It felt like only she and Naveed existed in this faraway snow-covered world.

He was pulling at his gloves, which, she now noticed, weren't waterproof. They were covered in snow from his many wipeouts. *Frostbite,* she thought worriedly. *Hypothermia.* But they hadn't been out for long; it didn't seem like either of those were likely.

"Here," she said, taking his gloves off for him. She removed her own gloves, too, then took his hands in hers. His palms radiated a reassuring warmth, but his fingertips were cold. Without pausing to think about it, she pressed his hands to her cheeks and covered them with hers, feeling the chill from his fingers transferring into her skin, her own heat penetrating into his.

Their eyes met. She thought for a second that maybe she should stop, but she didn't, and he didn't ask her to. He kept looking at her with that same conflicted expression. She felt herself leaning closer; she couldn't help that she was drawn to him, he was magnetic—

"Hey, slowpokes! Hurry up!" Cyrus called, and Naveed pulled his hands away.

"Um, thanks." He lowered his eyes. "That helped. Can I have my gloves back?"

"Take these," Andi said, handing him her waterproof ones. "They'll be warmer. They're too big for me anyway—I couldn't find mine so I had to borrow my dad's."

He tried to protest, but she didn't relent. She turned around and trudged on, sliding her hands into his slightly damp knit gloves. He kept a closer pace this time.

Finally, they emerged at the top of the hill. Cyrus whistled at its steep slope. "Nice spot, A. Who's first?"

"I'll take the sled," Naveed said. "Just to test it. Make sure it's still sturdy enough."

Cyrus and Roya were holding the two plastic saucers that Andi had dug out of her garage. Andi looked at Naveed. "I'll come with you," she said.

"That's okay, you don't have to. It feels pretty solid, but it's old, and we haven't used it in a while."

"I'm not going to stand up here alone while you guys all go," Andi said. "Besides, if you're about to hurtle recklessly toward an uncertain fate, you shouldn't be alone. I want to be there with you."

Was that a tiny smile trying to find its way onto his lips? "All right, then," Naveed said.

She sat cross-legged in front, and he settled in behind. Cyrus and Roya took off first, screaming as they spun down the hill.

"Ready?" Naveed asked.

"Ready."

He pushed off, then wrapped his arms around her waist. As they gathered speed, he shrieked in delight behind her, and the sled held beautifully, and they slid down over that frozen white world whooping with sheer joy and exhilaration. She liked the way their voices sounded in the air around them, twining together, no longer distinct. One voice, echoing back to them through the snowy forest.

February

Mikhail traced it backwards,
because that was the only way he could think now.

The death, the birth, the infection,
the ripped suit, the sunlit kiss, the greenhouse, the spaceship.

The only constant: the depth of their love.

How could he not have seen it? he wondered.
How could he not have predicted that they were destined for this?
That she would be the one to leave him,
to abandon him with this burden.
With this squalling burden that he could not quiet.

—Viktor Zolotov, *Keepers of the Moon*

Andi

MONDAY, FEBRUARY 8

ANDI AWOKE ON LUNAR NEW YEAR TO FIND A RED ENVELOPE BY her spot at the dining room table. She hadn't expected any acknowledgment of the holiday from her father, who had been so preoccupied with making music lately that he'd barely come up for air from his basement studio. He always slept late, and she never saw him in the mornings before she left for school. For a split second, she thought that maybe her mother had returned, that she'd planned some sort of surprise and was finally back home.

But when she opened it, she found a note along with a crisp $100 bill.

新年快樂! I'm sorry I can't be here with you today, but let's talk this afternoon. I miss you. Love, Mom.

Andi fixed herself some toast for breakfast and took it back to her bedroom; the kitchen was such a mess that just looking at it stressed her out. While she ate, she texted her mother, thanking her for the red envelope and suggesting a video-chat after school. It had been a while since she'd heard anything about how Ah-ma was doing, but she figured that no news was good news.

She was lacing up her boots at the door when a stream of texts from Naveed buzzed through.

Happy New Year!

Kourosh is cooking up a feast tonight

I'm in charge of steaming frozen potstickers

Should be hard to mess that up right? haha

Want to come over?

Your dad's welcome too of course

If you don't already have plans

Andi re-read the string again and actually sighed in relief. These were the most upbeat-sounding messages he'd sent in a while. He'd come down with the flu after last week's snow trip, and his replies to her texts had been terse and gloomy. The week had been incredibly busy at school and she couldn't afford to get sick herself, so instead of visiting him she'd dropped off little gifts on his back porch every day: a get well soon card, a bottle of Nin Jiom Pei Pa Koa cough syrup, a bouquet of fruit kebabs.

In truth, though, she was kind of glad to keep her distance. She knew she needed to have an honest conversation with him, but wasn't about to do that while he was once again battling illness and sinking back into the deep depression that always stalked him.

Part of her was exasperated with his unstable health. Why couldn't he just stay well? She felt bad for thinking that, though, because none of this was his fault. And she knew he was incredibly frustrated about it too.

But he must be feeling much better today if he was inviting her over, and she certainly didn't want to miss Cyrus's feast. She texted a response as she walked outside—I would love that. See you then—and didn't look up until she slid into the driver's seat of her mom's Sentra.

What she saw didn't make sense at first. The windshield was smeared with red. Little bits of soft, stringy... *somethings*... were stuck to the glass. At the bottom, wedged against the wipers, was a heap of black feathers.

A dead crow.

Andi's ears were ringing, but the world was otherwise devoid of sound. Something strange was happening; she was still in the car, but she was also stretched out on a rough, flat surface and the wind was blowing and there were crows everywhere and behind her something was rattling but she couldn't turn her head because it hurt too much—

It's not real, she told herself, but in a way it was, or at least it had been. And this crow was real, and it was dead, and drips of blood had congealed into streaks on the windshield that she was sure she'd never be able to stop seeing.

She gripped the steering wheel, trying to anchor herself in reality. The cold wheel beneath her fingertips. The familiar Sentra. The school day ahead. But part of her was still in the past, on that roof with the rattling cage, the wind, the crows, the woman in the white lab coat who had just bashed Andi's head against the wall.

No. Don't think about Dr. Snyder. She's not here. You're safe.

But even once she finally returned to the present, she didn't feel safe at all. She couldn't look at the windshield—so she turned toward the back seat, realizing that she hadn't checked the car before getting in, a habit she'd been trying to cultivate ever since the window-smashing incident. Nobody was there.

It was probably a hawk, she told herself, or some bird of prey who had attacked the crow and dropped it from the power lines above. A coincidence. An act of nature, nothing more.

She checked the clock on her phone to see that somehow fifteen minutes had passed, and she barely had enough time to get to class. She couldn't be late again. Her father's Highlander was parked right behind the Sentra, so she stood up and stumbled dizzily into it. She felt horrible, shaky and unstable, but figured things would be okay once she got out of here. Once she didn't have to see that mess anymore.

Before pulling away, she texted her dad, trying to make it sound like no big deal. Had to take your car to school. A hawk or something went to town on a crow and left a big mess on Mom's windshield. I'm running late so I didn't have time to clean it up. Sorry

She squeaked into first period as the bell rang. As the day wore on, she wondered why she had even come. The teachers might as well have been speaking Finnish; she couldn't hold onto a single word. Dizzy spells kept catching her as she walked in the halls, one of them so intense that she actually had to duck into a random classroom to sit down for a second. The few students inside—freshmen, from the looks of them—stared at her like she was crazy.

When lunch break finally rolled around, she retreated to her dad's car, where she could hide from everyone. She nibbled a protein bar while checking her texts. There were a few from Brooke wishing her a happy new year, several from Naveed expressing excitement that she was coming over, and some from her dad saying he was glad she'd taken his car because the cleanup had taken a while and was disgusting.

But it was the text from Cyrus that stopped her cold. You'll never guess what I saw when I stepped out the door this morning. A dead crow on our front porch. It was all torn up. Feathers and bird-intestines everywhere. Probably a psycho raccoon attack. Good thing I was able to clean it up before N or R saw anything. They would've freaked.

The words on the screen faded as she read them, and the next thing she knew her face was pressed against the steering wheel and someone was honking at her. As soon as she lifted her head, they stopped. Disoriented, she pressed the gas thinking that someone was waiting for her to go, but the car didn't move. Slowly she realized why: she was still in the school parking lot and her phone was on the floor and her body felt like jelly. She must have passed out for a second.

Without thinking, she turned the key in the ignition, started the car, and pulled away. Somehow she made it home. After she parked in front of the house, it hit her that she probably shouldn't have been driving, but she didn't regret leaving school. All she wanted to do was crash into bed and stay there forever and ever.

Unsurprisingly, her dad was in the basement. The sound of distorted guitars reverberated up the stairs; she didn't recognize the song, but was grateful he was preoccupied. She wasn't sure what to tell him about why she'd come home early. She'd used the headache excuse so many times lately—even though most of the time it was true—that he was bound to insist on taking her back to the doctor at some point. And she didn't want to deal with that on top of everything else. Besides, if she told him that she had passed out and had driven home right afterwards… she wouldn't be allowed to drive again for a long, long time.

Once she'd closed her bedroom door, she flopped onto her bed and texted Cyrus back. Wasn't a raccoon. I got one too

No response. He was probably in class. Just thinking about the crow— no, the *crows,* plural—made Andi feel like taking a shower, cleansing herself, but she still felt so shaky on her feet that it was probably best to stay in bed. Their deaths were no accident; someone had done it on purpose, had left the crows for them to find. As reminders. Or threats.

She drew the curtains in her room, once again thinking about Richard Caring. Had he sent someone to do this? Was someone watching her now? A nameless horror was stalking her, seeping under the doors, through the walls. And there was nothing she could do to keep it from coming in.

She curled up on the bed. It felt like she was still moving. Like she was drifting on a turbulent sea. She closed her eyes, letting fatigue overtake her.

Andi awoke to her phone ringing. Her mother was calling. She fumbled to answer it, hoping she didn't sound as disoriented as she felt. "Hello?"

"Xīn nián kuài lè! You having a good one so far?"

"It's okay," Andi lied. Maybe she could get her mom to do most of the talking. "You? How's Ah-ma?"

"She's having a good day. Only a week of chemo left, then they'll do some scans to see how things are looking. Do you want to video-chat? We're all here."

"Um" was all Andi could say. She really did want to see Ah-ma, but part of her wondered if it would be too painful right now.

Her mother must have sensed that something was wrong, because she asked, "Are you all right?"

Andi felt a miniature collapse inside. Her mother's voice, with its sweet soothing sound, made Andi want to believe that everything would be okay. She wanted to tell her, *No, I'm not, I feel horrible and something's happening to me and I'm scared.* But her mother wasn't here; she couldn't help. She couldn't even give Andi a hug.

"It's just good to hear your voice," Andi managed to say with only a slight verbal wobble.

"Oh, bǎo bèi," her mother said sadly. "I miss you, too. I hate not being together, especially today, but I'll be home soon, I promise. Here, let's get on video, so at least we can see each other."

Andi smoothed her hair and sat up, leaning against her wall. The room wasn't spinning anymore, which was good, but that familiar ache was spreading its way through her skull again.

She accepted the call, and smiled at the three beaming faces who showed up on her screen. Ah-ma looked very tired, but she was proudly wearing the wig that Andi had commissioned. Andi's mother had ended up chopping off her own hair and contributing to it, too.

Andi asked what they were up to, and they told her about the big feast they'd eaten at a friend's house the night before. That reminded Andi of Naveed's earlier invitation, but when her mother asked what she would do to celebrate the new year, she said she wasn't sure yet. At this point, she doubted she'd be able to drag herself over there.

"Well, I hope your father makes sure you get a good meal tonight," her mother replied. "How's school going?"

"Fine." At these words, a new pit of dread formed in Andi's stomach. She had completely forgotten about this afternoon's quiz in AP Government, one of the classes she had missed. It would be a miracle if she actually passed all her classes this year. The guidance counselor would probably be calling her mom soon to express concerns over Andi's falling grades, but he obviously hadn't yet.

"Not much longer now until you find out where you were accepted for college!" her mother said, which made Andi feel even worse.

"Yeah. Actually, I… I still have a lot to do today. I should get back to studying."

They talked for a few more minutes, then Andi signed off. She couldn't believe what a mess she'd made of everything.

She got up and shuffled into the bathroom, holding onto the walls as she went. It all felt so unsteady and her head was pounding again. Music still floated up from the basement; the song had changed to something quieter, more poignant. Something with… violins?

Yes. That *was* a violin. Was Patricia here? Her father hadn't mentioned collaborating with her, but Andi barely knew what he was up to lately.

In the bathroom, she reached for the bottle of painkillers that the doctors had prescribed for her headaches. That was odd; she'd thought there were more in the bottle, but now only six remained. Maybe she'd taken some without remembering. She shook one out and swallowed it, and thought that getting something to eat would probably be a good idea, but the kitchen seemed too far away. She only wanted to make it back to her room and let the drugs pull her away from reality, where she could float in a pleasant haze and pretend that everything would be all right when she woke up.

Cyrus

MONDAY, FEBRUARY 8

CYRUS WAS VERY DISTURBED WHEN HE RECEIVED ANDI'S TEXT after school. Wasn't a raccoon. I got one too. He'd never seen a dead crow that mangled before, but was hoping it was nothing more sinister than the everyday workings of nature. Andi's message proved him wrong.

He thought about it the entire way home. Whoever had done this must have been connected to Nutrexo—how else would they know what dead crows would mean to him and Andi? Tara Snyder was his first suspect, of course, but she was locked up in prison. So was Richard Caring—though this didn't seem like his style—as well as the others who'd worked at SILO like Zane and Erika.

Naveed was puttering around in the kitchen when Cyrus got home, doing dishes in his slow, apathetic way, coughing periodically into his sleeve. It was good to see him back among the living, and Cyrus didn't even consider knocking him off balance by mentioning the crows.

"Oh, hey," Naveed said when he saw Cyrus. "I started some rice. Andi said she'd come, but I'm not sure when. Can Shea make it too?"

"Yep. She's coming at six." It would be her first visit to the house, her first time meeting his family, and Cyrus was immeasurably nervous. Especially since Andi was coming too, which could make things awkward. Hopefully she'd show up early so that they could debrief about the crows for a few minutes in private. He sent her a text suggesting that.

Working in the kitchen helped calm his nerves a bit. He was glad to slip into concrete tasks like chopping vegetables and assembling sauces. Naveed backed him up by cycling through the dishes, though he did tag out for a while to go "get ready." Cyrus suspected he had just gone to lie down, because he looked exactly the same when he came back, but whatever. Even Roya came downstairs to help for a while.

The three of them fell into a comfortable rhythm that almost made Cyrus forget about the other difficulties bothering him. He and Dev still avoided each other at school. Cyrus had tried to make amends by sending an apologetic text. I'm sorry, can we please talk? And Dev sent a reply that still made Cyrus's stomach clench every time he thought about it. I would say no, but you'd probably lurk outside my window until I finally agreed, wouldn't you?

If Dev kept freezing him out, *D&C* was unlikely to survive. The show was still on hiatus, new subscribers had slowed to a trickle, and their earnings had dropped off precipitously. Not that Cyrus cared so much about the metrics—what really bothered him was watching this thing he'd built drift away, right along with the person who had helped him create it.

At least things were going well with Shea. They had hung out a few times, but the presentation was only a week away so she was busy putting all the finishing touches on the app. Cyrus had admitted he'd had a falling out with Dev, though he didn't go into any details. Even so, Shea kept trying to convince him to come back to the development team. Cyrus had no idea how he was supposed to do that if Dev wouldn't even talk to him.

Shortly before six, Cyrus got a text from Andi. Sorry but I can't come after all. The crow thing really got to me for some reason. I am such a mess right now. You think N would be too upset if I canceled?

Cyrus replied, No prob, it's creeping me out too. And N will be fine, don't worry about him.

Thx for understanding, Andi wrote back. Just can't deal with acting normal tonight.

I can bring over some leftovers later, he added. I'll come alone so we can talk if u want to.

Yes, please. And thank you, she wrote. Then, a few seconds later, But be careful out there.

He shuddered involuntarily, thinking about that crow carcass again, about all it implied. He looked up, hoping Naveed hadn't noticed, but his brother was frowning at his phone.

"What's wrong?" Cyrus asked.

"Andi can't come." Naveed paused to read another text that had just come in. "She forgot that she's working on a group project for school tonight."

"Aw, too bad." Cyrus hoped his disappointment sounded convincing. He was looking forward to debriefing in secret with Andi later. It would be like old times.

"I really wanted her to be here." Naveed sounded heartbroken.

"I know. Well, you'll have to show off your potsticker-steaming skills some other day, I guess."

Naveed turned away. Cyrus got back to work mincing ginger for the potsticker dipping sauce. "Could you grab the rice vinegar for me?" he asked.

Naveed brought it over, pausing after he set it on the counter. "Hey… Kourosh…." He drew the words out slowly. "There's something I wanted to talk to you about. I have… a favor to ask."

"What kind of favor?" Cyrus asked warily.

"It's sort of a long story. But you have to promise that you'll listen, that you won't just think I'm crazy—"

Roya bounded back into the kitchen, interrupting him. "When are we going to eat? I'm starving." She plucked out a piece of broccoli from the stir-fry.

Cyrus swatted her away. "Hey! Hands off. Not too much longer. Like, fifteen minutes, maybe."

"Fifteen minutes? That's forever," she groaned.

"All right, all right, I'll get you a potsticker." After he put one on a plate and handed it to her, he said to Naveed, "Sorry. What did you want to ask me?"

"Never mind. Later." Naveed drifted out of the kitchen. Cyrus was partly intrigued, but at the same time he wasn't sure whether he wanted to get involved in whatever crazy-sounding favor his brother needed.

Baba came through the front door as Cyrus finished chopping the scallion garnish, and Shea arrived shortly thereafter. Everyone seemed genuinely thrilled to meet her; Roya asked lots of bizarre questions that Shea seemed to find very amusing, and she held her own when subjected to Baba's grilling. Naveed—much to Cyrus's relief—was friendly, but not overly charming. He slipped into quiet mode after a while and kept coughing wetly into his napkin, which sounded disgusting and hopefully would deter Shea from falling under his spell. She didn't appear to be paying much attention to him, but kept shooting sly glances at Cyrus throughout the meal. He decided to take that as a good sign. Maybe tonight he could finally make his move... walk her out to her car later, kiss her goodnight beneath the streetlights....

After they ate, Cyrus and Shea went into the living room while Baba cleaned up. She sat on the couch and pulled out the laptop from the bag she'd brought with her. As she opened it up, she said, "Mmm, that food was really good. And your family's nice."

"So do we live up to all the hype?" he asked.

"Frankly, no. I expected you guys to be a little more... subversive."

"Ah. That's just because my mom's not here. Trust me, if she was, you'd be treated to a rant about some injustice or another."

"I guess I'll have to look forward to that next time, then."

Next time. He smiled.

"So I was hoping you could help with something," she continued.

"It's about the app... there's a bug none of us can fix and the program keeps crashing and the guys are freaking out and we wondered if you would take a look?"

"Oh." Cyrus deflated slightly. Was that why she was here? "I doubt I would be able to help. You guys are smart. You'll figure out how to fix it."

"We've tried everything. And what I really want—what *we* really want is—Cyrus, will you please come back? You should be up there with us at the presentation. You created this thing, after all. It wouldn't be the same without you."

"I don't know. Dev would probably kill me with eye-daggers before I could even get up there."

Shea typed in a lengthy password to unlock her laptop. "Are you two just fighting because he and Todd are a couple now?

Cyrus was taken aback. "You know? That they're, uh, going out or whatever?"

"Of course! Todd was crushing on Dev from day one."

Now Cyrus felt even stupider. Had it been that obvious to everyone but him? It was amazing, he thought, how easy it was to overlook things you didn't particularly want to see. "I didn't know," he mumbled. "That Dev was gay. He never told me."

"Oh." Shea was quiet for a minute. "So, you don't want to hang out with him anymore because of that? Is homosexuality not, like, allowed in your religion or something?"

"Whoa, no, that's not it at all. My family isn't even...." Cyrus was about to say they weren't religious, but Baba would be heading upstairs for evening prayers once he was done with the dishes, so that didn't feel entirely accurate anymore. "I'm not practicing, but lots of Muslims are super inclusive, and anyway it has nothing to do with that. I don't care that Dev's gay. But I kind of messed things up with him when I found out."

"Well, then, this would be a good way to earn back some points with him. If you save our asses with your bug-fixing superpowers, you'll definitely be back in his good graces."

"Okay. Fine," Cyrus said. He hoped she was right, because he really, really missed Dev. "I'll take a look at the code. But I might not be able to figure out what's wrong."

After an hour or two of troubleshooting with Shea, he managed to pinpoint the problem, which, he had to admit, felt pretty good. Afterward, he told her about Naveed's suggestion to make the game more accessible for people with mobility issues. She liked the idea, which gave Cyrus the courage to air his concerns about the heavy users and the addictive qualities of the app.

To his surprise, Shea didn't push back. "I get what you're saying. It's too late to make any design changes before the contest... but if this ends up going anywhere, we'll talk about it and figure something out."

That was about as good as he could hope for.

It was getting late, and Shea started packing up. Cyrus walked her out to her car, acutely aware of the darkness outside, of all the hiding places in their yard. He turned on his phone flashlight to scope out the bushes. No sign of lurking stalkers (good), but also no sign of a romantic goodbye (not so good). Shea just tossed her pack inside the car and said she'd see him later before zooming off.

Disappointed, Cyrus turned back inside. Maybe Shea wasn't into him the way he was into her. He mentally replayed their recent interactions, trying to examine them from a rational perspective, and was unable to find any hints that she thought of him as anything more than a friend.

That hurt a lot more than he wanted it to. He allowed himself a few moments of self-pity before the Dev-voice in his head started up. *Shea's a person with her own story and her own goals. She's not the Love Interest in your own personal rom-com.*

Akh. So painful. He wandered through the dark house, opening random cupboards and looking inside at nothing because he wasn't quite sure what to do with himself. Only when he opened the fridge and saw all the leftovers from their feast did he remember his promise to Andi.

He packed up some food and texted her before heading outside,

---

hoping she would still be awake. It was cold and quiet, and out here in the dark he felt it again, that icy fear that had invaded him when he'd seen the dead crow that morning.

Andi met him at the door. She was wearing pajama pants and an oversized sweatshirt, and something about her seemed off. Her eyes looked glassy and distant.

"Oh, food. Thank you. Yum." She set the dish on top of a stack of mail on the cluttered dining room table and started picking at the stir fry with her fingers.

Cyrus went to the kitchen in search of a fork, but was slightly shocked when he saw what a mess it was: the mountain of food-crusted dishes in the sink, the takeout boxes scattered across the counter, the trail of ants leading to a jam-covered butter knife. He was pretty sure the forks in the dishwasher weren't clean, and there weren't any in the utensil drawer, but he found a fresh pair of paper-wrapped chopsticks and brought them over. "Where's your dad?" he asked uneasily.

"I don't know. Maybe the basement, maybe he went out. He's busy, busy, busy." She kept eating with her fingers, ignoring the chopsticks.

Cyrus found that response even more unsettling. "Okay, so can we talk about it here, or do you want to go to your room, or what? Or do you not want to talk—should I leave? Tell me what you want me to do."

Andi looked at him with watery eyes, but didn't answer. She buried her head in her hands.

He sat down next to her when he saw her shoulders shaking. "What is it, A? What's wrong?"

"Everything," she said through her quiet sobs. "Everything is so fucked up."

If Andi was swearing, it must be bad. He wrapped his arms around her and held her while she sniffed into his coat, which he hadn't taken off yet. "Did something else happen?" he asked.

"No, not really." The words were muffled. "It's just that my life is falling apart and I don't know what to do and I can't talk to anyone about it."

"You can talk to me," he said.

She just cried harder, and he kept holding on. Finally, she spoke. "That crow. It was on my mom's car. The one I've been driving, the one that got broken into last week. And the crow was… mangled. Blood dripping down the windshield. Intestines stuck to it. And something weird happened… I had, like, this flashback or something, and it messed me up. I've felt awful all day, and my head… I had to take a prescription painkiller but I only have a few left and I can't imagine dragging myself to school tomorrow but I really can't miss it, I have to go, and I'm just so tired."

"Andi. Wow. Did you tell your parents? I think they'd agree that you need to take the day off."

"Can't tell my mom, she's got enough going on down in Berkeley. And my dad… he'll just freak out. Make me see a doctor."

"Okay, don't take this the wrong way, but maybe you should? At least then you'd have a legitimate excuse for missing school." Then, as he registered something else she'd said, he added, "Wait. Someone broke into your car?"

"Yep. They didn't take anything. But they emptied a bag of Blazin Bitz inside. Made a huge mess. Crumbs everywhere."

Well, that was strange. "Do you think there's a connection?"

"I've been wondering the same thing. I think there might be." She sat up and wiped her tear-streaked cheeks, then blew her nose into a paper napkin. "I know this sounds crazy, but… I think Richard Caring might be behind it. He was… I could tell he was really angry. When he got sentenced to prison."

"Well, of course he was—"

"No, I mean, angry at *me,* personally. And your mom, too. The way he was looking at us when the judge read the verdict…."

That threw Cyrus for a loop; he hadn't noticed this. He still thought it was extremely unlikely that Richard Caring was involved, but he didn't want Andi to feel like he was writing her off. "I guess it's possible that he sent some hired goons out to intimidate us or something. But why?"

"I don't know. I did publish that petition, and I've been working on an anti-Bitz ad to promote a boycott... but that's not official yet and... I don't know why they would even care." She paused. "Maybe it's retaliation. Maybe they like torturing us. They just want us to know this isn't over."

"But it is over." He *wanted* it to be over, anyway. "Maybe it's not them. Maybe it's someone else. There are plenty of other people who hate us. Like the trolls who comment racist shit on *D&C* videos." An idea struck Cyrus. "Actually, this one dude, fleshpuppet69, kept saying he knew Naveed, which I figured wasn't true—but maybe I was wrong. Judging from his comments, the guy was obviously unbalanced. Maybe he was at Englewood too, and knows all kinds of things about Naveed—and you—from group therapy or something. Did Naveed ever mention anyone who gave him a hard time?"

Andi closed her eyes. "There was someone... Naveed told me to stay away from him... I can see his face... can't remember his name, though. But I don't know. If this is about him, why did they break into *my* car, and leave a crow for me, too? It seems like a stretch."

Cyrus had to agree. They sat in silence until Andi said, "Please don't tell Naveed about any of this. I don't think he'd react well. He'd probably want to become my personal bodyguard, and if anyone tried to do anything—if he even *thought* anyone was going to hurt me...."

Cyrus drummed his fingers on the table. "You're right. If he overreacted and, like, attacked someone... that would violate his probation. Knowing his luck, he'd end up in prison this time. Or worse. But... I don't know, what should we do now? Tell the cops?"

"I guess I could ask my dad to file a police report about the crows. But they'd probably laugh me out of the station if I told them I suspected Richard Caring. I doubt they'll do anything about it. I'll just be extra careful, I guess. Lie low for a few days. Keep binge-watching self-defense videos. Buy some pepper spray or something."

"Good idea," Cyrus said.

To his surprise, Andi leaned over to side-hug him. "Honestly, Cy, I can't thank you enough for coming over tonight. The food is delicious, by the way."

He didn't stay much longer. As soon as he shut her front door, goose-bumps prickled his skin. It wasn't just the cold; he felt like he was being watched, but nobody was around, so he dismissed it as paranoia. All the same, he hurried through the alley as fast as he could, and didn't relax until he was safe inside his own house.

Roya

THOUGH ROYA HAD LEFT ENGLEWOOD WITH A BURNING URGE to search the Book of Shadows for the potion recipe Kass had mentioned, other things kept getting in the way.

For one thing, Naveed got sick. And it wasn't like before, where it was just nerve pain. This time it was an infection. The flu, Baba said. Every night when Roya crawled into her parents' bed after the bad dreams came, curling up in Maman's empty spot, he told her not to worry. "Enshallah, hamechi dorost mishe," he kept saying, over and over, like a prayer. *God willing, everything will be fine.*

It wasn't very reassuring, Roya thought, to leave it up to God's will, because who knew what He wanted with Naveed? So she would lie awake, listening hard, until she heard Naveed's percussive coughs across the hall. Only then could she relax. Coughing meant he was still breathing. Still alive.

The plan had been for Naveed to pick up Roya from school while Maman and Khaleh Yasmin were in Iran, but since he was too sick, Roya had to go home with her "friend" Madison. She lived down the street and their parents knew each other, but Madison had loudly complained about the arrangement right in front of Roya. "That's not fair, I wanted to go to Hailey's house! Nobody wants to play with Roya."

Madison's mom had compromised by inviting Hailey over too, which just meant that Madison and Hailey ignored her completely. It made Roya mad, but she held it in, because she knew Baba was counting on her to be good. She pretended to entertain herself with the Barbies in Madison's play room, but her mind was a hundred miles away. Roya wished she were back at Englewood right now, sneaking away somewhere to do the ceremony, so that Kass could finally ask her father the questions she needed him to answer.

By the weekend, Naveed was doing a little better, and Maman video-chatted with them from Tehran for almost an hour. Hearing her voice made Roya feel like she was being wrapped in a snuggly warm blanket, but when they ended the call she found herself missing Maman more than she had before.

The day after the big Lunar New Year feast, Naveed picked up Roya at dismissal time. He seemed very jumpy for some reason. As they walked, he kept looking around nervously.

"Is something wrong?" Roya asked.

"Oh—no. No," he said. "How was your day at school?"

"Terrible. Everyone hates me. Today in music we had to get into groups and the teacher had to force someone to be my partner, and of course it was Madison, and she told me that she doesn't like to be with me because I eat yellow food at lunch that smells weird, and I told her it's because of the saffron, and it's delicious, but she kept acting like I disgusted her, even though *she* eats gross-smelling stuff all the time."

"Mmm-hmm," Naveed said distractedly.

Roya sighed. Why did she bother talking to him when he didn't even listen to her? "How was your day? Did you go to the food bank?"

"No. Taking the week off."

"Oh. So what did you do?"

He coughed. "Nothing. Same as always."

Roya gave up trying to make conversation. Today, she decided. Today was definitely the day. He would probably go straight up to his room, giving her the perfect opportunity to escape underneath her bed and dive into the Book of Shadows.

But, to her disappointment, as soon as they'd taken their shoes off at the door, he shuffled into the kitchen. "Will you help me cook some turnips? You know, that old remedy Khaleh Yasmin suggested. I'll probably mess it up. But maybe if we worked on it together?"

What was this about? He had ignored her the whole way home, but suddenly wanted to spend time with her? Maybe, she thought with sudden dread, he had been waiting until he had her alone so that he could ask again about that night on Lopez Island. "Sorry, I have homework to do, so I'm going up to my room. Anyway, she just said to boil them and breathe the steam. That can't be too hard, right?"

"Please," he said. "At least keep me company down here? You can do homework at the table."

A fiery anger flared in Roya. She didn't know where it had come from or why it was so strong, but she needed to release it somewhere else before it exploded all over him. She made her way to the back door. "Okay. But first I'm going outside. To check on the chickens."

"No!" Naveed said it with such force that she stopped in her tracks. "You should stay inside. They're fine. I checked on them earlier."

Roya knew he was lying. Naveed never went near the coop. She was about to open the door anyway, but he turned the deadbolt and punched the button that armed the security system.

"What are you doing?" Roya almost screamed it, she was that close to boiling.

"Stay inside," he grumbled.

"Fine! I'm going to look for Pashi, then." She stomped up the stairs before he could respond.

Pashmak was curled up on a folded quilt at the foot of Roya's bed. When she heard Roya approach, she stretched out a paw and made a half-yawn-half-meow sound that was so adorable it slowed Roya's boil to a more manageable simmer.

"He's so annoying," Roya whispered as she stroked the cat. "What's the big deal about going outside? Why does he have to trap me in here? And he might barge in any second, and I just wanted to find the right potion in the Book of Shadows, but he always ruins it, Pashi!" She punctuated her rant by pounding her fist into a pillow, and that felt good so she kept punching, which caused Pashmak to leap off the bed and curl up on the rug instead, and before Roya knew it she was crying, which was dumb because she was angry not sad, but tears were confusing like that.

Once she felt calmer, she came back downstairs. Naveed had apparently given up on the turnips and was sprawled out on the couch. She tiptoed over and saw that he had fallen asleep—deeply, judging from the circle of drool on the throw pillow beneath his open mouth.

A smile spread across Roya's face. She was free.

She returned to her room. Once under her bed, she found the Book of Shadows and clicked on her flashlight. She paged through, hoping the potion recipe she needed would be obvious—maybe there would be a page labeled *Brews for Communicating with the Dead*. But the book was not organized in any particular way. It was a mixture of recipes, journal entries, drawings, spells, and descriptions of various rituals.

Zennia's handwriting was hard to read because it was in cursive, and there were lots of words that Roya didn't understand. Reading the book gave her a feeling like the sloshy stomach she got when she tried to read during a long car ride. But at the same time, a strange heat grew inside her, and she wasn't sure if it was from excitement, or nervousness, or maybe both at the same time.

Kass would have been able to turn to the right page, no problem, but Roya worried that she would accidentally skip over just the thing she needed. So she read carefully. There were many mentions of the peritassa tea they drank at the new moon ceremony that helped them contact the spirit world, but that was out of the question since the plant was illegal. Roya was about to give up hope that there were any alternatives when she stumbled across a note in a section about crop failure.

If the tea harvest is insufficient and the ceremony cannot be postponed, psilocybin mushrooms are a good substitute. However, the mushrooms MUST be identified by an expert (never forget what happened to Yvonne). Failing that, herbal cider can be used, though results have been mixed.

Roya knew better than to mess around with wild mushrooms, and was unsettled by the ominous mention of Yvonne. But the herbal cider sounded promising.

Naturally, the recipe was not written on that page, which sent Roya on another journey through the book. She re-read the part about the new moon ceremony when she passed it again. A few long paragraphs stressed how important fire was to the ritual because—just as Kass had said—*entire worlds exist within every flame.* Fire was a signal to spirits that they were being called, but also a gateway that allowed them to pass through to another world. Every flame held something vast and infinite within its tiny space.

It made Roya think of something Khaleh Yasmin had told her, about the Zoroastrian temple in Yazd with its everlasting flame, the fire that had been tended for more than a thousand years without ever going out. And even though it all felt too big and mysterious for her to fully grasp, at the same time it boiled down to something very straightforward. All she needed to do was light a candle, and all of this would be contained inside its glowing flame.

It was simple, but at the same time very difficult. Roya had no idea how she would sneak fire into Englewood. Maybe she could find a way to smuggle a candle and some matches in, but how would she and Kass be able to get away from the nurses long enough to do what they needed to do? How would she even get back to Englewood in the first place?

Roya was paging randomly through the book, lost in thought, when she finally happened upon the recipe for herbal cider. Eagerly, she read the ingredients. It contained several herbs she'd never heard of, but also a few things her family already had growing in their yard: yarrow, mint, juniper. And it looked easy to make. She just needed to mix raw apple juice with some honey and the herbs and let it sit for a week or two until it turned bubbly. That sounded doable. And she still had the apples from the cellar at Orcinia, which had kept well but seemed too sacred to eat. Because they were needed for this cider, she realized.

Still, an uncomfortable feeling nagged at her, a little voice saying, *this is not going to work.* The missing herbs might be the key ingredients. But she wanted so badly to do this, so that Kass could remember what her father had told her on the bluffs.

Although... maybe Roya could help figure out what he'd meant? Before giving the cloth book back to Kass, she had copied the whole thing down, because she knew she'd want to read it again someday. Now she was glad she had a copy: she could scour it for clues.

Even so, she knew the full answer wasn't in her grasp. Kass was the only one who could solve the mystery. All Roya could do was help.

Right now, though, she was tired of reading. She was ready for action, and the first step was to make some raw apple juice.

They didn't have a juicer, but Cyrus had taught her a trick for juicing beets that involved shredding them, then squeezing the juice out by hand, and she thought the same thing might work for apples. So she stepped quietly into the kitchen, bypassing her still-sleeping brother, and found a clean jar to hold the juice. As she scraped the Orcinian apple against the grater, she imagined how delighted Kass would be when Roya reappeared at Englewood with the potion and the candles and the matches, ready to call the spirits forth.

Naveed

FRIDAY, FEBRUARY 12

ON FRIDAY MORNING, NAVEED STARTED THE DAY WITH A SHORT meditation. When he reached the final exhale, he was surprised to find himself filled with an emotion he hadn't felt in a long time: excitement.

Other than picking up Roya from school, he hadn't left the house in ages; he'd scored a doctor's note that excused him from all his commitments for two whole weeks, to give him time to recover fully. But today, he actually had a pleasant outing to look forward to.

He closed his mind off to the panicky voice that kept reiterating all the reasons he should stay home, all the dangers he faced every time he stepped out the door. It was important that he do this—not for himself, but for Andi, who had left sweet gifts for him every day during his illness, and who had seemed kind of down the last time she'd visited. He could pull himself together for her. Besides, he finally felt okay again, and had made it through the last few hellish weeks without being hospitalized and/or having a mental breakdown. Nate hadn't even bothered him much lately. That alone was worth celebrating.

Nevertheless, something else had been haunting him. He couldn't stop thinking about Tim Schmidt. For one thing, there was Dr. Young's revelation that Schmidt didn't actually work at the CDC. Far more disturbing, though, was what had happened when Baba took Naveed to the urgent care clinic a few days afterward.

But he was tired of obsessively ruminating about that. Today, he was finally going to do something about it.

As soon as Cyrus started climbing down the ladder from his top bunk, Naveed said, "Morning, Kourosh."

Cyrus yawned, rifling through his dresser drawers for fresh clothes. "Morning."

"Hey... remember that favor I was asking you about the other day?"

"Oh. Sorry, I forgot all about that. Can we talk about it later? I'm back on the app development team and we've got a ton of stuff to get done before the presentation tomorrow. You're coming to that, right?"

"Um, yeah, sure, I can go. But—"

"Good, because Baba told me yesterday he can't be there. Some field inspection they have to do at work. You can bring Roya—I'll text you the details so you can map it. It's at the UW, in one of the big lecture halls."

"Okay. But... can I talk to you for a second? I really need to tell you something. And I need you to listen."

Cyrus turned around, concern flickering across his face. "What's up?"

Naveed swung his legs off the bed and pressed his palms to his knees. It was hard to say this out loud. He worried that Cyrus would immediately write him off as crazy. But if his brother couldn't help, probably no one could.

"Something strange happened at Englewood," he began. "While I was still an inpatient. Some guy who said he was from the CDC asked for my help with this research project on MRK. He wanted... I think he wanted... like, blood and tissue samples and stuff, and for me to release my medical records to them."

Cyrus looked horrified. "You didn't—"

"No. But when we visited the other week, Dr. Young asked if he'd tried to contact me again. She did some research and found out that he didn't work for the CDC. I hadn't heard from him... but... here's where it gets weird...."

Cyrus was giving Naveed his full attention now. "What happened?"

Naveed couldn't muster the courage to meet Cyrus's eyes. "A few days later, when Baba took me to urgent care, I... I saw him."

"Are you sure?" Cyrus sounded skeptical.

Naveed could still recall it vividly: he'd been sitting in the waiting room while Baba talked to one of the nurses, coughing into the mask they'd made him wear, and someone had sat down next to him. It was Tim Schmidt, looking the same as before, with his sandy blond hair and polished shoes. This time he was wearing a white lab coat with an ID badge hanging from its lapel, though it was turned the wrong way, so Naveed couldn't see the name printed on it.

Tim Schmidt had smiled at him sympathetically. "Quite a cough you've got there. Are you ready to help us yet?"

He'd handed over a clipboard full of forms, but Naveed hadn't taken it. He'd stood up, pausing to steady himself on the next row of chairs before walking over to Baba. "Help," he'd said wildly. "There's a man over there... Tim Schmidt... he isn't... with the CDC... he's not who he says he is...."

But by the time Baba turned around, the man was gone. "Naveed-jaan, no one's there. Don't worry, everything's all right."

"Why don't you have a seat and we'll check that temp," the nurse said, as if the number on the thermometer explained everything. But Naveed had been lost in feverish delirium before—he knew what that felt like, and this wasn't it. Tim Schmidt had really been there. He was certain of it.

Strangely enough, part of Naveed wished he'd just heard the man out. Especially after he started suspecting that what he had wasn't actually the flu. He'd gotten the flu shot, after all, and the Tamiflu they'd given him didn't do a damn thing except make him sick to his stomach. Plus, no one else in his family had caught it, which was unusual. It wasn't MRK, there was none of that characteristic bloody phlegm, but what if it was some disease that struck afterward? Symptom-wise, it felt just like what he'd come down with at Englewood, which they'd diagnosed as bronchitis. *Can you please tell me what's going on?* he wanted to ask the man who called himself Tim Schmidt. *What is happening to me?*

"I'm sure," he said to Cyrus now. "It was definitely him, and he was trying to get me to sign some forms. I didn't do it. Baba didn't believe me when I told him. That's why I need you. You have to figure out who he really is."

"Okay." Cyrus drew the word out slowly. "What did he say his name was?"

"Tim Schmidt." Naveed found his wallet on top of the dresser, then pulled out the business card. "Here—he gave me this. You can have it, if it helps."

Cyrus took it, frowning. "Looks legit. If he puts as much effort into covering his tracks as he did designing his fake business card, he could be really hard to find."

"I know. But could you just try? Please?"

"I'll see what I can do. But it'll have to wait until after our presentation tomorrow."

Cyrus left to get ready for school, and Naveed went downstairs to eat breakfast, doubly relieved. He'd finally gotten that off his chest, and Cyrus had promised to look into it. Now all he had to do was wait to see what Cyrus found.

He spent most of the day preparing for his evening out: cleaning himself up, panicking about leaving the house, doing yoga in an attempt to calm himself down, eating lunch, freaking out again, reassuring himself that it would be worth it, and listening to one last meditation before heading over to Andi's house. He slipped on a pair of sunglasses and Baba's suit jacket as he left. Even though it wasn't much of a disguise, it still made him feel a little safer.

Jake greeted him at the door and gave him the keys to his Highlander.

"Drive careful. And have a good time."

"We will," Naveed said. "Thanks so much for letting me borrow the car."

"Of course—thank you for doing this for her. I can't wait to hear how it goes."

Naveed drove to Andi's school. He was thankful for the tinted windows as he idled at the curb, but still kept his head down as the throngs of high-schoolers passed by. Jake, apparently, had been dropping Andi off and picking her up all week because she'd been having headaches again and hadn't wanted to drive. She hadn't told Naveed any of this, which bothered him.

Finally, she appeared. She was just one of the dozens of students swarming the sidewalk, but he picked her out instantly. She walked alone, dragging her feet, shoulders bent beneath the weight of her backpack, as if she were being marched to a prison camp.

Something tightened inside his chest. He'd never seen her look so dejected before. But—that was exactly why he was here. To cheer her up.

She got into the car without looking at him, setting her bag down and slumping into the passenger seat. "Hey, Dad."

"Surprise!" he said, and it happened so fast that he didn't even see it coming. She grabbed his hand, pulling his fingers apart while folding his wrist backward. It hurt so much that he cried out, desperate for her to stop.

She immediately let go. "Oh my God, it's you. What are you doing here? Why are you driving my dad's car? Is he okay?"

He rubbed his aching wrist, still in shock. "He's fine. He let me borrow it. I wanted to surprise you."

"Why would you want to do that?"

"Because I—"

"Never mind. Can we just get out of here, please?" She was covering her face now, and he noticed that a bunch of her classmates were staring at them.

He only peeled out a little bit in his hurry to leave. Neither of them spoke. He wished he'd thought to put on some music. The silence was palpable.

"I'm sorry," she finally said. "I hope I didn't hurt you. When I saw some guy in a suit and sunglasses driving my dad's car, I just… reacted. I never would've guessed it was you. I thought you weren't supposed to drive anyway."

"I can drive, I just generally choose not to. And I'm fine," he said, even though his entire right arm still felt dead. "I didn't mean to startle you. Those were some good moves, though."

He was trying to lighten the mood, but she didn't answer. "I know you've had a busy week," he continued, "And I wanted to do something special for you. To show you how much I appreciate you. I don't think I usually do a very good job of that."

She sank lower in her seat. "Where are we going?"

"You'll see. We'll be there in, oh, twenty minutes. You want to put some music on?"

She got her phone out and selected something mellow. "Jay Som. Always calms me down."

It was perfect, of course. "I missed you this week," Naveed said. "So what's new?"

She was quiet for a moment. "Well, my mom's talking about coming back soon."

"That's great." But she didn't exactly sound happy about it. "Isn't it?"

"Naveed, I think it's probably best if we… for a while… after she comes home… we should spend a little less time together."

He swallowed hard. "So… you don't want to come over anymore."

"Not, like, *never*, just… less frequently. I'm getting so behind in school, and it's really important to her—and to me—that I get good grades this semester."

"But it's not like we're… I mean, usually when we're together you're doing homework anyway."

"I know, but she doesn't get it. She thinks you're a distraction. That we're involved, you know. Romantically."

"But you've told her we aren't, right?"

Andi was looking out the window. "Doesn't matter."

"It's frustrating that nobody understands about us," he said. "That everyone assumes we're dating or whatever."

"Yeah." Was that a hint of bitterness in her voice? His stomach dropped. Their platonic relationship had suited him fine, and he'd figured she felt the same way. But... what if she didn't?

To mask his uncertainty, he barreled on. "It's like, everybody thinks romantic love is better than everything else. Friendship and family aren't as good," he babbled. "But romance, it just gets too... complicated. And it can die. Friendship can too, I guess. But family... you love them no matter what."

"That's not always true," Andi argued. "Some families hate each other. And just because you're born into them doesn't mean you get a free pass—you can't be horrible to people and expect them to still love you. You have to earn it. By respecting and being open with them. Trusting that they still care about you, despite your flaws. Helping them, and letting them help you."

She said the last part quietly. So quietly that he felt even worse, because he knew: he really hadn't done anything to earn her trust, her love. He could never give as much to her as she gave to him. And yet, without her...without her, he'd be lost. He was desperate to keep her, even though he realized how ugly that sounded. Like she was a thing to him, not a person but some sort of life preserver that he clung to in order to stay afloat.

"Are you... can we... is there anything...." He wasn't sure what he was trying to articulate, and it didn't seem to be helping. She was drifting further away every second. "I want you to be happy," he finally mumbled. This wasn't going the way he'd hoped at all.

"Me, too," she said.

Naveed didn't know what else to say. So he concentrated on driving, and she kept staring out the window. Eventually, he pulled up at their destination.

"Benaroya Hall?" she asked. "What are we doing here?"

"We"—he shot her a grin that she returned confusedly—"are going to the symphony."

Her smile faded. "Wow. I wish I could've changed out of my grubby school clothes first."

"Don't be silly. You look beautiful," he said as he circled the garage in search of a parking spot. "Besides, it's technically just a rehearsal. But they let you go down to the stage and talk with the musicians afterward."

They made their way into the sparsely populated theater, settling into seats in the front. As soon as the orchestra began warming up, Andi leaned forward, taking it all in, looking fascinated as the conductor spoke to the musicians.

They began to play—"Rachmaninoff!" Andi exclaimed in delight after listening for a few moments—and Naveed settled in as the music swelled around them.

At one point, he had to excuse himself to the bathroom when a tickle in his throat became a full-on coughing fit. When he returned to the theater, he spotted her in the audience, and paused there for a minute, buoyed by the rapture on her face.

When he slid back into his seat, she nudged his elbow. "Thank you," she whispered. "This is amazing." She placed her hand on top of his, and he knew that this had been the right thing to do after all, and his heart cracked open with joy.

Andi

FRIDAY, FEBRUARY 12

IF ANDI HADN'T KNOWN BETTER, SHE MIGHT HAVE THOUGHT she was on a date.

After the symphony, Naveed took her out to dinner at Cafe Flora, a fancy vegetarian restaurant. They were seated at a table in the atrium, an enclosed garden-like room, where Andi felt very much on display. It felt so strange to be doing this—just the two of them, eating together in public, surrounded by couples who were celebrating an early Valentine's Day.

The server asked what she wanted to drink, and she said she was fine with water since none of the beverages looked appealing to her, but Naveed ordered her a rosemary lemonade anyway. After they got their drinks and their coconut tofu appetizer, he asked how her music was coming, and it felt so good to talk about it that she managed to push down the unease that had been building ever since he'd surprised her at school. She was still mortified that she'd attacked him... and then, the conversation in the car afterward....

She wasn't going to think about that now. There would be plenty of time to dwell on it later, when he wasn't across the table dazzling her with his grin.

The food was amazing, and he seemed so happy. She allowed her worries to temporarily drop away, so that it was just the two of them, and this wonderful meal, and the bubbling fountain beside them. That was all there was, and all there needed to be.

But by the end of dinner he was fading, and when the check came he looked like he was about to fall asleep. For once, Andi didn't have a headache, so she offered to drive home. Thankfully, he accepted. She was a lot more comfortable with him in the passenger seat; his driving involved lots of jerky starts and stops.

"So can we spend some time together this weekend?" he asked as she drove along the lake. "Kourosh has that big presentation in the afternoon tomorrow. Want to come with me?"

"Sure." Andi wanted to support Cyrus, who'd been so sweet to her after the crow incident earlier that week. She had ended up missing two more days of school, and her father had made a doctor's appointment to get her headaches checked out, but she wouldn't go in for a few more weeks. Andi suspected they would have squeezed her in sooner if she'd mentioned the fainting, but she'd convinced herself that it was a freak one-time occurrence. Because of all that, she'd accumulated a lot of make-up work from her missed days, and she needed to spend some time this weekend catching up.

Naveed was talking, so she forced herself to pay attention. "Oh, I guess Roya has to come too... Baba has a work thing. But maybe we can do something together on Sunday?"

"Yeah, maybe," Andi said. The glow of that meal was fading now. She kept thinking back to their earlier conversation, when she'd finally gotten an opening to confess her true feelings for him, and he'd once again prevented her from talking about it openly. It had forced her into a realization that she didn't want to face.

Despite the fact that they both loved each other, their relationship was not healthy. He seemed to be satisfied with it; he was getting what he needed from her, but she was not, and she felt like she couldn't tell him so. Just saying that she wanted him to be her boyfriend wouldn't make him suddenly fall in love, she knew that. Still, she didn't know how much longer she could pretend not to feel that way. It was getting too painful to be around him.

But what would he do if she left? If she ended up going to college in another state? He depended on her for so much. If she were to go—

It would probably destroy him.

So. She was trapped.

"You want to come over now?" Naveed asked.

She didn't think she could handle that. Right now, she needed time alone. "That's okay. I think we should call it a night."

"Oh." He sounded disappointed. "So… see you tomorrow?"

Andi slowed as she approached his house, then put the car in park. She scanned the surrounding street and the bushes in the Mirzapours' yard.

"Andi?" Naveed prompted.

"Yeah. Tomorrow. Right." She noticed movement by the gate, but it was only a branch that had probably been jostled by a squirrel. Should she walk him to the door?

No. She was being paranoid; no one was lurking in the yard waiting for him. The lights were on in the house, and it looked very cheery inside.

"Are you… is everything okay?" he asked.

"Yep, everything's fine." Hilarious. She cracked herself up sometimes.

He breathed in sharply, like he was going to ask something else, but she didn't want to talk anymore. So she added, "See you tomorrow. Bye."

It wasn't until he'd gotten to his front door that she realized she should have thanked him for the evening. He'd obviously put a lot of thought into it, and she probably seemed like she didn't even care.

Naveed gave her a little wave and a tentative smile before he went inside. She raised her hand back, then waited for the door to close before coasting down the block and turning on to her street.

So tired. She was so tired of the emotional rollercoaster of this relationship, tired of being scared and overwhelmed and alone.

The Sentra was parked outside her house. She could still see the faint streaks on the windshield where her father had scrubbed away the dead crow's blood. But if the car was there, he was probably home. Good: she didn't want to be in an empty house right now. Andi held the tiny canister of pepper spray that now dangled from her keychain, ready to use it if necessary, and hurried to the front door.

But once she got inside, she still felt tense, even after she'd locked the deadbolt behind her. She made a cautious sweep of the house, wondering why it was so quiet. There was no music drifting up from her father's basement studio. Had he mentioned he was going out? She couldn't remember. But if he was gone, why hadn't he taken the car?

At least there were no signs of a struggle in any of the rooms on the main floor. Of course there weren't, because he was fine. He was fine.

"Stupid dark houses," she said out loud. "Why do you have to be so creepy? Here. Let's get some lights on. Ah, that's better."

Maybe he was down in the basement with his headphones on. Yeah. That was probably it. She walked down the stairs, noticing how loudly they creaked, and banged on the door at the bottom. "Dad! Are you in there?"

No answer. He must be listening to the music pretty loud.

Or maybe he was in trouble.

No! He was fine!

She banged on the door again. Still no answer, so she turned the knob. It was locked.

Strange. She went back upstairs and rifled around in the junk drawer where they kept the basement key. It was usually shoved into the very back, because they never locked the door. But she came up with nothing.

Andi pulled out her phone to text him, noticing that she had an extra set of keys in her pocket. Of course—her dad had given Naveed his keys when he borrowed the car. But the car keys weren't the only ones on that set. There was one that might have been the basement key, as well as his house keys. If he'd gone out, though, wouldn't he make sure he had house keys with him so he could get back in?

She wrote him a short text. Just got home. Where are you???

While she waited for a reply, she scrolled through her old texts to make sure she hadn't missed anything, but didn't find any recent messages from him. If he didn't reply in five minutes, she decided, she would call him. If he didn't answer, she'd try his keys in the basement lock.

Time ticked by slowly. When the five minutes were up, she called. No answer, of course.

So. Down to the basement.

Why did she feel such dread? What did she expect to see? Then she wished she hadn't asked herself that, because her mind responded by showing her grisly images that she prayed would not be waiting for her beyond that door.

But when she slipped the basement key into the lock and flicked on the light, everything looked normal. Well, normal-ish; it was messy, but not signs-of-a-struggle messy. He wasn't there, but he wasn't splayed out on the floor in a pool of his own blood or anything like that. So. That was good.

Andi scooted aside an empty pizza box and a few red Solo cups and sank onto the couch. She picked up the acoustic guitar propped against the wall and strummed an A-chord, listening to its cheerful vibrations travel through the room. She strummed another major chord, and another, and with each one felt calmer.

Maybe that was all she needed: more time to make music. She'd been so busy the past few weeks that she hadn't returned to the composition she'd been working on before she'd switched gears for the documentary score. After spending the afternoon listening to that incredible Rachmaninoff, she had some ideas for making it better. She was also starting to wonder if the release and freedom she felt while making music might have actually been keeping her sane.

The thought of going upstairs and getting to work relaxed her a little. At least it would pass the time until her dad called back. Which he would. Soon.

She clicked the latches open on the guitar's hard case—a habit deeply ingrained by a lifetime of her mother's nagging to always put instruments away properly—and was about to set it inside when something caught her eye.

A narrow piece of white paper was sticking out of the covered compartment underneath the guitar's neck, where her dad usually stored picks and tuners and capos. A note, maybe?

She opened the compartment and pulled it out. It wasn't a note, she saw when she turned it over, but a strip of pictures from a photo booth. Four frames ringed in white. Two people in each frame. Her dad on the left. Next to him, beaming a radiant smile, was Patricia.

Andi's shock turned to disgust as her eyes traveled down the series of photos. Both of them were laughing in the second frame. Clinking their beer bottles together in the third. Kissing in the fourth.

No. This couldn't be happening. She closed her eyes and counted to ten, as if this were a nightmare she could escape from.

It didn't work. Those four photos were still there when she opened her eyes.

Andi almost didn't know what was worse. The fact that her dad was cheating on her mom, or that he was drinking again.

She shoved the photos back into the case and managed to refrain herself from smashing it against the wall, from breaking everything of his.

What else was he hiding down here? Was he only drinking, or had he moved on to… other things, worse things? Andi hadn't noticed him acting stoned, but then again, he hid out in the basement constantly these days. And she'd been stupid enough to buy all of his lies.

She tore through the room, removing the contents of every drawer, every instrument case, not caring about the mess she was leaving in her wake. Relishing it, actually.

Andi found his stash buried deep inside a cabinet behind a box of cords and reverb pedals. Several bottles of vodka, a baggie of pot. No syringes, which came as a slight relief—until she noticed the pills.

They were in an unmarked bottle, but a quick image search confirmed her suspicions. Even so, she kept looking back and forth between the photos and the pills, studying their markings, wishing she'd been wrong. But there was no denying it. There they were in image after image, those exact same pills pictured next to bottles labeled *OxyContin*.

She carried everything she'd found upstairs, and had just set it all down in the bathroom when her dad finally texted back. Sorry thought I told you I was going out tonight? I'm at a show and didn't hear your call. How was your evening?

Ha. Ha. That text didn't deserve a response, so she set her phone down and opened the medicine cabinet.

She took out her own bottle of painkillers and poured the pills into her hand. There were still five left, as she'd expected. So he hadn't been dipping into hers, at least not recently. She supposed this wasn't too surprising. They weren't opioids. They weren't the good stuff.

She slid her pills back into their bottle, then threw it into her backpack. After hesitating for a second, she put the Oxy in there too.

Then she emptied the bag of pot into the toilet. All those dried green leaves floating in the water made her think of gōng fu chá for some reason. *I am brewing the biggest, most disgusting cup of tea imaginable,* she thought. It almost made her laugh. She flushed it all away.

Finally, she dumped the vodka into the sink. Or, most of it. She left a few inches in the bottom of one bottle.

All her life, she'd been the good girl. She'd dutifully taken her father's advice, never drinking, never trying so much as a single cannabis-infused brownie, since she knew how substance abuse had nearly ruined his life.

And now here he was, ruining things again. For himself, for her, for her mother, for their whole family.

She took a swig of vodka straight out of the bottle. It tasted good at first: smooth, almost creamy. Then came the fire, an intense, painful burn that was followed by a welcome hit of pleasure. A flood of well-being spread from her head through her whole body.

She swallowed again. Another sip. And another. So sweet, once you got through the burning. Pleasure and pain. Creation and destruction. All tangled up together, mingling inside the thick glass.

Naveed

FRIDAY, FEBRUARY 12

NAVEED CLOSED THE FRONT DOOR BEHIND HIM. HE WAS completely drained. And confused. He'd thought Andi had been enjoying herself—but when she'd dropped him off, it was like she couldn't wait to get him out of the car.

He collapsed onto the couch, letting his feet hang off the side since he still had his shoes on, before noticing that Baba was bustling around in the kitchen.

"You're back! How'd it go?" Baba set down the pan he'd been drying and joined Naveed in the living room.

"It was great."

"She liked the music?"

"Loved it."

There must have been something in his voice, in the flat way that he said those words, that made Baba ask, "You feeling all right?"

"Fine. Just tired." He tried to hold back a cough, but it came anyway, rattling through his sore ribcage.

"Make sure you take it easy tomorrow. Can't have you getting sick again," Baba said.

Naveed closed his eyes. *I'm never not sick,* he thought. He was starting to accept that he'd always be dealing with illness in some form or another, that symptom-free days were no longer his normal state, but rarities to be appreciated whenever they came. It was strangely freeing to surrender to the flow of the pain, to know it would swell and subside, instead of constantly fighting against it or pinning his hopes on some cure that may never come. Baba, though, was still under the impression that someday he'd be completely well again. "Don't worry, Baba. I won't overdo it."

Baba disappeared for a while, then returned with Naveed's evening meds and a glass of water. "I'm turning in. Need any help getting upstairs?"

"No, that's all right. Shab bekheir, Baba." Naveed took his meds, then tried to compose a text to Andi. But he had no idea what to say. It was like he was standing inside a hurricane, watching words fly by him, all of them fleeting and impossible to grab onto.

This happened sometimes, his thoughts getting tangled up and jumbled before straightening out again. He let them whip around, trying to imagine that they were leaves and he was the tree, steady in the face of the storm. Only this was a bad one. Strong enough to uproot him, maybe.

His phone buzzed some time later. Andi's text was only two words long. I lied.

That froze him. But before he could let it sink in, another one appeared. I'm not ok can u come over please i have something to tell u

Naveed was so disturbed by those words, by the obvious urgency of the sentence, that he was out the back door and passing through the gate into the alley before he even realized what he was doing. He opened his pocketknife, glancing into the shadows in case anyone materialized from them, walking faster and faster until he was running, arriving at her door breathless.

He gulped in the cold air, which made him cough again, and fumbled to put away his knife. Just as he was about to knock on the door, she opened it. "Hi," she slurred, and fell into his arms.

She was heavy. Limp. "Andi?" His heart thumped in his ears. "Andi. Andi."

He couldn't stop saying her name, but she didn't answer. He wedged himself inside and closed the door, her body so heavy in his arms, her head lolling against his chest, oh no no no what was going on what had happened to her what was he supposed to do?

He lowered her down, cradling her head on his lap, and leaned closer to make sure she was breathing okay. Her breath came shallow but steady—and soaked in an unmistakable scent. Alcohol.

It hadn't been that long since she'd dropped him off, an hour at most. How had she managed to get so drunk, so fast? When he glanced around the room, he found his answer on the coffee table, illuminated in the streetlights. An empty bottle of vodka.

None of it made sense, but right now he just needed her to wake up. He swept her bangs from her forehead. "Andi. Wake up. Please."

When his fingers brushed against her skin, her eyes flew open. She mumbled something that sounded like, "Your hands are cold."

Naveed pulled his hand away. He was about to ask if she was all right, but she obviously wasn't, so he said, "Do you need me to call... should I call an ambulance or something?"

"God, no." She struggled into a sitting position. "I didn't drink *that* much."

He wasn't sure about that, but she seemed coherent enough now that she was awake, and he would rather not get paramedics involved if he could help it. He decided to hold off, at least for now. "What's wrong? You said... you had something to tell me?"

She didn't answer. She regarded him with wide, desperate eyes. Then, in one swift movement, she grabbed his shirt and pulled him to her. One hand stroked the back of his neck and one still clung to his shirt and her lips touched his. He was so shocked that he opened his mouth and their breath mingled together, their breath and their lips and their tongues finding each other at last, and it felt like a wall was crumbling, like he'd been staring so long at bricks that he'd never even known about the garden beyond.

Part of him didn't want to stop, but he forced himself to pull away. "What are you doing?"

"Kissing you," she said, lunging in for another.

He turned his head just in time for it to catch him on the cheek. That made him feel really weird, somehow ill and wonderful at the same time. "No," he said. "No. We shouldn't. It's not a good idea... not now... you don't really want to anyway...."

"How would you know what I want?" She had a fierce look in her eyes. "Have you ever asked me?"

Her question tipped the balance inside. Now he just felt ill.

"I didn't want lemonade," she said. "I said I just wanted water! You thought you knew what I wanted, but you didn't! I don't even *like* lemonade!"

"This is all because I ordered you lemonade?"

She stared at him. On the coffee table, her phone started buzzing. The light from it sent aurora-like ripply lights onto the ceiling.

Then she started laughing. Hysterically. She didn't make any move to get the phone, she just laughed and laughed, and eventually it went silent. She kept laughing, or maybe sobbing, it was impossible to tell which. He didn't know if he should hug her or if she was mad at him or what, but when it became clear that she was crying, he put his arm around her and she buried her face in his chest. He let both arms encircle her and held on tight.

Her phone buzzed again, longer this time. But again she ignored it, and he didn't want to move, on precarious ground as he was.

After a while, her sobs quieted. "I'm sorry, Andi," he said. "I didn't mean to ignore what you wanted, or assume I know what you need. I'm trying, but I guess I'm not doing a very good job...."

"Stop," she said. "It's not all about you, okay?"

He took that as his cue to shut up. He honestly didn't know what to say anyway.

"I hate surprises," she said after a moment. "I hate them."

"Okay. Got it. No more surprises, no more lemonade." He hoped that might get a smile out of her, but no such luck.

Her phone buzzed again. "I think someone's trying to call you," he added.

"Just my dad." She spit the sentence out with unexpected venom. "He hates it when I don't answer."

"So should I...?"

"Let him worry. He deserves it, that... that...."

She didn't finish. Instead, she lurched forward and threw up on the floor. "Ohhh. Shit."

"It's okay." Naveed helped her up, supporting her as she teetered unsteadily beside him, and got her into the bathroom just in time for the next one.

He kneeled beside her, but she pushed him weakly away. "Leave me alone," she said.

He returned to the living room. Her vomit had green flecks in it from the salad they'd shared at dinner. Looking at it made him want to puke too, but he swallowed hard and kept it down. He held his nose as he wiped up the mess.

Her phone buzzed away. He was tempted to answer it, because he liked Jake and was starting to feel in over his head. But at the same time, he wanted to respect Andi's wishes, especially after the conversation they'd just had, and there was apparently something going on between them that Naveed didn't know about.

After he'd finished cleaning up, he spent a few minutes scrubbing his hands, and dug two cans of sparkling water out of the back of the fridge. Then he knocked on the bathroom door.

Andi cracked it open. She was leaning against the wall now, knees pulled up to her chest. He offered her one of the cans, and she took it. He lingered in the doorway at first, but sat down when she patted the floor next to her. They both sipped in silence for a minute.

"He's cheating on my mom," Andi said quietly.

Naveed almost choked on the sip of water he'd just taken. "What?"

"Yeah. With the violinist who helped me with the documentary score." She set her drink down quickly and retched into the toilet again.

"Oh. Andi." He rubbed her back, and when she finished she scooted closer, resting her head against his shoulder. "You're... you're sure? Maybe you should talk to him, maybe it's just a misunderstanding...."

"No. I'm sure. And it gets worse." She held the can against her forehead, then took another sip. "I found his stash. Decided to give his vodka a try."

"Wait, what? But he's sober...."

"He *was* sober. Eleven years."

"Fuck. Wow. I'm so sorry." Naveed didn't want to believe it. He'd always thought Jake was a great dad, easygoing and awesome. But... it did seem like he had barely been around lately. Like he'd kind of checked out.

"We need to leave," Andi said suddenly. "I don't want to be here when he gets home. When he sees what I did to the basement... to his stash...."

She stood up, steadying herself on the counter, then stumbled back to her room, where she started tossing clothes into her backpack.

"Okay," Naveed said. "You can stay with us. As long as you need."

She zipped up her pack, then paused in the hallway on their way out. She took one of the framed albums off the wall. "First printing of Nirvana's *Bleach*. Signed and everything. Probably the most valuable record he owns."

Naveed had a bad feeling about this. "Here. I'll carry it for you. Your bag, too. Let's go. You'll feel better in the morning."

"No, I won't," Andi said. "You can take my bag. But I want this one."

He didn't want to argue. They headed for the front door, but someone opened it just as they were about to turn the knob.

Jake took a step backwards, obviously startled. "Andi! Why didn't you answer your phone? I was so worried—"

"*You* were worried?" Andi said it with such slurred disbelief that Jake stopped talking immediately.

Naveed did not want to be caught in the middle of this. He stayed silent in the background.

"Andi, are you... are you *drunk?*"

"Yes, very," said Andi. "Hope you don't mind that I polished off the rest of your vodka."

"What? You found...."

"I found *everything*. And it's all gone now. Oh, except, I forgot to get rid of those photos of you kissing Patricia in the photo booth. Should've taken those to show Mom. Bet she'd like to know."

"Andi." Jake looked stricken.

"You told me you had the stomach flu," she said. "And I believed you. I took care of you! Even though you don't bother to take care of me! You are... you're just a washed-up rock star who has to steal your daughter's songs because you can't come up with your own... a gross old white guy who apparently has a thing for Asian women... a liar, a fucking liar, that's what you are. You *disgust* me." In one powerful motion, Andi threw the framed album onto the concrete stoop, shattering the glass. Then she pulled out the record and snapped it in half before Jake even had a chance to react to what was happening. She snapped it again, and again, into smaller and smaller pieces.

"This is how it feels!" she cried. "This is how it feels when someone breaks something you love, and it can't be fixed, it can't ever be fixed!"

"Please, Andi, you don't understand—you don't know how hard it's been, how guilty I feel about what happened to you—"

"*It wasn't your fault!*" she roared. "You think this is easy for *any* of us? Maybe you should try going to therapy instead of taking Oxy—but you'd never do that, would you? Because it's hard, and you're too lazy to do the work."

"Andi, we should go," Naveed said. This was already way over the edge into dangerous territory. "Jake, she's going to stay at our place for a few days, okay?"

Jake seemed to notice Naveed's presence for the first time. Naveed tried to steer Andi past him before she could say anything more, but as she walked out the door, she whispered to her father in a cold, brutal voice, "I can't believe I almost died trying to save you. You didn't even deserve it."

They stepped into the chill wind and hurried up the street, leaving Jake standing alone in the open doorway, surrounded by broken things.

Cyrus

SATURDAY, FEBRUARY 13

THE COMPETITION WAS ABOUT TO START. ALTHOUGH CYRUS WAS trying to gear himself up for their GameCodeX presentation, he could barely focus. Shea had given him a ride to the UW, and now they were sitting in an enormous lecture hall next to Dev and Todd. Dev hadn't even seemed to notice when Cyrus sat down.

This had gone on long enough. It was time to make amends.

"Hey Dev," he said over the roar of voices in the auditorium. "Can I talk to you for a minute outside? It's about *D&C*."

Dev seemed torn, but Todd scooted up in his seat, moving his gangly legs to the side so that Dev could squeeze through. Dev sighed and followed Cyrus out of the room. Many heads turned their way as they walked up the ramp; several people had approached Cyrus on his way in, saying they loved *D&C* and asking when the next episode would be released. He gave them an enigmatic answer, since he had no idea. *All will be revealed in due time.*

Cyrus led Dev outside. The brick courtyard of Red Square was slick from the rain that had fallen during the night. Cyrus kept walking, figuring it would be easier to talk if they didn't have to look at each other.

"So I wanted... I wanted to say... that I miss working on *D&C* with you," he said. "Well, I miss doing lots of things with you, I miss the way things were, but I guess we can't go back to that, and I'd understand if you don't want to work with me anymore. But if we quit, I feel like we owe our subscribers an explanation. I don't mean you have to... tell them... or anything like that. If you want, I'll make up some excuse about why I need to leave, and you can have the show. Take it in whatever direction you want."

"No," Dev said. "Can't have Devil without Cyborg. Either we keep working on it together, or we quit."

"Okay, then, so... what do you want to do?"

"What do *you* want to do?"

"I don't know," Cyrus answered truthfully. "Sometimes I'm not sure we can get the magic back with this weirdness hanging over us."

"*My* weirdness, you mean," Dev said. He didn't seem mad, though.

"No, that's not what I meant. It's like... unless we forgive each other completely, it won't be genuine anymore. People will be able to tell we aren't getting along, and it'll feel fake and hollow and that's not what the show's about at all."

"Yeah" was all Dev said. They walked towards a fountain that shot tall sprays of water straight up into the air.

"I still want to be friends," Cyrus made his mouth say. "I'm so sorry about the way I reacted. And I'm sorry if you felt like you couldn't tell me... things. I think you're awesome, no matter what. And Todd's all right too, I guess."

Dev didn't answer. They stopped at the fountain.

"Wouldn't it be terrible if we got lost?" Dev asked. The way he said it sent a flutter of hope into Cyrus: this was his brainstorming voice. "If we couldn't find our way back to the lecture hall? And we totally missed the presentation because we were wandering all over campus?"

"And then we realized that the buildings were rearranging themselves around us, because it was all an evil plan concocted by our arch-nemeses to cause us to lose the competition?"

Dev snort-laughed. "Wow. They'd need serious super-hacker skills to pull off moving actual buildings."

"Or maybe it was all in our heads." Cyrus wiggled his fingers in faux-mysticism.

"Okay, I think we have our next episode." Dev kicked a rock with his sneaker. "I missed you, too, Cy. But you're right, we can't just gloss over this and pretend things are the same as they were. It's not enough to say that you accept me. You have to show me, you know? And show all the queer folks in our audience—because there are a lot, if you didn't know—that you accept them, too. So I might call you out sometimes, but don't get all offended or think I hate you if you make a mistake. Just apologize, learn from it, and move on."

"Deal." Annoyance was already clawing at Cyrus, which was doubly irritating since it proved Dev's point. Obviously, this was not going to be easy. But—he'd figure it out. He didn't want to lose Dev ever again.

When they got back to the lecture hall, the lobby had cleared out and everyone was taking their seats. As Cyrus walked down to their row, he heard someone calling his name.

Roya waved at him, wildly trying to get his attention. Naveed was sitting next to her. Andi, though, was nowhere to be seen.

Cyrus had been surprised when he came home late last night to find Naveed on the living room sofa. Naveed explained that he'd given Andi his bed, and Cyrus had listened in disbelief as his brother told him why. He felt so bad for Andi, knowing more than Naveed did about the awfulness of her week, and had been extra careful not to disturb her as he entered their room. Not that it mattered—she was totally out. When he woke up in the morning, Andi was already gone, so he texted her. So so sorry to hear about what happened with ur dad. Want to talk about it?

She hadn't written back. Maybe she wasn't ready to talk yet, or maybe she just didn't want to bother him before the competition. She was thoughtful like that.

It was probably better to postpone catching up with her anyway. Cyrus couldn't help but wonder if "Tim Schmidt," the guy who was apparently stalking Naveed, had something to do with the crows and the car break-in. He had asked Todd if he could use his hacker skills to investigate, and Todd had promised to look into it as soon as the competition was over.

Cyrus and Dev took their seats as the lights dimmed and the competition began. Their talk was toward the end of the program, so in the beginning, Cyrus enjoyed listening to everyone else's presentations.

Well, he sort of enjoyed it. Cyrus thought the other groups' games were great, but the three judges picked every entry apart. He was beginning to dread their turn, even though Shea would be handling the meat of the presentation. His job was mostly to stand up there and look pretty.

Once they got onstage, Cyrus wished he had a more active role. He narrated while Dev and Todd played a demo, showing both the competition and cooperative modes, but after that he just had to watch the judges while they made notes, wondering what faults they were going to find. The demo didn't do the app justice anyway. Unless you played it yourself, it was impossible to capture the burst of pleasure that came from feeling those bugs pop satisfyingly beneath your fingertips.

After Shea ran through her impressive slide deck, focusing mostly on the usage metrics but touching briefly on the mood data, they wrapped it up and waited while the audience clapped. Once the applause died down, one of the judges, who peered over wire-rimmed glasses, spoke. "It's good to see such a high percentage of heavy users, but your data only covers a period of a few weeks. I'm not sure your app has staying power. It's cute, but it's derivative. Feels like something I've seen many times before."

The middle judge, a baby-faced dude in a baseball cap, added condescendingly, "To succeed in the crowded marketplace, you need to stand out with something original. But it's also important that your app gives value to the user *and* to the company."

"Right. Always need to keep your bottom line, and any investors you have, in mind," Spectacles added. "Which reminds me—the convenience store level, where the 'bad bugs' have dollar signs on their backs? That one's got to go. Can't be hostile to the guys who fund you."

Cyrus bristled. He didn't want to get rid of that—it was one of his favorite levels, and he remembered how much Andi had loved it too. This conversation was making him very comfortable.

"I don't think the ads fit in well, either," Baseball Cap said. "You should consider other ways to monetize. Like selling your user data to market research companies."

The hipster-bearded judge sitting farthest from Cyrus spoke up. "Business details aside, I think you've got a great game here. True, it's not the most original thing I've seen, but the cooperation mode is intriguing. Could you go back to that slide, the one about user mood?"

Shea pulled the slide up again. "There," Hipster-Beard said. "So you're showing that people who played in cooperative mode ended their games in more positive moods than when they started—but that's not true of competitive mode, or the individual option. And yet those who played competitively were more likely to be heavy users. That's interesting stuff."

"Maybe you should scrap cooperation mode, then," said Baseball Cap. "You don't want your users happy. You want them *hungry*."

To Cyrus's surprise, Shea laughed. The judges all turned to her, and she said, "Oh. Sorry. It's just funny, I didn't have time to go into it here, but I actually found strong correlations between ad click-through rates and certain moods. 'Snacky' was one of them."

Now they definitely had the judges' attention. "See, that right there," Baseball Cap said. "That's what I'm talking about. Thinking outside the box."

"There are some issues that you'll need to address. But I think the concept has value," Hipster-Beard said.

"I agree," said Spectacles.

That was about the most heartening response they'd heard from these fellows all day, so Cyrus decided to count it as a win. Even if it wasn't quite the feedback he'd been expecting.

Only a few more groups took the stage after them, then the judges left to deliberate. Everyone streamed into the lobby for the brief break, but Cyrus ducked away from his group when he saw Naveed and Roya approaching. Still no Andi—where was she?

"Good job, Kourosh! Yours was the best one," Roya said.

"Thanks." Cyrus was still unsettled by what the judges had said and worried that Naveed was going to launch into a loud and embarrassing rant, but his brother's expression was blank.

"Yeah, it was a good presentation," Naveed said in a monotone. "Hey Kourosh, can I borrow your car?"

Well, that was unexpected. "My car? Why?"

Naveed started to answer, but Shea was trying to get Cyrus's attention. "Um, sure, why not," he said to Naveed, and handed him the keys. He had never let his brother drive his car before. Frankly, he wasn't thrilled with the idea, but didn't want to look like a selfish jerk in front of Shea. "Just promise to be careful, okay?"

"I will. Promise," Naveed said.

Sincerely hoping he wouldn't regret this moment of generosity, Cyrus walked over to Shea, who introduced him to her mom, stepdad, and little brother. Dev's parents were also there, and Cyrus found himself wondering whether Dev had come out to them yet. Even though they were pretty liberal, Cyrus wasn't sure how they'd react to that revelation. He made small talk with everyone, all the while wishing that Baba and Maman could be there too.

He also half-hoped that a venture capitalist would swoop down out of nowhere and offer to acquire their game, but no one approached them. There was, however, a huge cluster around one of the other groups who had created an intricate game called Puzzlem, which Cyrus had to admit was pretty well done.

Soon enough, the judges finished deliberating and everyone filed back into the auditorium. As they announced the runners up, Cyrus held his breath. But the names they read were two games he didn't even remember.

Finally, Spectacles stepped forward and announced, "And the winner of this year's GameCodeX is… Puzzlem!"

Cyrus numbly clapped along with everyone else. Goddammit. They hadn't won. He turned to Shea, who looked similarly disappointed.

"What do you say, guys? Drown our sorrows with some coffee?" Todd suggested as they joined the sea of people heading up the auditorium's ramps.

"Sounds good to me," Cyrus said.

As they stepped into the lobby, someone tapped his shoulder. Cyrus turned to see the hipster-bearded judge behind him. "Nice work," the judge said. "I really think you have something there."

Then why didn't we win? Cyrus thought. "Thanks," he said.

"Have you considered getting more resources and building out a proper mobile gaming business?" the judge went on. "With the right structure, you could start churning out lots of apps every year instead of just focusing on one."

Suddenly, Cyrus no longer felt like a loser. "Really? You think so?"

"I do. And if you need a mentor, I'd be interested in helping out. You can get in touch with me through the contest organizers. Think about it. Oh—excuse me," he said, as Baseball-Cap came up to talk to him and the two men walked away.

Shea was standing there wide-eyed. "Whoa. Guys. Philip Bradley wants to mentor us? He sold his first app for, like, $50 million."

Cyrus was a little ashamed that he hadn't known the judge's name. But the offer was intriguing. Especially since Hipster Beard—no, Philip Bradley—hadn't been the one harping on how they needed to sell their user data and tailor the app to appeal to investors.

After they had walked outside together, Cyrus said to the others, "So. What do you think?"

"Let's do it," Dev said decisively. "We've got plenty of ideas for scaling up already, right? Like you were saying, Cy, there's a lot we could do to build in more accessible features, and maybe we should run with this whole cooperative gaming concept. We should see where we can take this thing."

"I agree," Todd said.

"Same," said Shea. "Cy, what about you?"

Cyrus hesitated. After hearing the judges' feedback, he was uncertain how he felt about plunging into this industry, about the compromises they might need to make in order to build something marketable.

"Come on," Shea prompted. "We can't do this without you, you know."

Cyrus looked at their expectant faces. Staying involved was the only way he'd be able to retain any creative control. Besides, he couldn't think of anything he'd rather do than spend his spare time working with the group of coders standing before him.

He returned Shea's smile. "Hell yes. I am so in."

Andi

SATURDAY, FEBRUARY 13

ANDI AWOKE IN AN UNFAMILIAR PLACE. SHE SAT UP, MOMENTARILY panicked, as she tried to make sense of her surroundings. Slowly, she realized she was in Naveed's bed. He was not there, but Cyrus was snoring in the top bunk above her.

Her head was pounding, and her throat was scratchy with thirst, and she only felt worse as details from the night before hit her all over again. The photos of her father and Patricia. The bottle of vodka. Texting Naveed to come over… wanting to hold him, to kiss him, to lose herself in him… but she couldn't remember much after that. Oh God… she hadn't *actually* kissed him, had she?

Then there was her father. She vaguely remembered yelling at him, which he absolutely deserved after what he'd done. Still, she was ashamed of the way she'd acted, and did not want to face Naveed, who must have witnessed the whole thing.

Andi threw the bed covers aside. She was still wearing the same clothes she'd had on the night before. They felt rumpled and sweaty, so she grabbed her backpack from the floor and headed to the bathroom to change.

According to her phone, it was 6:30 a.m. She shouldered her backpack and tiptoed down the creaky stairs into the living room. A kettle was boiling—someone was already awake. Naveed?

No, he was asleep on the sofa by the front door, a throw pillow over his head. Sam was the one brewing tea. He caught her eye, so Andi stepped reluctantly into the kitchen.

"Good morning," she muttered, not knowing what to say. She wished Mahnaz was here instead; Mahnaz would listen to her problems and hug her and reassure her that everything would work out. Andi didn't know Sam nearly as well, and wasn't about to open up to him.

"Naveed told me what happened," Sam said in a low voice. "I'm so sorry, Andi. You can stay here as long as you need, all right?"

"Thank you," she whispered. What had Naveed told him? Her face flushed in embarrassment.

"Would you like some tea?" he asked.

What she really wanted was escape. "That's okay. I think I'll go for a walk. To clear my head. Could you tell Naveed…." She wasn't quite sure how to finish that sentence, so she finally said, "Tell him that I need some time alone today. I'll call him later."

"Sure thing." Sam walked her to the door and punched in the alarm code so that she could leave. For a second she worried that the beeping would wake Naveed up, but he remained still. She slipped on her shoes and headed outside.

It had rained in the night, but the sky was clear now. Andi summoned the courage to return to her house, where her mother's car was still parked. Her dad's car was gone, but even so, she didn't want to go inside. What if it was a trick, and he was in there, waiting?

She got into the Sentra and drove south. She was tempted to take one of her painkillers to deal with her pounding head, but she got pretty drowsy on those. It wouldn't be safe to drive after taking one. Besides, this was just a hangover headache, and she felt like she deserved the pain.

After driving aimlessly through Renton for a while, she pulled over at a café by the transit station. She ordered herself a coffee and a croissant, then set up her laptop so that she would look like a normal person working diligently, even though she was really just staring into space and typing at random intervals.

She did feel better—physically, anyway—after the coffee and the food, but didn't know what to do next. What she really wanted was to get in the car and drive away with the music up loud. Forget about everything and just watch the road go by. She couldn't run forever, she knew that, but... couldn't she at least have one day off?

Thankfully, she'd thrown her MIDI keyboard into her backpack—she was proud of her drunk self for having the foresight to know she might need it. She decided to camp out somewhere and work on a new song, pour her frustrations into her music. Then she could go for a run, or take a nap, or whatever. Buy a little more time while she worked up the courage to face Naveed again. And maybe by tomorrow she'd be able to talk to her father. But today... not today. Not yet.

She had just gotten into her car when the phone rang. Her mom was calling.

Andi's first instinct was to ignore it. She didn't want to be the one to tell her mother what was going on. But her dad was probably too much of a coward to tell her himself, plus her mom was coming back soon. It wasn't right to keep this from her.

So Andi accepted the call. "Hi, Mom."

"Oh, Andi." Her mother's voice sounded heavy. "I'm so glad you picked up. Jake called me this morning and filled me in. I'm so sorry, bǎo bèi, are you doing okay?"

It felt so good to hear her mother that Andi wanted to cry. The use of her dad's first name threw her off, though. Usually he was *your father* or just *Dad*. "I'm... well, I guess I'm okay, but I... I hate him," she said.

Her mother sighed. "I understand. I'm angry too, but, you know, it's been an ongoing struggle. Addiction is a disease, and staying sober was never easy for him."

"Yeah, but... I mean, if he really cares about us, he should be able to pull himself together."

"It's not that simple," her mother said quietly. Then she added, "Andi, I'm sorry. This is... I think a lot of this is my fault."

"It's not," Andi said. "He cheated on you! Did he tell you that? So don't blame yourself for his... his... behavior." That made him sound kind of like a three-year-old, but that was exactly how she thought of him right now. A little tyrant who did whatever he wanted, without caring what it meant for anyone else.

"He didn't cheat on me." Her mother sounded weary.

"Did he not tell you about Patricia? Because I saw it, Mom, I saw pictures—"

"I know about Patricia," her mother said. "But he wasn't—oh, Andi, I wish I was there right now. I didn't want to do this over the phone, it's part of the reason I made him promise not to tell you."

"Tell me what?"

"I'm moving to California," she said. "I'll be back for a few months to get things in order, but I've already accepted a new job at UC Berkeley that starts in June—working on graphic design and photography for their website. It's important to me to be close to Ah-ma right now."

Andi felt like she'd been struck in the forehead with a brick. Her mother continued, "Jake and I... we're very different people. We've tried to make things work, but both of us are ready for a change. Especially now, when we're headed in opposite directions. I don't have any desire to tag along with him while he's on tour, and he doesn't want to make Berkeley his home base. But... you've been through so much this year. The last thing you needed was more stress. So I thought we should wait to officially split up until after you'd graduated. He thought that would be dishonest, and wanted to tell you as soon as possible. But

I convinced him to put it off until I got home and we could make a plan in person."

Now it wasn't Andi's head that was hurting so much as her chest, which felt like it was being crushed. Of course: *On Peak Hill.* She had forgotten all about the song her father was playing when he picked her up at the airport... those depressing lyrics about spiraling into existential despair after getting dumped.... He had tried to tell her through music, the way they'd always communicated best, but she'd been too wrapped up in her own troubles to notice.

Her mother kept talking. "But now that it's out in the open... I'm planning to come home next week, and he's looking for a place to rent until he leaves for the tour. He doesn't blame you for being angry with him, but figured it would be for the best if he moves out sooner rather than later."

"Oh" was all Andi could say. Her whole life was crumbling away in front of her. Her family, her home—gone. Just like that.

"I wish I was there to give you a hug," her mother said.

For some reason, this made Andi recognize how mad she was. "What about me?" she asked. "Where am I supposed to go?"

"You can move down to California for college," her mother said. Suddenly, that strange stipulation in her grandparents' Christmas gift made sense, as Andi realized how long they had all known. How long they had kept it from her. "But you'll always have a home with me or your father, no matter where we are. We love you, Andi, we both do, and want you to know this has nothing to do with you."

It sounded so trite, like something straight out of the *How to Talk About Divorce with Your Children* handbook, that Andi grew even more disgusted. "You know what? I wish you and Dad respected me enough to let me make my own decisions. What if I don't want to go to college in California? What if I don't want to go to college *at all*?"

Her mother started to interrupt, but Andi kept talking. "Sorry, Mom, but I'm not going to pretend that I'm fine with all this, because I'm not.

I'll see you when you get home, but until then, don't call me. I need some time to think."

Andi hung up and powered her phone off. She had nowhere to go. But she didn't want to stay here any longer, so she turned her key in the ignition and started to drive.

Roya

SATURDAY, FEBRUARY 13

ROYA CHECKED THE MAILBOX AS SHE AND NAVEED HEADED OUT for Cyrus's presentation. Usually they got nothing but junk mail—but today, the only envelope in the box was a letter from Kass.

Even though her fingers itched to open it right away, she tucked it into her coat pocket. Naveed was in his own world, as usual, and didn't notice.

They walked to the train station in silence. Roya thought about the herbal cider bubbling away in a jar inside her closet. She'd have to figure out a way to get it to Kass before it went bad. But how was she going to convince someone to take her back to Englewood? Though she'd been tempted to use the athame and the Book of Shadows to get her family to do what she wanted, she was afraid of messing up and making things worse somehow.

As it turned out, the answer was in the letter from Kass, which Roya read while they sat on the train.

Dear Roya,

How are you? I am okay. They let me work with the horses now. The other day I braided chestnut's mane and it looked really pretty but they made me brush it out again. I guess some things aren't meant to stay.

I'm writing because I have some bad news that you will probably want to share with your brother. I don't know what's gotten into Koffka, but when I was throwing a stick around with him in the woods the other day, something happened. He got upset, started growling, and then he attacked me. He bit my arm, not hard enough to break the skin, but it left a big bruise. They had to lock him up. I overheard Becky say they can't trust him with the patients anymore. It's really sad. I liked that dog a lot.

I have to go now, sorry this was so short. I miss you. Will you come visit me soon?

Love, Kass

The part about Koffka was weird, but Roya figured it wasn't true. That dog was so gentle—there was no way he'd hurt Kass. Roya understood exactly what Kass was really saying: the whole letter was basically a secret message, one Roya decoded with ease. *Show this to Naveed. It's your ticket to Englewood.*

"Naveed," Roya said. He was staring out the window and didn't answer. She said his name again, and when he still didn't respond, she nudged him in the shoulder. That got his attention. His eyes came into focus and he turned to her.

"I got a letter from Kass. She had some not-so-great news about Koffka." Roya tried to sound somber.

He looked very upset as he read the letter. Once he'd finished, he handed it back to her and took out his phone. "We have to do something."

Oh no—he was going to call them! "Wait." Roya thought fast. "I know what we need to do. We'll go up there, and I'll distract them while you find out where he is and break him out. It'll be a rescue mission!"

He shot her a skeptical glance. "No. They're reasonable people—let me talk to them. We'll work it out."

Roya sat back in her seat, her heart pounding rapidly while he searched for the number on his phone. She couldn't think of a way to stop him without being obvious, so she bit her tongue while he dialed.

"Hi, Becky?" he said into the phone. "It's Naveed Mirzapour."

Roya couldn't hear what Becky was saying, but her heart continued its frantic rhythm. Kass had come up with such a good way to lure him there, but now it would be ruined when he found out it was a lie.

"I'm fine, thanks. Just calling because—I heard about Koffka."

There it was. Roya waited for confusion to show on Naveed's face. But to her surprise, he added, "Kass wrote my sister a letter about it. So he can't stay at Englewood anymore? What are your, um, plans for him?"

Roya couldn't believe it. Koffka had really attacked Kass?

"Well, you know, I'd be interested…." he was saying. "Yes. I understand. I know that. But if he can't… I just thought…."

And then something changed. Naveed sat up straight and started speaking so loudly that several people sitting nearby glared at him in annoyance. "Really? Yes, definitely! I'll do whatever you need me to do, if there are waivers I need to sign, or more paperwork, or if there's a fee—let's make this happen. How late are you there today?"

A cautious hope grew inside Roya. Naveed hung up a minute later and burst into a grin. "I can't believe it," he said. "They said I might be able to adopt him! I can't… it's too… now I just have to find out a way to get there today. I don't want them to change their minds."

Roya hugged him. "Wow! That's amazing!" She decided not to remind him about how she'd desperately wanted a dog for her seventh birthday, but their parents had given lots of excuses about why she couldn't have one, including the fact that it was against Muslim tradition. At the time,

Baba wasn't even practicing, so that reason had stuck with her as being particularly unfair. Roya figured Baba would make an exception for Koffka, though he might not be so excited if he found out about the biting. "Can I come too?"

"Sure." It seemed like Naveed could barely sit still. Neither could Roya.

Soon enough, though, the next problem dawned on her: she hadn't come prepared. All through the train ride, the walk to campus, and Cyrus's presentation, she tried to think of excuses to go back home so she could collect the supplies she needed.

But that, too, worked itself out when Naveed asked Cyrus to borrow his car. Cyrus had gotten a ride to the competition, so his car was still parked at home. Perfect.

As soon as they got the keys from Cyrus, Naveed started walking towards the auditorium doors, but Roya stopped him. "We have to find out if Kourosh wins," she said. She expected him to, because his game was amazing, and wanted to see him accepting his prize. It was going to be the best day ever for all of them.

So they stood in the back, waiting for his name to be called with the winners. But it wasn't. Roya was mad about that and wanted to tell him that he deserved first place, but she'd have to do it later. Naveed was already opening the door to leave.

The train ride home seemed to take forever. When they finally walked up to the house, Naveed went straight for the car, but Roya said, "Wait! I have to go to the bathroom. And I'm hungry." So Naveed unlocked the front door for her and she ran upstairs.

She stuck a book of matches and two thin beeswax candles into the waistband of her leggings. Then she poured the herbal cider into a plastic baggie and pushed the air out of the top, sealing it up tight. She stuffed that in too. It looked too lumpy in the shirt she was wearing, so she changed into a dress that hid the top of her leggings better. She really hoped that they wouldn't pat her down, but they never had before. Why would they? They had no reason to believe she would smuggle anything in.

She grabbed a box of crackers from the kitchen before running out to the car. "What took you so long?" Naveed asked.

"Just finding something to eat," she said innocently.

When they ran into traffic on the freeway, he got really crabby. He snapped at her to stop eating so loudly, but it wasn't like crackers could be eaten any other way, so she closed the bag but still he found other things to be annoyed about. Like the person who left their blinker on but never changed lanes, and some political bumper sticker that someone had on their car. Roya tuned him out after a while and closed her eyes while the car lurched forward, stopped, lurched forward again.

Eventually the traffic cleared, and they made it to Englewood as darkness was beginning to fall. It had been clear all day, but the wind had picked up and clouds were rolling in. There were only thirty minutes left until visiting hours were over.

Roya made it through screening just fine. The front desk lady was talking to some parent who had come to visit, so she distractedly handed Naveed a bag where he put his phone and pocketknife. Then she gave them a quick wave with the metal detector wand and buzzed them through the door.

Roya rushed into the dining room, where Kass was sitting in her usual spot. But there was no way Roya could give Kass the supplies here. They needed to go somewhere private, away from the eyes of the nurses.

"Okay, Roya, you stay here," Naveed said. "I have to find Becky, but I'll be back in a minute."

Kass had just spotted her and was waving excitedly. "Wait," Roya said. "Can me and Kass come with you? I want to take a walk outside."

"Um, I guess. Let me check with a nurse to make sure it's okay."

Roya walked over to Kass. "Your letter worked!" she whispered when she got close enough. "But did Koffka really bite you?"

Kass pulled up her sleeve to reveal an ugly black-green bruise. "I tricked him. He was wrestling with a stick, so I just... replaced it with my arm."

"Wow," Roya said. "Did it hurt?"

"A little. But you're here now. So it was worth it."

"Yeah, it was—they're going to let my brother take Koffka home! He's so happy."

"Good. Koffka was sad without him. Those two were meant to be together." She leaned closer. "So. Did you bring anything?"

"Yes. But we can't do it here. I asked Naveed if we could go outside with him."

As if on cue, he appeared. "Hi, Kass. They said it's all right if you two want to come with me. I'm going to Becky's office, but you can play in the courtyard outside her window."

They followed him outside. The courtyard was better than the dining hall, but it still wasn't the best place for their ritual. Too many windows, too many people streaming through. There was a path off to the side that led to the woods, though. Maybe they could sneak away….

Naveed opened a door on the opposite side of the building. "Becky's office is right there. Stay close so we can keep an eye on you, okay?"

"Of course," Roya said. She and Kass sat on the edge of a raised garden bed while he went inside. Roya waved to him through the window. He waved back, then started talking to Becky.

"Come on," whispered Kass. "We can go to the barn. They usually close it up before dark, so no one should be there right now."

"Not yet," said Roya. "Let's walk around the courtyard for a minute. Pretend like you're showing me stuff."

Kass veered her over to a sage plant and plucked a few leaves off. "We'll need these for later," she muttered. "You should pick some too."

Roya stuffed a few sage leaves into her coat pocket, then followed Kass as they strolled through the garden beds. The wind blew stronger now, and it was getting darker: a storm was definitely coming in. Soon, they were the only people outside. Roya noticed Naveed glancing their way a few times, but then he seemed to get drawn deep into conversation with Becky and stopped looking out the window.

"Now," Roya said. They made their way casually onto the path leading to the woods.

"Come on. Let's go the back way." Kass stepped off the path into the thick trees around them. Roya thought it was a good idea to stay hidden, even though everything seemed deserted now that the weather was turning.

They made it to the barn as rain began to fall. Kass peeked inside the back door to make sure it was empty, then waved Roya in.

Kass led Roya to a far stall, where they crouched behind a stack of hay bales. Roya liked it in here. It smelled horsey, but also sawdusty, like Baba's workshop. Plus, it was warmer than outside, and the gentle whinnying of the two horses calmed her.

She wanted to ask which one was Chestnut, maybe see if she could feed them a treat, but there was no time for distractions. "What did you bring?" Kass asked.

Roya lifted her dress and pulled the baggie out first. "I made this herbal cider stuff with some apples I found in your root cellar. It smells kind of gross, but I followed the recipe." Mostly. She left out the fact that she didn't have all the right ingredients. Maybe part of the power was in Kass believing it would work.

"Herbal cider! That's great. I haven't had that in a long time. What else?"

Roya held up the beeswax candles. They were soft since they'd been pressed against her skin for so long. Next, she pulled out the matches.

"Perfect!" Kass exclaimed. "This is perfect, Roya."

"But I didn't bring any candle holders. All of ours are metal. So, I don't know, maybe we shouldn't light them?" Roya was starting to feel nervous about this.

"No, it's fine. I know what to do. But first, I'll need to charge them and purify the space. Can I have your sage?"

Roya took the leaves out of her pocket and Kass gathered them into a bundle. She lit a match and held it against the leaves until they started to catch, though they didn't burn very well because they were so fresh.

"Hold the candles over the smoke," Kass commanded. Roya did as she said. After the sage smoke faded, Kass sprinkled a few drops of cider onto the candles and massaged it into them.

Kass lit the candles and used one to cast a circle around them. Then she dripped two pools of hot wax on the barn floor and steadied the candles on top. They remained upright after the wax hardened. With the candles burning and the circle of protection around them, Roya relaxed. After all, Kass had grown up using candles all the time, and knew how to stay safe around fire.

They settled in facing each other. Kass stretched out her arms and chanted, "Hail, Hekate, Chthonia. Hail, Hekate, Enodia. Hail, Hekate, Astrodia. Mother of Mysteries, to you I turn. Traverse the threshold with me. Guide me with your torch as we venture into the dark."

Roya wished she could've brought the Hekate chalice to drink from, but Kass just opened the bag of herbal cider and tipped it straight into her mouth. "Ah," she said. "Tastes like home."

Roya wasn't planning to have any, but Kass suggested she try some, so she reluctantly took a sip. It tasted fermented, but still sweet. Like a stronger version of the kombucha tea Maman drank sometimes. It made her head feel funny, as if her brain were floating up into the sky. But not in a bad way.

She drank a few more sips and passed the bag back. Kass drained the rest. The candles glowed. They were so beautiful. Roya wasn't sure what she was supposed to be doing, so she closed her eyes and thought of Lopez. She pictured the bluffs where she and Kass had met. The place where this all began. She peeked at Kass, who was swaying a little, humming, as if she were going into a trance.

A moment later, Kass spoke. "Hekate," she said. "What did Father tell me on the bluffs?"

Roya listened carefully. No answer came.

"How does he expect me to remember?" Kass asked, louder now. "I was only five! Why didn't he just write it in his note?"

It was very quiet, except for the raindrops lashing the roof above. Roya didn't dare speak. She watched the flickering flame and thought about everything that tiny light contained. Thresholds. Gateways. Worlds within worlds. The horses stood guard inside their stalls, shaking their great manes. They looked so soft. She wanted to touch them.

Then Kass drew in her breath. "I saw him."

Roya startled at the sudden noise. "What? Here?"

"No. I found a memory. Not the one I was looking for, but... I remember. I saw him. Right before he died. He lost his hand in the 'accident,' and it was all bandaged up but it wouldn't stop bleeding. He kept telling Mother that we had to leave. He said Alastor had done it. She told me it wasn't true, that it was the fever talking. She made me go away. But before I did, do you know what he said to me?"

"What?"

"He said, 'Come outside, Katerina.'"

"Like in the book," Roya breathed.

"What was he trying to tell me?" Kass's voice was very small.

The answer had to be in the book somewhere. But before Roya could say this out loud, she heard a noise. A quiet *scritch-scritch-scritch*. As if someone were scraping the other side of the wall.

Kass's head snapped up. "He's here."

"What? Your father?" Roya's skin prickled.

"He wants me to come outside. Hekate will lead us to him. Let's go."

Kass pried one of the candles off the floor, hastily tracing an invisible doorway in their circle before hurrying outside. The back door slammed shut behind her. Roya wiggled the other candle off the floor, intending to follow. When she stood up, though, she got really dizzy and had to steady herself against the wall of haystacks. As she did, the candle tipped and hot wax spilled all over her hand.

"Ow!" She let go of the still-burning candle instinctively, before she even realized what she was doing. It fell from her fingers—and landed on a hay bale next to her.

Roya stared at it, bewildered. Already, the flame had caught, and a small section was smoldering. "No," she said. "No, no, no, no...."

She tried to blow it out, but that only made it worse. The dry hay soaked the fire up. She called for Kass, but Kass was gone, out in the woods following the light of Hekate's torch, chasing after the ghost of her father, and Roya was all alone.

By now the room was filling with smoke, and it made her eyes water and her lungs ache. She had to get out—and so did the horses. It was up to her to save them.

They neighed loudly, stamping in their stalls. Roya made her way to the closest one and lifted the latch. The horse stepped forward and Roya got out of its way, then opened the other stall door. She had to cough after that, the smoke hurt and she could taste it in her mouth and all she wanted was a clean breath of air, so she sank to the ground where it was clearer.

When she looked up, she realized that the horses were still inside. Of course they were. None of the outer doors were open.

Okay, so she just needed to open them, and they would all be free.

But the horses were panicked. They paced back and forth against one wall. Roya figured the front door must be there, but she could barely see it through the thick smoke and her streaming eyes. Knowing that they all needed to get out as fast as possible, she ran toward them.

Which turned out to be a mistake.

Her sudden movement only terrified them more. One of them reared up and charged.

Roya tried to get out of the way but she stumbled and fell, and the horse came down and there was a violent explosion inside her leg, which made no sense but nothing did anymore, there were flames inside her too now, the fire was inside and outside and everywhere.

A roaring sound filled up her ears. Smoke filled up her eyes. But she couldn't just lie here—she had to get out. She clawed at the ground, digging her fingernails in, and a scream escaped her mouth as she pulled herself closer to the door, it hurt that much just to move.

So close. The door was right there. She could almost touch it.

She dug in again, tried to pull herself forward, but this time the pain was unbearable, like she was dragging her leg across a floor made of hot knives, and now all she could hear was screaming, her own and the horses', they would all be trapped inside this burning barn until the end, unless she made it to the door.

The door. She just needed to open the door.

It was so close. Just there, beyond the smoke.

So close.

If only she could reach it.

Naveed

SATURDAY, FEBRUARY 13

NAVEED WAS A TOTAL MESS BY THE TIME HE SAT DOWN IN BECKY'S office at Englewood, but he was trying hard not to let it show.

For one thing, he hadn't heard from Andi all day. He wanted to give her the space she'd asked for, but also needed to talk to her about what had happened the night before. He was still turning it over in his head. That kiss, that astonishing kiss—but also the way she'd exploded at Jake. All the rage she'd been holding inside.

He'd always thought Andi could handle anything, so it had been shocking to see how viciously she'd lashed out at her dad. But some of that anger was actually Naveed's fault. Because he had hurt her, too. By not listening. By not seeing how miserable she truly was.

Cyrus's presentation had also unsettled him. He wasn't sure whether it was more disturbing that tech companies were perfectly willing to sacrifice the well-being of their users in order to make more money—or that everyone else was so complacent about it.

To top it all off, Maman had sent a bunch of photos from Farhad's wedding. Despite the conversation they'd had before she left, she looked like she belonged. And even though he knew it was irrational, he felt like Maman was rubbing it in. He had missed her intensely, especially while he was sick, but there she was smiling at him in photo after photo as if saying, *look how happy I am when I don't have to deal with you.*

The thought that he might be able to adopt Koffka was the only thing keeping him from losing it, though he was afraid to even hope that anything this good could happen to him. Something would probably go wrong. Like always.

Becky welcomed him in to her office. Outside, Roya and Kass wandered the courtyard.

"I know you're here about Koffka," Becky was saying, "But there's something I wanted to ask you first—I wanted to make sure that your parents' contact information is still the same." She handed him a printout showing their home address and phone numbers. "Are these correct? I've been trying to reach them about some billing questions, but haven't been able to get ahold of them."

"Oh—um, this all looks right," Naveed said. "Maybe I could help? If it's about my insurance, I have the card in my wallet, I can give you all the info—"

"No, no, this was regarding the out-of-pocket costs. Just have your parents contact me as soon as possible. We'll get it straightened out."

"Okay. I will." There had to be some mistake, Naveed figured. Maman had told him his stay was fully covered by their insurance, so there shouldn't have been any out-of-pocket costs aside from a minimal copay. She was usually the one who handled all of his medical stuff, but he didn't want to bother her about this while she was out of the country. Hopefully Baba could figure it out.

"Thank you." Becky set the printout down and turned her focus to Naveed. "So. Koffka. As I mentioned on the phone, the biting incident makes this more complicated. Adopting him out to a former patient... it's not... ideal."

Naveed felt like pacing—he had to get his nervous energy out. He bounced his heels, but that didn't diffuse it enough, so he wrung his hands together in his lap. He hoped she didn't notice. "I know. But like I said, I'm willing to do whatever it takes. If he needs more training, I'll make sure he gets it. If you need me to sign something that shows I know what happened and accept future liability, I'll sign it. I can't stand to think of him locked up. So please, *please* let me take him home."

"I understand where you're coming from," Becky said. "And... well... between you and me, I don't believe that this was an act of aggression so much as an accident. There weren't any witnesses, so we have to take Kasandra's word for it, but she's... given her history, I mean... we can't be sure what really happened. But we can't risk it happening again, of course, so he can't stay here. Still... I'm not sure this is the best solution...."

"I want to see him," Naveed said. "Where is he? Just let me see him for a minute. Please."

Becky seemed to sense that he wasn't going to back down, and probably didn't want him to freak out on her. She stood up. "All right. Follow me."

She led him to a back room, where Koffka was curled up on the floor of a small crate.

Naveed's breath caught in his throat. He could feel it in the air here: that dejection, that hopelessness he knew all too well.

Koffka lifted his head as they approached. When he recognized Naveed, his black mouth curved upwards. Naveed rushed forward to kneel in front of him, and Koffka licked his hand between the bars.

Get me out of here, Koffka said with his eyes.

"I will," Naveed promised, realizing too late that he'd whispered it aloud. He didn't care if Becky heard, though. He didn't care about anything but freeing Koffka from that cage.

They sat together in the dim room, Koffka nuzzling his head against the crate and Naveed petting him as best he could. After a few minutes, Becky said from the doorway, "All right. Let's go. I'll get the paperwork drawn up."

Naveed turned to her. "Really? He can come home with me?"

She nodded. "I honestly don't think he's likely to hurt anyone, and given the connection the two of you have, this seems like the best option. I'll put you in touch with someone who can do individualized service dog training, so that Koffka can learn specific ways to help you. But you can't take him through the patient areas. So let me get things ready, and we'll meet you in the front—it should take me about fifteen minutes."

"Oh, thank you! Thank you," Naveed found himself repeating. He could hardly believe his good luck. To Koffka, he said, "I'll see you in a few minutes, okay?"

The dog seemed to understand, and gave Naveed's hand a final lick. As they were walking back toward Becky's office, Max stepped into the hallway.

"Oh, hey Naveed. What're you doing here?" Max asked.

"They're letting me adopt Koffka!" Naveed blurted.

He half-expected Becky to interrupt, to say that he had misunderstood somehow, but all she said was, "See you in front. Fifteen minutes."

"Wow. Nice," Max said once she had left. "So Koffka's yours now, huh?"

"It's amazing. I still can't believe it." They walked toward the doors to the courtyard.

Oh shit—the courtyard. Naveed had forgotten all about Roya and Kass. The skies had opened up, and it was pouring now. Maybe they'd gone back to the dining hall? Naveed headed for the door.

"What are you doing? Let's stay where it's dry," Max said.

"No, I have to go check the dining hall. My sister was visiting with Kass. They were in the courtyard. I was supposed to be watching them."

"Wait, really? Your sister's hanging out with *her*?"

Naveed stopped. "What do you mean?"

"Have you ever talked to Kass? About why she's here?"

"No." Naveed stared at the dining hall windows, but it was pouring so hard that he couldn't see through them clearly.

"Yeah, well, she ended up in group with me," Max said. "Apparently she grew up in this 'retreat center' out on one of the San Juans... sounded more like a cult to me, though. I forget the name. Something to do with whales, I think?"

Naveed steadied himself against the wall. Orcinia. It had to be. Still, he could hardly believe it—Kass was from Orcinia? The place Alastor had come from, the place Viktor Zolotov's body had been found, the place Naveed could picture in his own mind, mounds of dirt and scraps of police tape, a wooden cabin, an open door, a deep dark hole—

But no, that last part wasn't real. He'd only imagined it.

Hadn't he?

"Anyway," Max was saying, "They got her out of there and sent her to live with a foster family. I don't know what her foster dad did to her, she never shared any details, but she told us how she got back at him—she was really proud of it. One day she built a fire while he was gone. In the living room. And then she *stepped into it*. I guess a neighbor saw the smoke and called 911, and when the firefighters found her she was standing there, real calm, in the middle of the fire."

Well, that was horrifying. But Naveed was still trying to piece all of this information together. Kass... and Orcinia... and Roya. How much of this did Roya know?

Only one way to find out.

Naveed pushed the door open. He didn't even feel the rain as he crossed the courtyard and burst into the dining hall.

No sign of Roya or Kass.

He thought about asking a nurse, but didn't want to admit that he had no idea where they were. He had to find them before someone else did, or the staff might decide he wasn't responsible enough to adopt Koffka.

Where would they go? He returned to the courtyard, where Max was huddled under an awning. "Not there?"

"No, will you please help me?" Naveed asked over the rain.

"Kass likes the woods." Max started toward the path. He and Naveed generally walked at a similar sluggish pace, but now they were practically running.

"Roya does too," Naveed panted. "It seems like she would have gone inside in this weather, though...."

He trailed off, because he didn't want to think it. There was only one building at the end of this trail.

The barn.

Naveed slowed down. It figured—of all the places to hide, they had to choose the barn. At least Max was here; he could go in and get them. Then, Naveed would demand answers on the way back and finally figure out what the hell was going on.

It seemed like a good plan—until he smelled something in the wind. Not the barnyard smell that had triggered panicky flashbacks before. Something even worse.

Smoke. Thick, acrid smoke.

He rounded the corner to see the burning barn. He didn't just see it, he *heard* it. Flames crackling. The horses braying in fear. Someone howling. A voice he knew very well.

Roya. She was inside.

His legs wobbled. He grabbed at the air, but there was nothing nearby to support him, and he came down on the muddy ground. He reached into his back pocket. His phone. He had to call for help.

But his phone was gone—he'd turned it in at the front desk.

Fuck.

"I'll go get someone." Max had turned back down the trail before Naveed could say a word.

There was that howl again. They were so far away from everything out here... how long would it take for a fire truck to arrive?

Too long. And his sister was inside.

He knew what he had to do, but knowing wasn't doing, and his body was frozen. He couldn't go into that barn. If he went in there now, he would die. That's just the way it was: he knew it with total certainty.

But if he didn't—then *she* would die. And if it was a choice between him and Roya, he knew who deserved to live.

He couldn't stand up, though. Couldn't move at all.

I'll just run in and get her, he thought to himself. *No problem. No problem at all.*

Nope. Didn't work—he still couldn't get up. So much for the power of positive thinking.

He closed his eyes, frustrated. His thoughts were the only things that moved, running through a perfect circle. *I can't go in there / I have to go in there / I can't go in there / I have to go in there.* Round and round and...

STOP.

He just needed to stop.

Focus on the breath. Just for a minute. Four in. Hold. Four out. Hold. Draw a box. Reset.

I am sitting up, he thought.

I am standing. Another breath.

I need to go meet Becky in front, he told himself as he got to his feet.

She's waiting with Koffka. Don't overthink it. Just keep moving.

I'm going to take him home. One step forward.

He can sit in the back seat with Roya. Another step.

She'll like that. Another.

Before he knew it, he was standing in front of the barn. But there was no time to feel triumphant for breaking through the paralysis of circular thoughts and panicky dread. Movement was all that mattered now.

He grabbed the metal handle of the barn door. It didn't budge at first, so he held on with both hands and put all his weight into it. The horses brayed on the other side, so loud, but he couldn't hear Roya anymore.

He kept heaving and pulling until the door came unstuck and rolled open. The horses burst outside, galloping away into the cool rain.

Naveed took a gulp of fresh air before stepping through the doorway. It was hard to see through the smoke and flames devouring the place, but there was no sign of Kass. Roya, though, was huddled on the ground just inside the door.

When he tried to gather her up, she let out a horrible scream. He froze: the agonized, animal voice didn't even sound like hers. That was when he noticed that her leggings were different colors: one side was sky blue and the other—

Blood red. And her leg—it was floppy and—bending in the wrong places—

Everything started to go dark. Naveed fought to stay conscious. He couldn't distract himself with breath now, better to hold it in than breathe the smoke, don't breathe, don't think, just *get out of here.*

He pictured Koffka in his mind. Sitting out in front with Becky, waiting to go home with him. Yes, that was where he needed to be. He stood up, cradling Roya in his arms, and staggered back through the open door.

An unexpected euphoria seized him as he stepped into the rain. It was so strange; fear had stalked him every day for many months, but in this moment at least, he was free from it.

Others were running up the trail, coming to help, but it was all going to be okay now. Naveed had gone into the barn, but he wasn't dead, and neither was Roya; they were both alive and water was falling from the sky and the air was clean, and everything—all of it, every last detail—was such an absolute miracle.

Cyrus

CYRUS LIFTED THE FORK TO HIS MOUTH. THE SLICE OF GERMAN chocolate cake looked delicious, but it was the first time in months that he'd eaten a food item prepared by strangers. Part of him worried that one of the workers at the café was secretly out to get him and had garnished his plate with a dash of poison.

Do you even hear how ridiculous you sound right now? he chastised himself, and shoveled the bite in. Rich chocolate, sweet coconut, toasted pecans… he was instantly in heaven. Not the one you had to be dead to get into, though. The one that existed on earth in the form of perfectly crafted baked goods.

He applauded himself silently, celebrating this small victory over irrational fears, before turning back to Dev's laptop. Their post-competition coffee date had turned into a work session, and they'd been hashing out the next *D&C* episode while Shea generated some stats about optimal video length.

Todd sat across from them, clicking around on his hacker laptop, following Tim Schmidt's meandering rabbit hole. Cyrus wanted to ask how it was going, but didn't want to break Todd's concentration.

As Cyrus was about to take another bite of cake, Todd tore off his headphones and looked up.

"What is it? Did you find something?" Cyrus asked.

"Uh, yeah. But prepare yourself. It's kinda disturbing." Todd turned his laptop around.

Cyrus studied the message board open on Todd's screen. There were photographs on it, grainy zoomed-in images of the same person over and over again, doing various mundane things: sitting inside a car, crossing the street, sipping a drink at a café. Nothing scandalous, but they still made Cyrus's heart lurch, because he recognized the face centered in the frame of each photo.

Andi.

Worse, *much* worse, were the comments below. Cyrus had grown accustomed to the bluster that followed Naveed around, but this was another level entirely. The posts were predatory, racist, graphic—just reading them made little pieces of his soul shrivel up and die.

With mounting dread, Cyrus realized he'd never seen Andi at GameCodeX. And she hadn't been with Naveed and Roya when they'd asked to borrow the car. So... where was she?

Cyrus texted her, then tried Naveed. Do u know where Andi is??? Pls text back asap this is very important!!!!!

As soon as the text whooshed off, Todd said, "So, um, Cy... I found Tim Schmidt. Sort of."

"You did?" Cyrus set his phone down.

"I started off with Englewood," said Todd. "Oddly enough, there was already a back door into their system. I think Schmidt might have opened it—maybe he used that meeting with your brother as cover so he could gain physical access. Anyway, I found some emails he sent to the staff. He spoofed a CDC email address, but it didn't take me long to get into his real account and find out about these message boards he created—like the one I showed you about Andi. There's one for Naveed, too. And Mahnaz—your mom, I mean. Don't feel left out, you have one too, but the others are a lot more... active."

Cyrus swallowed hard.

"He's not working alone, either. It looks like he's been paying a few people to feed him information."

"Like who? Did you find any names?" Cyrus asked.

"Just their message board handles." Todd read out a few that didn't mean anything to Cyrus, but the last screen name was familiar: fleshpuppet69.

"Oh shit, I know that one," Cyrus said. "He kept trolling our videos. I think he's met Naveed. It's possible he was an Englewood patient, actually."

"Hmm. That's concerning...." Todd trailed off.

Cyrus's phone buzzed with an incoming call, and everyone at the table literally jumped. But it was just Baba. Cyrus accepted the call. "Hello?"

"Hi, Kourosh." Baba's voice sounded strained. "Are you at home?"

"Uh, no. I'm at a café in the U-District. Is something wrong?"

"I just got a call from Englewood," Baba said slowly. "There was an accident. A fire. Naveed's okay, but Roya... they're taking her into surgery."

"Oh my God," Cyrus choked out. He was so confused. Why did Roya need surgery? What the hell were Naveed and Roya doing up at Englewood anyway? And a fire... how random was that?

Unless it wasn't random at all....

"I'm leaving work right now. Can you meet me up there?" Baba continued.

"Sure—oh, wait, no. Naveed borrowed my car. Can you come get me instead? I'll text you the address."

"Okay. Be there soon."

Cyrus hung up and shoved his phone into his coat pocket. His hands were shaking.

"Is everything all right?" Dev asked.

"It's my sister," Cyrus said. "An accident. A fire? She's going into surgery, I guess? I don't... I can't... my dad's picking me up. I have to go."

They all asked him a bunch of questions he couldn't answer. After texting his dad the address, Cyrus told them he'd send an update later and gathered up his stuff. He left his half-uneaten slice of cake on the table.

Baba arrived soon afterward and filled him in as they drove. Apparently Roya had been inside Englewood's barn when a fire started, and the horses trapped inside with her had trampled one of her legs. The doctors thought she would be all right as long as the surgery went well. So that explained about one-tenth of the things Cyrus was wondering about. The whole way there, as Baba muttered prayers in Arabic, Cyrus couldn't stop thinking about Tim Schmidt. Did he have anything to do with this?

Also—where was Andi? Still no answer from her, but he figured Naveed would probably know. Annoyingly, his brother still wasn't responding to any texts, so Cyrus would have to ask him once they finally arrived.

Traffic was terrible, and it took them over two hours to get all the way to the hospital where Roya was being treated. They entered the doors to the emergency department, but before they made it to the check-in desk, a woman with long silver hair stopped them.

"Dr. Young," Baba said.

"Sam." Her eyes were red-rimmed. "I am so, so sorry."

"How did it happen?" Baba's voice shook, betraying his anger. "She shouldn't have been in that barn in the first place. How did the fire start? Why was no one around to help her?"

Dr. Young looked supremely uncomfortable. "We found Kasandra—one of our patients—in the woods afterwards. She says it was her fault. The girls had snuck away during visiting hours, and Kasandra accidentally started the fire. She panicked and left, but got lost in the forest trying to find help."

"How did she manage to start a fire? I'm assuming your patients don't have access to matches."

"Of course not. We don't know how it began. All Kasandra will tell us is that she started it with her mind."

Baba let out an exasperated sigh. Because really, what was there to say to that?

"But Naveed found Roya. He—" Dr. Young shook her head. "We were never able to get him near that barn. But tonight, he ran inside. He saved her. He saved the horses. I don't think it can be overstated how big a step that was for him."

Leave it to a therapist, Cyrus thought, to be thinking about shit like that at a time like this. Dr. Young continued, "They've already discharged him. He burned his palms on the barn door, but didn't breathe much smoke. His labs and vitals look fine. Just to warn you, though, he was fairly agitated after the medics arrived, so they gave him some sedatives—"

Baba cut her off. "Where is he?"

"In the waiting room. With Koffka."

"Koffka?" Baba asked.

"The dog," Cyrus reminded him.

"That's right. I'm so glad the adoption worked out. Koffka will be a huge help for him while his hands heal." Dr. Young handed Baba a stack of papers, one of which was titled, "Service Dog Adoption Agreement."

Well, that was an interesting development. Naveed hadn't told them he was adopting Koffka—but at least it explained why he had gone to Englewood.

"I want you to know that we feel terrible about what happened," Dr. Young continued. "If there's anything we can do…."

"Excuse me," Baba said. "I'd like to go see my son now."

"Yes, of course." Dr. Young stepped aside, and they walked over to the waiting room.

Naveed was sitting in the corner. His eyes were closed, his hands bandaged, but other than that he looked all right. Smelled like a campfire, though.

Koffka sat at attention beside him. He regarded Baba and Cyrus curiously, as if doing some sort of robo-dog scan to make sure they were on the good side.

Cyrus held out his hand, letting Koffka sniff it for a second before giving him a tentative pat on the head. Koffka allowed it. Cyrus hoped that meant he had passed the test.

A nurse came over to Baba and asked to speak with him, so he followed her back to the registration desk. As soon as he was gone, Cyrus nudged Naveed. "Hey. You awake?"

Naveed cracked his eyes open and gave Cyrus a hazy smile. "Kourosh! What are you doing here?"

"Uh, I came to pick you up, obviously. You okay?"

"The fucking best!" He chuckled. "They gave me something. No idea what. But it is some good shit."

"That's great, I'm really glad you're all right, but I need to know— where's Andi?"

Naveed's smile instantly disappeared. "Andi. Do you know where she is?"

"That's what I just asked you. So… you haven't seen her? Or heard from her?"

"Been texting. Told her about Koffka. Because I promised. No surprises, no lemonade. But she hasn't answered. All day." He paused, closing his eyes again. "Do you know where she is?"

Okay, this was going nowhere. Cyrus stood up just as Baba reappeared.

"Kourosh, let's go," Baba said. "I'll bring you to Englewood to get your car. Then you can take Naveed home. I need to stay here, so I can be with Roya once she gets out of surgery."

Cyrus fished through Naveed's bag of belongings for the car keys, then they helped Naveed out to the car. As Baba drove them back to Englewood, he attempted to grill Naveed about what had happened in the barn and how Koffka's adoption had come about, which turned out to be futile since Naveed kept talking in nonsensical circles.

After a while, Cyrus stopped listening. He remembered the last time they'd been on this road, that day when they'd gone sledding and Roya had convinced them to make this detour. He really didn't want to picture his little sister unconscious in an operating room, so instead he tried to imagine her laughing as she spun down those snowy slopes. But then he could only think about how she wouldn't be able to do that again for a long time. And how the "friend" she'd gone to visit had abandoned her in a burning barn.

Once they made it to Englewood, he was surprised how relieved he was to see his own car again. It was dark in the parking lot, so he'd have to inspect it in the morning for new dings and scrapes, but it actually appeared that Naveed hadn't done any damage. Well, except that the back seat was covered in cracker crumbs. "Where did these come from?" he grumbled as he cleared space for Naveed and Koffka.

"Roya's snack," Naveed said. "Sorry. Want me to clean...?"

"Just get in." Cyrus's heart broke a little at the thought of Roya obliviously munching crackers. He closed the door behind Naveed and hugged Baba goodbye.

Baba handed him a paper bag. "Put some fresh aloe on his burns when you get home, okay? There are dressing changes in the bag. His inhaler's in there too, but they said that if he starts to have trouble breathing you should call 911 right away."

"I will. Hey, could you text me when Roya's out of surgery?" Cyrus asked.

"Of course. Don't worry, sounds like it's going fine," Baba said. "Text me when you get home."

Naveed curled up in the back, his arm draped over Koffka, who sat in the footwell resting his head on the seat. Cyrus hadn't had much time to let Koffka's presence sink in, but he really liked the idea of Naveed having a companion like that.

Cyrus was pulling away from the curb when Naveed said, "Kourosh... I have a bad feeling about Andi. Something's wrong. I can feel it."

Cyrus could feel something too, a change in his brother's energy from that heavily drugged mania to a focused anxiety. Worry was expanding inside Cyrus, too. It really was not like Andi to ghost them. "I'm sure she's fine," he said hollowly. "Let's just get home. She might be waiting for us there."

Naveed coughed, but didn't respond. Cyrus peeked in the mirror and saw him running his bandage-mittened hands along Koffka's back.

After a few minutes, Naveed said slowly, "I've been thinking about Dennis."

"Who the hell is Dennis?"

"He was at Englewood with me. He said things, he made... comments... about her and... I don't know. I'm probably being paranoid."

Oh crap. Dennis must be the patient Naveed had told Andi to stay away from, and was likely the troll also known as fleshpuppet69. Cyrus was just wondering if he should pass this information on to Todd when his phone buzzed. He glanced at the screen. It was a text from Andi.

He held out his phone to Naveed. "She just texted. What does it say? My passcode—"

Naveed pulled himself into a seated position in the back. "I can't— damn bandages—"

"Sorry. Forgot." Cyrus pulled onto the shoulder and put the car in park. He opened his phone, and his stomach dropped when he saw her message. It was a single word.

Help

"Shit," Cyrus muttered. He started writing, Where r u? but hadn't yet sent it when another cryptic message came through.

I cracked I'm up north side of road to coffee dinner by e

"She... cracked? What does that mean?"

Naveed was reading over his shoulder. "I have no idea."

Cyrus read it again, but the message was a word salad that made no sense. He wrote back, Where? I don't understand

They waited, but nothing came through. No blinking dots. Nothing at all.

He wrote another text. We'll be there as soon as we can but where r u?

WHAT IS COFFEE DINNER???

Can u share ur location w me?

Still nothing.

Andi are u ok??????? he wrote.

Send location

Please we're worried

While he waited, Cyrus's thoughts pinged all over the place. He couldn't just sit there and do nothing, so he pulled up his contacts and dialed Todd.

"Hey. What's going on?" Todd asked when he picked up. "Your sister okay?"

"I think she'll be all right, but something's up with Andi. Can you do me a favor and look into someone for me? His name is Dennis...."

"I don't know his last name," Naveed said from the back.

"I think he's fleshpuppet69," Cyrus told Todd. "And he was a patient at Englewood. Does that give you enough to go on?"

"Possibly. I'll check it out."

"Thanks. Find anything else yet?"

"Not yet. Still digging. I'll message anything important, so keep your phone nearby."

"Thanks, Todd. You're the best."

As soon as Cyrus hung up, Naveed said, "We need to go. It's going to take forever to get back to Seattle."

"Just a sec. Let me look at that text again." He pulled it up and read it out loud. "'I cracked.' Okay, maybe that was autocorrect. 'I'm up north side of road. To coffee dinner by e.' Who's 'E,' and why are they making a coffee dinner?"

"She still hasn't texted back. Something must be really wrong. We have to hurry."

"I know!" Cyrus snapped. "I'm trying to figure this out. Do you have any insights? You know her better than I do...."

He trailed off. The text had been sent only to Cyrus. Why not Naveed?

Cyrus rifled around in the bag of Naveed's belongings until he found his brother's phone. Maybe she had texted him separately? Or maybe they were sharing locations with each other and he could track her down that way?

"What's your passcode?" he asked Naveed, who recited it for him. But Cyrus didn't find any helpful text notifications or location clues when he opened the phone. He scrolled up through Naveed's previous messages to Andi, looking for any hints to where she might have gone, but didn't make it very far. The text string went on forever. They texted each other all the time, obviously, which made it seem even more strange that she had reached out to Cyrus, not Naveed, for help.

But what if....

What if she had sent that text to Cyrus because she knew he was the only one who would understand the message?

"Holy shit," he said, as pieces fell into place. *Up north. Side of road to coffee dinner by e.* That bit must have been autocorrect—she meant diner, and "e" had to be Englewood. She was on the side of the road leading to the diner where the two of them had coffee the day they went sledding.

"I know where to go," he told Naveed. "It's close. I have no idea what she's doing up here, but—let's just find her." Cyrus found the diner on the map and had his phone navigate them there.

Within ten minutes, they were approaching the diner. Cyrus scanned the road for her, but it was deserted. There was nothing here, nothing but woods all around.

"What's that?" Naveed asked suddenly.

"What's what?"

"Stop! I saw something back there."

Cyrus pulled onto the narrow shoulder. He hadn't seen anything—but, he now noticed, the opposite side of the road had no shoulder at all. It plunged into a deep ditch.

"I'll go look—you stay here," he said. "I'll be back in a minute, all right?"

Cyrus grabbed his phone before stepping out of the car and locking the doors. It wasn't until he crossed the road that he saw it, the gleam of metal winking at him from the bottom of the ditch.

No. There was Andi's car, her mom's car, whatever—the front end wrapped around a tree trunk. *Crashed,* he realized with horror. Not *cracked.* Crashed.

Cyrus was dialing 911 before he even got down there, answering the dispatcher's answers in a daze because he was so frantic to get to Andi. He couldn't see anything through the broken windshield and the still-inflated airbags inside, so he threw open the driver's side door as the dispatcher asked if anyone was hurt.

Andi was not inside. But there were bloodstains on the fabric seat.

"Yes," he told the dispatcher. "Someone's hurt, and you need to send help *right now.*"

He had just hung up when he heard the scream coming from deep in the woods.

Andi

SATURDAY, FEBRUARY 13

ANDI HAD NO IDEA WHERE SHE WAS GOING. THE FREEWAY stretched endlessly in front of her, leading everywhere yet nowhere.

She kind of wanted to talk to someone. If Brooke were here, Andi would have gone straight to her house and told her everything—but Brooke had left, and it was probably better to spare her the drama. Naveed wasn't an option either. She was far too ashamed of her drunken behavior to face him right now. She wondered if he'd filled Cyrus in on all the gory details. The thought made her want to puke.

The rhythm of the freeway calmed her, though. Since she didn't want to turn on her phone, she made her own music by singing to herself. It felt a little crazy at first, but it wasn't like anyone was watching, and soon she was screaming out the angriest songs she could think of, bobbing her head to the chords playing only in her mind.

She was driving nowhere in particular, heading north on pure autopilot, when the sun hit the windshield wrong and she saw it again. The blood.

The dead crow. All of the crows, the roof, Dr. Snyder in her white lab coat coming closer—

The road was fading away. Andi turned on the AC, and the cold air blowing on her face helped bring her back—just in time for her to realize that she had started drifting into the left lane.

She snapped back to attention and checked her blind spot. No one there.

Still shaking from the near miss, she merged to the right and took the next exit. It wasn't until after she'd pulled into a parking lot and let exhaustion roll over her that she noticed everything looked familiar: this was the exit she'd always taken to get to Englewood.

Maybe her subconscious was trying to tell her something. *You need help.*

She probably did. Maybe she should go to Englewood. It could be just what she needed... like a retreat, a place to get away from messed-up parents and overwhelming school and a confusing relationship that was starting to feel like a prison.

Once she had collected herself, she drove the rest of the way there. But the parking lot was nearly full. Of course: visiting hours. She had forgotten it was a Saturday afternoon.

She pulled into a parking space, but couldn't work up the nerve to get out of the car. What was she going to do, march inside and tell them she needed to be admitted? This was a place for people with real problems and serious psychiatric diagnoses. For people like Naveed, with his many mental and physical health issues, and Max, who'd tried to blow his own head off. Not for someone who was a little freaked out over a dead crow.

The more she thought about it, the stupider she felt for coming here. She didn't necessarily want to be admitted anyway... it was just... she wanted someone to listen. But she wouldn't find that here. This place wasn't a walk-in clinic.

Still, she was nervous about driving anywhere else. It had been a while since she'd eaten—she hadn't had anything since the morning croissant, but it was almost 4 p.m. now. That was probably why she'd had that little episode in the car. She just needed food, that was all.

After digging through her backpack and finding no stale energy bars lurking in its depths, she decided to go back to that diner where she and Cyrus had coffee before heading out to the snow. She drove there carefully, and once seated ordered a chicken sandwich with fries.

She debated turning on her phone, but ended up leaving it off. She didn't want to hear her parents' voicemails or read any of their texts. Not yet. Let them worry.

The dilapidated copy of *The Grapes of Wrath* that she'd been reading for English was still in her backpack, so she hid behind it as she ate. The food was greasy and sat heavily in her stomach, and she ate it slowly enough that the fries eventually grew cold and inedible. But she didn't want to leave. Especially when a torrential downpour started around five, and not long afterward, a caravan of emergency vehicles screamed by. The sustained wail made Andi's head hurt. She felt like she could see the flashing lights long after they'd passed by the windows.

While everyone else was distracted, wondering what was going on—she got the impression that such things were far less commonplace here than in her south Seattle neighborhood—Andi searched through her backpack for her bottle of painkillers. She'd held out all day, but the sound of wailing sirens... it kept shaking unpleasant memories loose inside her head.

Before she found her own painkillers, though, her fingers closed around the bottle of Oxy she'd taken from her dad. Hazy images from the night before tried to push their way back, but she was so tired of thinking; she just wanted it all to go away. She shook one pill into her palm and swallowed it with a gulp of water.

It didn't take long for her to feel different. Better. Things didn't seem so dire anymore; she was filled with a comfortable warmth. She got the server's attention and ordered two slices of pie. One apple, one cherry. No ice cream, thank you.

The server looked confused, or maybe surprised, but Andi didn't care. She leaned back with her book. She didn't know where she would go next, but right now she didn't care. It felt good just to be here, eating as much pie as she wanted.

She sampled one slice, then the other. If it weren't for the cinnamon, they would have tasted almost identical, but it didn't matter. The restaurant got louder as more people came in, then quieter as they all left after the dinner rush. She kept drinking coffee and water, kept ordering whatever random food suited her fancy—garlic bread, a side of fruit salad, a warm chocolate-chip cookie. Kept staring at her book, turning pages occasionally, letting her mind wander through the blissful haze.

But it couldn't go on forever. After a few hours the pleasantness started wearing off, leaving her feeling worse than before. Her stomach churned from the vast amounts of food she'd shoved into it, and she rushed to the bathroom to throw up. When she returned to her booth, one of the servers asked impatiently if she was ready for her check. She glanced at the clock—it was already after eight.

So she paid for her food and slothed her way out to the car, grateful that the rain had stopped. It was time to suck it up and make her way back to the Mirzapours'. If that went okay, maybe she'd work up the nerve to face her father tomorrow. Maybe.

Andi was about to start the car when she heard movement behind her. She watched in the rearview mirror as a shadowy figure rose from the back seat.

"Drive," said a deep voice. Something cold touched the base of her neck. She didn't have to look in the mirror to know it was a gun.

She wasn't scared, that was the weird thing. It felt kind of inevitable: she hadn't checked the back before getting in, so of course something horrible would happen.

Andi started the car and put it in reverse, trying to catch a glimpse of her captor's face as she backed up, but he was wearing a ski mask and she couldn't tell who he was, or if she even knew him. The pepper spray on her keychain tapped against the dashboard as the car moved, useless now.

She pulled out of the diner parking lot, hoping she'd be able to catch the attention of any passers-by, but no one was around. Numbly, she started along the country road that led back to the highway. *Well, this is stupid,* she thought. *Worst possible place to get hijacked. The middle of nowhere.* The barrel of the gun was warming up, now, from the heat of her skin. She replayed all those self-defense videos in her mind, but she hadn't practiced the moves properly, except on Naveed that one time—yesterday, actually, that had been only yesterday. Too bad she hadn't reacted the right way when it really mattered. Now, she might never see him again.

The thought jolted her into alertness. Even if her dulled reactions had gotten her into this mess, that didn't mean she couldn't find a way out of it. She'd been through worse. Right?

The road was dark. Wet from the earlier rainstorm. Andi pressed harder on the gas and cleared her throat. "Who are you?"

"You know who I am." He pulled off the mask and grinned terribly at her in the rearview mirror. She could just make out the dimples in his cheeks.

What? The person holding a gun to her head was *Dimples*?

As Jed ruffled his hair back into place, the gun briefly lost contact with her neck, pointing towards the windshield instead. *Now,* she thought, and jerked the steering wheel forcefully to the right.

The Sentra careened across the asphalt, and everything was spinning and somehow she was falling and then there was a tree, where had that tree come from, and she tried to slam on the brakes but there was no stopping it and then came a bone-rattling impact and a very loud noise and then—

Then, nothing.

Andi raised her head, groggy. The air smelled wrong—like motor oil and singed wire—and her face was numb. *Oh,* she realized. *Oh. I did it. I crashed the car.*

She moved her limbs. They all worked, though her feet felt cramped, like she'd moved the seat way too far forward. The rest of the car slowly came into focus, the ruined windshield, the inflated airbag, the backpack upside-down in the passenger footwell.

The gun. Where was the gun? She tried to turn around, but she couldn't quite force her body to bend the way she wanted. She could see Jed, though, sprawled out in the back. Dead, she dared to hope for a minute, until he moaned quietly.

She shuddered as she reached in her pocket for her phone, because the action really hurt for some reason. While it powered up, she tried to swivel in order to check for the gun under the seat, but sharp pain exploded through her abs and she had to stop. How was she going to get away from Jed? She wasn't sure she'd even be able to stand up.

Andi stared at her phone's screen, waiting for it to warm up, and noticed that her hand was bleeding. The cut looked minor, thankfully. She wiped it on the seat as her phone came to life, emitting a buzz and displaying notifications of the many calls and texts she had missed.

In the back seat, Jed stirred. She froze, but he didn't get up. Dialing 911 would be too loud; she couldn't talk in here without him waking up and probably shooting her, but maybe she could text someone else to send help. Who, though?

Cyrus, she decided. He knew where the diner was. She sent a quick plea, Help, and was trying to explain where she was when Jed moaned again. Then she realized she could send Cyrus her location—but before she had a chance, she heard Jed sitting up.

No time to finish. She sent what she'd written just as Jed knocked the phone out of her hand. It slid into the passenger footwell with her backpack, out of reach.

"I don't think so." Jed looked furious and—as far as she could tell—mostly uninjured, though his eyes were unfocused and blood trickled lazily down the side of his head. "Nice try, but you're not getting rid of me so easy this time."

He felt around under the seat and found his gun, holding it up to her temple. She almost wanted to laugh, it was all so ridiculously awful. Part of her expected him to pull the trigger and end this right now, but deep down she knew he wouldn't. Not until he got what he wanted from her.

She did not want to know what that was.

"Come with me," he said. "Too cramped in here. Let's go into the woods. Quietly, unless you want a bullet in your brain."

That wasn't exactly an appealing option, so Andi found herself following him. It would be too hard to fight back against him in the car, anyway. Easier for her to get away if she had more room, more places to hide.

But once she was out, she found it hard to straighten up. So dizzy. And her stomach hurt so badly she wanted to stay doubled over. He pulled her up. She recoiled from his touch, but stopped resisting when he nuzzled the gun into her neck.

They didn't walk too far into the woods before he let go and she sank to the ground. She curled up on her right side, because a sharp ache had started stabbing her left shoulder. She didn't bother hiding her pain; it would be better to appear weak. That would make it more surprising when she saved up enough strength to fight back. Which she would. She would.

Jed crouched beside her, settling his free hand on her aching shoulder. She would have punched him if she hadn't known how badly it would hurt to do it—and how much he would make her pay.

"You. Fucking. Bitch," he said, tightening his grip with each word. "You lied to me, *Sasha*. You made a fool out of me that night at the club." He forced her onto her back. She cried out, and he covered her mouth. "Making me think you were into it, then abandoning me right when it was starting to get good. Laughing at me. Humiliating me in front of everyone. I couldn't let you get away with that. Especially when I found out why you looked so familiar, after that fat-ass friend of yours called you by your real name."

"Wait," Andi tried to say, but it came out muffled. He pressed harder. Her lips were growing numb.

"I didn't know you were one of those social justice warriors." His mocking tone caught her right in the gut. "But that's the beauty of the internet, isn't it? I found out everything I needed to know about you online. And I found like-minded people who hate you just as much as I do. Powerful people. People with the resources to make things happen. People who knew things about you, so that I could make sure that everything I did *really* hurt."

Richard Caring, Andi thought. But she said, "It was you?"

His hand was still over her mouth. He relaxed it slightly, and she said, "You broke into my car."

"That was me. I put a tracking device on it, too. Which came in handy today. But I was getting pretty tired of waiting for you to come out of that diner. What were you doing in there for so long?"

He'd been following her all this time? Andi's insides squirmed. "Wait, the crows... what about the crows? Was that you, too?"

"Oh, that was a favor. For someone who wants you to remember. Not an easy thing to pull off, but definitely worth it to see your reaction."

"Who?" Andi's voice rose. "A favor for who?"

He shifted, and for a second she thought he was going to stand up. But then he repositioned the gun against her jaw and straddled her, pinning both arms underneath his legs. His weight against the pain in her belly made her see stars, but she bit her tongue to keep from crying out. She wished she could kick him—but the angle was all wrong. A kick would be futile. If only she'd thought to grab her keys from the car, she could use her pepper spray... but of course she'd forgotten about that, too, when it really mattered.

"Tell me! Who was it? Richard Caring?" Andi said, frantic, because he was running one of his fingers along the waistband of her jeans, the same way he had that night in the club. Brooke had rescued her then, but her friend was hundreds of miles away now. No one knew where Andi was.

She hadn't given Cyrus nearly enough to go on. She had to find a way out on her own, but there was something really wrong inside her, a crushing pain causing all her thoughts to break into useless shards.

Jed didn't answer her question. "Enough. Foreplay's over. Now we finish this."

Andi felt a chill as he pulled her shirt up, and his cold hand found its way under her bra. His fingers fondled the sensitive skin of her nipple. She closed her eyes so that she didn't have to look at his face. He still had her pinned with his legs, and the pain shooting through her whole body made it impossible to twist free. "I'm sorry," she said, desperate to stop this. "I wasn't laughing at *you*. I was having a bad night... and it just... started coming out...."

She thought she heard something in the woods. Her name. But that couldn't be. No one was here. No one knew where she was.

"Stop talking," Jed commanded. He took his free hand off her breast, but there wasn't even a moment to feel relief, because then he was unbuttoning her jeans, unzipping her zipper, unbuckling his belt.

Andi was sure she heard rustling now. *Even if he kills me*, she thought, *at least I tried*. She drew in a breath and screamed louder than she ever had in her life.

Naveed

NAVEED AND KOFFKA WATCHED THROUGH THE CAR WINDOW as Cyrus sprinted across the road. They watched him stop. They watched him take out his phone and race down into the ditch.

Staying in the car was not an option—Naveed had to know what was going on. He still felt sluggish and groggy, thanks to all those drugs they'd pumped him with in the ER, but he'd have to push through. Finding Andi was the only thing that mattered now.

He pulled at his bandages with his teeth until they loosened and he could unwind them. His fingers and palms were red and blistered, but not oozing. Koffka sniffed at the wounds, whimpering.

"Don't worry," Naveed assured the dog. "It'll be fine. I'll wrap them up again when this is over."

He turned on the dome light and searched the front seat until he found the plastic bag Iris had given him at Englewood. The one with his knife inside. He cursed its design as his clumsy fingers laboriously pried open the sharp blade. Then he opened the car door.

Naveed could hear Cyrus's voice—he was on the phone with 911, from the sound of it.

With Koffka's help, he stumbled across the road, his heart thumping a frenzied beat. It thumped even faster when he saw the Sentra crumpled in the ditch, and faster still when the terrified scream echoed through the woods.

Cyrus was heading towards the forest, calling Andi's name. He turned when Naveed slid down the steep slope. "I told you to stay in the car," he hissed.

Naveed ignored that. He and Koffka crossed the ditch and climbed up after Cyrus. When Naveed got to his feet, still gripping the knife, he said, "Where is she?"

They listened. Rustling leaves, hushed voices. Not far away.

Naveed wanted to follow the sound, but it was so dark in the forest. He'd never be able to make it through this thick brush without some light to help him see his feet. "Turn on your phone flashlight," he whispered to Cyrus.

"Bad idea. We should wait till help gets here."

"By then, it'll be too late." Naveed stepped forward, holding onto Koffka's harness with his left hand and the knife with his right. Light or no light, he needed to find her. Right now.

Cyrus sighed audibly. Seconds later, light flooded the forest around them. Naveed pushed through the underbrush without looking back.

"Who's there?" an unfamiliar voice called out.

Naveed moved closer as Cyrus swept his flashlight into a nearby clearing. It took him a moment to process what he was seeing. Someone was on top—on top of Andi, holding her down, a gun in one hand while the other fumbled with his belt—

Koffka was barking furiously now. The man pointed his gun in the dog's direction. Before Naveed could react, though, the man suddenly fell forward and the gun dropped from his hand.

Andi was sitting up—she must have twisted out from underneath and knocked him over somehow. The man cursed loudly as he turned to face her. Which gave Naveed the opportunity to slam into him from behind and pin him to the ground.

Naveed dug his knee into the man's back, forcing him to remain face-down on the pine needles. Out of the corner of his eye, he saw Andi struggling to button her jeans. She looked like she was about to fall over. Cyrus helped steady her, then retrieved the gun from the ground.

Rage flooded Naveed. He grabbed the man's shaggy dark hair and bashed his face against the forest floor. "Who the fuck are you?"

The man didn't answer. Naveed held the knife against the man's throat. "I said, *who the fuck are you?*"

Still no reply. As the man struggled to get up, his hair fell away from his face. On the right side of his head, beneath his hair, a gash was leaking blood.

Naveed averted his eyes quickly. The world was trying to fade out. All he could hear was radio static. *Stay here,* he demanded himself. *Stay, stay, stay.* He repeated it with each breath; he watched the man's stubbly throat, the knife pressed into his skin, the pulse throbbing beneath. The static faded. "Did someone send you here?" Naveed asked wildly. "Tim Schmidt?"

The man chuckled. It was a horrible sound. "Tim didn't send me. Oh, he has big plans, *big* plans, but this doesn't have anything to do with him. I'm here for Andi. She owes me. It was time for her to pay up."

"What are you talking about?" Naveed pressed the flat side of the knife, hard, against the man's neck.

"Stop." Andi's voice was all wrong. Ragged and hoarse. "Don't, Naveed. Don't do it."

Naveed wanted to, though. He wanted justice. This man didn't deserve life, and Naveed wanted to be the one to take it away.

But—he also wanted to listen to Andi. Because she deserved to be heard.

He hesitated. Sirens blared in the distance. Then, out of nowhere, an abrupt burst of pain between his shoulder blades knocked him off balance. He fell to the ground, but couldn't move because Cyrus was holding him down—

The man was getting up—

He was running away—

Then the quiet woods shook with a sudden explosion of sound.

The sharp blast of gunfire.

Panic built in Naveed's chest as he looked back towards Andi. But she stood in the shadows behind him, the gun extended in her hands.

The forest was still once more. The man was no longer moving. All Naveed could see when Cyrus swept his flashlight through the trees was a dark heap on the forest floor.

Andi wobbled. Cyrus sprang up to catch her. He took the gun from her hands as she fell against him.

Koffka was barking again, and Naveed could hear movement in the woods, other people, police maybe. But all he wanted to do was hold Andi. He crawled over to where Cyrus had lowered her.

"Sorry about that," Cyrus said to Naveed. "But I was afraid you were going to... and the police are coming... and no offense but you look, um, well, I didn't want the cops to think you were the crazy one and shoot you or something but holy shit, I had no idea Andi was going to do that."

Naveed barely heard him. He scooted closer to Andi and took her into his arms.

"I'll go talk to them," Cyrus said, indicating the cops and paramedics who were making their way into the woods.

Once he'd left, Naveed brushed Andi's bangs aside. "Oh, Andi—thank God you're okay." He was about to kiss her forehead when she pulled back.

"Don't," she said. "Just—don't do that, please. Not right now." She closed her eyes. "Did I kill him? Is he dead?"

Naveed could no longer see the huddled body on the ground. The paramedics were blocking his view. "I don't know."

"I hope he is." She nuzzled her head against his shoulder. "How did you get here so fast? And why do you smell like camping?"

"Did you get any of my texts?" he asked. She shook her head, so he added, "We were at Englewood to get Koffka. They let me adopt him. And then—well, never mind, it's a long story, I'll tell you later."

"I'm glad Koffka's yours." She reached out to stroke the dog, who had come to sit next to them. But she quickly pulled her hand away, moaning softly as she pressed it to her stomach.

"Do you need something?" he asked. "Did he hurt you?"

"The crash," she said. "I think... there's something wrong inside. He made it worse."

"I'll go tell the medics," Naveed said, though now that the adrenaline was wearing off, an intense fatigue was descending on him, and he didn't want to go anywhere. So he was glad when she said, "Wait."

"What is it? What do you need?"

"I don't want you to come with me," she said.

He had no intention of leaving her, so it hurt to hear that. But she went on, "I want you to go home. Come see me tomorrow. I need the doctors to figure out what's wrong and make the pain stop. I need to talk to a counselor. I need the police to tell me that he's dead, because I don't want to see him ever again, and I need to tell them exactly what happened so that you don't get in trouble." She paused. "That's all."

"Okay," he said. One of the medics was walking over now. "Andi. I love you."

"Even if I'm broken?" she whispered.

"You're perfection," he said. "Exactly as you are. And I love you no matter what. Always."

The medic arrived and started asking Andi questions. Naveed wanted to say more, to find the right combination of words that would convey how much she meant to him, but something so deep and wide and infinite was impossible to explain. Right now, it was enough just to be here in the midnight forest, holding her as long as he could.

Andi

SUNDAY, FEBRUARY 14

ANDI HAD TO WAIT IN THE WOODS FOR WHAT SEEMED LIKE A long time. They had taken Jed first, so she was stuck there answering the police's questions. She fully owned up to the fact that she had shot Jed. "It was self-defense," Cyrus kept saying, nervously and unnecessarily. Of course it was—but Andi couldn't deny that it felt perversely good to be the one who had taken him down in the end.

By the time the ambulance came and whisked her away, she was completely spent. The police were starting to ask Naveed questions by then, but he told them he was exercising his right to remain silent and refused to say another word. Andi worried they'd think he had something to hide, so when Cyrus tried to follow her out to the ambulance, she told him to stay with his brother. "Don't leave him alone with them," she said.

He nodded. "Don't worry about us, A. We'll come see you as soon as we can."

"Tomorrow," Andi said. "Come see me tomorrow."

At the hospital, she was about to rate her pain in the "moderate" category, but ended up choosing "severe." Because emotional agony counted as pain, too. She made sure they knew she didn't want to see her dad until she'd talked to a counselor, because part of her wanted him there and part of her didn't and she couldn't possibly explain any of that to him while everything was such a confused jumble. But as soon as the narcotics hit her system, bringing their sweet comfort, she relaxed into them and fell asleep.

It was a dim, superficial sleep, because they were examining her and taking scans and people kept saying the word "spleen," which she found hilarious because it was such a funny word, but it hurt to laugh because—as she finally put together—she had a ruptured spleen. They had to give her a transfusion because she had bled so much internally, but they thought it would heal without surgery. Still, she would need to stay for a few days while they monitored it. They also suspected that she'd suffered another minor concussion, which wasn't great given her history, so they would need to watch that too.

At some point a counselor came in, and everything poured out of Andi in a flood. When she finished, she added, "I'm not usually like this, I swear. It was just a bad day, everybody has bad days, some people have way worse days than that all the time. And it's not like Jed even, you know, went all the way. It could've been a lot worse. I don't know why it's getting to me so much."

To which the counselor said, "Andi, you've been under a tremendous amount of stress, and what happened to you was incredibly traumatic. Even if Jed didn't go 'all the way,' he still stalked, abducted, and sexually assaulted you. It counts, okay? So don't tell yourself that your own feelings aren't as important as someone else's—they matter. *You* matter."

Those words just burst her open. The counselor held her hand as she cried, but it wasn't enough. "I want to see my dad," she said through her sobs.

He was waiting outside. Respecting the boundaries she'd set, even though he probably hadn't wanted to. When he entered the room, he didn't look drunk or high or hungover, so she let him hug her and cried into him, and he kept saying how sorry he was, that she was right, that he'd fucked up and fallen into old habits because he didn't know how to cope any other way, and he was so ashamed that he tried to hide it, which of course only made things worse, and he was going to get help so he could be the father that she deserved.

Even though she had no idea if he'd actually follow through, she appreciated his apology. She hugged him back, too tired and overwhelmed to say anything out loud, but hoping the gesture communicated, *Thanks for saying that. Now show me that you mean it.*

After he left, she crashed straight into sleep. This time, it felt endless, stretching longer and thicker and deeper, going on for what felt like many days.

When she finally opened her eyes, someone was sitting next to her holding her hand. She blinked. Was it really…?

"Good morning, bǎo bèi," her mother said, smiling.

"You're here? What day is it?" Andi asked groggily.

"It's Sunday. I flew up first thing this morning."

"Where's Dad?"

"He's taking care of some things at home. Oh, Andi, I'm so glad you're okay."

Details from the night before returned with fresh clarity. Andi suddenly felt very awake. "Mom, I'm sorry, your car—wait, what about your car? Did anybody get my backpack? My computer was in there, my keyboard… and did they find my phone? He took it from me—" Thinking of Jed made her want to vomit. "I hope it didn't break."

"Your father found it all in the car," her mother said. "The Sentra was totaled, but don't worry about that. Your phone's fine; he's charging it at home. He'll bring it later."

Andi felt horrible about wrecking her mom's car, but there was something else she needed to know. "Jed." Her voice shook just saying his name. "The... the guy who... attacked me. Is he dead?"

Her mother pressed her lips tight together. "No. He's still hanging on."

"So... do they think he's going to live?"

"He has a serious brain injury. They don't know the prognosis yet."

"Good. I hope he—"

"Whatever happens, you're going to be all right," her mother interrupted. "But I don't want you talking to the police anymore. Not unless our lawyer's there," she added.

"Why not?"

Her mother didn't respond, and the reason slowly dawned on Andi. If Jed didn't survive, this could become a murder investigation.

Oh. That wasn't good.

"It's just a precaution, bǎo bèi," her mother said. "I don't want you to worry about anything."

But Andi had started to feel squirmy. The clock on her wall said it was already one o'clock. Naveed and Cyrus were supposed to visit today. Where were they?

She was about to ask about them when her mother continued, "I am so sorry. I should have been more honest with you. I should have been here. Maybe then... maybe then it wouldn't have gone this far."

It had gone pretty far, Andi thought. You knew you'd stooped low when checking yourself into a mental institution actually sounded appealing.

"Don't worry about it, Mom," Andi mumbled. She searched her bed for that little button they'd given her, the one that would deliver a sweet blissful dose of morphine straight to her veins. But it wasn't there.

"Where's my..." What had they called it? Oh, yeah. "My PCA?"

"You don't need it anymore," her mother said curtly. "Do you want me to call a nurse?"

The nurse came and gave Andi something, but it really wasn't as good. It kept her head way too clear. But it did make her drowsy, so she was relieved to escape back into sleep for a while.

When she woke up, Cyrus was sitting next to her bed. He smiled when he saw her opening her eyes. "Well, if it isn't Andi of the Ruptured Spleen. *Spleen.* I love that word."

"Me, too!" she said with so much excitement that they both laughed. It felt good, even though it hurt.

"So Naveed's fine," Cyrus said, answering the question she hadn't asked out loud yet. He held out a box of chocolates. "He made me buy you these—happy Valentine's Day, by the way. Care for a cherry cordial? Or something. I don't actually know what's in here."

"Don't mind if I do." Andi hadn't given Valentine's Day a second thought, but sitting in a hospital bed eating chocolates delivered by her ex-boyfriend seemed a fitting way to celebrate her messed-up love life. Cyrus opened the box and handed her a square chocolate, which turned out to be filled with a delicious chewy caramel.

Cyrus set the chocolates on her bedside table. "So yeah, Naveed sends his love and all that, but it was a rough night and he needs to stay home today. He feels awful about it, of course, because he really wanted to visit you and Roya—"

"Roya? What happened to Roya?"

Cyrus looked stunned. "Oh. I guess we didn't get a chance to tell you, but last night was… eventful. Naveed and Roya went to pick up Koffka at Englewood yesterday, and somehow a fire started in the barn and Roya was trapped inside. Naveed got her out. But the horses trampled her leg and she had to have surgery. Naveed and I were driving home from the hospital—this hospital, actually—when we got your texts."

Andi wanted to think she'd heard that wrong—it all seemed so unbelievable—but she could still remember being held by Naveed last night. It had felt like she was engulfed in a cloud of wood smoke. "Is Roya okay?"

"She's all right. They think she'll come home soon. Still watching for infection, but so far, so good. She'll have a full-leg cast for a few months, though."

"Wow. That's horrible. Poor Roya."

"Yeah, but you know her. She's a trouper." Cyrus leaned forward. "Okay, A, so I'm breaking the strict promise I made to your mom, who didn't want me to talk about real stuff. She only let me in here because I said I'd make bland remarks about the lovely weather we've been having. So we didn't have this conversation, all right?"

"All right? But you'll have to go slow. My brain's a little scrambled."

"That's okay. You're sure you're up for it? It has to do with Jackass T. Jerkington."

She almost smiled at the nickname. Almost. "Yes. I'm up for it."

Cyrus glanced behind him, as if to make sure no one was listening. "So—they kept us at the police station for hours last night. Didn't get home until this morning, actually. It all seemed routine at first, but when Baba came to pick us up they still wouldn't let us go. After a while it was obvious they thought Naveed had fired the gun—they were stalling, waiting to see if Jed was going to die. They were probably thrilled at the idea of a potential homicide investigation with a high-profile family like us. Naveed was actually holding it together pretty well, considering. You know how he feels about cops. It's a good thing Koffka was there to calm him down, and that he was still kind of spacey from those sedatives they gave him after the fire. Otherwise he might have done something stupid."

"Wait, but I told them I shot Jed. Why did they think Naveed did it?"

"They thought you were covering for him. Naveed didn't want to answer any questions without a lawyer there, and we obviously couldn't reach one in the middle of the night, but I explained over and over that he'd never even touched the gun. They didn't care. He's the one with the criminal record."

"But they didn't arrest him? They let you all go home?"

"Eventually. They didn't end up charging us with anything. Thank God, because Naveed was super on edge by the time they finally said we could go. As soon as we got into the car, he completely lost it. It was not a peaceful ride home, let's put it that way."

Andi winced. "So… it all worked out okay?"

"For now. But I think it depends what happens with Jed. If he dies…."

He didn't finish the thought. Instead, he continued, "They'll be checking out our stories today. That's why I need your help. I need to know if Jed said anything to you. About his… motivations, I guess."

Andi told Cyrus about the night at Neumo's, and Jed's comments about finding powerful like-minded people online. She told him that Jed put a tracking device on her car after the break-in and had been stalking her ever since. Cyrus typed notes into his phone as she spoke.

"God, I hate him so much," he said when she was done. "And I'm so, so sorry. But I have to ask you one more question. Did Jed say anything to you about a guy named Tim Schmidt?"

"No." Andi took another caramel and chewed it for a moment before adding, "All he said was that he'd been in contact with people who had lots of information about me. People who apparently knew what the crows meant to us, and 'wanted us to remember.' Actually… I thought he might have been talking about Richard Caring."

"Huh. Not sure about that, but this Tim Schmidt guy is definitely involved somehow. Naveed actually met him at one point… it's a long story, I'll fill you in later. Todd's been working all night trying to figure out who he really is, but so far, no luck. I'll have him look for connections to Caring. Maybe that'll turn up some new leads. Or maybe the FBI will track him down in the meantime."

Andi's head was spinning. "I hope so."

Her mother came in then, and Cyrus quickly changed the topic. "So by the way, Brooke has been texting. She says she 'feels terrible about Dimples,' whatever that means. And that she hopes you feel better and wants you to call as soon as you're up for it. Oh, hi, Joyce. Is my time up?"

"That's it for now. She needs to get some rest," her mother said.

Andi wished they could have kept talking, but at the same time was glad to have some quiet space to turn everything over in her head.

"Thanks for coming, Cy. Tell Brooke I'll call her soon, and send Naveed and Roya my best."

"Will do. Bye, A. Take care of that spleen, now."

Once he'd gone, her mother sat down. "I hope he didn't say anything that upset you."

"No. Not at all," Andi lied. But she couldn't resist adding, "You don't think Naveed did it, do you? Shot Jed, I mean. Because *I* did. I wasn't lying. I shot him."

Her mother kept her eyes on the closed door. She was quiet for a long time. "I think you should get some sleep," she finally said, stooping to give Andi a kiss on the forehead. Then she left, closing the door firmly behind her.

Roya

MONDAY, FEBRUARY 15

ROYA STARED AT THE CEILING ABOVE HER HOSPITAL BED. SHE'D asked the nurse to turn the TV off, because the cartoons on the screen were so loud and flashy they made her head hurt. Roya preferred to watch the ceiling instead. She liked its blankness. It felt as far away as the moon.

There was a knock at the door. By now Roya was used to people knocking while barging in at the same time, the endless stream of white coats and blue scrubs. But this time, the face that poked inside her room was a welcomed one.

"Naveed!" She scooted herself up as her brother entered the room, Koffka trotting alongside him. The dog settled in next to her bed so she could pet him. Since he was wearing his service dog vest, she had to wriggle her fingers underneath to feel the soft fur on his back. "They let you bring him in?"

"Yep. He's officially on duty." Naveed ambled inside, holding a notebook underneath his arm. He set it down on the table and perched on the side of

Roya's bed, then scooped her up into a gigantic hug. She still had oxygen tubes poking into her nose because she'd breathed in so much smoke, and the burns on her back ached, but he figured out all the obstacles and held her just right.

"Where's Maman? Is she home yet?" Roya asked Naveed's chest.

"She's on her way," Naveed said. "But she has a long layover in Dubai. Probably won't make it here until late tomorrow."

Roya couldn't wait to see Maman again, but felt guilty for making her leave Iran early. She pulled away from Naveed and stroked Koffka's ears. "Does Pashi get along okay with Koffka?"

"Actually, she doesn't seem to mind him at all. Pretty much ignores him. I think she just wants you to come home. She keeps meowing at your bedroom door."

It made Roya sad that Pashmak had noticed her absence and was probably confused about where she was. But, at the same time, it felt good knowing that someone missed her. "What about Baba?" Roya asked. "What does he think?"

"He's still weirded out to have a dog in the house, but he's getting used to it. He can see how much Koffka's helping. And he's glad Koffka will be able to help you, too, when you come home."

"Good." Roya would need all the help she could get. At first she'd thought it might be fun to walk on crutches while her leg healed. But when she actually tried them, she quickly changed her mind. Even just getting out of bed was way harder than she thought it'd be.

"Does it hurt?" Naveed waved a hand at the big cast on her leg.

When most people asked her that question, she usually answered that it wasn't too bad so they would praise her for being tough and brave. But this was Naveed: someone who understood pain. Who didn't mind talking about it. "Yes. It really, really, *really* hurts."

"What does it feel like?" he asked, and listened while she told him about the aches in her pieced-together leg bones, about how much the burns stung, about how sometimes it felt like she couldn't breathe.

He listened, and didn't brush it off with a *you'll-feel-better-soon*, because he knew as well as she did that feeling better was still a long way off.

She snuggled into him once she had finished talking, glad he was there. "Did you go see Andi already?" Roya had heard that Andi was at the same hospital because she'd been in a car crash the same night that the barn burned down.

"Not yet. I wanted to see you first. I brought the notebook you asked for." He started coughing, which made her cough too, and they hacked together for a minute.

"Are you okay?" She touched his chest. "The smoke probably wasn't good for you."

"It's not good for anyone," he said. "But, yeah, I'm all right. Didn't breathe much smoke, actually." He held out his bandaged hands with a smile. "And the good thing about nerve damage is, the burns don't hurt at all."

"Thank you for finding me," she said in a small voice. "And I'm sorry, there were so many things I should've told you, but... did you read the story I copied into the notebook? *Katerina and the Little Strangers*?"

"Yes." Naveed leaned against her bed, and Koffka settled his head down beside them. Roya stroked it. "That story was the sequel to a book I loved. *Keepers of the Moon*. Where did you find it? And what happened to the original copy? I have some theories, but—tell me. Tell me all about it."

So she did. She started from the very beginning: the day she met Kass. He didn't interrupt, but she was too nervous to watch him react so she kept her eyes on Koffka. She ended with what had happened in the barn, telling him, as she'd told everyone who asked, about the matches and candles she'd brought. About accidentally dropping the candle on the hay bale. About Kass, how she had left before the fire started to find her father, who was calling from the woods.

"So I need to read *Katerina* again," Roya finished. "To see if I can figure out the hidden message, and then I need to talk to Kass. Just one more time."

"I don't think that will be possible," said Naveed. "I heard they were transferring her to another institution. One that will be safer for her."

"No!" Roya yelled. "No. Englewood was perfect! How could they make her go somewhere else?"

He side-hugged her. "I know, Roya. Don't feel like this is your fault—if anything, it's mine. I should have kept a closer eye on you. I was just... distracted and...."

"But I told them I was the one who brought the candles. And started the fire."

"It's out of our hands, Roya. She's a ward of the state—they have the final say in where she goes."

"But is she still at Englewood now?"

"I think so."

"Then we still have time to figure it out. So do you have any ideas? About what Kass's father was trying to tell her in the story?"

"I don't know," Naveed said. "I can't believe Zolotov was Kass's dad. And I'm still not sure what to make of *Katerina*. In a way, I'm kind of disappointed, because I liked Mikhail—"

"You *liked* him? But he was so mean."

"No, not in this story. In *Keepers of the Moon*. Mikhail was a good person back then... in general, I mean, though he did have an unhealthy obsession with Natasha... but anyway, after he lost her... I guess he just couldn't recover."

"Something bad happened to him and he became bad." Roya hoped she was following this.

Naveed seemed so sad. "I didn't want to believe he would kill—or try to kill—Katerina when she was born. But he was so... so blinded... by the despair... by the loss of the person he loved more than anything in the universe...."

Roya wasn't sure why the story was affecting him so much. When he didn't say anything more, she added, "Kass said that her father wrote this for her. That she was like Katerina. So does that mean

Mikhail was someone in real life too? He seems like Alastor. He even had a long beard."

"Mikhail was Alastor," he said slowly. "Yeah. Mikhail was Alastor."

"But that doesn't make sense. Alastor was Kass's granddad. Not her dad."

"Well, it might not line up perfectly. Dr. Belinsky was the real father figure—he was definitely the one speaking for Zolotov."

Roya thought about that. "Can I see the notebook?"

He handed it to her. Before she opened it, she said, "What do you think Katerina decided to do at the end?"

"I'm not sure," he said. "Maybe she killed Mikhail, but... I hope she was able to get away. I hope she found freedom somewhere. But maybe she couldn't find peace until she killed him. Still, she didn't know what he was like before, the good he had in him... but how could she see that, when she only knew him as the tyrant leader who tried to kill her as a baby?" He lowered his face into his mitten-hands. "Akh, Roya, I feel like it's exploding my brain."

Roya didn't know what to say, so she paged through the copy she'd made of *Katerina and the Little Strangers*, paying close attention to everything Dr. Belinsky said. Something caught her eye this time.

"Ilyana Petrokova!" she exclaimed. "In the story. That's it! That has to be it!"

"What?"

She showed him. "Dr. Belinsky said that Katerina could live with his sister Ilyana. And this—maybe it's her address! 'She lives near the Volga River in Syzran...' Did Zolotov have a sister? Maybe Kass could go live with her! That way she won't have to go to an awful new institution...."

"Wait. Doesn't anyone know that Kass is Zolotov's daughter? Wouldn't they have looked for his relatives already? And the Volga River's in Russia. It wouldn't be a simple thing for her to move overseas... plus I think she needs a lot of, um, support, after what she's been through...."

"Maybe Kass didn't know his real name. Everyone took different names in Orcinia. So they wouldn't have known where to look." Roya grabbed his forearm. "Please," she said. "Please, please, go to Englewood and ask them to look for Ilyana. She would be good to Kass. I know it. I just know."

Naveed opened his mouth, like he was going to say another grown-up-ish thing about how impossible it was, but Roya didn't want to believe that. She wanted Kass to be free. "You owe her," she added. "Kass is the reason you have Koffka—she made him bite her so that he could be yours. And now you have a chance to help her. So... will you? Please?"

He raised his eyebrows. "Really? She did that on purpose?"

"Yes. She did it for you." *And for me,* Roya thought but didn't say.

Slowly, he nodded. "All right. I'll talk to them."

"And will you tell her to write to me? I have to know what happens to her."

"I'll have them tell her." Naveed paused. "Roya, you know... I wish you'd told me all of this. It wasn't... good for me... when you made me think that stuff on Lopez didn't really happen. So please, don't do that again. Please be honest with me from now on."

"Okay," Roya said. "I will. I promise."

Koffka licked her hand, and Naveed pulled her in for another hug before he left. Once he was gone, she leafed through the notebook again. It was strange to read the story in her own writing, as if she had been the one to make it up in the first place.

She found a pencil on the tray by her bed and turned to the next page of the notebook. *I took the lighter from Mikhail's hand,* she wrote. *Then I got on the rocket ship with Dr. Belinsky. We slammed the door in Mikhail's face and he couldn't get in.*

We fired up the ship. We blasted off. Then the moon got very small as we flew away through the stars to our new home. Earth.

Naveed

NAVEED OPENED THE GATE INTO ANDI'S BACKYARD. SHE HAD TOLD him to meet her outside, but she wasn't sitting in the patio chairs like he'd expected her to be. The yard, as far as he could tell, was empty.

He paused just beyond the gate. Koffka stepped closer, as if sensing his anxiety.

"Naveed. Over here." Andi's voice came from an overgrown part of the yard.

Relieved, he crossed the lawn and kneeled down to find her sitting cross-legged on the ground beneath a woody butterfly bush.

"What are you doing?" he asked.

"Hiding."

"From?"

"From everything." She patted the ground beside her. "Come on. We don't have much time."

Koffka looked at Naveed quizzically as he crawled into the hedge.

"It's all right," he reassured the dog. Koffka settled in, sitting at attention outside the thicket.

"What's going on?" Naveed asked as he eased in next to her. The ground was cold, a little damp. "Are you sure you should be down here?"

"I just wanted to get away," she said. "To be on my own for five minutes. You know?"

He wrapped his arms around her. "I do. Andi—I'm so glad you're home."

Andi scooted closer and moved her legs so that they were draped over his lap. A strand of hair from her bangs was caught in a branch. He tugged it free and smoothed it back into place.

Their eyes met, and he felt it again, that ecstatic soaring, like his heart had taken flight. Like he could hold onto that lightness forever if he just kissed her.

He could see it in her eyes too: the longing, the hunger. But he was afraid, so afraid that he would mess this up, afraid of crushing her, of hurting her, of dragging her down with him during his inevitable fall. So he stayed as he was, frozen, and they sat there under the bushes while the wind shook raindrops from the leaf-buds onto their heads.

"I have something to tell you," Andi said. "And it's really hard for me to say, so don't interrupt."

"Okay. I'm listening."

"I love you," she said. "And not like a brother. I *love* you, and I want to be with you for real—I want to kiss you, if that's okay, and I want you to tell me what feels good to you and what doesn't, and I promise to listen, and I want you to do the same for me. I want to be able to tell you everything. No secrets, no surprises. And I know you're happy with the way things are, but I'm not. I've felt so trapped, because you told me who you wanted me to be, the role you wanted me to play, and I tried to make you happy by being that person. But now you've seen the real me, and you're still here, and I don't care if it makes no sense and everything is breaking all around us and we're always running out of time. I want you. For however long I can have you."

Her words broke his heart and held it together at the same time. How was that possible? How was *she* possible, this astounding person who could speak to him when no one else could, through her words, her music, her presence? All he wanted was to love her the way she wanted to be loved.

He let that feeling fill him up, let the pressure build until it exploded. No need to overthink this: she had told him what she wanted, and he wanted the same thing. He leaned in and kissed her softly. She answered his kiss with her own, and that reciprocation was so incredibly satisfying, he actually felt like he was floating into the branches. It made no sense to him, really, why he couldn't stand to have anyone touch his face, yet right now he didn't feel squeamish at all. But it didn't have to make sense. It was astonishing and liberating and perfect, and that was all that mattered.

Naveed was finding it hard to breathe. Not in a bad way, for once, and he didn't want to stop. But eventually, he was thwarted by a cough that couldn't wait.

Koffka had reminded him to take his inhaler before leaving the house, and he was thankful for that now, as he found it in his coat pocket and took a brief hit. It was probably the unsexiest way to interrupt a kissing session ever, but Andi didn't seem to care.

The second he finished, she lunged in for more, but he found himself saying, "Wait. I love you, too, Andi. But I wanted to think of you as a sister because… because I want you and me… to be forever, and I'm so afraid that if we're a couple, I'll end up hurting you and the thought of that, the thought of losing you, is just… unbearable. I don't think I have a happy ending. Trouble follows me, and I don't want it to follow you, too. You deserve to be with someone way less messed-up than me."

The sadness was returning to Andi's eyes, but her cheeks were still adorably flushed. "Maybe *you* deserve to be with someone less messed-up than me."

"Andi. I don't want to be with anyone else," he said. "But… I'm not really sure if I can...." The next part came out in a rush. "Some of my meds, they have these side effects and sex is, like, incredibly frustrating, and I'm afraid I won't... I won't be able to...."

"I am so not in the mood for *that* anytime soon," Andi said. "One thing at a time. Right now let's kiss each other some more, because it feels amazing, and let's not think about the future or anything else, let's just... be here, now."

Her reaction came as a huge relief. Even though she'd shown him over and over that she accepted him despite his flaws, it still felt like a miracle every time. Maybe this could work after all—maybe they could have a romantic relationship, even with all the issues he brought to it, because they understood each other. They could figure out how to make it work.

For now, it was enough to be kissing in this hidden spot—but he felt doors opening, a sense of plunging into something vast and wonderful, like he was about to discover new worlds he had never known before. And he absolutely could not wait.

After what seemed like no time at all, Andi pulled away. "Let's go sit on the patio. My mom will freak out if she can't find me."

One last kiss, then he helped her up and supported her while she walked unsteadily to the chair.

"I forgot he was here," Andi said as they walked, indicating Koffka. "He's so quiet. Like your shadow or something."

Naveed liked the comparison. Even though he'd only adopted Koffka a week ago, it was hard to imagine life without him. It was kind of amazing how much safer he felt having the dog around.

True, Naveed didn't have to worry about Jed, who remained in critical condition at the hospital. Or Dennis, who, according to Max, had been readmitted to Englewood. Regardless, Naveed continued to bring his knife everywhere he went—and whatever happened, he was sure that Koffka would protect him.

Tim Schmidt, too, seemed to have disappeared without a trace. Naveed still didn't understand what that whole thing had been about, and had been strangely disappointed that the post-MRK research project had been a ruse. But after doing more research, it became obvious that no one was studying the long-term effects of MRK because the need to contain the current epidemic was so great. Through Vanesa, he had reached out to Ramón and Marisol, and after talking with them to figure out the needs of the farmworker community, he'd started a grassroots fundraising campaign to assist with medical bills. It was just one tiny piece of a very complex puzzle, but it felt so good to be doing something to help other people.

One reason this finally felt possible was that, aside from the shortness of breath and occasional coughing fits that had been bothering him since the fire, he'd been feeling better physically than he had in a long time. While in Tehran, Maman had learned a lot about tebbe sonnati, traditional Iranian medicine, and had brought various herbs, tinctures, and plant essences home with her. As a result, she'd been detained at customs for hours, but they eventually let her go and only confiscated a few things. Naveed had been following the complicated regimen faithfully, mostly because he knew how much trouble the medicines had caused Maman, but they really did seem to be working. All of this made it easier to accept that there wasn't some sinister MRK-related illness still lurking in his body, that his flu and bronchitis had just been run-of-the-mill respiratory infections. He was cautiously optimistic that, now that spring was coming, he could keep getting better.

The fact that he felt hopeful about anything seemed miraculous, really. Koffka had helped a lot to improve his mood, but it was more than that. Almost like he had reached some sort of tipping point, like he'd endured so much trauma that he'd finally figured out how to take it in stride. Or maybe he'd been so concerned about Andi that everything else got pushed aside, and would resurface later. That was always a possibility.

As Naveed and Andi sat down on her patio chairs, he realized she wasn't wearing a coat. Her thermal shirt had soaked up all the raindrops they had shaken free beneath the butterfly bush. Her bangs were still messy, too, but when he reached over to smooth them she jerked away and ran her fingers through her hair. "My mom might be watching," she said.

"I don't care," said Naveed. "If we're going to be—together—then she should know."

Andi furrowed her eyebrows. Koffka settled his head in her lap.

"Do you want to go inside?" Naveed asked. "You must be cold."

"No," Andi said.

Naveed unzipped his coat and draped it over her shoulders. She pulled it tight around her.

"Okay, so there's something else I have to tell you." Andi didn't give him time to respond before she rushed on. "My mom decided it's not safe for me in Seattle anymore. I'm moving to California with her next month."

Everything froze. Leaves paused mid-flutter; birds hovered above, unmoving. Or at least that was how it felt, like nothing could go on as it had before, like her announcement had shattered time itself.

"But—but you can't." The world around him came unstuck, but Naveed felt like he'd just been stabbed. "What about school? You only have a few months left, why can't you live with your dad until you graduate? Or you could stay with us, I'm sure it would be fine with my parents—"

"I'm not going back to that school." Andi wouldn't look at him now. Her voice sounded robotic. "I'm on cognitive rest for two more weeks. Already hopelessly behind. And it's different this time, it's really hard for me to remember things. Important things. Like the fact that we're moving—my mom swears she told me a bunch of times in the hospital, but I don't remember it at all. So the doctors want me to take it extra slow, and my mom talked to my teachers and they're going to work out a way for me to finish up online. Just so I meet the minimum needed to graduate—no AP tests or anything. Plus I dropped a few classes."

One stab after another. He could feel vitality draining from him, like he was rapidly losing blood.

"I can't stay with your family," Andi went on. "I'd love to, but my mom would never go for it. She won't even let me live with my dad, even though he's going through that detox program and says he's going to stay sober. He'll be too busy when the album releases in a couple months—he won't have time to take care of me, too. Especially since I can't drive right now."

Naveed had to get out his inhaler again, because it felt like his lungs were being squeezed.

"So this month might be all we have," Andi said. "I don't want to waste it. I want you to come over every day, and when I'm finally allowed to leave the house, I want to go on, like, the most epic date we can imagine, and we'll take lots of pictures so that I can remember it when I'm in Berkeley."

Naveed finally found his voice again. "I'll move down there. As soon as I can." But even as he said it, he knew how far away that was. His probation wouldn't end until October. Eight long months from now. And there wasn't any hope for negotiating even a short trip out of the state; he was on shaky ground thanks to his involvement in the Jed incident. Still, he added, "I want to be with you, Andi. I want to be there for you."

"I know. But it won't be that long until I see you again. I have to come back up for the trial this spring."

He didn't even want to think about the trial that was supposedly starting in a few months. *The People v. Tara Snyder.*

"And I'll be eighteen in July," Andi was saying. "Maybe I could move back up here, but if I get accepted to college, and if my head's working better by then… I'll probably stay in California. I just don't know what's going to happen yet."

"We'll figure it out," he said, not wanting to think about that. Not wanting to think about any of it, really. Wanting to go back to their hideaway under the bushes and stay there forever.

"We will," she said. "When have we ever let teensy little obstacles stop us before?"

Naveed got up and wedged himself into her chair. She settled in on his lap, pulling his coat over both of them like a blanket. Then he kissed her again, not even caring if her mother was watching. He didn't want to waste a single second of the time they had left.

Andi

TUESDAY, MARCH 15

A FEW DAYS BEFORE ANDI LEFT FOR CALIFORNIA, SHE SAT IN HER almost-empty room. Every poster and photograph had been removed from the walls. Everything she owned, except for necessities like her laptop, MIDI keyboard, and a few changes of clothes, had been packed into boxes. Now that nothing was left except the furniture, a slight echo reverberated whenever she spoke.

She scanned the bare walls, noticing all the scars she had inflicted on this room. The hole in the ceiling from the mosquito net canopy she'd hung over her bed when she was ten. The dings in the paint from the time she'd rearranged her room and scraped a long slash with the corner of her desk. They would soon be spackled up and painted over, leaving no trace of her or her previous selves.

Her phone dinged, and she couldn't pick it up fast enough. It was a text from Naveed. Done with my probation appt! The PO praised me for staying out of trouble. Haha not really but he did say I "appear to be making progress" & since he usually treats me like garbage that feels like a win.

What time can I pick you up?

Andi scrolled back to their previous conversation. Her memory had improved lately, but it still helped to revisit details over and over to make them stick. Can you come w my family to Chaharshanbe Suri? he had written a few days ago. We're getting together on Alki Beach w a bunch of friends to jump over bonfires (an old Zoroastrian tradition). Happens the Tues evening before spring equinox to kick off the Nowruz celebrations.

Andi read through the rest of the string again before replying. How about in an hour?

He responded with a flood of celebratory and fiery emojis. Andi texted him a blushing smiley and a few hearts, then set a reminder so that she wouldn't forget. She wanted to change out of her now-standard sweatshirt-and-leggings combo, but first she'd have to muster the energy.

To kill some time, Andi opened the notes app on her phone. She'd gotten into the habit of jotting things down throughout the day, so that she'd be able to remember every possible detail about her last weeks in Seattle. The first entry had been written nearly a month earlier. She kept it at the top so that she could read through it every time she opened her notes.

> **Feb 20:** We kissed under the butterfly bush. I CANNOT BELIEVE how good it felt. Like turning on the radio and your favorite song is playing. Like watching a video where a glass breaks but then it reverses and all the shards knit themselves back together again. But none of that captures how satisfying it actually was. He listened and he understood and he didn't run away to protect himself from getting dragged into all the crap I'm going thru. I love him so much.

She had been hanging out with Naveed a lot lately, so he was a main focus of nearly all the entries.

> **Feb 26:** Volunteered at the food bank with N. We scooped a ton of rice into smaller bags and unloaded crates of bread. Most fun I've had in a long time (not being sarcastic! It really was).

March 1: N and I rented a canoe today and rowed through the lily pads in the arboretum. We docked at one of the beaches for a picnic lunch. It was so beautiful. Sparkles of light on the rippling water. Sweet grapes bursting in my mouth. Naveed squinting into the sun as he threw a ball to Koffka. K looking adorably nervous as he tested the tippy boat with his front paws before lumbering back in. As we glided through a wooded inlet, I kissed Naveed beneath the willow trees. Felt like I was in a movie for a second, imaginary violin music swelling in the background, the two of us silhouetted against the sunbeams piercing through the leaves.

March 5: Can I just say how much I love Koffka? Yesterday N was in a mood but K somehow made it more bearable. N said sometimes he feels like he's forced to carry something super heavy for a really long time, but K helps lighten the load. I used to feel so much pressure to be the one who did that for N, but now I don't have to worry as much about him or fear that he'll totally self-destruct when I leave. I can't even express how much of a relief that is.

Andi closed her eyes. It was a minor miracle, really, that they'd been able to spend so much time together without her mother giving her a hard time about it. Maybe she knew it was futile to try to keep them apart. Maybe she didn't care since she knew it would be over soon anyway. Maybe she was finally starting to like him... or maybe she just liked the fact that everywhere they went, they were accompanied by a huge, intimidating-looking German shepherd. Whatever the reason, Andi would take it.

Of course, there had been plenty of less-pleasant times too, which she recalled as she read the next series of notes.

March 7: Spent the weekend in Ballard w/Dad at his new apartment. SO AWKWARD, esp when he was showing me some pictures on his phone and Patricia called and he tried to send it to voicemail before I noticed. But I noticed. He brushed it off by suggesting we do some songwriting, but I worked up the nerve to confess that I feel like he always steamrolls me whenever we collaborate (remember to tell therapist this, she will be proud!!). He seemed shocked at first, like, what? I'd never do that! but he actually apologized. So that was... something. Also seems like the detox thing is working out and he's clean again (for now) but I doubt that'll last when he goes on tour. I guess I'm not as mad at him anymore bc now I know how tempting it is to escape and it's easy to see how quickly that could spiral out of control. So I know it's not entirely his fault but still I don't know if things will ever be the same between us.

March 9: N was driving me home from therapy and the light turned yellow so he slammed on the brakes too fast and I felt so panicked, just flooded with fear, remembering things... things that happened with Jed... things I don't want to write down bc I'd rather NOT remember. I asked Mom and she told me Jed's at a long-term care facility now. Drs think he might have to stay there for years. When I shot him in the leg he fell and smashed his head into a rock or something, which was bad because he'd already injured it in the accident, I can't remember what they said, something about a skull fracture, some sort of hemorrhage... anyway the brain damage is irreversible and severe and even though my inner Ah-ma wants me to go all Buddhist and have compassion for him, I don't think I'll ever be able to. I mean, I am glad he didn't die but only because now there's no murder investigation drama, though the police are still looking for some guy named Tim Schmidt who was involved somehow. But anyway none of us were charged with anything.

The problem, Andi thought as she rested her eyes again, was that Jed wasn't some random person acting alone. He was just a symptom of a larger disease. Even if he couldn't hurt her anymore, there was no shortage of lonely, insecure men out there who thought themselves entitled to pursue her, to stalk her, to assault her. If anyone tried anything in the future, she wanted to be ready. Cyrus had tightened up her phone and laptop's security settings, and given her a crash course on protecting herself online. As soon as she moved to Berkeley, she was going to enroll in self-defense classes, too.

Wanting to cleanse her brain of Jed thoughts, she read through another note on her phone, this one titled "Things I'm Thankful For."

Mom. For taking care of me.

Naveed & Koffka & Cyrus & Roya. All the Mirzapours, really.

Ah-ma is feeling much better, and Mom says the doctors are hopeful that her cancer is now in remission!!!

The songs I recorded for the documentary turned out amazing. Vanesa said she was so impressed by how professional they are & that they fit the film perfectly. She'll keep me posted on whether it gets accepted to the Seattle International Film Festival in the spring! Also: the awe on N's face as he listened to them for the first time was EVERYTHING.

Blazin Bitz boycott kicked off on 3/1 with the satirical ad the artivist collective put together (featuring a short jingle I wrote)! Who knows if it's affecting sales, but at least people are talking about the Nutrexo scandal again, and about factory farming and its connection with MRK. N said his farmworker fundraising campaign got a huge boost when the boycott started.

The first twinges of a headache pulsed behind Andi's eyes. Enough reading for now. She needed to get ready, anyway.

She stood up slowly and changed into jeans, a soft white t-shirt, and a mustard-yellow cardigan. She had just finished giving her eyelashes a quick sweep of mascara when her mom called from the living room. "Andi?"

The uncertainty in her tone worried Andi, so she twisted the mascara tube back together as she walked out to the living room. But her mom only looked inquisitive. "Just picked up the mail." She held up a large envelope. "You applied to USC?"

Andi blinked. Over the past few weeks, she'd received rejection emails from Stanford and Davis, and hadn't bothered logging into any other schools' application portals to check on decisions. She wasn't exactly a competitive applicant anymore. What if she didn't get into any of them?

Heart beating faster now, she took the envelope from her mother. She felt like she should sit down for this, but the couch was strewn with cardboard boxes and crumpled newspaper from their ongoing packing spree, so she settled in on the armrest. "Yeah, didn't I tell you?" she asked her mother, although now that she thought about it she remembered *not* telling her, since she'd applied to the music program and had figured the chances of getting in were so remote as to be laughable.

Andi did laugh as she read the first sentence of the letter inside, out of shock as much as delight. *Congratulations! You have been accepted to the USC Thornton School of Music.*

"I got in!" she said in disbelief, holding the letter in her hand tightly while her mother shrieked and hugged her.

"I'm so proud of you, bǎo bèi! Ah-ma and Ah-gong will be, too—should we call and tell them the good news?"

Andi's excitement quickly fizzled. "Not yet. Mom… I applied to the music composition program. I really didn't think I'd get in, and I know it might not be a practical major, but… it's what I love more than anything else. I honestly don't think I could handle pre-med right now. It's so hard to concentrate on anything, but with music… for me, it's like an escape, or maybe a kind of therapy even. It feels like something I can handle. Something that I *want* to do."

"Andi." Her mother cleared a spot on the messy sofa and sat down. "I know. I can see how absorbed you get when you're working on a piece. But I wanted to save you from following in your father's footsteps, if you know what I mean. Or getting sucked into a dead-end job the way I did. You know what, though? Part of that was me, falling into inertia, afraid to take a risk or put my own interests first, because I had to take care of you. And Jake, in a way. But I'm finally about to start a job that I'm excited about, one where I'll actually get to work on my photography again, and you're all grown up and… I trust you to choose your own way. I do think you should wait to make a decision until we hear back from Berkeley, but if you want to go to USC, you'll have my support. And your grandparents'.

We love you, Andi. We want you to be happy."

Andi wished she'd waited on applying mascara. "Thank you, Mom," she choked out. "But... what if they don't want me anymore after they see my updated GPA? My grades are terrible... and I'm finishing high school online and...."

"Don't worry about that. Can I see the letter?" As her mother read, Andi leafed through the other enclosures in the packet, the glossy brochures and USC decal stickers, but could barely absorb any of the information.

"It says here that you were 'selected due to the strength of the compositions you submitted with your application,'" her mom said. "They love your music, Andi. If they're concerned about your grades, we'll explain the situation. And they'll let the admission stand. I know they will."

Andi hoped that was true. Still, it was a lot to process. So much change all at once. And Naveed would be coming over any minute. She let her mom congratulate her once more, then laced up her boots, zipped up her coat, and went out back to wait for him.

Naveed and Koffka picked her up right on time, and she walked alongside them through the alley with a heart both heavy and light. How was she supposed to break the news? Ease him into it somehow, or just come out and say it? She knew she couldn't keep it from him for long, but decided to wait until they had some time alone later.

Once Mahnaz, Sam, and Roya were ready to leave—Cyrus had spent the afternoon at Dev's and would be arriving separately—they piled into the car and headed over to West Seattle. Across the water, the downtown skyline glimmered in the dark. A large crowd had already clustered on the sand. Someone had set up an amplifier playing traditional Persian music, filling the air with its driving drumbeat and undulating vocals. Andi and Naveed got Roya settled on a camp chair, then helped his parents unload supplies from the car.

"Is Roya going to be okay with all the fire?" Andi asked Naveed as they watched people build three small bonfires in the sand, which was still damp from earlier rain.

Naveed wrapped Koffka's leash tighter around his hand. "Maman and Baba thought about skipping this year, but Roya wasn't having it. Not that she'll be jumping over any fires this time." He kept his eyes on his sister, and Andi followed his gaze. Several women were exclaiming over her cast, and Roya seemed to be soaking up the attention. "She just... blows my mind sometimes. The way she sees things, how she figures stuff out. Like her friend Kass, you know, the one at Englewood—did I tell you they found her aunt? Apparently she emigrated from Russia to the U.S. a few years ago, and ended up in Tacoma, of all places. So now Kass has a place to go when she gets released."

"That's good," Andi said distractedly. She had heard her name, and searched for the source—it was Cyrus, who was standing on the periphery with Dev. By the time she turned back, Naveed was having a conversation in Persian with a couple of men who seemed curious about Koffka, so Andi excused herself and walked over to Cyrus.

"Hey, A, what's up? Seems like it's been a while," he said.

"I know. You guys have been busy, huh?" Andi punted the conversation back to them, not wanting to break the news about USC until she'd talked about it with Naveed. "How's the business plan coming?"

"Akh. Painful," said Cyrus.

"It's not *that* bad," said Dev. "I really like the angle we're taking for our company. The world needs more prosocial, accessible games and content, don't you think?"

"Totally." Andi nodded and listened as they kept throwing jargon around. Even if she didn't understand half of what they were saying, she liked the way they lit up when they talked about it.

Dev's phone buzzed and he stepped away to take the call. Once he'd gone, Cyrus said, "I can't believe you're leaving. Will you still be here on Sunday? Got quite the feast planned for Nowruz."

"We head out on Friday." Andi did not want to think about that now: she had only two more full days here.

"End of an era." Cyrus sighed. "We're going to miss you, A."

"I'll miss you too. But you'll still see me plenty." She tried to keep emotion out of her voice, but it showed up in her teary eyes anyway. "Cyrus... will you... just make sure that Naveed...."

She didn't even have to finish. "Of course," Cyrus said. "I'm sure he'll mope around for a while, but he'll adjust. Don't worry."

She was too choked up to say anything more, so she gave him a thank-you shoulder squeeze and headed back through the crowd in search of Naveed. She couldn't find him, so she walked toward Roya, who was now sharing a chair with her mother. Sam sat next to them, his arm around Mahnaz, the three of them laughing about something. The sight only made Andi sadder, so she veered away from the crowd instead, heading up the stairs onto the sidewalk.

Then she spotted Naveed, sitting on the steps in the distance. He was taking a breath from his inhaler, something she hadn't seen him do in a while. Koffka sat beside him, watchful.

"Hey." She stepped up beside him. "You all right?"

He nodded, but started coughing again and had to take one more hit before he could answer. "Yeah. Just standing in the wrong place. Got a lung full of smoke."

"We don't have to do this." She sank down beside him. "We can just stay here. Talk. Or whatever."

"Well, I'm always up for 'or whatever.'" He shot her a sly smile. "But no, I'll go back in a minute."

"Are you sure?" she asked.

"Yeah. It's important. It's like...." He zipped open Koffka's service dog vest and slid his inhaler inside. "When we jump over the fire, we say these verses. They're about taking all the bad things out of yourself and giving them to the fire, and feeling everything good coming from the fire into you. 'My sadness to you, your joy to me; my weakness to you, your strength to me'—stuff like that. And this past year has been so... I don't even think there's a word for it. If there was ever a time that I needed to do this, it's now."

That made perfect sense to Andi. "Okay. But let's not go back yet." She was practically bursting—she couldn't keep it inside any longer. "So, I have some news. I just found out that I got into USC. The music composition program."

He breathed in so fast that she thought he'd start coughing again, but instead it came out as a sputtery, joyful laugh. "You did? That's amazing! Congratulations!"

"Thanks. I still can't believe it."

"Wow. This is huge!" He paused. "So... where exactly is USC?"

Andi was surprised he didn't know, but she supposed he hadn't spent as much time researching California universities as she had. "It's in LA."

"Oh. That makes sense." He sounded less effusive now. He ran his hand along the ridge of Koffka's back. She decided not to say anything more. Just let him sit with it for a minute. "It could be a nice place to live," he said eventually. "I've always wanted to see Tehrangeles."

She wasn't sure if he was saying it to her or himself, but she added, "Lots of acting jobs in LA, too."

He kept one hand on Koffka's back. "Yeah. Those too."

"I don't know for sure if I'll go there yet," she said. "Still waiting to hear back from Berkeley."

"And UW?"

"And UW. But the USC program sounds like the perfect fit. Plus, if I get my Bachelor of Music there, I'm automatically accepted to their graduate program in scoring for movies and TV. It's, like, my dream school."

"I'm not going to pretend I wasn't secretly hoping you'd go to college in Seattle," he said. "But if this is what it takes to make sure that the world gets to hear the transcendent music of Alexandria Lin, I definitely don't want to stand in your way. So. You choose, and I'll support you, no matter what."

She rested her head on his shoulder. "Thank you."

A raucous cry sounded from the crowd. "I think it's starting," he said. "Shall we?"

"One more thing first," she said, pulling him in for a kiss. She would never tire of the thrill of kissing him.

Eventually, they walked back, the damp sand shifting beneath their feet. They took their spot in line. Naveed tried to teach her the Persian verses to recite as she jumped, but she couldn't quite commit them to memory before it was their turn. Koffka was obviously uncomfortable around the fire, so Naveed handed the dog off to Cyrus. Then he and Andi turned to face the bonfires before them.

Naveed extended his hand. His face glowed in the firelight. "We have to go fast. No hesitating—that's how you get burned. Are you ready?"

She paused, taking it all in: the merry chaos and bright flames, the joyous music, the strong grip of his hand in hers. So much behind them. So much ahead.

"Ready," she said. And they leapt over the fire into the new year, together.

ACKNOWLEDGMENTS

As I revised this book during the winter of 2020 and the spring of 2021, I found myself constantly distracted. There was so much happening all the time, so many interruptions, so much turmoil in the wider world. Words flowed like sludge. I was pretty sure it would never be done. And yet, after chipping away at the manuscript for months, it was eventually complete—but this wouldn't have happened without the support of many others.

Many thanks go to my editorial/sensitivity/content-expert team: Janice Kao, whose insightful questions led me to re-think entire storylines; Pam O'Shaughnessy, who kept Roya out of the Box; Melanie Peterson, who helped make this book 82% less confusing; Pontia Fallahi, who taught me about Persian home remedies and healing traditions; Kristel Peterson, who helped me dream up Englewood; and Joe Fahr, who provided valuable, much-needed feedback on Cyrus's chapters. As always, however, any mistakes that remain are my own.

To Jacob Covey, the alchemist, for running with the "worlds within worlds" theme and creating yet another gorgeous cover. A pomegranate truly is a universe within itself, and I'm always amazed by your ability to distill concepts like this into eye-catching designs.

Much gratitude also goes to Anthony Campbell and Su Harambe, who graciously provided away-from-home writing space when I needed it most.

My respect and gratefulness for teachers has grown exponentially this past year. Thanks to all of my teachers, especially: Mr. Jeppson (4th grade), Ms. Kuhles (5th grade), Ms. Cox (6th grade), Ms. Kirst and Mr. Harrison (English), Mr. Herald (Anatomy & Physiology), and Ms. Wells (Poetry). I had quite a few amazing professors during college, including Drs. Waugh, West, and Diment, from whom I learned the delights of Russian literature; mentors including Drs. Derek Wood (Microbiology) and Neli Ulrich (Nutritional Epidemiology); and all of the preceptors who helped me complete my dietetic internship. This list doesn't even scratch the surface, though! Thank you all for everything you have taught me.

To my parents, Meg and Hal, for always cultivating my creativity. Thank you for saving every manuscript I wrote during childhood, including the one about the magic unicorn who foiled a robber's evil plot, so that I may now look back upon them and cringe (but smile at the same time).

To my sisters, Kristel and Holly, who ignited my love of storytelling. Because of the years we spent creating intricate fantasy worlds together, I can now play Paper People inside my mind!

A huge thanks to my in-laws, John, Jean, Nicole, and Justice, who have always offered unending and unconditional support. I'm so lucky to have you in my family.

To Brett, who has been the best quarantine buddy imaginable (and who, incidentally, can make a kickass loaf of sourdough). To Cora and Desmond, whose words of encouragement never fail to send me soaring all the way up to the moon.

And, of course, a heartfelt thank you to #TeamCrowbie and all of my readers. I can't even express how much it means to me that you continue to pick up these books. It is truly an honor to share them with you.

ALANNA PETERSON is the award-winning author of the Call of the Crow Quartet, a series of young adult eco-thrillers. The third installment, *Within Every Flame*, was inspired in part by her work with food justice organizations, her childhood travels to the Bay Area, and a long-ago music festival she attended in Seattle's Georgetown neighborhood. She lives on occupied Duwamish land with her family and a cat who occasionally wakes her up by sniffing her face.